HE WALKS AMONG US

The "After" Life of Elvis Presley

by

Christopher Wood

DORRANCE
PUBLISHING CO
EST. 1920
PITTSBURGH, PENNSYLVANIA 15238

The contents of this work, including, but not limited to, the accuracy of events, people, and places depicted; opinions expressed; permission to use previously published materials included; and any advice given or actions advocated are solely the responsibility of the author, who assumes all liability for said work and indemnifies the publisher against any claims stemming from publication of the work.

Dorrance Publishing Co
585 Alpha Drive
Suite 103
Pittsburgh, PA 15238
Visit our website at www.dorrancebookstore.com

ISBN: 978-1-6376-4254-2
eISBN: 978-1-6376-4570-3

ORIGINAL STORY IDEA AND CONTRIBUTIONS
BY JOHN ALBERT TARTER (1952-2015)

FAME DOESN'T TAKE YOUR SOUL RIGHT AWAY.
IT PLEASES, TEMPTS, AND TORTURES YOU FIRST.

CHAPTER ONE

It was a warm and sultry evening. The line had begun to form early in the morning. People from all walks of life were there to pay homage to their fallen idol. An elderly woman in a wheelchair clutched her treasure, an original vinyl. As she mouthed the words —"Love me tender, love me sweet"— the wistful look in her eyes was as telling as the '50s-style glasses that somehow still looked stylish on this night. She was there, what seemed like 30 short years ago, screaming wildly as The King turned young girls and women alike to jelly. Nearby a group of younger men looked just as stylish with faux sideburns as they relished in their attempts to mimic the knee-buckling swagger of their hero. Reverence was in the air as well. Many fans simply held their vigil candles in hand and moved forward in the ever-growing throng, waiting to pay homage in their own, silent way. Tomorrow morning, August 16 in the year of our Lord 1987, marked the 10th anniversary of the death of one of his true angels, Elvis Aaron Presley.

Nick Sartain had watched the crowds gather at Graceland all day. Now he was standing guard in plain clothes as the line shuffled past his security post just inside the main entrance to Ellis Theatre, where a performance for all time was being held: 10 Elvis impersonators playing every single one of his 40 Top 10 hits, including all 18 that reached #1 on the Billboard charts.

Nick huffed on a Marlboro Light and watched the plume of smoke disappear into the night sky. Nick had quit several times. It seemed to work until something major shook him up, like having to pull his gun in the line of duty. He chain-smoked for weeks after gunning down that drug dealer, not that the bastard didn't deserve it.

"God, what I wouldn't give for a Camel stud right now," he muttered to himself, noticing how the grey-white wisps of smoke seemed as fleeting and elusive as the ghost he had been chasing for the past 10 years. Could it really have been that long? He caught his reflection in the marble wall to his right. The image that stared back had shrunk to under 6 feet tall as he approached 60, his once full head of sandy hair barely covering the bald patches. He'd just as soon scream obscenities as yell "Oorah" after his stints as a grunt in Korea and later as a decorated NCO in 'Nam, but being a Marine had taught him to stay fit. He didn't look like a bad ass, which was just fine. He'd been around long enough to know that looking like a tough guy just meant some other tough guy was itching to put you to the test. He preferred to be wiry, relentless, and sneaky strong, more of a badger than a tiger. His grit had been put to the test these past 10 years. The greyish green eyes that stared back from the black marble looked tired—and a little ghostly themselves.

"What the hell am I doing here?" he thought.

One of the reasons for his presence materialized just then.

"Man, y'all are a dumb-ass city boy if you think Vegas Elvis was better than The King was in the early days!"

Nick turned to see three men in their early 20s, obviously drunk, and working toward disorderly as they staggered through the main gate. The loudmouth of the group wore fake sideburns and had made a lame attempt to spin his hair into a duck tail and paint it black. That's going to look even worse when he wakes up with a hangover in the morning, Nick thought to himself.

The loudmouth must have forgotten he was in a line that was moving at no more than shuffling speed as he banged into a middle-aged woman in front of him and nearly sent her to the ground. The woman's male companion held her up and shot a menacing glance at the loudmouth.

"What the hell you lookin' at?" the loudmouth challenged.

2

That was Nick's cue to get into position. He sliced through the crowd and quickly was within striking distance. He still had a slight hitch in his gait from the helicopter accident that shattered his pelvis just a year and a half earlier, but Nick could still move. One of the loudmouth's buddies noticed Nick's approach and tried to keep things calm.

"Hey, Kevin, just keep your mouth shut," he told his buddy.

"Screw you, Jim," the loudmouth slurred as he took a wild swing at his friend.

Amateur hour, Nick thought, and he wasn't going to exert any more effort than required. He stepped back as the two wrestled toward him and let them fall flat on the concrete. With one quick move he cuffed the loudmouth and had his friend pinned face down.

"You can go to jail with your friend here, or settle down," Nick said.

"I'm good, man. I won't do anything," Jim said.

Nick pulled Jim to his feet while being mindful to keep a foot on the back of the loudmouth's back as he remained prone.

"We'll be escorting you two off the premises, and don't think of coming back," Nick said to Jim and the third member of the trio, who amazingly had managed to keep his mouth shut and stay out of the fracas.

"And you, my friend," he informed the loudmouth, "will be spending a little time downtown tonight."

Two uniformed Memphis police cops arrived shortly and followed Nick's orders precisely. Nick had briefly retired 5 years ago to a life of leisure after 20 years with the Memphis Police Department. Retirement was more like being sentenced to a life of boredom. If he got old and fat, he feared he would end up stone cold like his partner, Eddie Baxter, who suffered a massive heart attack just six months after retiring while weeding his garden. He yearned to get back to work after just a few months of being "gone fishing." Nick tried going solo, but he soon realized a private investigator's day consists mostly of chasing down deadbeat dads and other assorted assholes. Providing private security for the Manko brothers, Sid and Johnny, had given Nick plenty of work. He was certain the Mankos were into some illegal shit, gun-running and other small-time hoodlum activities. They hadn't killed anyone—at least no one who didn't deserve to be dead. Most important to Nick, they had checked out clean with his sources at Memphis PD as not being part of the burgeoning drug gangs. When Priscilla Presley rid Grace-land of the remaining members of the Memphis Mafia—Elvis' infamous band of male companions—she often hired the Mankos to provide security at various events. Nick was among the detectives who had interviewed Priscilla during the hectic days following the fateful morning of August 16, 1977, and she was cordial with Nick, almost friendly, whenever he was on the job at Graceland. He volunteered for every gig at Graceland and eventually was hired as part-time security at the mansion. Nick's motives were strictly to feed his obsession to find the truth, however. Working night shifts gave him access to the mansion and any leads that might show up there. Nick had been more than suspicious during the investigation into Elvis' death, but everything that could be proved—fingerprints, dental records—checked out. The one thing that had never been satisfied was his cop's sixth sense, that gnawing feeling in his gut that something wasn't right. He'd fought the urge to say screw it and dedicate the rest of his life to bettering his bass-fishing and beer-drinking skills as hundreds of leads evaporated. Chasing the ghost had damn near gotten him fired from the force. Baxter and other cops he respected had called him a lunatic, or worse, more than once. Jenny had threatened to walk out on him several times. Why couldn't they understand? Giving up wasn't an option. Several times Nick had almost seen the ghost materialize—other than in his fitful dreams—but each time the promise of a discovery turned to dust. Then the break finally came last summer. The tape.

"He sounds the most like Daddy!"

Lisa Marie Presley was quoted in a newspaper account of her and Priscilla viewing more than a thousand tapes of Elvis impersonators as part of the year-long preparations for the 10th anniversary. Mother and daughter had chosen 10 impersonators to perform various tributes. At first, "he" had rebuked their invitation to be the final act or even to participate at all. But "he" hadn't accounted for Nick Sartain's obsessive pursuit of the truth. "He" had gotten careless. "He" had allowed Nick to get close, and now "he" was slated to be the final act—and Nick damn sure would be there to meet him. Jenny was immersed in the moment as she clutched her prime ticket, third row, seat 23. Nick was there for her, as he had been throughout nearly 20 years of marriage, but her mind was wandering back to a magical time. She was just 14 years old when her parents hauled her on a 10-hour road trip to Fort Wayne, Indiana, in 1957 to see their idol.

The warden threw a party in the county jail.
The prison band was there and they began to wail.
The band was jumpin' and the joint began to swing.
You should've heard those knocked out jailbirds sing.
Let's rock, everybody, let's rock...

Jailhouse Rock was always her favorite. While her friends grooved to The Beatles and The Stones, her heart stayed with The King.

"This is so exciting! Can't we go in?"

"Jen, you go ahead," Nick replied. "I have to hang here and make sure everyone checks out. I'll catch up to you."

He felt a slight pang of guilt at the realization that he planned to do nothing of the sort. Nick would be positioned near the corridor leading from the stage, waiting and watching. When "he" made his exit from the stage, Nick would be ready to make his move.

CHAPTER TWO

JOURNAL ENTRY: SEPT. 14, 1977

Note to self: Dr. Smythe thinks writing down my thoughts will help me transition to my new life and my new looks. Writing occupies my brain at night, which is the loneliest time for me now. I take Sundays off is all, so I can pray.

It's strange, but my mind has captured details that I never would have imagined. I can remember every step, every conversation, on the path that has brought me to this moment in time, all the way back to my childhood. I'll start there.

I was raised in a pretty decent home, and I was always made to behave. We never had any luxuries, but we were never hungry. I knew the average side of life, not having anything, but not knowing what it was like to have anything. I never felt poor. There was always shoes to wear and food to eat—yet I knew there were things my parents did without. Music wasn't a huge part of my life yet, but I loved watching the choir at church. Mama liked to tell the story of when I ran down the aisle of the First Assembly Church of God and stood in front of the choir, singing along and mimicking their movements. When I was 10 years old, I entered a singing contest and won $5 in fair rides even though I only placed 5th. When I turned 11, I wanted a bicycle for my birthday—one of those 5-speeds with a banana seat and long handle bars—but Mama got me my first guitar instead. I guess she always knew what was best for me.

JOURNAL ENTRY: SEPT. 15, 1977

There are lots of stories about what was my first actual recording, but the first one was just for me and Mama. Mr. Phillips wasn't in that day at Memphis Recording Studio, but his assistant, Mr. Keisker, helped me out. I recorded *My Happiness* and *That's When Your Heartaches Begin* on acetate for a cost of about $4. Then I took it home and gave it to Mama as a late birthday present. I don't recall when they renamed it Sun Studio, but I went back there to record another acetate, and this time Mr. Phillips was at the controls. I guess he liked what he heard because that summer he teamed me up with Scotty Moore and Bill Black to do some real recording. Mr. Phillips was looking for a certain sound, and we weren't getting there on the first few songs we did, so he told us to take a break. I was just messing around with an old blues tune, playing it twice as fast as normal. Mr. Phillips stuck his head out the door of the control room and said, "What are you doing?" I think it was Scotty who said, "I don't know." I thought we might be in trouble or something.

Mr. Phillips said, "Well, back up, try to find a place to start, and do it again." *That's All Right Mama* was on the radio two days later and came out as a single two weeks after that.

JOURNAL ENTRY: SEPT. 16, 1977

All of a sudden, I had so many things, so fast. That first year and a half I was all mixed up. I couldn't keep up with what was happening.

The first time I appeared on stage it scared me to death, man. I didn't know what I'd done. To the manager, backstage, I said, "What'd I do!? What'd I do!?" He said, "I don't know, but whatever it was go back and do it again." I really didn't know what the yellin' and screamin' was about. I didn't realize my body was moving. It was a natural thing to me. Some people tap their feet, some people snap their fingers, and some people sway back and forth. I just sorta did 'em all together, I guess. We we're all getting something out of our system. Nobody knew what it was, but nobody was getting hurt, and we were having a wonderful time.

JOURNAL ENTRY: SEPT. 17, 1977

Me and Scotty and Bill started playing all sorts of places, but we didn't quit our day jobs until a few months later. Actually, I thought I might be a truck driver for the rest of my life after we pretty much flopped during our debut at the Grand Ole Opry. Scotty was our manager, and he got us a gig on the radio show *Louisiana Hayride*, which played every Saturday night from Shreveport. Later I signed to do 52 weeks on the *Hayride*.

Bob Neal took over as our manager on New Year's Day in 1955. He was a nice guy, but I knew from the start that he wouldn't be a match for the sharks of the music business. The first time I saw one of those circling was when I met Colonel Tom Parker for the first time a few weeks later. I think he saw what he wanted from that first meeting, but The Colonel never was one to tip his hand. The Colonel took over for good in the fall of 1955. He got me a contract with RCA, and the ride just kept getting faster. One of my idols, the genius James Dean, jumped off his ride when he died in a car crash that year. I've wondered many times since if it wouldn't have been easier to just flame out.

JOURNAL ENTRY: SEPT. 19, 1977

I had my first No. 1 hit in the winter of 1956, *Heartbreak Hotel*, and I appeared on the *Jackie Gleason Show*. Damn, he was a funny dude! My first album came out in the spring, and then the TV people really started to take notice. I did the *Milton Berle Show*, which caused those publicity people to go crazy. They made me sing to a hound dog for some reason on the *Steve Allen Show*. I should have said right then and there that I perform the *way I want* to perform, but that kind of gets lost when you got so many people pulling at you. Ed Sullivan said he would never have the likes of a singer like me on his show, but I think he changed his mind when he figured out everyone was watching me on the other channel. He had me on a few times and the last show, even though they only showed me from the waist up, Mr. Sullivan said, "This is a decent, fine boy." That was good for my name, but I learned you got to expect the bad along with the good. Those publicity people have a job to do, and they do it. The more popular you are, the more criticism you get. I did my first movie in 1956, *Love Me Tender*, and the publicity people had a heyday criticizing my acting skills.

Mama didn't care about any of the people who bad-mouthed me. She bought her a big green scrapbook and asked me to send her stuff whenever I got the chance. For the first year or so, I didn't send her a thing, and the scrapbook was empty, except for a couple of clippings she got out of the Memphis papers. Then one day I saw this article about me not being a very good singer. I cut that out and sent it to Mama, and she wrote back and told me I didn't want to fill my scrapbook with things like that. But I wrote back and told her, "Mama, anyone can fill a scrapbook with good things. But what good does it do? I'd like to know the things people don't particularly like and study them and try to make myself better if I can."

So that's how the original Green Book got started.

JOURNAL ENTRY: SEPT. 20, 1977

Daddy never pushed me to do anything, to be anything, other than what would make me a happy man. I remember when I was just a pup, maybe 10 or 11, he asked me to go hunting with him. I said, "Daddy, I don't want to kill birds." He could have tried to shame me into going, but he never said a word about it.

Like any good father, he always wanted me to be thinking about what I would do when I became a man. When I was still in high school, I remember telling him, "Daddy, I want to be an entertainer. I want to sing with a gospel quartet." I didn't know what to expect.

"You do whatever you want to do," he said, "and we'll help you all we can."

I had him over to the house a few days before the end, and we just sat and talked for hours. Finally, he said, "Son, I have to go home now and get something to eat."

I was so ashamed to have him see me in poor shape even though he never really believed that I was into taking drugs.

"I know, Daddy," I said, "but I want you to know that I've really enjoyed this." I knew it was the last time that I would see him alive.

JOURNAL ENTRY: SEPT. 21, 1977

It wasn't long before I found out that popularity had its price. What I always missed most was just being one of the guys, doing regular things like taking a girl down to Arcade Restaurant or for a cruise around town, going to church, or to the movies when there are actually other people there. I think the first time I figured I'd never be a regular guy again was when I had that new Seville and it ran out of gas downtown. Those people were crazy! They all wanted a piece of me, but not one of them offered a gallon jug of gas. If I run across a fella who's out of gas, the first thing I'm gonna do is fill his tank. Not those folks. All they wanted was my autograph. After that I figured, well, let's face the facts. Anybody that's in the public eye, their life is never private. I mean, anything you do, the public knows about it. And that's the way it's always been. That's the way it'll always be. So, I bought a mansion in Memphis for $100,000 to find some peace and quiet. Graceland would be my home until the very end.

JOURNAL ENTRY: SEPT. 22, 1977

I guess I was just like everyone else when Mama died on August 14, 1958. It doesn't matter who you are when you feel like everything you really had goes into the ground. I don't know why she had to go so young, but it made me think about death. That's why I had to get what I could from every day. Things like that can make you a better human being. The worst thing about that is people come around the house, bring you some comfort food, and all you can wonder about is what they really want from you.

You know, I had lots of friends, but I don't know how many good ones. Red was a good friend, at least in the beginning. One night in Vegas we'd had some death threats, serious ones I was told, but we finished the show. At the end, I knelt down in a karate pose to make myself a small target, just in case anything was coming my way. Red, he stood there in front of me, trying to be as big as he could—and Red wasn't all that big. When he thought drugs were getting the better of me, Red really tried to make me stop. That was hard to watch, him thinking he was losing a friend and nothing he could really do about it. But then he turns around and writes that damn book of lies. He even admitted that part of it was for the money. Hard to call a guy a good friend after that.

Sonny said he never wrote the book for the money, but only he knows for certain. I never let on that I knew Sonny flushed all those pills down the toilet at Graceland to keep them from me. Funny thing is I always knew when the packages arrived and left them right out in the open for him to discover. Anyway, Daddy fired them both for a pittance. I always wished I could have made things right with those two, but that would have just left more loose ends.

JOURNAL ENTRY: SEPT. 23, 1977

Mama was always worried about us boys in the early days, but I loved being on the road with Scotty, Bill, and DJ. Bill was the oldest by quite a bit, but you would never know it. Scotty was more like a big brother to me, and Mama always asked him to be on the lookout since he had already been in the Navy and all. I was really lucky to have those two boys, because they were really good. Each one of them had an individual style of their own.

Bill—Blackie everyone called him—was nine years older than me, but you'd never know it. He had squinty eyes, a round face and that big grin, kind of like the Cheshire Cat. No wait, the Cowardly Lion! That's it, yeah, but he was never one to back down from anything. Sonny said Bill was the craziest dude he'd ever met. He did look a little crazy when he'd get to smacking that bass, but it always got the crowd going. When we all broke up in '58, I figured I'd hook up with all of them again someday. Bill pretty much went his own way, though. I think he always was a little pissed at The Colonel over the money split, and I can't really blame him. The doctor said he had a brain tumor, and he was gone, just like that. I decided not to attend the funeral, not because I didn't want to say goodbye to Blackie, but because I didn't want people to cause a scene because of me. That hit me hard as I sat at home thinking about it. Too famous to attend a friend's funeral. That's a hell of a thing.

There were just lots of guys that were fun to have around. Of course, there were plenty of girls hanging around, too. I was pretty close to a couple of them, especially Anita and Ann, but I couldn't see any way I could be with someone anywhere near as famous as me. That would just mean more people hangin' around, and I can get awful lonesome—even in the middle of a crowd.

JOURNAL ENTRY: SEPT. 24, 1977

I figured I'd be a regular guy when they put me in the Army, but you know, after they made a nice publicity stunt of shaving off my hair, they didn't even put me on KP like the rest of the grunts. I was in a funny position. Actually, that's the only way it could be. People were expecting me to mess up, to goof up in one way or another. They thought I couldn't take it and so forth, and I was determined to go to any limit to prove otherwise—not only to the people who were wondering, but to myself. When I landed in Germany, there was a crowd of people screaming and carrying on just like I was on stage. I know some of the guys didn't like that I got to live off base in a nice house with Daddy and Gramma there with me, but I got along good with some of those boys. I guess when I became a Sergeant, they didn't have much choice but to try to get along with me, too.

I heard the East Germans were afraid of my presence, and they even created the Lipsi, a dance that was intended to take attention away from my shimmy. It didn't work, of course, especially with the girls.

JOURNAL ENTRY: SEPT. 26, 1977

The best thing about being in the Army was meeting my darling Priscilla. You know, I kinda feel like I'm writing to you, my dear, when I make these journal entries. Maybe I'm dreaming that you'll get to read them someday. You were the most beautiful thing I had ever seen, but we didn't get to spend much time alone since you were just 14. I didn't see you again until I got out of the Army, and then we talked your daddy into letting you come to Hollywood to finish high school. When you graduated, I didn't even dare go to the ceremony for fear of making a scene. That was your day, and I sure was proud of you.

JOURNAL ENTRY: SEPT. 27, 1977

I got back to the States in 1960 and started making movies. I made me a lot of money, and it was fun at first. I met Ms. Marilyn Monroe in 1962 while filming *G.I. Blues*. We had a lot of fun, but still, it was a job. That's how I treated it. The publicity people said I didn't care if the films were any good or if I was any good in them. Well, I cared to the point that it would make me physically ill. The fact was at a certain point I had no say-so in anything, no approval of the script. The contracts had been signed years in advance, and I had no choice. And they all became very similar. I'd read 4-5 pages, and I knew it was the same movie, just with a different name and some more mediocre songs. I'd go someplace, meet some girls, fight some guys, and sing some songs. I remember The Colonel saying we strayed from that formula one time and the movie didn't make any money, so let's just stick to the script. I was stuck doing things that I didn't believe in, and that was hard on me. I thought they might give me something to show my acting ability or do a creative story. But they didn't, and it was not going to change. It was not going to change! So, I became very discouraged, and they couldn't have paid me any amount of money in the world to make me feel any self-satisfaction.

JOURNAL ENTRY: SEPT. 28, 1977

The music world changed while I was busy making movies and singin' all those mediocre songs. If I was The King of Rock 'n' Roll, well, these new boys were taking over the throne. I got to see what it was like for someone else to have all those girls going crazy and screamin' every time they appeared. We actually had The Beatles come up for a visit in the Bel Air house on Perugia Way in the summer of 1965. Hard to believe, but even those guys found an occasion to just sit and stare at me.

Finally, I said, "If you guys are just going to sit around and stare at me, I'm going to bed." That cracked them up, and then we had a great time. John and I were talking about Peter Sellers and our favorite scenes from *Dr. Strangelove*. We swapped some stories, played a few songs and just had ourselves a real nice time.

They invited us down to their place, but I didn't dare go out with all the publicity people hangin' around. One of my boys, Jerry Schilling, went and visited and came back with a great story for me. "See these sideburns?" John had asked Jerry. "I almost got kicked out of school for trying to look like him. Please tell Elvis that if it hadn't been for him, I wouldn't be here."

JOURNAL ENTRY: SEPT. 29, 1977

I made some other friends through show biz. I hung out with Muhammad Ali when he was still Cassius Clay, and we exchanged gifts. I gave him a boxing robe, and he gave me a signed pair of gloves. Evel Knievel was fun to party with, and I had to laugh at his quote about me: "All Elvis did was stand on a stage and play a guitar. He never fell off on that pavement at no 80 miles per hour."

JOURNAL ENTRY: SEPT. 30, 1977

Priscilla gave me the honor of becoming Mrs. Elvis Presley on May 1, 1967, and that was one of the best days of my life. She may not believe me, but I took to heart those words: "'Til death do us part."

Our world changed just as much as the one outside when Priscilla made me a daddy. I remember telling her: "She's all we have—she is our most prized possession. I want Lisa Marie to know what the important things in life are. Money is not important—it is fleeting and all this is just vanity."

JOURNAL ENTRY: OCT. 1, 1977

Those movies sure got me into a rut. I tried all sorts of other things to get my engine running—slot cars, horseback ridin', you name it—but music— *good* music—was the only thing that was going to do the trick. I rounded up a lot of the old boys, and we talked about all sorts of plans. Maybe we'd go around the entire world on tour. By summer we were ready to do some sessions for the Comeback Special. It was supposed to be a Christmas deal, but this creative young dude, Steve Binder, had other ideas. I remember he basically told me he thought my career was in the toilet and this show had to be great to bring it back. Well, we nailed it pretty good despite me being more nervous than ever about being on stage in front of a real audience. The publicity people even had some nice things to say about The Comeback.

JOURNAL ENTRY: OCT. 3, 1977

The world changed for the worst in 1968. Folks were all stirred up about the war in Vietnam. The Reverend King was assassinated and so was Bobby Kennedy. It reminded me of how sad the country was when JFK was assassinated in 1963. Such tragedies. The Reverend King was killed just nine miles from my home at Graceland. That tragedy inspired me to end the Comeback Special with a tribute, "If I Can Dream."

JOURNAL ENTRY: OCT. 4, 1977

I'll never forget my first gig in Vegas. It was way back in '56 as an opening act for Freddie Martin and Shecky Greene. One of the publicity people wrote that I may be pretty popular with the young girls, but they don't shoot craps. Well, I had changed a bunch between then and 1969, and I guess the craps shooters had changed some, too. On opening night at The International the place was more than packed. I don't think they could have jammed one more high-roller in there. I had a standing ovation before I even opened my mouth. So, I just struck a pose, twitched a knee, and the place went crazy. After that

The Colonel signed a contract for me to do 57 more weeks at The International. I got out on the road again in the fall for a tour, and I guess things were just rolling along, but not for me.

I had figured that getting back to performing for real would fill up my heart again, but it didn't.

JOURNAL ENTRY: OCT. 5, 1977

I made the cover of the *Rolling Stone* for the first time in 1969. Ironically, I didn't appear on the cover again until my "death" in the September of 1977 issue. 1969 was a hell of a year. We had a man walk on the moon and another man, Charles Manson, convince his followers to butcher a bunch of folks in L.A. because he said "Helter Skelter" by the Beatles made him do it.

JOURNAL ENTRY: OCT. 6, 1977

One of the things that I took really seriously was my karate. I started out in the Army, and before I got out an instructor at Fort Campbell, Hank Slomanski, made me a Black Belt. He kicked my ass more than a few times first. I remember he sent back word to The Colonel: "Your boy ain't pretty anymore, but he's a black belt."

I trained with Ed Parker, a Hawaiian who made millions from his karate schools, from 1960 almost until the end. It was just acting when I beat up all of those bad guys in the movies, but I could have got the job done if it was for real. I never was much for fighting competitions, though. Ed lined me up to take part in one once, and then I found out his real plan was to use my name to promote the event. I guess fame can even taint something that's supposed to be as pure as the martial arts. Priscilla took to karate as well, and made a serious go of it. That was good. Of course, karate was why I introduced her to Mike Stone. That turned out really bad.

JOURNAL ENTRY: OCT. 7, 1977

Larry Geller helped initiate me into Kriya Yoga and introduced me to my "spiritual mother," Sri Daya Mata. I wanted to spread her teachings to the world through my fans, and she helped me see that I could do that through my calling as an entertainer. She was a beautiful person, and I kept in touch with her for years. In fact, she was one of the first people I went to for advice after my divorce. Turns out she didn't have the ultimate answer for me. What I really wanted to know was why God had made me Elvis Presley.

JOURNAL ENTRY: OCT. 8, 1977

I had always been fascinated by lawmen, in the movies and in real life. I collected all sorts of badges, and once word got out, I had all sorts of people givin' them to me after shows. I wanted one that I really thought would do some good, though. I ran into Vice President Spiro Agnew in Palm Springs toward the winter of 1970, and the idea hit me. I wanted to be granted the position of Federal Agent at Large. I think it was The Colonel who gave me this advice: If you want something, go to the person who can get it done. I figured the guy who could get it done was President Nixon. It was just before Christmas, and I got into a spat with Priscilla and The Colonel over spending too much money on presents—more than $100,000 for 32 handguns and 10 Mercedes-Benzes—but like I always told Daddy, "Don't worry about money because I can always make some more if we need it."

I didn't want to stick around the house, so I headed for the airport and caught the first plane out of Memphis, which happened to be bound for Washington, D.C. I met Sen. George Murphy of California on that plane, and we got to talkin' about the drug culture and how bad it was getting, especially in California. I wrote down some notes right there and later typed up an official letter to President Nixon all by myself. Sen. Murphy had been in show business, a song-and-dance man and a pretty famous one before he got into politics, so he was keen to talk to me about anything. God had made me Elvis Presley, but what I wanted to know was if Sen. Murphy could tell me how to make myself into someone else.

"Well, I don't know about that, son, but I can put you in touch with someone who does know," he told me during that flight.

Sen. Murphy pulled out his little notebook and scrawled a name and number: J. Edgar Hoover, FBI, 202-555-3745.

"That's Mr. Hoover's private line. His secretary will answer, but you tell her the Keeper of the Candy Desk wants Mr. Hoover to get in touch with you. Leave a phone number—make sure it's a private line—and an exact time when you can be contacted. He'll call you back."

I checked into the hotel—to this day I ain't sayin' which one—and sat there starin' at the phone. The thought of talking to the Director of the FBI made me more nervous even than being on stage. "What if he thinks *I'm* on drugs?" my mind teased me. "These FBI guys can make you disappear in a bad way ... dang it, Ace, get ahold of yourself!"

I watched my finger slip into the circle for "2" and begin to dial.

"Director Hoover's office, how may I help you?" the woman answered, in a tone just as matter-of-fact as if I was calling the front desk for more towels. I told her exactly what Sen. Murphy instructed, at least that's what I heard my voice say as I still couldn't believe I was sitting in a hotel room attempting to have a secret conversation with one of the most powerful men in the world. "Thank you, sir. I will relay the message to Director Hoover."

I gave myself only 30 minutes to prepare for the return call. Any longer than that would have seemed like forever. I paced a bit and then flipped on the TV, but that didn't work. The *Washington Tour Guide* magazine on the hotel desk offered little distraction. Then I reached down and slid open the desk drawer to pull out the Gideon Bible that I knew would be there. I've always been a believer in omens, but before that moment I'd never really felt God had spoken to me personally. Slowly, being careful not to look nor choose any section in particular, I opened to a page and my eyes were drawn to a passage:

Matthew 16:26

"For what will it profit a man if he gains the whole world and forfeits his soul? Or what shall a man give in return for his soul?"

Then the phone rang.

"Uh, hello?" I heard my voice say.

"Mr. Presley, this is J. Edgar Hoover. I understand you would like to speak with me on a personal matter."

"Yes, sir."

"Tomorrow is Sunday, but be at FBI Headquarters, the front desk, Monday morning at 8:30. Don't be a minute late. Someone will be there to meet you." Click.

My out-of-body experience ended as I carefully hung up the phone. I couldn't help walking to the hotel window, pulling back the curtains and making sure no one was lurking on the balcony. Sleep would be impossible tonight.

I checked out of the hotel, booked a cab for Washington National, and caught the red-eye headed for L.A. I called Jerry Schilling to have him pick me up at LAX, and asked him if he would fly back to Washington with me that night.

"Are they actually going to give you that Narc badge?" he asked.

"You better believe it."

"Well I'll be damned, boss!"

We made it in time to show up at the White House gate at 6:30 A.M. My personal letter was delivered to one of President Nixon's aides, Egil "Bud" Krogh, who just so happened to be a fan. He loved the idea of the Leader of the Free World meeting the King of Rock 'n' Roll, and convinced White House Chief of Staff Bob Haldeman to make it happen. The meeting wouldn't happen until around noon, giving me plenty of time to check in at FBI Headquarters, which was in the Department of Justice building, just six blocks from the White House. I had the perfect alibi for a trip to Washington, a meeting with President Richard M. Nixon. The publicity people were sure to eat that up.

Jerry was tired after taking the red-eye and accompanying me to the White House gate, so he had no objections about hanging out in the room that morning while I slipped out for some "sightseeing."

"Just be careful out there, boss, and stick to your disguise," Jerry cautioned as I headed out. I walked briskly down Pennsylvania Avenue and blended in nicely with the crowd of tourists who were busy gawking at the many sights in our nation's Capital. I entered the Department of Justice building through a side door, closest to the FBI offices, and made my way to the main entrance without being noticed. I didn't even make it to the front desk before a serious looking man in a black suit made my acquaintance.

"I believe you are here to see Mr. Hoover," he said.

"Uh, yes, I am."

"Follow me."

The man in black used a security key to open a side door and beckoned me inside. We walked down a long corridor, accessed another security door and stepped into a large foyer. Helen Gandy, Director Hoover's personal assistant, moved from behind a large oak desk to greet us.

"Thank you, Agent Spaeth. I'll take it from here," she said, and the man in black turned and exited silently.

"Welcome, Mr. Presley. I must say Director Hoover is very excited to see you. I, uh, well, I'm a big fan, too. Would you mind signing this?"

Ms. Gandy held out a cover of my original album and handed over a stylish fountain pen.

"I'd be delighted," I said, and scrawled, "Your friend always, Elvis Presley" across the cover.

"Thank you so much!" Ms. Gandy said. "I'll tell Director Hoover you are here."

Another man in black appeared from nowhere and opened the large wooden door with "J. Edgar Hoover, Director of the FBI" attached on a large brass plate.

"The Director will see you now, Mr. Presley," he said.

I walked into a spacious office with large glass windows overlooking The Mall and Washington Monument. Director Hoover moved slowly from behind a mammoth desk that made him look smaller than I expected. He held out his hand and shook mine firmly.

"Nice to meet you, Mr. Presley. Deputy Director Tolson will be joining us shortly. Please, have a seat."

"Why, thank you kindly, Mr. Director," I said, hoping to look at ease though I was far from it.

"I understand you would like an honorary badge as a Special Agent At Large?"

"Well, you can give me whatever title you want, but yes, I'm a collector of law enforcement badges, and this one sure would be special."

Director Hoover nodded and pushed his intercom.

"Ms. Gandy, please have Deputy Director Tolson join us now."

Clyde Tolson entered from an adjoining office and moved into the room with an air of authority. He had been Deputy Director as long as Director Hoover had been in charge of the FBI, going on 40-plus years. Tolson was a handsome man with a long, angular face that was framed by a distinguished, chiseled jawline.

"Nice to make your acquaintance, Mr. Presley," he said. "Your reputation precedes you."

This was all a bit formal for my Southern upbringing, but I managed to keep my manners intact. "Likewise, Mr. Tolson," I said, regretting that I had forgotten his title, which seemed to be awfully important to these folks.

"I believe we can accommodate your request, Mr. Presley," Director Hoover said. "I'll have Deputy Director Tolson see to it that an honorary badge is delivered to the White House for your meeting with President Nixon. I'm sure he will be delighted to present it to you."

The realization that I was going to receive the badge to beat all badges got the better of my manners.

"Hot dog! That sure would be special!" I said before I could get my "mister this" and "title that" in front of my tongue.

"Well, we're glad to be of service," Director Hoover said without using any courtesies, which made me feel better. I guess I always did have a way of disarming folks. Just when I thought the old boy might be warming up a little, though, he turned serious again.

"Now, you understand, Mr. Presley, that this badge is strictly an honorary token from the FBI," he warned. "It does not confer privileges to conduct any official business on behalf of the agency."

"I understand fully, Director Hoover," I said, my manners back in charge.

"Okay, very well then. Is that all, Mr. Presley?"

"Well, I, uh, there is something else I wanted to know," I said.

J. Edgar Hoover, one of the most powerful men in the world, leaned forward and gave me a thorough sizing up.

"Yes, Mr. Presley?"

I'd been practicing this speech for days, but what came out was from the heart all the same. "Well, I'm sure you know what it's like to have people starin' at you all the time if you want to go out in public, maybe just to grab a bite, go to church, see a movie, or whatever. Well, for me, they stare and all, but then they get to screamin' and carryin' on to the point where even the other folks who are just tryin' to mind their own business can't have no peace. I still love my music, and being up on stage, but I'm just plain dog tired of all the crap that goes with it."

"Yes, fame can be a double-edged sword, Mr. Presley," Director Hoover said. "There is no doubt about that, but I'm not sure what you are wanting from me."

"Well, sir, I figure that if anybody would know how to get out, how to disappear, start a new life, get away from all the ruckus once and for all, it would be you. I'm just wonderin' what it would take *not* to be Elvis Presley anymore."

Director Hoover sat back in his large leather chair, sized me up again, and said nothing for what seemed an eternity. Then he leaned forward and pressed the intercom.

"Ms. Gandy, please bring me the Presley file," he said.

I guess the stunned look on my face gave away my thoughts.

"Yes, we have a file on you, Mr. Presley, just as we do on all famous people," Director Hoover said. Ms. Gandy entered with three manila folders in tow and laid them neatly on Director Hoover's desk. He opened one and scanned the contents momentarily, but I could tell he was just thinking of where to go next.

"Mr. Presley, if you are serious about what you describe, starting a new life as you say, well, this is very serious business," he said. "Of course, the agency has the means to make people disappear. The notion of starting a new life, a quiet unassuming existence, is a delicate matter, however. I'll need some time to consider, and will take up the matter with Deputy Director Tolson. Our findings will be right here, in your files. Then we will be in touch. In the meantime, you need to consider just how serious this request may be. I suggest we visit this at a future date. If anything should happen to me between now and then, Deputy Director Tolson will act on my behalf. Understood?"

"Yes sir, I'll give it some thought. You bet I will. And I can't thank you enough for gettin' me that badge."

Director Hoover and Deputy Director Tolson rose to shake my hand goodbye and summoned Ms. Gandy to show me to the first entrance. An agent appeared to escort me through the gauntlet of hallways and out a different door than the one through which I had entered. I stood in a narrow alley, looking both ways to make sure I was clear before heading for the main street. If nothing else, I'd have a badge later that day and a good story, even if I didn't dare share it with anyone.

JOURNAL ENTRY: OCT. 10, 1977

President Nixon turned out to have some "morality issues" later on, but he seemed like a pretty regular guy when we met in the Oval Office. I have to say it's one of the few times when I was the one who felt intimidated. I hope I didn't sit and stare at him, like so many dopes have done to me. We had some pictures taken, and I've heard the shot of us two together is one of the Smithsonian's most requested photographs.

JOURNAL ENTRY: OCT. 11, 1977

The highlight of 1971 came early when I was honored as one of the nation's 10 Outstanding Young Men of America by the United States Junior Chamber of Commerce, the Jaycees for short.

The rest of 1971 brought more of what had become the usual for me—engagements in Vegas and Tahoe, and a 12-city tour in the fall. One night in Vegas fans rushed the stage, and I chipped a tooth as I fought my way out of there. Later that year management invented the saying "Elvis has left the building" as a way of getting fans to realize I was gone and they weren't going to get a piece of me. I really would exit through a private back door as quickly as possible and head to my private hotel somewhere else in the city. We were always changing routes and had several vehicles leave in different directions, so no one was sure which one was carrying me. I felt more like a living piece of precious cargo than a human being.

JOURNAL ENTRY: OCT. 12, 1977

The music world was jolted again in 1971. We lost so much talent when Jimi Hendrix, Janis Joplin, and James Morrison all died from overdoses. People have told me all of them said I had an influence on their music. I can sorta see it with Janis, but not the other two. Still, I was flattered. All of this came after The Beatles had separated in 1970. I was still doing my usual thing, but rock 'n' roll was welcoming a new breed.

JOURNAL ENTRY: OCT. 13, 1977

New Year's Eve had always been special, with parties uptown or later in the Jungle Room at Graceland, but something was missing during the countdown to 1972. I really felt that Priscilla didn't love me anymore. Of course, that feeling was confirmed less than two months later during my Vegas engagement when she admitted her affair with Mike Stone. What really made me sad was knowing deep down inside that it was my own fault. I had driven her away with all my fooling around, so I couldn't really blame her. I sure was pissed at Mike, though. I had asked him to train my wife, not to screw her. Still, I figured it was just a phase, that Priscilla would come to her senses and forgive me, like she had always done whenever I messed up. Even later, when the divorce papers came, I didn't want to face the truth that we were really done. Still, the shock of realizing she was with another man was enough for me to seek some more advice from Director Hoover.

I had more than a month off before a two-week tour scheduled for April, plenty of time to set up another meeting with Director Hoover. I made a call to Ms. Gandy and waited anxiously for a reply. The return call came three long days later.

"Mr. Presley, this is Helen Gandy."

"Yes, ma'am," I replied. "I've been waiting to hear from you."

"Director Hoover would like to see you next week. Are you free on Wednesday afternoon?"

"Absolutely."

"Director Hoover will be expecting you at 1 P.M. at his office. Of course, he wants you to come alone."

"I'll be there."

"Thank you, Mr. Presley. We look forward to seeing you." Click.

Director Hoover didn't rise from behind his mammoth desk this time as I entered his office. Deputy Director Tolson had already joined us, sitting to my right—and watching.

"Nice to see you again, Mr. Presley," Director Hoover said. "You know Mr. Tolson. I've asked him to join us this afternoon because I'm certain he will play a key role in your proceedings."

Rumors of Director Hoover's declining health due to heart problems had been a subject for the publicity people, and he looked pale and more frail than he did just 16 months prior.

"I'm sorry to hear about the status of your relationship with Mrs. Presley, which I assume is the motivation for this meeting."

"I guess word gets around fast these days," I replied.

"Information is power, Mr. Presley, and we control both. Now then, I've laid out a plan to proceed with your wishes."

"I'm not sure just yet what my wishes are, Director Hoover, but I'd like to know what you have in mind."

"Of course, Mr. Presley, you will have the final decision whether to proceed. If and when you decide to proceed, there is no going back. Any second thoughts could have disastrous results for you and your family. Of course, this office will need to protect its reputation at all costs. Do you understand, Mr. Presley?"

"I do indeed, sir."

"Very well, then. If you decide to pursue a new life, all remnants of your former existence will be off-limits. You will be a new person, with no contact with anyone from your current existence. Of course, a plan of this magnitude will take some time to develop. First, you will need to build financial assets that will be available to you in your new life and untraceable from your current existence. We have plans in place to assist you in creating an offshore bank account and funding it generously."

"Just how much are we talkin' about?" I asked with no hint of formality.

"A sum of $30 million will be required to take care of proceedings prior to your demise and to ensure your well-being in the future," Director Hoover said with no intention of negotiation. "It will take at least three years, perhaps more, to build assets that will satisfy our requirements and ensure you have funds to live comfortably for the rest of your new life. Money isn't the only variable, however. Your health will have to be such that a sudden death will not be questioned. We have medical experts in place who will guide you in making the public—and those people who are closest to you—believe that your death was inevitable. Of course, your health will be in no serious danger. The official cause of death will be heart attack brought on by congestive heart disease."

"I guess I won't have to cut back on the peanut butter and banana sandwiches like the docs are wanting me to then, eh?"

"Your current diet won't prompt anyone to question the weight gain we advise, in the latter stages of your proceedings, of course. The real culprit will be your growing need for prescription medication."

"Now, wait a minute, Director Hoover. I can't be doing anything that gives the publicity people more opportunities to spread those lies about me," I replied.

"Actually, we're counting on the media to do just that, Mr. Presley. You don't really think you can keep your reputation intact, die suddenly, and embark on a new life, do you? This is going to require sacrifice on your part, Mr. Presley, and your reputation is going to suffer the most."

"I guess that's what God was talkin' about," I said.

"Excuse me, Mr. Presley?"

"Well, you see, the last time we met I pulled out The Bible while I was pacin' around my room, trying to get some sleep before I met with you and President Nixon. I opened directly to Matthew 16:26: What shall a man give in return for his soul?"

"You alone will have to answer that question, Mr. Presley," Director Hoover said. "Once we've established your bank account and planted evidence of your failing health, we have a plan in place to carry out your death—and resurrection, since religion seems to resonate with you—in a seamless operation."

Director Hoover had laid out the plan like a surgeon himself, and he was just getting started. "Years ago, I had an agent who worked for me by the name of George Gant," Director Hoover continued. "The name has special meaning to me and to the FBI, but is of no real significance to anyone else in this world. He was a fine agent, one that I trusted. George was married to a wonderful woman, Melanie, and together they had a son in 1935. Both George and Melanie were only children and unfortunately after their son Dale was born, Melanie was unable to have any more children. Other than the three of them they had no other known relatives. This family suffered more tragedy than any should have to bear. Dale came down with a severe case of influenza and died in 1944. Heartbroken, George immersed himself in his duties with us, and Melanie became very reclusive. In 1946, while apprehending a fugitive, George was killed in action. This was another severe blow to Melanie, who I believe to this day died of a broken heart less than a year later. As unfortunate as this sounds, it provides the perfect solution to your identity. I have already initiated the steps to remove Dale's death certificate, and have proceeded to place records into the Social Services system showing that Dale spent the next six years of his life in a home for boys. School records and everything that is necessary to establish a background for Dale will follow. This will allow you to have a history from the time of birth to the present. You will have a Social Security card, employment records, tax returns, and a residence history in place for you. From the minute your death is staged, you will become Mr. Dale Gant."

"But I'm still Elvis Presley for the time being, and I'm not quite certain I'm ready for that to end," I replied honestly. "How much time do I have to think it over?"

"As much time as you need, Mr. Presley, but I'm afraid my time frame may not match yours," Director Hoover said. "Your file will be updated, of course, and will be passed on through proper channels should I not be present."

I glanced at Deputy Director Tolson, who met my gaze without blinking. Director Hoover pushed the intercom button on his desk and summoned Ms. Gandy.

"I'd like the contents of Mr. Presley's file updated and moved to my personal collection," he instructed. "You will be briefed on the details of today's discussion at the conclusion of our meeting."

"Yes, sir," Ms. Gandy acknowledged and turned to leave without being asked.

"If and when you decide to proceed, we will be ready," Director Hoover continued. "The amount of time needed to complete the proceedings cannot be altered, however. We require three years, minimum. This will be the last meeting that will take place at this office. If and when you commit, you will call from a secure line to this number," Director Hoover said and slipped me a piece of folded paper. "You should commit that to memory. The fewer loose ends, the better. If everything is proceeding normally, the person on the other end will reply, 'This is Cousin Billy.' Then, and only then, arrangements will be made for a meeting. Do you understand?"

"Yes, sir," I replied.

"Very well then. If by chance I am no longer in service when you make your decision, Mr. Tolson will act on my behalf."

"Thank you, kindly, Director Hoover," I said. "You'll be the first to know when I decide."

"Of course, we will, Mr. Presley. It's our business to know."

JOURNAL ENTRY: OCT. 14, 1977

Director Hoover died suddenly just before my big summer tour. They let Deputy Director Tolson lead the FBI for one day before President Nixon appointed a new acting director. Hoover and Tolson always were a strange pair. There were lots of rumors going around about them being homosexual lovers. I don't know about that, but I could tell that Clyde Tolson cared deeply for his boss for all those years they were together. Hoover even left his inheritance—half a million bucks—to Tolson. I didn't attend Deputy Hoover's funeral—that would have been a big mistake—so I didn't get a chance to speak to Tolson about Director Hoover's passing and my pending "personal matters." I only had one option. I pulled out the folded piece of paper Director Hoover had given me from a hidden compartment in my desk drawer—the idea of memorizing the number seemed too risky to me—and dialed.

"This is Cousin Billy," a familiar voice answered.

"Mr. Tolson, is that you?" I asked.

"Yes, Mr. Presley, it is," Clyde Tolson said. "Director Hoover had the foresight to have this number dispatch directly to me."

"He was a smart man. God rest his soul."

"Yes, he was. Now what can I do for you, Mr. Presley?"

Even after his retirement, Tolson knew a whole lot about what was happening in Washington and probably everywhere else in the world. You don't get that close to the top—and stay there for 40 years—without having connections.

"Well, Mr. Tolson, I just wanted to make sure you were still the person handling my proceedings," I said.

"Your information is safe, Mr. Presley, I assure you," Tolson said. "If you decide to pursue the matter any further, get in touch with me. And if for some reason I'm not around—you know my health isn't great these days, either, and it's not going to get any better at my age—you may contact your assigned Agents."

JOURNAL ENTRY: OCT. 15, 1977

I did 15 shows in 15 nights on the summer tour, and I guess it was pretty good because later they made a documentary type movie from those performances. In July, our separation was made formal—whatever the hell that means—and that's when I met Linda. All the guys really liked her—for more than her gorgeous looks—and we got along pretty good together.

She was pretty young when we met, but I never took advantage of her. At first, I think she was concerned that I was still married. When I told her we were separated, she said I should have married a Southern girl. In the end, I think it probably made her a better person, though. I stayed faithful to her for a while, but then I started to have some "indiscretions" as she called them. I'd deny it at first, and then say I was so sorry and that she was my true love, and she would always forgive me. The last time I spoke to her in person I gave her a big speech about her being the only girl in my life. Well, that wasn't true since we were in San Francisco and I'd had a new girl flown out from Memphis who was just waiting for Linda to head back home. Linda had a good soul, and we talked about getting married sometimes, having kids, all the good things in life that she deserved. Maybe that would have changed my mind about leaving this life.

JOURNAL ENTRY: OCT. 17, 1977

When 1973 rolled around we all got out of town and headed for Hawaii to film a big show. "Aloha from Hawaii" was beamed by satellite to a billion people worldwide, one third of the Earth's population and more people than watched live on TV when those astronauts first walked on the moon. I'd been to the Islands before, but I really fell in love with the place while we toured and taped the show. We got to meet some of the natives, see how a lot of them still lived in the traditional island lifestyle, and that made an impression on me. Just the simplicity of their lives was something that I craved, even more than being on stage. When we got back to the mainland, it was time to go back to Vegas. I remember sitting in my hotel room and just reflecting all night on the difference between the places. Hawaii was clean, natural, virtuous, and beautiful. Vegas had none of those qualities.

JOURNAL ENTRY: OCT. 18, 1977

The publicity people hounded me with drug rumors while we toured all over the damn country that summer. I was back in Memphis when Priscilla made me go back to the Courthouse to get more out of the divorce. Turns out she wanted more money, and that was just fine with me because that day I came to peace with the idea that it was time to start stashin' some cash of my own. The very next day I pulled out the folded slip of paper again.

"This is Cousin Billy," the familiar voice answered.

"Mr. Tolson, is that you?"

"Yes. What may I do for you, Mr. Presley?"

"Mr. Tolson, I've made my decision. It's time to put my proceedings, as Director Hoover called them, into motion."

"Okay, Mr. Presley, you know what you are required to do overall, but we need to proceed methodically and in a very detailed way. When can we meet in private?"

"I've been wondering that since about 1954," I joked.

Silence.

"Mr. Presley, if I'm going to be involved, this has to be a very serious matter."

"Yes, sir. Well, I planned on renting out the theater, The Memphian, you know, a couple nights this week to watch some picture shows. I can make up a story that your boys want to talk to me in private about doing a movie; maybe that one they've been wanting me to do with Ms. Streisand. Yeah, I think that would work. What do you think?"

"Two agents and I will meet you there Wednesday night at 1 A.M. Good afternoon, Mr. Presley." Click. Just like his boss, I thought of the abrupt ending.

I went to The Memphian just after midnight, about my usual time. I told Sonny and Red the story about meeting some movie producers, and they didn't bat an eye. I was sitting in my usual seat, center seat of the center aisle in row 23, the exact middle of the theater. Somehow sitting exactly centered made me more at ease, but it would take a lot more than numerology to make me comfortable tonight. I sensed two figures enter my row from either side.

"I'm Agent Monroe," the black outline on the left said.

"I'm Agent Schmidt," the black outline echoed from the right.

"Listen carefully, Mr. Presley." The voice came not from either visage to my sides, but from the row behind me. I tried to turn around and see who it was, but the suits grabbed my forearms and held me tight in my seat.

"My name is Agent Johnson," the voice said. "I need to keep my identity protected in this matter, so please continue to look forward as we speak."

"Uh, I don't appear to have much choice in the matter," I said. "Of course, I could call my boys in here in one second, and we could just work it out."

"I assure you that would be very unwise, Mr. Presley," Agent Johnson said.

"Where is Mr. Tolson?" I demanded.

"Mr. Tolson was not feeling well enough to make the trip to Memphis, so he requested I come instead," Agent Johnson said. "Of course, since Mr. Tolson is no longer with the FBI, this is now a personal matter rather than a government matter. Therefore, I think you can appreciate the need for me to keep my involvement quite confidential."

"I'm more concerned with my own well-being at the moment," I said.

"We'll get to your well-being, so to speak, Mr. Presley, if you will allow me to proceed."

"I'm listenin'."

"We know you have been taking prescription Demerol as a sleeping aid for some time now. Perhaps you have an addiction, as the papers say; perhaps you don't. That doesn't matter, at least not right now. What matters is that you will convince your doctor that you are addicted to Demerol and get him to record that as part of your official medical records. It will be much easier to feign drug addiction in the future once the initial diagnosis has been recorded."

"How am I supposed to fake being addicted to Demerol?" I asked. "I've been acting most of my life, but I'm not sure I can take on that role."

"We will replace your prescribed drugs with placebos, Mr. Presley. You will receive instructions from our doctor. Remember, Mr. Presley, this will be a long process with details that must be followed precisely if you wish to be successful in your pursuit."

"I understand. Is that all?"

"For now."

Just as quickly as the two FBI agents had appeared, they vanished. I sat in the dark, in my centered seat, feeling like I was lost in the middle of the universe.

"Can I really pull this off?" I asked myself.

"Pull what off, boss?" Sonny asked.

He had moved into the seat behind me without me noticing at all.

"Just this role they are talking about," I said. "It's a long way from being a singin', fightin' playboy, but we'll see."

"I'm sure you will do fine, boss," Sonny assured me. "You need anything at the moment?"

"Just my sanity, but I don't think you can get that for me, old friend."

I laughed to ease the quizzical look on his face and went back to munching my popcorn. Sonny rose to leave, then paused and said, "Those are some pretty sneaky dudes for movie types, boss. I could swear we only counted two of them coming in, but I know there was three when they were sitting around you. Damned if I know how the third guy came and went without any of us noticing."

JOURNAL ENTRY: OCT. 19, 1977

I received a nondescript package at Graceland in early October from a Dr. Martin addressed from a P.O. Box in Washington, D.C. The boys weren't suspicious as I was receiving things all the time from all sorts of people and places. The contents included a bottle of pills and a phone number, nothing else. I went to my bedroom, locked the door and dialed.

"Mr. Presley, this is Agent Johnson."

"Uh, yes, sir, I received a package with a bottle of pills and this phone number."

"Good. When you are ready to proceed, clear your schedule for the next four days. Take the pills before you go to bed. The pills will bring on minor respiratory distress, nothing to worry about, but you will be a little uncomfortable. Enough to get you checked into Memphis Baptist Memorial Hospital. We'll know when you arrive. We have contacts there, but you won't know who they are. We'll make sure toxicology tests are ordered. When your doctor arrives, the levels of Demerol on the report will lead him to conclude you are addicted. We'll make sure his report indicates as such. Understood?"

"What happens when I get out?"

"The effects will wear off on the fifth day. You'll receive further instructions." Click.

I hung up the phone and had to admit I was a little scared, but also excited. I had always been interested in police work. This was the other side, definitely illegal on several levels, but no less intriguing.

JOURNAL ENTRY: OCT. 20, 1977

After my "incident," I took it easy the rest of the year and surprised Linda with a new mink coat for Christmas. Before I could begin to stash some bucks, I had to have plenty of cash on hand. I received instructions from Agent Johnson to work as much as possible without raising suspicion to maximize my cash accounts.

I opened 1974 doing two shows a night at The Hilton in Vegas and managed to behave myself most of the time. The band hit the road for a 20-day tour through the South in the spring. I made sure the boys saw me taking the pills, but I had replaced most of the real Demerol with harmless placebos. It didn't matter to the publicity people because they were going to write about my pill-popping no matter what I did. I faked a few bad shows during my Tahoe engagement, just to make sure none of the publicity people would write that I was back on top of my game. Lisa Marie came to visit in Tahoe, and the last night she got to meet Michael Jackson. I'm not sure she really knew who he was at the time, the kid was just 11 years old, but she sure liked him. We made 15 stops on a cross-country tour in early summer, and once again I managed to stay out of trouble for the most part. Agent Johnson called before my August engagement in Vegas and told me it was time to raise some more doubts.

"Mr. Presley, I see your bank accounts are getting quite flush."

"How do you know that?"

"We have access to more than know, Mr. Presley. I want you to interrupt one of your shows—it would be fitting if the former Mrs. Presley was in attendance—and lament the rumors of your heroin addiction."

"I ain't heard no story about a heroin addiction!" I shouted.

"You will."

"Now, wait just a damned minute! Does Mr. Tolson know about this?"

"Mr. Tolson is sick. He's not going to get better. I will be handling this operation, but rest assured that I have consulted with Mr. Tolson and he is in complete agreement."

"Well, I'd prefer to hear that from Mr. Tolson. Prescription drugs are one thing, you know, but I ain't goin' along with no story about heroin!"

"You don't have to go along with it, Mr. Presley. You have to refute it, onstage, in a most forceful manner."

"I'm not sure I want to do that."

"Mr. Presley, what you want, what you told us you want, is to be free. In order for that to happen you have to follow the script. It's time to go back to your acting days, Mr. Presley. We'll be watching. You'll receive further instructions once you return to Memphis." Click.

JOURNAL ENTRY: OCT. 21, 1977

I realized just how creepy these FBI guys could be. Cold and calculating, too. I thought about pushing the abort button on the whole plan, but then I hadn't really experienced anything in the 100 or so shows I had already done that year to make me reconsider my desire for a new life. I had 29 shows scheduled at The Hilton spread over 15 days, and each time I took the stage I wondered how I was going to follow orders. Then I saw the story about the heroin. Usually I don't pay attention to that trash. I'd quit reading any of my reviews, good or bad, but that one pissed me off. There wasn't much acting going on when I stopped the show and addressed the audience on closing night.

"I don't pay attention to rumors. I don't pay attention to movie magazines. I don't read 'em, because they're all junk. I don't mean to put anybody's job down. I'm talking about they have a job to do and they've got to write something. So, if they don't know anything, they make it up! In this day and time, you can't even get sick. You are strung out! Well, by God, I'll tell you something, friend. I have never been strung out in my life, except on music. When I got sick here in the hotel, I got sick that one night. I had a 102 temperature. They wouldn't let me perform. From three different sources, I heard I was strung out on heroin. I had a doctor, and I had the flu. I got over it, and it was alright. But all across this town people were whispering that I was strung out! If I find or hear the individual who has said that about me, I'm going to break your goddamned neck, you son of a bitch! That is dangerous. Thank you very much."

I followed that up by stumbling out of my limo as I arrived at a show in Baltimore, the opening night of a two-week fall tour. A few weeks later I went to see Dr. Elias Ghanem in Vegas, and he diagnosed me with ulcers in my stomach. I don't know what Dr. Ghanem had to do with anything because I really think he was trying to help me. He prescribed a new diet and sleep regimen and tried to get me off the "pills." But packages kept arriving from other doctors, one from Palm Springs and one from Hollywood. A notation on one of the bottles said "to keep sanity." I made sure to keep that one in plain sight.

JOURNAL ENTRY: OCT. 22, 1977

Even though my birthday was two months out, *The National Enquirer* ran the headline "Elvis at 40: Paunchy, Depressed, and Living in Fear"—dated Nov. 19, 1974. That's one of the few clippings I kept from the later years. I took out a piece of blank paper and wrote my own headline: "Elvis at 43: Lean, Happy, and Living in Paradise."

I have to admit turning 40 wasn't any fun, but what man can't say that? It sorta made me feel like a regular guy, looking for gray hair and wrinkles, wondering if I still had my sex drive. Of course, most guys who hit middle age don't have much choice but to just keep doing what they've been doing. I had the cash to buy me some new toys, and that's exactly what I did. It was all part of the plan, building for my future life, Agent Johnson told me, but it was pretty fun, too. I received a call at Graceland a few days after turning 40 with a belated gift.

"Mr. Presley, we've arranged for you to purchase a jet airplane, a Boeing 707," Agent Johnson said. "The selling price will be $200 million. Of course, we've negotiated a tidy discount from that sum that will be deposited in your offshore bank account. Happy birthday."

"A jet airplane? Damn, I was expecting maybe a birthday card or something from you, but this is a surprise!"

"Enjoy your new ride, Mr. Presley." Click.

JOURNAL ENTRY: OCT. 24, 1977

I had almost two months to burn before my next Vegas engagement, and I found out how I would spend some of it when another nondescript package arrived from "Dr. Martin." Linda discovered me having trouble breathing—she came to the rescue more than once—and I checked into the hospital in Memphis on Jan. 29 with what was officially termed "shortness of breath." I was still there when Daddy suffered a heart attack. They put him into the room right next to mine. Dr. Nick agreed to let me out on Valentine's Day and set me up with a new regimen that meant only he or his nurse would bring me my pills. I much preferred the nurse because she was a cute little blonde. I think the boys got a laugh out of the arrangement because they knew the supply of pills was pretty much non-stop. I made sure to flush most of the real ones and take plenty of the placebos. I was getting pretty good at acting groggy and dazed. Some of those publicity people might say I did a pretty good job of that during all of those mediocre movies I made. It gave me a chuckle to think I was putting one over on those scum suckers.

JOURNAL ENTRY: OCT. 25, 1977

The publicity people said I was looking a little better when I opened in Vegas in early spring of 1975. Agent Johnson had worked out a plan to take a cut from each show that not even The Colonel could track, so my offshore account was growing steadily. Ms. Streisand came to see my show a few times, and her people got to talking with The Colonel and me some more about making a new picture, actually a remake of *A Star is Born*. I think The Colonel figured I wasn't up to it, given my drug problem and all, so he made them an offer they had to refuse.

After I finished my Vegas engagement, I heard the news of Clyde Tolson's death. I pulled out the folded piece of paper Director Hoover had given me three years earlier and dialed the number, having no idea who might answer.

"This is Cousin Billy," a familiar voice said.

"Agent Johnson," I said. "I should have known it would be you."

"As you know, Mr. Tolson is dead. Fine man," he said. "That leaves me in charge of your operation. How do you feel about that, Mr. Presley?"

"I trusted him more than I trust you."

"Trust is a luxury in this affair, Mr. Presley. What matters is that you realize we are the only people who can deliver what you want. Do you realize that, Mr. Presley?"

"I trust you guys know what you are doing," I said.

"We do indeed, Mr. Presley. Once the date of your demise has been established, we will have procured a double to take your place. Your fingerprints and dental records will have been switched to match perfectly with the dead body."

"*Dead body?* Nobody said anything about no dead body!"

"Why, Mr. Presley, did you think we'd put a wax dummy in your coffin? We will take care of the procurement of a suitable match for you. No need for you to worry about that."

"Well, I'm not too keen on being the cause of death, you know?"

"*Someone* has to die, Mr. Presley, and we've established that you prefer it not to be you," Agent Johnson said coldly.

"I'm a religious man, and Thou Shalt Not Kill is right up there on God's Ten Commandments."

"I assure you we won't be procuring anyone who has positive contributions to make in this life. And, of course, we will take care of the *proceedings*," Agent

Johnson said with the assurance of someone who'd signed more than one death order during his tenure.

"Well, swapping fingerprints and dental records is one thing, but how are you going to make this, uh, *dead body*, look like me?" I asked.

"There are many people in the world who aspire to mimic your appearances, for obvious reasons, Mr. Presley. We will be able to find someone who resembles you enough facially and has similar body characteristics. Cosmetic surgeons will take note of your scars, moles, birthmarks and other identifying characteristics and match them perfectly on the corpse."

"You're going to put scars on a dead guy?" I asked with disgust.

"He will be quite alive when the procedures take place, but I assure you we will take measures to make sure he feels no pain," Agent Johnson said. "We will deliver the double to Graceland and inject drugs that will bring about the desired result. Your private bathroom appears to be the most secure location. The actual time of death must come shortly after the last time you are seen alive. By the time the dead body is discovered, you will have been secreted away from the premises and on your way to a new life."

"My God!" I gasped. The plot was gruesome, but I must admit exciting, too, with its elements of danger and deceit.

"Of course, the autopsy will confirm the dead body as having your identity. Toxicology reports will show potentially lethal levels of various drugs, which will match the testimony of anyone present that day concerning your actions."

"I'm not sure what you're gettin' at there, Agent Johnson," I said.

"You will have particular trouble sleeping the night and early morning prior to your demise, Mr. Presley, and, therefore, will be seen ingesting large quantities of drugs to help you relax. This will not be out of the ordinary given the documented rumors of your drug abuse."

"I guess there's no way for me to come off looking like a saint, eh?" I asked.

"As I've already stated, Mr. Presley, your reputation has to be one of the casualties of these proceedings; if they are to be believed. After the medical proceedings have been completed, we suspect the dead body will lie in state for family, friends, and your fans to say their goodbyes. Heavy makeup will have been applied to the corpse, which is normal, and no one will be too suspicious if you don't look exactly like your living self after a sudden death. The corpse will be buried according to your family's wishes, and all of the necessary arrangements will be complete. Of course, then comes the matter of your re-entry into the world."

"Yeah, I've kinda been wonderin' about that."

"You will receive details when the time is right. From now on, we'll be contacting you, Mr. Presley. And now, like my predecessors, this line is dead." Click.

JOURNAL ENTRY: OCT. 26, 1977

Agent Johnson arranged for me to buy new plane, and nobody thought twice about me having more than one. I'd already established a pattern for buying in bulk when I got into a hobby. The price for this one was less than $100 million, but I had it decked out with gold bathroom fixtures, a queen-size bed, and a full audio-visual system. I'm sure plenty of the cash for the extras ended up coming back to my offshore account. I had TCB painted on the side for my slogan, "Taking Care of Business." I took to riding in the jets to most of those stops. Sometimes I'd be in one and have the boys use the other to bring in some girls. I think Agent Johnson had a nice little deal going to skim the top off the price for jet fuel because we always filled up at pumps with the same name on them.

JOURNAL ENTRY: OCT. 27, 1977

Jerry Scheff had rejoined the band at the beginning of the tours, and I could tell he was shocked by what he was seeing. Not being able to be true to the band was the hardest part of this scheme, and I got frustrated with it. Maybe that's why I ripped into Kathy Westmoreland and the black backup singers one night on stage. Sure made an impression on the crowd, though, and that was always a good way to get the publicity people stirred up. I made an impression on Dr. Nick, too, when he tried to cut off the pills. I was waving my Beretta around backstage, and the damn thing went off. Ping! Ping! Ping! The bullet ricocheted around the room and caught Dr. Nick right in the chest. Didn't hurt him seriously, but it did knock him on his ass and drain all the color from his face. I think I even laughed when he pulled his hand back from his chest and looked down to see he wasn't bleeding. I had a few weeks to burn before my next Vegas engagement, and the FBI boys had me set up for a spending spree.

"We've got a special discount for you at the Cadillac showroom in Vegas," Agent Johnson said. "Your account will be credited a tidy sum for each purchase, so don't be shy, even with complete strangers."

Well, no one had to tell me that! I bought 14 Caddies that day. I know the salesman had to be in on it because he didn't faint or nothin'. I even bought one for this black lady who was just walking by and happened to look through the window with a wishful eye. I walked right out and escorted her into the showroom.

"Ma'am, how'd you like one of these?" I said, sliding my hand over the hood of a black Seville.

"Mister, I don't know what you think you're doin', but there ain't no way I can afford one of those."

"Well, sister, I'm Elvis Presley, and it's not going to cost you a penny," I said.

Another salesman came out to set her up, and I told her I wasn't leaving until I saw her drive off in that shiny new automobile. I'm pretty sure she was a setup, probably ended up with $500 bucks or so to sign the title back to me through one of Agent Johnson's agents. Spend your money like a madman and pad your private account at the same time! It was quite the racket, and a helluva lot of fun. I bought another Cadillac, three more jet planes, and a bunch of three-wheeled motorcycles in the next few weeks. I never really saw how they cooked the books, but I know my offshore account was getting healthier as I was convincing people that my health was going in the opposite direction.

JOURNAL ENTRY: OCT. 28, 1977

I was scheduled for another engagement at The Hilton toward the end of summer. I laid down on stage one night to do some songs, and that didn't sit too well with The Colonel. He canceled the rest of the engagement, and I checked back into the hospital in Memphis with what was called "fatigue." I figured that fit just fine because I was pretty damn tired of the whole mess. I didn't know which was harder, trying to deal with the pressures of being famous or tricking people that I was falling apart. I guess Linda got tired of trying to figure out where I was coming from—or who I was leaving with—because she decided to stay in Hollywood. Dr. Nick figured I needed some exercise to cut the flab from my shanks between shows, so he came up with the idea of putting in a racquetball court at home. I took to the game and had a pretty wicked forehand because of the strength training I'd done with my hands and forearms for karate. I wore white tennis shoes, shorts, and safety goggles, which were huge, because Dr. Nick didn't want anything to happen to my eyes. Me and the boys would have matches all night and then head out on motorcycles to cruise around town, hit the movies, or try to sneak unnoticed into the nightclubs.

Agent Johnson must have been watching what was going on because he called with another idea to fatten my offshore account.

"Mr. Presley, racquetball is becoming quite popular throughout the country, not just in Memphis."

"What y'all gettin' at?" I asked.

"We can make use of our contacts to pad the price of cement in your hometown and skim some revenue for you, but it would be much more beneficial if we could duplicate the process," he said.

"I'm listenin'."

"We'll set you up with a contractor who will build racquetball courts across the country—with your name on them, of course. We'll be in touch." Click.

JOURNAL ENTRY: OCT. 29, 1977

I felt like I was sleep walkin' through an entire Vegas engagement at The Hilton just before the holidays. I had a good view of the sunrise over the desert mountains from my private bedroom. I think that's the only time I ever saw any real beauty in Vegas.

There wasn't much beauty around Graceland for the holidays. Linda was in Hollywood, and I was alone with the boys, Daddy, and some relatives. I'd been watching *A Christmas Carol* a few nights before His birthday, and that must have gotten to me. On Christmas Eve I had a terrible nightmare.

I was bankrupt, and everyone had left me. I called out Priscilla's name, and I thought she was coming to be with me. I saw her face at first, soft and innocent, like the day we met, but then it turned ugly. Her face changed in a flash into Linda's and then into all of the women I had been with, but they weren't beautiful like I wanted them to be. Just ugly, and cold when I reached out to clutch their arms. Then I could see myself, cold and lifeless, too, but my eyes were open. Their ugly faces had swirled into a ghostly tornado, but instead of carrying me up to heaven, their ugliness had enveloped my body and was sucking me down, eyes open ...

I glanced frantically around the room, trying to shake myself from the dream world and recognize anything that would assure me I was still in my bedroom, safe in Graceland, guarded by the facade of a life I had built. My eyes stopped at Mama's picture on the nightstand.

"Tell me it's going to be alright, Mama," I pleaded.

JOURNAL ENTRY: OCT. 31, 1977

After the New Year—which gratefully was kind of quiet and uneventful—I wanted a change of scenery, someplace fresh to celebrate the beginning of the year. We rounded up the jet airplanes and headed for Colorado, and I talked Linda into coming out and joining us. I'd been made an honorary member of the Denver police force a few years earlier, and those boys hooked us up with some nice condos in Vail, out of the way but close enough to the slopes and ski bunnies—though Linda had agreed to fly out from L.A. and join us. At least that's the story I had laid out for the boys, not that any of them were one damn bit suspicious of just about anything I came up with these days. I thought about skiing, but it was new to me and I didn't like being no good at any sport, nor much of anything else for that matter. Besides, skiing was pretty much of a day sport. By the time I was up and around most days, the boys had hit the slopes and were back in the hotel room looking for various ways to get warm, whether by drink or companionship.

The real reason for my visit was a face-to-face update meeting with Agent Johnson. I had received specific instructions on the meeting time and place. Funny how those Denver cops had led us to a convenient spot to make the connection. The boys were too tired to object when I took a few post-midnight forays on a snowmobile prior to the meeting date. Getting out alone on the meeting night would be no problem. I followed the map that was delivered by mail—in a non-descript package, return address from a Washington P.O. Box—and made sure to come alone, no tails. As instructed, I stopped 100 yards short of the dimly lit log cabin, by the split-topped pine tree.

"Good evening, Mr. Presley."

I'd barely heard the voice before I was knocked off my snowmobile and pushed down, face-first in the snow. I gasped for breath as a black hood was thrust over my head and tied loose enough at the neck to let me breathe. My arms were pulled back and cuffed. I could feel several hands brushing the snow from my body as I was pulled to my feet. I tried a leg sweep, but was knocked to the ground by an elbow smashing into my chest.

"Our karate is better than yours, Mr. Presley."

The knee grinding into my kidney assured me this was true. I relaxed and was yanked to my feet again.

"Can you walk?"

"As long as you don't knock me on my ass again, Ace."

"I assure you, we mean you no harm, Mr. Presley."

"Then lead the way, because I sure as hell can't see which way to go."

Strong hands clasped my shoulders and led me forward through the snow. I could hear muffled voices inside as we mounted a short set of stairs. I heard a door open, was pushed inside onto a hardwood floor, and heard the distinct sound of a dead bolt sliding into the locked position.

"Good evening, Mr. Presley."

Agent Johnson's voice sounded even creepier than before.

"I hope my colleagues weren't too rough with you."

"What the hell ..."

"Quiet, please, Mr. Presley. It's quite late and sound travels for miles in the cold of winter."

"Take this damn thing off, you son of a bitch!" I hissed.

"I'm afraid I can't do that, Mr. Presley. I need to maintain my identity. I will, however, have Agent Schmidt uncuff you, but do promise to remain calm."

"I'm not itchin' to go anywhere."

"We need to discuss the matter of payment, Mr. Presley. It turns out the original margin of $30 million won't cover our expenses. The sum is now $50 million, which will be distributed in a 50/50 split."

"I always knew you were a snake," Agent Johnson. "What if I pull the plug on the whole thing right now!?"

I received another chop to the shoulder blade as a reply.

"We want you to realize, Mr. Presley, that we've come too far, all of us, including you, to change our minds now. Do you agree, Mr. Presley?"

"What if I don't?"

"Well, let's just say some people who are very close to you, your ex-wife, perhaps even your daughter, may run into some unforeseen 'difficulties'."

"I know some people, too, you son of a bitch. You do anything to hurt my family, hurt anyone I know, and I'll have you strung up."

"No reason to get excited, Mr. Presley. We're just protecting our investment, so to speak. Let's not forget that what you want is to start a new life, and we're providing you the means to do so."

"I'm not sure what I want exactly," I said.

"We share that concern, Mr. Presley, but you already made that choice when you headed down this path. It's too late to turn back now, at least not without grave consequences. Just continue to take the placebos, continue to perform and behave erratically, but don't do anything radical. Understood?"

"I hear ya."

"Good. Agent Schmidt is going to have to handcuff you again now, Mr. Presley. Don't breathe a word of this encounter to anyone back at your cabin, or we will know. You'll receive more instructions soon. Goodnight, Mr. Presley."

I was yanked from my chair, handcuffed behind my back again and hauled to the porch. They put me behind a rider and tied us together, back-to-back, for the return ride. I could hear the whine of several machines as we took off. We rode for what seemed like a half mile or more, certainly farther than the distance from where I stopped by the split-topped tree. We stopped, and I was untied, uncuffed, and pulled to my feet. By the time my hood was removed the three men escorting me had donned full-faced ski masks.

"Mr. Presley, your cabin is straight down this trail, about a half-mile. Head straight there."

Through the muffler I couldn't tell if the voice was Agent Schmidt's. I hopped on my snowmobile and headed straight back for our cabin, as instructed. I'd had enough of messing with FBI agents for one night. Before we left Colorado, I spent another $70 grand on three more Caddies and two Lincolns for members of the Denver Police Department, though.

JOURNAL ENTRY: NOV. 1, 1977

That contractor Agent Johnson had mentioned did get in touch with me after we returned to Memphis, and we built a bunch of racquetball courts all across the country. I kind of lost interest in the sport, but what really mattered was that each slab of cement that was laid meant a few more greenbacks were being added to my offshore account. Agent Johnson played it just right, making sure the publicity people printed that I had lost all sorts of money on the racquetball venture before it was taken over by Don Kessinger, a baseball player for the Chicago Cubs. We "lost" some money, alright.

JOURNAL ENTRY: NOV. 2, 1977

The Colonel booked two short tours that spring and another 10-day engagement in Tahoe. I kept up my act during all the shows, making sure not to do anything too erratic, just as Agent Johnson had advised. I'm sure my behavior was being noticed because Daddy canceled plane tickets for Sonny's family to join the tour down in Fort Worth. Not long after that Daddy fired Red, Sonny, and Dave Hebler. That must have pissed 'em off because those three took to writing a book that would tell all of my secrets, the drug addiction and all. I pretended to make a big stink about it and even offered to buy them off not to write the book, but secretly I knew it couldn't hurt my cause to make people believe my health was in real danger. I stayed on the road most of the fall, with drug rumors and the publicity people following me to every stop. One of the new members of the entourage, George Klein, brought Terry Alden, the new Miss Tennessee, out to Graceland just before the holidays, but I fell for her younger sister, Ginger. I took her on a date to Vegas, with her parents' permission, of course, and arranged for her to fly out to San Francisco to spend some nights with me on tour. I'd still been seeing Linda off and on, and she was in San Francisco with us. I tried talking her into heading back to Memphis for some beauty rest, but she knew what was going on. She didn't believe that I would have another plane flown out there just to take her home. No, she knew the "cargo" included a lot more than I was letting on. We'd talk on the phone from time to time, but that night in San Francisco was the last time I ever saw Linda's face.

JOURNAL ENTRY: NOV. 3, 1977

Christmas at Graceland was mostly depressing, but I got out of there real quick for a short tour that ended up New Year's Eve in Pittsburgh. By the end of 1976, I'd been on 11 separate tours and performed 129 shows.

I kept searching for something that would keep me interested in this life. Deep down I knew it was the beginning of the end, though. Even If I wanted to remain Elvis Presley, Agent Johnson and his boys weren't going to let that happen. I celebrated the last birthday of this life with Ginger and her sister, Rosemary, in Palm Springs. I convinced Dr. Max to come down with his fiancée' and get married. Larry did a real nice ceremony. A few days later I asked Ginger if she wanted Larry to do the same for us. I guess that didn't go over too well because Ginger didn't give me the answer I wanted, and we ended up fighting is all. Back in Memphis, I put together a ring myself from what I had laying around and made a formal proposal. Ginger accepted in the bathroom at Graceland, which turned out to be quite ironic in the end.

JOURNAL ENTRY: NOV. 4, 1977

I signed my will over to Daddy, leaving him in control of everything I owned before heading off to Hawaii for vacation. The real reason for my trip was another secret meeting with the FBI. I'd received word to ditch the boys and be ready for a helicopter ride to the Big Island. I got up early and was able to exit our private vacation home just north of Waikiki without being noticed. We were on vacation, and the boys wouldn't be up early. As instructed, I walked to the corner of Diamond Head Road and Makalei Place to await my ride. At precisely 7 A.M., a black Hummer heading north pulled to the curb in front of me, and the large door swung open.

"Please get in, Mr. Presley." I could barely make out the face, but the thick forearm that braced the door told me this was a large man. I climbed in and the Hummer headed south toward Honolulu. We entered what looked like a military compound through an armed security checkpoint, and the Hummer pulled up to a helipad.

"We're hopping over to the Big Island, Mr. Presley," said the pilot, who introduced himself as Agent Martin.

"You ever flown in one of these before, Mr. Presley?"

"Yes, sir, way back when I was in the Army."

"Well, hang on, because we've got some wind shear up there, today."

I climbed into the back with two black suits, who buckled up and didn't bother to introduce themselves.

"We'll be your escort, Mr. Presley," the smaller one with sharp, close-set eyes said. "No need for handcuffs and hoods *this time*, at least not yet."

The bigger dude stayed silent, but I could see a slight grin on his face at the words "this time."

"So, you two ever been to Vail?" I asked with no attempt at hiding the insinuation.

"A time or two, Mr. Presley," the small one said as the big one smiled broadly.

Agent Martin steered the chopper into a steep dive as the dark outline of the Big Island appeared through the haze of the morning marine layer. I think he wanted to see if I could hold my breakfast. Those FBI guys do enjoy their petty games. I held on fine and could see two large, black Hummers awaiting our arrival. We touched down with a bump, and Agent Martin cut the motor.

"Mr. Presley, I think you know the drill," the smaller Agent said as he pulled out a black hoodie and a pair of handcuffs. "We'd like this to go smoothly."

The smirk on the big one's face assured me it would, no matter whether I planned to cooperate. No need to resist, I thought, and turned to put my hands behind my back. The hood slipped over my head, and I could feel the cold steel of the cuffs cut slightly into my wrists.

"Take it easy on the hands, boys. I ain't plannin' to go nowhere, and these hands are worth more than you'll make in a lifetime."

I was lifted out of the chopper and placed feet first on the ground.

"Nice to, uh, *see* you again, Mr. Presley," Agent Johnson said with a hint of pleasure in his tone.

"Can't really say I share that view," I said.

I was loaded into the backseat of one of the Hummers and could feel the presence of agents on either side of me.

"We're at Pohakuloa Training Area, Mr. Presley," Agent Johnson said from the direction of the front seat. "We are heading for a secure compound where, when the time comes, you will be debriefed and prepared to re-enter civilian life."

"Debriefed? I'd prefer to just pay you guys and never see you again," I said.

"This is a very delicate affair, Mr. Presley, the type of thing that can end careers—and not just singing ones—if it's not handled properly. Once we are satisfied that your cooperation is guaranteed, you will be granted some freedoms."

"I'm kinda used to doing what I want, you know?"

"Well, Mr. Presley, our aim is to make sure dead men tell no tales—even if they come back to life." I heard the front door open and close. A hand slid behind my back, and I was uncuffed. As the hood was pulled away, I saw my escorts from the helicopter had joined me on either side in the back seat of the Hummer. Agent Martin was in the driver's seat. Agent Johnson had moved to the second vehicle.

As the Hummer headed down a steep mountain road, I made note of the road signs and landmarks, just in case that might come in handy. We passed Pu'u wa'a wa'a Cinder Cone State Park. Hawaii Belt Road turned into Mamalahoa Highway, Palani Road and back into Hawaii Belt Road as we entered the town of Kailua-Kona. The Hummer turned north on Queen Kaahumanu Highway, following the coast to our left. We exited onto Ala Nui Kaloko and turned onto a road that had no name, just "Private Drive - NO TRESPASSING" in large block letters. Agent Martin slid a security key through the electronic sensor to open the 10-foot high iron gate. The Hummer proceeded down a narrow lane with dense shrubs growing to the edge of the asphalt on both sides. A quarter mile down the lane, the Hummer pulled up to a white plantation style home that sprawled over several acres of open land. As we exited the vehicle, I could smell the ocean. Two men approached from the house and introduced themselves as Agents James McMahan and Richard Gatewood. They both seemed friendly, dressed in shorts, casual shirts and sandals, and this was the first time one of the FBI types had bothered to include a first name when shaking my hand.

"Good morning, Mr. Presley, and welcome to Kona," Agent McMahan said. "We'd like to give you a tour of the premises."

"That sounds great. Will Agent Johnson be joining us?"

"Just us three, if that's okay with you, Mr. Presley."

"Actually, I'd prefer it that way, Agent McMahan. Or may I call you James."

"Please do, and follow me."

We walked through the main entrance into a spacious open-air home decorated in traditional Island style. The large front windows looked out over a golf course and the cobalt blue waters of the Pacific in the distance. I noticed a thick row of shrubs and a 10-foot stone wall separating the compound from the green grass of the adjoining fairway. Agent Gatewood opened the sliding door to a large deck overlooking the view.

"Let's sit and have a chat before we continue the tour, Mr. Presley," he said.

We sat down in comfortable lounge chairs around a glass table with an umbrella to provide shade. A group of golfers rolled by in carts and waved. A woman dressed casually entered from the left carrying a tray of drinks and set them on the table.

"Mango-lemonade, Mr. Presley, an Island favorite," Agent McMahan said. "Thank you, Keloa." The woman, who appeared native to the Islands, bowed slightly and returned inside.

"Mr. Presley, I apologize for all you've been through, but I'm sure you understand that a level of security is necessary in this situation," Agent McMahan said. "We'd like this to be your home as you get acclimated to your new life, and Agent Gatewood and myself would like to be your personal bodyguards in that endeavor."

"You make it sound as if I have a say in the matter, James," I said.

"You will be allowed only certain freedoms in the beginning, Mr. Presley, at least until you are comfortable in your new surroundings," Agent Gatewood said. "After a period of time, you will be free to live your new life on your own terms. I assure you that the precautions we are taking in this matter are for your protection and for the safety of your family."

"Agent Gatewood, uh, Richard, may I call you Richard?"

"Please do."

"Well, Richard, I'm paying a very high price for my new life, in more than money, and I'd like to live it on my own terms," I said.

"We understand, Mr. Presley, and you have our word that our presence here and you living here, is in your best interest," Agent Gatewood said.

"I thought Deputy Hoover and Deputy Director Tolson had my best interests in mind, but they're both gone now," I said. "I don't trust Agent Johnson."

Agent McMahan placed an envelope on the table. My name had been hand-printed on the front. The letter was dated and sealed with the FBI logo.

"Go ahead and open it, Mr. Presley," Agent McMahan said.

The envelope contained a typed letter:

"Dear Mr. Presley:

If you are reading this letter, you are sitting with Agents McMahan and Gatewood at our FBI safe house in Kona, Hawaii. I'm sure you can see what a beautiful place it is. Following our last meeting, I approached Agents McMahan and Gatewood with a proposal for what would be their final assignments. They are both fine men and outstanding agents who have served faithfully for many years. By the time you are ready to proceed to the next stage, they will have reached retirement age. Both have given their lives to their careers, and neither have family. I have arranged for them to serve as your private bodyguards in retirement. You will be allowed to live at the safe house for as long as you like, as part of your payment, with Agents McMahan and Gatewood at your service. I trust you will find this arrangement agreeable. I wish you all the best in your new life."

Sincerely yours,
J. Edgar Hoover, Director the FBI
Dated: April 24, 1972
cc: Clyde Tolson, Deputy Director

I put the letter back in the envelope and stuffed it in my pants pocket.

"Director Hoover speaks very highly of both of you," I said.

"He spoke highly of you too, Mr. Presley," Agent McMahan said. "We were present when he placed that letter in your file. I was hoping we would get the chance to be here when you opened it."

"Okay. I still don't trust Agent Johnson, but I'll put my new life in your boys' hands," I said.

We rose and shook hands again, a silent agreement sealed by three nods of approval. We toured the rest of the compound, which included comfortable living quarters, a state-of-the art exercise room, personal movie theater, and even a recording studio. I couldn't imagine a better place to begin my new life. We stopped on the patio to take in the view once more before heading back to the Hummers.

"You play golf, Mr. Presley?" Agent Gatewood asked as another foursome rolled by in their golf carts and waved at us.

"Not much, but I've been meanin' to learn," I said.

"I think we can get that done, boss."

Agent Johnson maintained his disguise on the return trip, and truth be told I really didn't want to see his face anyway. I preferred the image of him in my mind's eye, a shrewd-looking little son of a bitch who needed to have his ass kicked. But the little voice that accompanied my visions reminded me that a man like Agent Johnson would always have enforcers nearby to do his bidding.

JOURNAL ENTRY: NOV. 5, 1977

We cut the vacation short as I complained of an infection from sand in my eye, which provided more fodder for the publicity people. The Colonel had a tour booked soon after we got back from Hawaii. I'd studied enough about cops and criminals to realize that the person pullin' off a caper is always itchin' to tell someone. The cops will tell you that is usually how criminals get caught. My mind was tellin' me to stay calm, stick to the plan, don't do anything out of the ordinary—whatever the hell that was these days. Well, I must have had that itch to leave some clues because I changed the first verse of "Can't Help Falling in Love" to "Wise men know when it's time to go" as I closed out a show in Alexandria, Louisiana. I gave the publicity people some more to write about by canceling the final four stops. The Colonel was pissed, of course, but I wouldn't have to keep him happy for much longer. I received more instructions from Agent Johnson and checked into the hospital again for a few days. The official diagnosis this time was "exhaustion," but secretly I was more excited than ever. Priscilla and Lisa Marie came to visit, and when I got back to Graceland, I overheard the boys arguing about what to do about the pills. Some of them wanted to give me placebos instead of the real stuff. It made me feel pretty smart to know that I was at least one step ahead of them. I headed off to Vegas for a short rendezvous with a bank teller I met in Memphis because, you know, I still planned to live a little before I "died."

JOURNAL ENTRY: NOV. 7, 1977

I made it through two more tours in May and June, and apparently I didn't care too much what my fans were thinking because one night I left the stage for a half-hour just to take a piss. The book Sonny and Red had been working on was coming out in other parts of the world, and that kept all of the publicity people busy. I figured the more lies, the better. It hit the bookstores in America in mid-summer, and maybe that is what put me completely over the edge. I'd been planning to leave this life and enter a new one for some time, but it all seemed like some sort of dream, or maybe a nightmare—probably somewhere in between. Pulling the trigger, so to speak, was going to be the hardest thing I had ever done. I couldn't bear the thought of not being able to see Lisa Marie, my Little Injun, and her missing her daddy. Agent Johnson was vile enough to make good on his threats, though, and that made me realize I had to leave Lisa Marie to her mama. Somewhere in my dream/nightmare visions I still believed I'd wake up, and those two would be there. We'd be together, like I always wanted. Then my "reality" voice would always get in the way. I looked for all sorts of meanings in my books on omens and such to pick just the right day for my "death." Then it hit me. August 14, the day Mama died.

I called Agent Johnson with the news of the date for my demise, but he had other plans.

"Mr. Presley, while it would be poetic and somewhat believable to pass away on the same date as your mother's death, it might also cause some undue suspicion," he said coldly. "I see you are scheduled to leave on a tour on Aug. 17. I don't think you will be making that trip. The day before should be perfect timing."

"Well, I guess I can hang on for a few more days."

"Very well then, Aug. 16. Agreed?"

"Yes, that will do."

"Okay, you will be receiving detailed instructions, which of course must be kept in the utmost secrecy." Click.

JOURNAL ENTRY: NOV. 8, 1977

I went about life as usual and prepared for the tour without a hint of anything unusual. I made a short trip to Tennessee to catch some new movies in a private screening. The new James Bond flick, *The Spy Who Loved Me*, was especially entertaining. Secretly, I wished I could come up with a much more stylish way to go out, something befitting a man of adventure like Agent 007. Maybe a hang-gliding accident, the ticker overheating in the middle of a hot threesome, or flying one of my jets into a mountain top. I knew Agent Johnson would make me stick to the plan, though. He called the evening of Aug. 12, four days before my demise, to make sure everything was proceeding to order.

"I trust you are ready to proceed, Mr. Presley," Agent Johnson said.

"Yeah, I'm doin' fine, thanks for askin'," I said in my most sarcastic tone.

"The matter of your health will be resolved shortly, as you know, Mr. Presley. We have secured a suitable replacement for you. Preparations are being made as we speak to make sure he is a perfect match."

"Anyone ever told you what a cold son of a bitch you are?"

"I've been trained to complete the task at hand, Mr. Presley, nothing more, nothing less. Now then, let's get to the details, shall we?"

"I'm listenin'."

"Very well then. You will make a phone call the morning of Aug. 15 to this number: 555-1687. If anyone looks up the number subsequently, they will see that it matches to Lonnie's TV Repair."

"1-6-87?" I asked.

"That is correct. I do hope you wrote it down, though. A man with your proclivities for drug use may be prone to short-term memory loss."

"I wasn't repeating the number for you, Ace. 1-6-87. August 16, 1987. Don't you think that might raise some suspicion?"

"We thought you might enjoy the irony, Mr. Presley. After all, we have been very strict with you to proceed according to our plans."

"Okay, I'll go along with your little game. What else?"

"The repairmen will arrive on the morning of Aug. 16, precisely at noon. Since you called for the service, people will expect their arrival. Their van will pull up to the back entrance, allowing ease of access to the back staircase that leads upstairs to your living quarters where your televisions are located. They'll be working on the TV in your private bathroom, of course. Your job is to create a diversion so the agents can escort your double up the back stairway to your private bathroom without being noticed."

"You mean the poor bastard will still be alive?" I asked in dismay.

"Alive, yes. Coherent, no. He will be drugged—fatally, of course. The actual time of death has to be very near to the last time you are seen alive, so to speak. We wouldn't want people to discover a body that is already stiff, now would we?"

"What a sick prick you are."

"Be that as it may, Mr. Presley, once the agents have delivered your double to the bathroom, and they have made for his final arrangements, so to speak, you will address Ms. Alden before entering the private bathroom yourself. Do be sure to close the door this time, Mr. Presley. Then you will switch clothes with your double and leave with the agents down the back staircase. The van will exit Graceland with two agents in the front and you hidden safely in the back. The van will proceed to a private airstrip, where a plane will be waiting. Understood?"

"What if I decide to blow the whistle on this whole thing? What then?"

"Well, Mr. Presley, we have agents tracking your ex-wife and daughter at this very moment. They have instructions to stay within striking distance until I give the order to clear. Now do you understand?"

"Touch either one of them, and so help my soul ..."

"You are in no position to threaten, Mr. Presley. And remember, this is what you wanted."

"One more question. What's preventing you from making me disappear and keeping all the money for yourself?"

"The FBI has well established protocol for protecting everyone's interests in a delicate matter such as this," Agent Johnson said.

He explained that all transactions would be handled through Swiss bank accounts with extreme security measures in place. Bank representatives would be meeting Mr. Presley in person to confirm the following terms. Payments would take place only after Mr. Presley had alerted Swiss authorities for approval. Mr. Presley would have complete access to all personnel files and would choose from among 19 bank executives to make the call for approval. Mr. Presley would choose a new executive whenever he wished, including every month if that made him more comfortable. In the event of Mr. Presley's death, for whatever reason, the remainder of the account would be transferred to an heir of Mr. Presley's choosing, and this person would remain anonymous to the FBI.

"So, Mr. Presley, we have everything to gain by keeping you alive."

"I still don't trust you completely, Agent Johnson, but okay. I make the call the day before to your cute little number. The van arrives the next day at noon. I make sure the coast is clear for the agents to scale the back staircase. I switch clothes and get the hell out of Dodge while some poor bastard chokes his guts out and dies on my bathroom floor. I think I've got it."

"Your description is quite dramatic, Mr. Presley, but yes, there will be vomiting followed by convulsions that will cause discoloration in the face, bulging eyes, and the tongue to swell and protrude. All of which will help conceal the corpse's true identity and work to your benefit. You will receive no further instructions, but remember, we'll be watching." Click.

JOURNAL ENTRY: NOV. 9, 1977

The morning of Aug. 15, I made the call to Lonnie's Repair Service. Some cold FBI bitch actually answered and stayed on the line while I requested immediate service for my broken set. I went to see Dr. Hoffman for a routine dental checkup the night before I "died." It seemed like a strange way to spend my last night of this life, but I had already made the appointment. I respected Dr. Hoffman's time, and I'm sure Agent Johnson wouldn't want me to do anything out of the ordinary. Of course, the dental records had already been switched to match the poor soul who would die—for me.

CHAPTER THREE

The message crackled through Nick Sartain's police radio at 1:57 P.M. Dispatch was requesting all available units, including detectives, for backup at Graceland.

"Probably some lunatic trying to break in and see Elvis," Nick muttered to himself.

It certainly wasn't the first time that fans had gotten out of control while trying to catch a glimpse of their idol. Nick had been following up some leads on a bar fight that left two thugs dead. One of them was Charlie "Big Thumbs" Sarkowicz, one of the Manko brothers' enforcers; so Nick figured the trail could lead to Memphis' organized crime scene, which paled to operations in cities like Chicago and New York but still provided enough action to keep the detectives busy. Nick had become a "suit" in 1972, after 10 years as a patrolman assigned to the heart of the city. He'd worked both vice and homicide, and in Memphis it was hard to separate the two. The blues joints on Beale Street produced the best music scene north of New Orleans—some say even better than the Crescent City—but tunes had been synonymous with drugs in Memphis since the beginning of the Cultural Revolution of the '60s. Nick's mostly clean-cut, straightforward approach didn't serve him well when the job called for going undercover, but Nick preferred it that way. He'd grown up in a blue-collar family on his own terms in Dent, Ohio, a suburb of Cincinnati that sits just north of the Mason-Dixon Line. Perhaps that's why Nick never adopted any "Southern charms" and he spoke with no hint of an accent. He'd escaped the boredom of the Midwest right after high school by joining the Marines. Uncle Sam shipped him off to a stint in North Korea, where Nick took a bullet in his left shoulder, an injury that still caused some sleepless nights. After Korea, Nick advanced through the ranks while stationed at Camp Lejeune in North Carolina. He returned to Southeast Asia before U.S. involvement escalated in Vietnam, but Nick still saw enough gore—both the political and battlefield varieties—to realize he wasn't a career military man. Nick still liked the ideals of duty and honor and he always had an eye for detail, so police work was a natural fit. Memphis PD seemed like as good a place as any to start a new career—and they were hiring. Nick was older than most rookies and not as brash. He still took too many chances according to his hard-ass Sergeant, but that changed dramatically—and for the better—three years into the job. Nick and his partner surprised three guys cutting a drug deal in Robert Church Park. One of the punks wheeled around while reaching into his coat pocket, and Nick didn't hesitate pulling the trigger on his .357 K-frame revolver. He'd killed before, but that was while facing fire from enemies who damn sure we're trying to kill him. Turns out the drug dealer was packing nothing more harmful than a switchblade, but the dumbass hadn't given Nick any choice but to use deadly force. An inquiry absolved Nick of any wrongdoing, but soothing his conscience was another matter. For months he awoke in raging night sweats, unable to purge the image of all that blood hitting the wall.

The incident made Nick more careful—even Sergeant Pike acknowledged as much—and he had a good reason to watch his ass when he met Jenny Wilkinson in the spring of 1966. She was 11 years younger and fresh out of college, but mature beyond her years. Jenny had been reared in Collierville, an upper middle-class suburb of Memphis with plenty of Southern charm. Like Nick, she had managed to avoid Southern mannerisms, though. Jenny looked and sounded like she was from anywhere else. The one part of Memphis that was imprinted on her soul, however, was an undying love for Elvis Presley. Nick and Jenny met through mutual friends at a cop party and were married less than two years later. Jenny couldn't have children, which suited Nick. Not that he didn't want kids around, but it's enough stress on a cop worrying about coming home to just a wife. Jenny would have been a wonderful mother, but having each other was enough.

Nick thought of Jenny as he rolled his dirt brown 1971 Ford Galaxie toward Graceland. He could see a swarm of people and cars around the front gate, blocking any entrance by car.

"Looks like it's something big," Nick told Eddie Baxter, who was partnering on the homicide investigation and riding shotgun.

Nick pulled near the curb and jammed the Ford into park. Everyone they could see was either crying or looked like they were ready to do so. One middle-aged woman was on her knees, looking to the sky and wailing.

"That broad is puttin' up quite a fuss," Baxter said in his Mississippi-born-and-bred drawl. "Shore as hell, somethin' ain't right."

The detectives walked down the entrance road and found a uniformed cop, who was visibly shaken and even appeared to have a tear in his eye.

"Officer, what's the situation?" Nick asked in his usual cut-the-crap manner.

"Ain't you heard? They're sayin' Elvis is dead!"

"Holy crap!" Eddie bellowed.

The news nearly floored Nick, too, but his analytical mind was already assessing the situation.

"Who is saying that Elvis is dead?" he demanded while shaking the cop's shoulder.

"Well, uh, I don't know. Just everybody. They found him lyin' on his bathroom floor. They're sayin' he had a heart attack."

"When did you arrive?"

"I heard the first call for an ambulance request at Graceland, and I was just a few blocks away," the cop said as Nick's interrogation had a mind-clearing effect. "That was at 1:33."

"What happened after that?"

"The ambulance pulled up a few minutes later and those medic boys rushed right in. A little while later, a lady came out. She looked like a cook or some-thin', and she was cryin' and carryin' on real bad. One of the guards asked her what was wrong. She kept sayin': 'He's gone! I can't believe he's gone!'"

Nick glanced at his watch and announced the time so Eddie would take note: "2:24 now. Officer, did you see anything else that you can confirm?"

"Well, just lots of people were comin' out of the house, and they was all upset."

"Who is the officer in charge?"

"I'd say it's you, sir."

Just then the commotion around the main entrance exploded. What looked like Graceland bodyguards were clearing a path. The medics were still working on the victim as they loaded the stretcher into the back of the ambulance. Nick was able to reach the driver's side door and flash his badge before the driver jumped in.

"What is his condition?" Nick demanded.

Without speaking, the medic shook his head from side to side. Nick had been around enough battlefields and accident scenes to know a medic's triage skills were never wrong when they signaled no chance for life.

As the ambulance driver blared its siren and cut a swath through the growing crowd, Nick took control as best he could. Eddie and Nick both held lieutenant ranks, but they also both knew who was the lead cop.

"Eddie, we're going to need some tape. When you're down at the car, could you call the Captain and see what he needs us to do?"

"You bet, Nick."

Four more uniformed cops had made their way up the entrance, and several other officers were already working crowd control on the streets. Nick whistled and motioned the nearest officers to gather for a conference.

"Gentlemen, we need a barrier around this entrance. Nobody else gets in."

"Yes, sir!" rang out in unison.

With the perimeter sealed, Nick went about surveying the scene outside the mansion and making note of the people still gathered there. They all checked out as bodyguards, cooks, attendants, groundskeepers, etc.—save for one man dressed in a gray suit.

"Sir, what is your name?" Nick asked the conspicuous fellow.

"Agent Carter, FBI," he responded while flashing his shield.

"What is your business here, Agent Carter?"

"Routine surveillance. Mr. Presley had been receiving some threats of late. Nothing unusual."

"Perhaps you could use some help here, Detective."

"I think the officers can handle crowd control, Agent Carter. Nothing to investigate here."

After a noticeable pause, Nick gave a low whistle.

"Heart attack," he said while shaking his head. "I guess the doctors will be doing the rest of the investigating."

Nick was clearly alluding to the reports of Elvis' drug use and deteriorating health that had been chronicled in all the gossip and entertainment rags.

"I would say so, Detective. Now, will you excuse me? I have a report to file myself."

"Oh, yes, go right ahead. Do you have a card, just in case something comes up?"

"I'm afraid I'm all out at the moment, Detective. You can reach me at our Memphis Bureau, however."

As the man in the gray suit moved to head down the entrance, Nick gave the okay sign for the officers to let Agent Carter pass. Detective Sartain wasn't done fishing, however.

"Agent Carter. Got it," Nick said loud enough to make sure the man in the gray suit turned and saw Nick writing the name on a notepad.

Eddie had returned with the tape, and the detectives made their way to the interior of Graceland.

One of the cooks sensed their intent and pointed upstairs. Nick could smell death, or was the suggestion of the moment tricking his senses? Nothing appeared out of the ordinary in the master bedroom. The king-sized bed was unmade, but that matched what Nick had heard about Ginger Alden waking up and discovering Elvis' body in the bathroom. Nick noticed the large TV console that looked brand new. Various drug vials were visible throughout the room. Making sure not to disturb anything, Eddie made his way to the bathroom door.

"Jeezus! That doesn't look good."

Nick peered inside and saw what looked to be a mixture of blood, vomit, and urine staining the plush yellow carpet in front of the black commode.

"Okay, Eddie, let's leave this to the examiners."

Nick nudged his partner to break his stare from the bathroom scene, and the detectives made their way downstairs. They heard commotion from upstairs as they reached the main entry, and heard a voice give clear instructions.

"Lock it down! No one else gets in here. Understood?"

Nick and Eddie exited the main entrance and walked into a mob scene. More cops had joined the effort at crowd control, but hundreds of people had already made their way through the main gate. Nick heard the whir of a helicopter and saw the bird, circling overhead. It reminded him of a vulture.

"The media is already here," Nick told Eddie. "This is going to be one long night, partner."

Nick and Eddie stayed on the scene as the crowd swelled. Memphis Police called in reinforcements from nearby precincts to keep the peace. Nick was relieved of his post at 8 P.M. and wanted nothing more than to get home and soothe Jenny. His Ford was parked smack in the middle of the huge crowd, and Nick knew he wouldn't be driving it away anytime soon. He pulled the Ford closer to the curb and radioed for a patrol car to pick him up a half-mile north of Graceland. Nick checked inside to make sure he wasn't leaving any lethal weapons in case someone got inside, and locked the Ford.

Nick walked against the flow of mourners who seemed drawn to the death scene. Most were crying, some were wailing. All had the unmistakable look on their faces of the shock of losing a loved one.

Nick's tongue was silent, but his mind was still whirring from the day's events when Officer Thompson dropped him off at the modest three-bedroom home he shared with Jenny in the Mud Island district of North Memphis. The location was close enough for Nick to be downtown in 15 minutes if traffic was light—and far enough that Jenny's parents rarely made any unannounced visits from Collierville.

Jenny had been in the front yard, watering her prodigious flower beds, when Mrs. Kratzert burst out of the house next door and blurted: "Oh, my God, Jenny, the radio is saying Elvis is dead!" Jenny dropped her water pitcher in the middle of a patch of daisies and stared at Mrs. Kratzert in disbelief.

"It's true!" the elderly woman screamed.

Jenny stumbled into the house and stopped short of snapping on the transistor radio in the kitchen that kept her company while she prepared meals. The clock on the radio showed 3:04 P.M. "Maybe I'm just hallucinating," Jenny mumbled to herself.

Slowly, she twisted the "on" dial for the radio, which was always tuned to one of the Oldies stations. There was no music, just the frantic voice of a female reporter providing details.

"... Inside Baptist Memorial Hospital, where an ambulance arrived just over an hour ago. There has been no official word on Elvis' condition, but wait, doctors appear to be coming out now. There are three men at the podium. One of them appears to be an associate of Mr. Presley. He's mumbling something, but I can't make it out. He's obviously emotional and distraught now. They're leading him to a chair. A hospital official, I think, is stepping to the podium now. He has identified himself as Dr. Maurice Elliott. I believe he is one of the hospital administrators. Hard to make out over the noise and confusion, but I heard the words 'heart attack.' Yes, Dr. Maurice Elliott has just confirmed that Elvis Presley is dead ..."

The radio report continued with details of the tragic event, but Jenny's mind was spinning too fast to make sense of it. She fainted in the middle of the kitchen floor.

Jenny heard a voice and slowly opened her eyes to see the worried face of Mrs. Kratzert kneeling over her.

"Jenny, dear, are you okay?"

"I think so," Jenny whispered.

Mrs. Kratzert helped her to a chair and hastily brought a glass of water.

"Here, dear, drink some of this."

Jenny took a drink and set the glass on the table.

"My God, it's true!" she wailed. "He's really dead!"

"I'm afraid so, my dear," Mrs. Kratzert said. "Are you feeling better now?"

"Yes, but I don't know what to do. Is Nick here?"

"I'm afraid not, dear, but I'll stay with you. Why don't we go into the living room, and you can lie on the couch?"

Mrs. Kratzert steadied Jenny as she arose and led her to the living room. Jenny knew exactly where she needed to be at this moment, and it wasn't the couch. The leather rocking chair had belonged to Jenny's grandmother, and a 14-year-old Jenny sat in it and cried for hours when Grammy Flo passed away. Jenny's parents made sure she would keep the chair from then on. Jenny was sitting in that chair when she played the very first Elvis album she had bought with her own money. She had listened to every album The King had made since while sitting in that chair. Her mind wandered back through the pleasant memories of sitting and listening to his angelic voice. As Jenny slumped into the comforting and well-worn seat, she also thought of the many nights she had sat in that chair and waited for Nick to come home when she was worried about him working the night shift.

"Where is he?" she wondered aloud.

After a while, Jenny assured Mrs. Kratzert that she would be okay, and the elderly woman relented her caretaker's role. Finally sitting alone, Jenny pulled out a collection of Elvis' greatest love songs and gently touched the needle on the record player to vinyl.

Elvis' unmistakable version of "Always on My Mind" was playing as Nick walked through the door at just before 9 P.M. He knew Jenny would be in the living room, in her listening chair. She'd finally quit sobbing when she heard her husband come through the front door, but Jenny's tears hadn't really stopped since she realized her idol was gone. Jenny didn't say a word when Nick's figure appeared in the living room.

"Jenny, honey, are you okay?"

"I've been here, waiting," Jenny said in a distant voice.

"I know, baby, and I'm home now."

"Why weren't you here when it happened?"

Nick knew the stages of grief all too well from his years in the field. He felt a sharp pang of guilt as he watched his wife entering stage three: Anger. Nick had been working the late shift when Jenny's father passed away suddenly three years ago. She was alone for hours after hearing the devastating news, and Nick wasn't sure she had ever forgiven him.

"Damn you!" Jenny said as her mood changed suddenly. "You're never here for me when I really need you."

Nick also knew the technique for dealing with the effects of sudden shock, but only the direct approach that would bring a soldier back to reality after seeing one of his buddies blown apart on the battlefield. Unfortunately, Nick knew no other way.

"Jenny, look at me," Nick said in a stern tone. "You've had a shock, and your systems are reacting to it. I'm not going to tell you everything will be okay, but what you are feeling now will pass. I'm here for you, and I love you."

Jenny's feelings of anger were replaced by numbness and a vague sensation of being disconnected from her body. The part of her consciousness that knew Nick was telling the truth, that he did love her, that he would be there for her, was reassuring.

"Oh, Nick, I'm sorry," Jenny said as she arose and held her husband in a tight embrace. "I know it's not your fault. It's just ..."

"I know, honey," Nick said. "It's hard for everyone to understand."

Nick held his wife's hand and led her to the couch. He knew that the listening chair, which would help her cope with this tragedy in the future, in her own way, was not the best place to be right now given her traumatized state. He poured each of them a snifter of brandy, and held her close while the music continued.

Make the world go away
Get it off my shoulder
Say the things you used to say
And make the world, make it go away.

The crowds had swelled to an estimated 50,000 before a white hearse escorted by a motorcycle brigade cut through the throng and made its way to the front entrance of Graceland just before noon on August 17. As the copper casket was carried from the hearse through the main entrance, emotions reached a crescendo. Later reports indicated in excess of 200 people collapsed at the sight and needed medical attention. Throughout that day, tens of thousands of mourners filed past Elvis' coffin as The King lay in state in the main foyer of Graceland. Many more jostled and pushed and made vain attempts to catch a glimpse inside. Some even jumped the security fences and made a mad dash for the mansion. If ever there was a day Nick was thankful for trading in his uniform to be a plainclothes detective, this was it. He pulled rank to make sure Jenny made it through the line that allowed mourners to see The King lying in his copper coffin. And Nick made damn sure that he didn't leave her side for a second. Jenny stared with a mixture of shock, reverence, and disbelief on her face as she looked at the body.

"It doesn't look like him," Jenny said after they'd emerged from the foyer and back into the stifling Tennessee heat.

Nick filed the comment in his mental case drawer. A good detective had that cerebral stash, a place in the deepest recesses of gray matter where key details would be forever preserved.

Just two days after the news that shocked the world, a procession including a white hearse and 17 white limousines rolled to Forest Hills Cemetery in midtown Memphis so Elvis' copper coffin could be laid next to that of his beloved mother. Many thousands of fans lined the route of the funeral procession, and Graceland remained a magnet for huge crowds of mourners in the days that followed.

The particulars in the Presley case, those believed to be the last people to see him alive, had already been interviewed at the hospital or downtown:

- Fiancée' Ginger Alden, who was the first to discover Elvis unconscious in his private bathroom.
- Bodyguards Billy Smith and Ricky Stanley, who had been playing racquetball with Elvis in the early morning hours and delivered the last of the opened packets of medications that were discovered throughout the house.
- Private physician George C. Nichopoulos, the infamous "Dr. Nick" who allegedly was the source of Presley's flow of prescription drugs and who made a frantic effort to revive the corpse.
- Private nurse Tish Henley, who allegedly administered the last packet of prescription drugs that Elvis ever took, approximately two hours before his collapse.
- Father Vernon Presley, who remained distraught, and even 9-year-old Lisa Marie, who just wanted to know where her daddy had gone.

Nick and Eddie had been assigned to mop-up duty on the Presley case. Truth be told, Nick bugged the hell out of Capt. Summerfield to get the assignment. Eddie would have preferred to be tracking down whoever knocked off "Big Thumbs" Sarkowicz than talking to people who couldn't seem to quit bawling over a dead entertainer.

"What the hell we doin' down here, Nick?" Eddie pleaded. "Let's wrap up this shit and go after some criminals."

"I'm sure there are plenty of lawbreakers among these beatniks," Nick replied.

"We might catch someone stealing flowers, but that's about it," Eddie said.

Nick ignored his peevish partner and went about his business. They were assigned the forward end of the investigation, to interview anyone who had anything to do with Elvis Presley in the 48 hours preceding his death, aside from the aforementioned particulars. While Nick kept his eyes and ears open,

Eddie's best sense was always his nose. Right now, it was leading him to the smell of some good southern cookin' coming from Graceland's expansive kitchen. Nick decided to let his partner take the lead on this one.

"Howdy, ma'am," Eddie said as he stepped into the kitchen and addressed the cook, an elderly black woman.

"Howdy to y'all, officers," the woman replied.

"Well now, how'd you know we was police, ma'am?"

"Well, sir, it's pretty dang hot to go paradin' around in them suits, so I figured you wouldn't be doin' that unless it was yo' uniform."

"You read us like a book, ma'am," Eddie acknowledged. "I'm Detective Baxter, and this is Detective Sartain. What's your name, ma'am."

"Gracie Lewis," the old woman said as she glanced at their badges, but kept on kneading a batch of homemade dough that was destined to frame some southern-style pot pies. A vat of vegetables was boiling on the stove next to a batch of simmering giblet gravy.

"Well ma'am, we don' mean to keep you from fixin' the fine lookin' meal you have goin' there, but may we ask you some questions?"

"I don' mind," Ms. Lewis said.

"Okay, were you here during the days just before Mr. Presley passed away?"

"Well, I'm here jus' about all the time, 'cept Sunday mornin' when I'm at the Hopewell Baptist Church. I sing in the choir, you know."

"I'll bet you are somethin' to hear, ma'am. Detective Sartain and I, we're just wonderin' if you saw anything out of the ord'nary in the days prior to Mr. Presley's death?"

"Sonny, I been cookin' here goin' on 20 years. Now you tell me, what do y'all consider ord'nary around this place? I seen just about ever'thing a person could see. Lord, have Mercy!"

"I'm sure you have, ma'am. But did you see anythin' or anyone that seemed peculiar during that time?"

"Well, them boys that delivered Mr. Presley's new TV set that mornin' seemed a bit out of place."

"Which mornin', ma'am?"

"The day he died," the old woman said as she bowed her head and wiped away a tear with her apron.

"What did you see?"

"Well, I was here in the kitchen, and I saw 'em come through the back way and head upstairs. I don' think they saw me, but they was lookin' around, kinda like they was makin' sure no one was watchin'."

"And they headed straight upstairs?"

"Yessum, they was carryin' somethin' that looked kinda heavy, but they had it covered with a blanket."

"How long were they upstairs?"

"Oh, I'd say only 'bout 10 minutes or so. I ain't got no fancy TV set, jus' an ol' black and white, but seems to me it would take longer than that to set up a brand-new colored set."

"Did you see them come back down, ma'am?"

"No, sir, but I heard 'em head back out. They jumped in their van and was gone in a hurry."

"Was anyone else aroun', ma'am. Did anyone else see them, you think?"

"No, I don' think so. It was pretty quiet roun' here for a change. I guess it's always kinda quiet 'fore somethin' bad happens like that."

"Do you have any idea what time of the mornin' it was when you saw these men, ma'am?"

"Well, I'd done cleaned up all the breakfast dishes an' put 'em away, so it had to be gettin' on close to noon."

"Okay, well, thank you, ma'am. We'll let you get back to your cookin' now."

"I guess I'm needin' to do that. Now don' you fellas go sweatin' to death in them suits."

"Thank you kindly, Ms. Lewis, and we'll come aroun' again if we need to ask you any more questions."

Eddie bowed slightly to Ms. Lewis and led his partner out of the kitchen. Nick was impressed, as always, by Eddie's approach. Baxter looked and sounded like a good ol' boy to the casual observer, but he had a way of getting information out of these people that Nick could never copy. Paired with Nick's bulldog approach, Eddie provided the finesse that formed their chemistry. The two detectives stopped near the back entrance, and each instinctively looked up and down the stairway leading to the private residence upstairs.

"I guess we need to get a look at the security tape and those delivery boys, eh?" Nick said.

"Yeah, they've got me a little interested, too," Eddie replied.

Nick added a note to his mental case drawer: Eddie thinks something is strange, too. He was pleased that his partner also had a case of the curiosities.

Elvis Presley had gone to see his dentist, Dr. Lester Hoffman, late Monday evening, an estimated 16 hours before the time of death. Nick and Eddie both thought getting your teeth drilled just before midnight was pretty damn weird, but apparently most of Presley's visits were late at night to avoid any commotion from fans. Still, a visit with Dr. Hoffman definitely was on their mop-up list.

"You know, I read a story that Elvis gave this Dr. Hoffman an organ and a brand-new Cadillac, just for the hell of it," Eddie said as they pulled up to the dentist's office in their dirt-brown Ford. "Damn, maybe someone will give us a new Chevelle or somethin' to replace this piece of shit one day, jus' for bein' nice guys."

"Don't count on it," Nick said as they walked through the glass doors and were greeted by a receptionist at the front desk.

"May I help you?"

"Yes, I'm Detective Sartain and this is Detective Baxter. We're here to see Dr. Hoffman."

"Please have a seat, and I'll let Dr. Hoffman know you are here."

Five minutes later, the receptionist parted the batwing doors to the back offices and invited Nick and Eddie to be seated in a small conference room.

"Please make yourselves at home, gentlemen," she said. "Dr. Hoffman will be with you shortly."

"First time I've ever been in a dentist's office without the fear of God in me," Eddie said with a chuckle. "Always hated goin' to the damn dentist's office, but I guess it's better than not havin' any teeth. There's a few of them folks hangin' aroun' my family tree."

Dr. Hoffman entered the small conference room and gave the reassured smile he'd rehearsed—daily—for the past 20 years.

"Now, what can I do for you gentlemen?"

"This is Detective Baxter, and I'm Detective Sartain," Nick said as the detectives gave a cursory flash of their badges. "We're here on routine business, Dr. Hoffman. We're just following up on Mr. Presley's death and talking to folks who interacted with him in the days prior. We understand he came to see you for some dental work the night before he died."

Dr. Hoffman wasn't the sort who needed to be led into conversation. Working on Elvis Presley's teeth was his 15 minutes of fame, and he didn't mind talking about it. He regaled the detectives with stories of Elvis' generosity and the many times he had made appointments at all hours of the night to avoid any fanfare.

"The guy couldn't even go to the dentist in peace," Eddie marveled as Dr. Hoffman detailed The King's dental hygiene.

Dr. Hoffman could sense the detectives hadn't come just to hear about late-night laughing gas and gifts of organs and Cadillacs, however.

"So, what's all the interest in Mr. Presley's dental records?" Dr. Hoffman asked.

"What do you mean, doctor?" Nick replied.

"Well, two guys from the FBI were here yesterday looking through his file."

"I see. Dr. Hoffman, what procedures did you perform on Mr. Presley during this recent visit?" Nick continued as his demeanor returned to all business.

"Nothing big, just a cleaning and two small fillings, if I recall," Dr. Hoffman said.

"Mind if we take a look at the file?" Nick asked.

"Not at all," Dr. Hoffman said as he arose from his chair and leaned into the hallway. "Polly, bring Mr. Presley's file, would you?"

Dr. Hoffman opened the manila folder and thumbed through a pile of x-rays and other papers.

"That's strange," Dr. Hoffman said with a furrowed brow. "I don't see anything from the recent visit."

"Are you sure, Dr. Hoffman?" Nick asked.

"Nothing. It should be right here in the back. We file everything chronologically."

"What should be there, Dr. Hoffman?"

"We took some x-rays to pinpoint the recent decay. I made notes of the procedures, that sort of thing."

"Dr. Hoffman, has anyone else besides you and your staff had access to this file since yesterday?"

"No sir. We closed early when we heard the news," Dr. Hoffman said. "Everyone was quite upset, naturally. No one has had access to those files since. Just our staff here and the FBI agents."

"Did you or anyone else watch the gentlemen from the FBI go through the files, Dr. Hoffman?" Nick asked.

"We were in the other conference room, across the hall," Dr. Hoffman said. "I received a phone call, so I excused myself for a moment."

"Who called you?" Nick asked.

"It was a call from Dr. Miller's office, one of his receptionists, I believe. She asked me to wait on the line for a minute. Then she came back and said that Dr. Miller had been called away, but that he would get back to me. She said it was nothing urgent."

"Then you returned to the conference room?"

"Yes, I walked back in and sat down. They thanked me for my time and left."

"Do you recall the names of the gentleman from the FBI, Dr. Hoffman?"

"Uh, let me think ... Carter, Agent Carter. Not sure the other one introduced himself."

Eddie and Nick turned to make eye contact, but they made sure not to derail the interrogation.

"Did either of them leave a card for you or anything else?" Nick asked.

"No. They just said they would be back in touch if they needed anything else. It seemed a little tense, but you know, I guess FBI agents are pretty serious."

"Indeed, they are, Dr. Hoffman," Nick said with a hint of suspicion in his voice. "We'll be in touch. In the meantime, please let us know immediately if the FBI shows up again."

Nick handed a card to Dr. Hoffman as he and Eddie exited the doctor's office. Nick made another note in his mental case drawer, which was expanding with unexplained details surrounding the death of Elvis Presley.

"Well, Eddie, what do you make of that?" Nick asked as the detectives climbed into the dirt-brown Ford.

"I don't know, Nick. There have been stories for years of Elvis being involved with the FBI in one way or another. Hell, there are all sorts of strange stories about Elvis, and you know the tabloids are going to ride this for as long as they can. Maybe the Feds are just tryin' to protect his reputation."

"They don't give two shits about reputations—except maybe theirs—and you know it, Eddie."

Someone apparently was protecting The King's legacy, however, as the initial autopsy report from the Shelby County Medical Office stated "there was no indication of drug abuse." The autopsy had been performed fewer than six hours after the time of death. Media reports indicated that further results would be available after doctors received results from a series of lab tests. Nick knew from experience that process would take at least a few weeks, and the public may never know what was inside Presley's body the day he died.

Nick and Eddie made another visit to Graceland to find out if anyone other than Gracie Lewis had seen some mysterious TV repairmen on the morning of Elvis' death. Al Strada, who had been on duty the day Elvis died and was one of the first people to respond to Ginger's screams for help, was still handling security in the aftermath of the death and the funeral proceedings. Cameras had been planted all over the grounds through the years, and the various bodyguards on duty could monitor them from the master control room downstairs. Nick requested to see all angles of the main entrance and the back stairway for a 24-hour period backward from 2:30 P.M. Tuesday.

"No problem, detective," Al Strada said in a genuinely helpful tone.

Strada showed the various camera angles, how each could be viewed on the main screen, and how to rewind with the time and date stamps showing.

"Now, would you allow us to view the tapes in private, Mr. Strada?" Nick asked.

"Sure thing, detective. I'll be right outside if you need anything."

Nick had worked some video surveillance systems in the Marines and picked up this system quickly even though the technology was much more advanced than what he had used in the military. Nick rolled through the tape for Monday afternoon and evening, and on through the morning hours of Tuesday, Aug. 16. He clicked the stop button when the surveillance tapes showed an ambulance rolling through the front gates of Graceland at 2:36 P.M. Nowhere to be seen was a TV repair vehicle. Eddie looked at his partner and tried to read his thoughts.

"So, what now?" Eddie asked.

"Damn! I don't know," Nick replied. His analytical mind was already weighing the options, though. "I guess we should get sworn testimony from Ms. Lewis, but I don't know what good that will do. There is absolutely nothing here to corroborate what she said she saw."

"She seemed to be tellin' the truth, though, and she had no reason not to," Eddie said.

"Exactly, but the tapes tell a different story. So, I guess we have two possibilities. One, she was hallucinating and didn't really see anything. Two, she saw what she said she saw, but the tapes have been altered to show nothing."

"I'd pick door number two, partner," Eddie said.

"Yeah, me too, but where does that leaves us?" Nick replied. "We have the testimony of one person against visual evidence. And if the second option is true, if someone did alter the tapes, they sure as hell don't want Ms. Lewis telling her story. We could put her in real danger if we share her story."

"Yea, but you know we still have to talk her again, Nick."

The two detectives exited the video surveillance room and thanked Al Strada for his cooperation. They walked to the kitchen and encountered a different cook working over some legs of lamb and chopping vegetables.

"Excuse me, ma'am, this here is Detective Sartain and I am Detective Baxter," Eddie said as the middle-aged white woman looked up from her duties. "Would Ms. Lewis be on duty today?"

"I been here since yesterday," the woman said. "I ain't seen Gracie at all. Mr. Esposito said she might not be aroun' for a while, and I'd be on duty for the rest of the week."

"Thank you kindly, ma'am," Eddie said.

The two detectives exited the back door and scratched their chins in unison.

"Well, I hope Ms. Lewis will be back soon," Nick said with more than a hint of suspicion. "Eddie, I think it's time to go visit the FBI."

"Jeezus, Nick! I admit there's some strange shit goin' on here, but what do you expect? One of the most famous entertainers in the world is dead—probably the most famous entertainer in the world. Don' you think people who was around him want to protect his legacy, make sure they keep sellin' records?"

"Yeah, that's all it is, partner. Still, I think we need some answers from Agent Carter and whoever else has something to hide at the FBI."

"Shit. You know, I could be on vacation right now? It's so damn hot aroun' here already, and now you want to go pokin' around with the Feds. I may just go tell the Captain that I'm on extended leave and get the hell out of here."

Nick had known his partner long enough to be sure that Eddie wasn't going anywhere. It was just his way of saying maybe they should leave this mess alone. Eddie had a good sense of where to tread and where to steer clear. Sometimes Nick wished he had enough sense to follow his partner's lead.

"I'll pick you up in the morning, and we'll go see if we can track down Agent Carter," Nick said.

"I was afraid of that," Eddie said. "I'll bring the coffee."

When Nick pulled up in the dirt-brown Ford in the morning, Eddie climbed in with a steaming thermos of black brew. Nick merged onto Highway 240 and headed for the FBI offices located east of Memphis. He had called ahead and requested a meeting with Director Aimes. The two detectives showed their badges to a suit at the main entrance and were directed to a conference room. Director Aimes and two other suits entered the room 10 minutes later.

"What can I do for you, detectives?" Director Aimes asked as he took a seat at the circular table with the suits seated on his flanks.

"We're just trying to tie up some loose ends with the Presley death, sir," Nick said.

"Loose ends, detective? And what might those be?"

"Well, Detective Baxter and I were in the area when the 911 call came through that day. We arrived at Graceland shortly after the ambulance arrived."

Director Aimes shifted forward in his chair and made no attempt to hide his annoyance.

"Detective Sartain, I'm a very busy man. Please get to the point."

"Yes, sir. Well, we encountered an Agent Carter at the scene who identified himself with FBI credentials."

"We have many agents, on many assignments, at all times and locations throughout the country, detective. So, what is your question?"

"We thought it was strange that an FBI agent just happened to be at Graceland at the precise moment that Mr. Presley met his demise," Nick continued.

"Like I said prior, detective, we have many agents in the field, assessing a variety of risks. It doesn't seem uncommon at all that one of those agents would be conducting surveillance at the residence of a famous entertainer."

Eddie could see that his partner was getting nowhere with this exchange.

"This same Agent Carter made a visit to Mr. Presley's dentist," Eddie interjected.

"It's, uh, Officer Baxter, correct?" Director Aimes asked.

"Yessir."

"Was our agent in need of a teeth cleaning?" Director Aimes asked, gaining a smirk from both suits.

"No sir, but I'd say some cleanin' was done," Eddie said. "The dental records from that visit seem to have gone missin'."

The direct assault landed squarely with Director Aimes, who shifted backward in his leather chair.

Nick glanced at his partner approvingly and continued the attack.

"Our question is, Director Aimes, may we speak to Agent Carter?" Nick asked.

Director Aimes shifted to his right and made a silent request of the suit in that direction. The suit arose and exited the room.

"We'll look into that request immediately," Director Aimes said. "Will you excuse us for a moment?"

"By all means," Nick said.

Director Aimes arose and exited the conference room with both suits in tow.

"Are these dudes like robots, or what?" Eddie said with a laugh.

"Robotic, maybe, but they always seem to have a purpose," Nick replied.

Ten minutes passed before Director Aimes returned alone.

"Detectives, we have no record of an Agent Carter with this bureau, nor with any bureau within a reasonable distance. There are several agents with that surname within the agency, but none of them could have possibly been at Graceland on August 16, nor would they have been able to visit the local dentist to which you refer. I can't help you any further. I believe that concludes this conversation."

Nick and Eddie both wanted to grill Director Aimes further, but one of the cardinal rules of investigation was to know when to step back.

"Thank you for time, Director Aimes," Nick said. "We'll be in touch if we have any further questions."

Nick and Eddie were led out of the FBI building and climbed back into the dirt-brown Ford.

"So, we've got a missing FBI agent, a missing cook who says she saw some TV repairmen enter Graceland—but no video to back it up—and a dentist's visit with no files on record," Eddie said in quick summation of their investigative work. "Crazy as hell, Nick, but not much to go on. How 'bout we file a report and move on?"

"We're going to file a report alright, partner." Nick said. "And we're going to show it to the Captain. I don't know what's going on down here, but someone is hiding something."

"And you plan to keep diggin', right?" Eddie asked.

"Can't quit now, partner. They've got my curiosities up, you know?"

Eddie knew exactly. He'd been Nick's partner long enough to know his bulldog nature wasn't cut out for backing off, even if every indication signaled otherwise. The two detectives headed back to the department, and Nick plopped down in front of his Underwood Touchmaster Five to type up the report. He laid it out in chronological order, from the time they answered the 911 call at Graceland on Tuesday afternoon. Nick's reports were succinct, but thorough.

"Hey, Eddie, you want to look this over before we show the Captain?"

"No, man, I'm sure you've got it all there. Not sure we want to push this one, though. I mean, what we goin' to gain from this crap, Nick? The dude is dead. People are upset. Why can't we jus' leave well enough alone and get back to business?"

"I'll go in alone if I have to, Eddie."

"Damn. Okay. Let's get it over with."

Nick led the way into the office of Captain Martin "Marty" Summerfield. The Captain didn't like surprises, and he expected to hear some progress on the downtown killings when the detectives knocked on his door.

"Come on in, boys," Capt. Summerfield said. "What's the status from that mess downtown?"

"Well, boss, we're going to get on that shortly, but we got some information from our investigation into the Presley death," Nick said as he plopped the report on the large oak desk.

"I suspect this is going to tell me The King is dead, and we've got a hell of a mess in town trying to keep all his fans from going crazy over it," Capt.

Summerfield said as he picked up the report and dropped it just as quickly. "This … I don't really need to know. What I do need to know is what my best detective team is doing about keeping the peace downtown."

Eddie just glanced at Nick with his best "told you so" smirk and said nothing.

"Well, sir, like I said, we're going to get right on the downtown case, but you need to see what's been going on since Mr. Presley expired," Nick said. "Something fishy, that's for sure."

"Why don't you just give me the short version and I'll save this for later, when I need to visit the latrine," Capt. Summerfield said as he moved the report to his "I'll get to it later, much later" pile.

"Well, sir, it appears some surveillance tapes have been tampered with, covering up the business of alleged TV repairmen who visited Graceland Tuesday morning, just hours before the time of death. Some dental records from Mr. Presley's visit to Dr. Gene Hoffman on the night preceding the death are gone, too. And there's an FBI agent who was at both scenes, but apparently he doesn't exist as far as the Bureau is concerned."

"Something fishy going on, huh?" Capt. Summerfield said. "Well, Jesus Christ! I've got the Mayor and Sheriff Barksdale crawling up my ass about people getting gunned down on the streets of this city. I need my two best detectives to give me some progress on that. Instead, they bring me something that I can read in the damn *National Enquirer*!"

Nick opened his mouth to continue describing the mystery, but Capt. Summerfield cut him off with a wave of his hand. Capt. Summerfield and Nick had been partners for a short time when Nick first made detective. Capt. Summerfield knew Nick was a good cop, perhaps his best in a sticky situation, but right now the boss had too many balls in the air to worry about a dead entertainer, even the most famous one of all time.

"Downtown. Now," Capt. Summerfield said as he pointed to the door. "And I expect to see a report on this desk about what's been going on down there first thing in the morning. Understood?"

"Yes, sir." Nick said. "But when you get a chance, just read through the report. Okay?"

"Alright, Nick. I'll check it out when I get a chance. Now get on it, guys. We need to clean up that downtown mess before it gets any messier."

Nick and Eddie steered the dirt-brown Ford toward Beale Street. They'd drop in on a few of their informants, see what the word was on the street about the Sarkowicz shooting. The two detectives ducked into Murphy's Tavern, a known hotspot for Memphis Mafia affairs.

"What'll it be, boys?" the barkeep asked as Nick and Eddie slid onto their barstools.

"I don't know about my partner here, but I'm ready for a cold one," Eddie said.

"Yea, Molly, make it two beers," Nick said.

Before their suds arrived, Eddie grabbed the tabloid sitting on the bar. There was a picture on the cover of Elvis in his coffin and a banner headline that said: "The King is Still Alive!" Eddie read the subhead aloud.

"Elvis Presley photo a fake! The King is alive and well in Hawaii!" Eddie exclaimed. "Would ya' believe that shit! The man's been gone only a few days and already these scumbags are goin' crazy. What in the hell is this world comin' to?"

Nick scanned the cover and had a much more subdued reaction.

"Hmm. Interesting," the veteran detective said. "You know, that adds up with what we've run across so far."

Eddie made a scene of damn near falling off his barstool and smacked his forehead in mock dismay.

"Holy shit, Batman! That's it. He faked his death and headed off to paradise. Now why didn't I think of that?"

"Well, Eddie, you've got to admit something isn't right about this whole thing."

"Yeah, Nick, and it says right here that a farmer up in Ohio got kidnapped by aliens!" Eddie said as he pointed to the secondary story on the tabloid cover. "Maybe we ought to head up there and check it out, pard!"

"Yeah, and maybe you ought to kiss my ass."

The two detectives finished their beers and decided there wasn't any Mafia business going on tonight.

"Eddie, I'll be in a little later tomorrow, but before noon. I got some things I want to check out on my own."

"Yeah, okay, I'll get somethin' typed up for the Captain and see what else I can find out about what's goin' on down here," Eddie said. "Now you go on home and get some sleep, but watch out for those aliens."

Nick wanted to swing by Graceland in the morning, just to see if anything was going on and find out if perhaps Gracie Lewis was back at work. The cook who had replaced Ms. Lewis was in the kitchen and reported she "hadn't seen hide nor hair of Gracie since Mr. Presley passed away." Nick planned to look up her address when he got to the office and see if he could locate Gracie himself.

As he entered the precinct, Nick could hear the snickers from his colleagues as he walked into the detectives' room and approached his desk. Someone had plastered copies of the *Weekly World News* all over his desk and typewriter. The headline screamed: "Elvis abducted by Aliens!" Every guy in the department had been the butt of a practical joke, including Nick, but he wasn't amused this time. Nick ripped the taped papers loose, rolled them in a ball, and tossed it at the snarky grin on Detective John Horton's face before heading for the door.

"Screw you, Eddie," Nick said to his partner as he walked out the back door.

"Hey, Nick! Come on, man, it was all in fun," Eddie called after him.

Nick climbed in the dirt-brown Ford and hopped on the gas to burn some rubber as he peeled out of the police parking lot. He wasn't pissed at Eddie—he knew he'd find a way to return the favor to his partner soon enough—but this whole thing was just bugging the hell out of him. Capt. Summerfield hadn't said a thing about his report. Nick seemed to be the only one concerned that some sort of cover-up was afoot in the death of Elvis Presley.

Nick decided to take the day off and treat his wife to lunch. Eddie and the rest of the department could go to hell—at least for one afternoon. Jenny was still in the stages of grief, so a nice lunch on the waterfront would do her good.

"Hey, babe," Nick said as he showed up at their home unannounced.

"What, may I ask, are you doing home so early, Mr. Sartain?" Jenny replied sweetly.

"Well, I have some free time, and I thought you might like to go to lunch down on the waterfront."

"I'd love to, honey. Let me grab my purse."

Jenny seemed to be in better spirits, so Nick made sure not to upset her.

"What are you in the mood for?" Nick asked as they headed for downtown Memphis.

"Oh, something not too heavy, but nice."

"How about that seafood joint, Murphy's, down on the wharf."

"Sure, babe, that sounds good. It'll just be nice to spend some time with you."

Nick figured he could be on the lookout for any of his informants in case they happened to be hanging around and still give the Captain something of a report on the murder investigation. What he really wanted to do was make sure he and Jenny didn't hear anything about Elvis Presley's passing. That would be hard to do anywhere in the world, of course, but impossible in downtown Memphis. As they waited to be seated, Jenny scanned the news racks that were still all about Elvis.

"I guess it's going to be awhile before things get back to normal around here," Jenny said as the waitress seated them at an outdoor table overlooking the river.

"I'm not really sure what normal is right now," Nick said, chiding himself for not changing the subject immediately.

"All of these vultures are coming up with all sorts of stories," Jenny said.

"Well, it's a mystery, and you know how they love that," Nick said.

"A mystery? You sound like one of them, Nick."

"I've come across some real evidence that needs to be addressed, but I seem to be the only one who doesn't want to put this to rest."

"Evidence? Evidence of what?"

Nick launched into his list of "things that didn't add up" about the Presley death and wished for all his might that he was talking about the nice weather instead.

"All I know for certain is somebody is hiding something," Nick said in summation.

"Nick Sartain! I don't like hearing about this, least of all from you!" Jenny said in a voice loud enough to draw some stares from adjacent tables. "Why can't you just leave well enough alone? He's dead! Gone!"

Jenny rose to head for the ladies' room, and Nick kicked himself, figuratively, and not nearly as hard as his loving wife would have done had she been given the opportunity. Nick looked at the roiling, brown waters of the Mississippi.

"It's water under the bridge," he told himself, all the while knowing he couldn't just let his suspicions flow downstream. Jenny returned to her seat as the waitress brought their lunch.

"Nick, I don't want to hear another word about it, at least not from you. I can't escape all the media reports, but I damn sure don't need to have it coming home to roost. You understand, detective?" Nick had been around Jenny long enough to know when it was time to heed her call. She'd put up with plenty, just like any cop's wife, but this was personal.

"Okay, babe. Not another word."

Nick kept his promise at home and tried to stay busy at work on the downtown case. Nearly a week had passed when he heard the call come through on the scanner. Three dudes had been arrested at Forest Hills Cemetery on suspicion of trying to steal Elvis Presley's corpse. Nick gave Jenny some excuse about some trouble downtown and headed for the crime scene. He heard the call come through that everything was secure at the scene, and the alleged perpetrators were being escorted downtown. The dirt-brown Ford changed course immediately and headed for the Memphis County Jail.

"Where are they, Bobby?" Nick said to the jailer.

"They've got 'em in a holding cell, detective. 3C."

Nick headed down the hall and encountered a cluster of cops, both uniform and plainclothes, gathered in front of the holding cell.

"I thought you'd still be after those extra-terrestrials, Sartain."

It was Detective John Horton making sure that the previous incident still had some run. Nick imagined kicking his ass, but decided to take the high road.

"Very funny, John. What have we got?"

"Well, we don't have anything," Horton said. "Miller and I have three dickheads in here who made one dumb-ass attempt at breaking into Elvis' mausoleum. They might just be drunk and stupid because they didn't have any chance of breaking through those cement walls."

"Who are they?" Nick demanded.

"You can read the report in the morning like everyone else, Sartain, but rest assured the situation is under control."

The report detailed three petty criminals—Raymond Green, Eugene Nelson, and Ronnie Adkins—caught outside the mausoleum. The beat cops had received a tip that an attempt would be made to rob Elvis' grave, and the perps hadn't even tried to run. Nick made sure to point that out to Capt. Summerfield first thing in the morning.

"Captain, these guys were planning to get caught all along," Nick said as he dropped a copy of the arrest report on his boss' desk. "They were sitting ducks, and they didn't have any tools or anything. There's no real evidence, unless you count loitering at night in a graveyard."

The Captain gave Nick the benefit of the doubt against his growing desire for all this Presley bullshit to just go away.

"Alright, Nick, so what does it mean?" Capt. Summerfield asked.

"I'm not sure, sir, but it has to lead somewhere."

"Well, detective, when you find out where that *somewhere* is, please let me know. In the meantime, let's get back to work. Okay?"

The three alleged grave robbers were eventually freed on lack of evidence. Nick couldn't make any connection whatsoever to the string of peculiarities he had already encountered in the Presley case. He read a story a few weeks later in the *Memphis Commercial Appeal*. Vernon Presley, father of the deceased megastar, was appealing to the Memphis Board of Adjustment to have the bodies of Elvis Presley and Gladys Presley moved from Forest Hills Cemetery to a permanent resting place on the grounds of Graceland. The Board was expected to approve the appeal at its Sept. 28 meeting. The word on the street was the attempted grave robbing was a set up to influence the board. Executors of the Presley estate saw plenty of opportunity in having The King's gravesite located at Graceland, where fans could pay plenty of dough to pay their respects in the future. Nick spent the next three weeks trying to gather more evidence on the Presley case while helping Eddie investigate the downtown murders. With the date of the appeal fast approaching, Nick saw an opportunity to plead his case. He went to Capt. Summerfield with a request that even Nick himself thought was an extreme longshot. Since Elvis Presley's body likely would be exhumed and moved to Graceland, why not get a warrant to check the corpse against known dental and fingerprint records?

"What judge in his right mind would grant that!?" Capt. Summerfield bellowed loud enough for everyone in the department to hear through his closed office door.

"Come on, Marty, just give this a chance," Nick said as he used a ploy that had worked in the past: Get familiar with the Captain, get him thinking like a detective on the street again, instead of a boss in the office.

"I'll tell you this for certain," Capt. Summerfield said as he scrutinized Nick, his former partner.

"When that body gets relocated—if it gets relocated—the Memphis Police *will not* be requesting any further tests be done to confirm the identity of the deceased. I have enough of a damn circus around this place already. But, against my better judgment, I'll check with my contacts at the County Medical office and see what was included in the original autopsy report."

Capt. Summerfield went on to explain that fingerprinting is pretty standard practice in a high-profile case, but dental x-rays usually aren't taken unless the body needs to be identified. He'd be surprised if they were included, especially since the autopsy was done so hastily after the death.

"Ah hell, Nick, I'm not telling you anything you don't already know. But know this: If you make a mess out of this it's your own ass, not mine. Got it?"

"Absolutely, sir."

"Okay, I'll get back to you when I hear something. Now, please, get on the downtown case, will you? And light a fire under Baxter, too."

"Yes, sir. Thank you."

Nick couldn't help but smile as he walked out of Capt. Summerfield's office. He'd expected to be thrown out, at least figuratively, but the Captain was somewhat receptive. Nick knew that meant the report from his investigation had triggered the bloodhound in Marty Summerfield as well, even if the Captain wouldn't admit it.

Nick and Eddie heeded the demand to follow up on the downtown murders. Eventually, they caught up to Sid Manko and got the low down on "Big Thumbs" Sarkowicz.

"Hey, Nick, you wanna know why they called him 'Big Thumbs'?" Sid asked. "I wouldn't know for sure, of course, but the story goes that Charlie didn't like to shoot people, so he'd strangle guys if it came to that. Instead of wrapping his hands all the way around a guy's throat, Charlie would knock the guy down with a punch, pin his arms, and crush his windpipe by applying pressure with his thumbs. One of the cops who was checkin' some of Charlie's handiwork allegedly said, 'Whoever did this would have really big thumbs.' So there ya' go."

"So, what the fuck does that do for us, wiseass?" Eddie asked. He always took the bad cop role when he and Nick were dealing with their "sources."

"Why you gotta be such a hothead anyway, Baxter?" Manko asked. "Our boy Nick here, he treats us real good and we do the same. That's how it should be."

"That's all fine, Sid, but I got a boss breathing down my neck to figure out what's going on down here," Nick said. "We could hang around more often, beef up patrols, whatever needs to happen ..."

"All right, guys, here's what I know. It seems Charlie's thumbs ain't the only big part of his anatomy, ya' know?" Sid said as he chuckled and nudged Nick in the ribs. "The word is Charlie was dippin' into the girlfriend of one of the Branch gang out of Nashville. The word is one of them took care of business with Charlie."

"So, you're telling me we don't have to worry about any escalations over this?" Nick asked. "We can go back and tell the boss everything is status quo?"

"Yeah, there ain't no beefs goin' that I know of," Manko said. "Just us guys tryin' to make a livin'."

"Yeah, and let's keep it that way, punk," Eddie said as he stood and brushed past Manko.

"Thanks, Sid," Nick said. "You keep us in mind if anything comes up."

Nick and Eddie cleared out and agreed that Manko was telling the truth about "Big Thumbs" Sarkowicz. Drugs. Sex. Money. One or more was always involved when someone ended up dead. The good news was rival Memphis gangs wouldn't be hitting each other any harder than usual over the demise of "Big Thumbs." Nick delivered the official report to Capt. Summerfield in person three days later.

"Good work, Nick," Capt. Summerfield said as he scanned the report. "I've got some news for you, too."

Capt. Summerfield pulled out a manila envelope with "CLASSIFIED" stamped in red letters on the front and slid it across the desk.

"They wouldn't release the report itself—not without cause and a warrant—but I was able to get the fingerprints and dental records. Apparently, they did a full set of dental x-rays. Pretty unusual if you ask me, but I guess that's their call."

"Don't bullshit me, Marty," Nick challenged. "You've been trying to figure out why they would do dental x-rays since you saw they were included. Once a detective, always a detective."

"Yeah, Nick, I admit it does pique my curiosity, so to speak," Capt. Summerfield said.

"Well, it doesn't surprise me at all," Nick said. "Ever since you told me you would try to get the report, I've been thinking about what might be in it. Fingerprints for sure. Dental x-rays, all the better."

"All the better for what, Nick?"

"Well, sir, to make sure the corpse in that coffin is positively identified as Elvis Presley, according to fingerprints and dental records on file, if the question should ever arise."

"And you have reason to believe that question should arise, Nick?"

"No, sir, I can't go that far. Hell, I don't know. The whole thing seems pretty surreal. But I was thinking, if you had a body and you wanted everyone to know that body was a certain person, you'd make sure all of the means of identification matched between the two. You'd make sure all of the records on file jived. And if one of those records didn't jive, if one of those records showed a discrepancy between the events of this person's life and evidence on the body, you'd make sure that record was destroyed."

"You mean like a dental x-ray on the body that might not show work done from a visit to the dentist the night before the person died?" Capt. Summerfield asked.

"Yeah, boss. I knew the old Marty was still in there."

"Well, it's still just a story, Nick, and a pretty fantastic one at that," Capt. Summerfield said. "I know you'll follow up on all the records in existence. My hunch is they will all match exactly with what you have in your hands."

"I'd bet on it, too," Nick said. "I'm still going to check it out, though, in case there is a discrepancy out there somewhere."

"Nick, if there's any truth to your story—and for the record I think it's nothing but a story—then one big 'discrepancy' exists," Capt. Summerfield said. "Elvis Presley is alive and living somewhere under an assumed name."

CHAPTER FOUR

"**W**elcome to the Big Island," Mr. Gant.

Dale slowly opened his eyes and rubbed his temples. The world was coming back into focus after a 10-hour flight from Memphis that seemed like a dream to Dale. The last thing he remembered clearly was two men entering his bathroom at Graceland and leading him downstairs and into a van.

"What the hell did you guys give me?" Dale asked as the figures around him became clearer.

"Just a sedative to keep you comfortable during the flight," Agent McMahan said.

Dale recognized the voice and face. James McMahan held Dale's forearm and helped him gain his bearings on the ground.

"Are you feeling better now, Mr. Gant?" McMahan asked.

"I'm getting there, James, thank you. Remember, I told you to call me Dale."

"Ah yes, very well then, Dale. Are you ready for the trip to your new home?"

Dale's thoughts flashed to Agent Johnson. The SOB has to be around, he figured. Agent Johnson would be proud that Dale had passed his first test. He had referred to himself as Dale Gant, not Elvis Presley.

"Ready when you are, James," Dale said.

He was helped into the back seat of a black SUV with Agent McMahan at his side and Agent Gatewood behind the wheel. Another agent Dale didn't recognize was riding shotgun. A second vehicle of the same shape and description followed as the SUV headed down the mountain from Pohakuloa

Training Area. Dale recognized some of the winding route through the lava flows above Kona and the secluded road with hedges guarding both sides as they approached the security gate. Agent Gatewood nodded to the security guard, and the SUV glided through the heavy iron gates. Dale recognized the white plantation style house, but it felt far from home at that moment.

"Here we are, Dale," Agent McMahan said. "After you."

Dale still felt like he was in a dream as he nodded to Keloa and walked through the front door of his new home. Dale stopped in the expansive entryway and had no idea what to do next. His mind whirred through the events of the past seven years that had brought him to this point.

"Now what?" Dale asked to no one in particular.

"Your bags and everything else will be handled for you," Agent Gatewood said. "Why don't we go to the back veranda, and Keloa can bring us a glass of that mango-lemonade that you liked so much on your first visit?"

Dale tried to focus on the events of his first visit. That was what, six months ago? For Dale, it could have been six years ago, or six days ago. Time frames, past or future, had no significance at this moment. He heard his voice reply to Agent Gatewood, as if he were watching this scene in a movie.

"Uh, yeah, I guess that sounds good."

"Don't worry, boss, you'll be feeling at home in no time," Agent Gatewood said. "The Islands have a way of making you feel welcome, no matter the circumstances."

Dale did feel a little better as he sipped the mango-lemonade and looked past the golf course to the cool blue waters of the Pacific in the distance. The sun was just beginning to melt into the horizon.

"It sure is beautiful here," Dale said. "The view never gets old."

He thought back to all the good times he'd had on the islands—good times with Priscilla and Lisa Marie. As the glowing orange sun merged with the Pacific and became a dark purple disk before waving goodnight, Dale's countenance changed, too, from somewhat sunny to confused and paranoid.

"I gotta go, guys," he said and rose suddenly from his patio chair.

"Uh, boss, where are you planning to go?" Agent McMahan asked.

"Lisa Marie will be going to bed soon," Dale said with a blank look in his eyes. "I need to kiss her goodnight."

Agent McMahan held Dale's forearm and talked to him directly with the savvy of a field agent who'd dealt with many disoriented subjects.

"I think we better get you off to bed," he said as Agent Gatewood slipped a needle into Dale's other arm.

Dale slept for what seemed to him like weeks. When he slowly opened his eyes, he was sideways in a king-sized bed, uncovered but not cold despite a breeze that flowed over his body. He could hear voices outside his bedroom, which was decorated in the island style, much to his liking. Fresh flowers were abundant, and murals on the walls depicted beach scenes. The events of the previous day seemed like another lifetime as Dale looked at the clock on the nightstand: 9:15 A.M.

"Jeezus, it seems like noon," Dale said to himself and realized jet lag must be partly to blame for the fogginess in his head that was clearing by the minute. Dale could smell food, and he was starving. Dale pulled a pair of jeans and a short-sleeve shirt from the suitcase that lay open next to dresser drawers. He followed the scent of bacon through the unfamiliar hallways. Keloa had a full plate of Hawaiian-style ham, bacon, and eggs waiting for him in the open-air kitchen.

"Mmm, that smells good," Dale said as he settled into a seat at the breakfast bar.

"I thought you would be hungry this morning, Mr. Gant," Keloa said with a shy smile.

"Indeed, I am, my dear," Dale said as he waded into the meal. He could see the genuinely good side of Keloa from the first time they met. She exuded the simple side of life that he yearned for, the Island style, natives called it. Dale ate heartily and imagined one day he would find the peace that he saw in Keloa. She offered more sustenance, but Dale was satisfied.

"I'd better stop now, or who knows where this waistline will end."

Agent McMahan stepped into the kitchen from the veranda and offered Dale a healthy alternative to Keloa's cooking.

"Well, Dale, maybe the best thing for you would be to get started with our training regimen," he said. "It's time to get you back in shape."

Dale patted his ample midsection and knew he was ready to do some reducing.

"Lead the way, James."

The downstairs floor of the plantation home included a full gym, replete with state-of-the-art workout gear. The martial arts mat caught Dale's eyes, however.

"Let's start there," he said with a challenge to Agent McMahan.

Dale stripped off his shirt and shoes. He wished he was wearing a pair of his favorite silk sweats, but jeans would work for this first session. Agent McMahan kicked off his sandals and tossed his print shirt aside. Both men struck a defensive pose and sized up the other.

"Your move, boss," Agent McMahan said.

Dale hadn't trained or even attempted a karate move in at least six months, but the techniques hadn't left his brain. Connecting the brain waves to his body proved to be more of a challenge, however. Agent McMahan easily blocked Dale's first thrust, dropped a knee into Dale's thigh and flipped him onto his backside.

"I guess our karate is better than yours, boss," Agent McMahan said as he withdrew his clenched fist without driving it into Dale's ribs.

"Uh, yeah, thanks for not making that point too clearly," Dale said.

Something deep inside the recesses of Dale's brain was trying to make a connection. He'd heard that phrase somewhere before.

"What was that you said about your karate?" Dale asked.

Agent McMahan seemed puzzled by the question.

"Oh, I guess you're just out of practice," Agent McMahan said.

"No, you said 'our karate is better than yours.' Why would you say that?" Dale asked.

Again, Agent McMahan appeared puzzled by the query.

"Uh, I don't know," he said. "It's just that you were, you know, in a prone position … maybe you haven't trained in a while? … uh, I really don't know."

Dale sat and stared at Agent McMahan. His mind was trying to reconnect to the phrase that he could swear he'd heard before. Dale decided it was best to let it go and wait for the memory to connect when his mind was ready.

"Good move, James," Dale said. "I need to get in shape before we try this again."

"Sure, boss," Agent McMahan said. "You have everything you need to get that done down here. It doesn't happen overnight, though. When you're ready we can map out a workout plan. I've seen some of your clips when you were in tournament shape. That bad-ass is still in there."

"Well, it's more like a fat-ass at the moment, but I'm ready to change that," Dale said.

Dale walked back upstairs and out to the veranda, where Agent Gatewood was reading the *Honolulu Star-Advertiser*. The front page, like that of most every newspaper in the free world, was plastered with news of the shocking death of Elvis Presley and its aftermath throughout the world. THE KING IS DEAD was splashed across the top of the front page in four-inch-high bold type. At least they had chosen a good picture of a Vegas performance for the main photo. Agent Gatewood dropped the Comics section on top of the front page purposely and slid the pile of print out of the way.

"How are you feeling, Dale?" Agent Gatewood asked with genuine concern.

"Much better, but I'm afraid James got the best of me on the karate mat downstairs," Dale said. "I have a lot of work to do to get ... my *body* ... back in shape."

Dale looked over at the pile of newsprint as he hung on the key word of the day.

"Yes, well, that will come in time," Agent Gatewood said. "I know your penchant for hard work when it comes to the dojo. You'll have the upper hand in no time."

Agent Gatewood arose and opened his arms to the blue waters in the distance.

"Perhaps you'd like to take a walk with me down to the shoreline. There's nothing like the clean ocean air to clear your mind. By the time we return, Keloa should have lunch prepared."

"Sounds like we get three squares a day around here," Dale said as he patted his still full stomach. "Yeah, a walk would do me some real good."

The path to the beach was about a quarter-mile, with thick brush on both sides. It opened up to a jagged, black cliff that overlooked the ocean.

"Quite a view," Dale said. "How do we get down to the beach?"

Agent Gatewood showed the way to a wooden staircase that paralleled the cliff and led down to the water's edge. The beach was several hundred yards wide and protected by rocky outcrops that protruded into the churning surf at both ends.

"Pretty exclusive," Dale said as he looked up and down the white sands that were devoid of any signs of human existence.

"It's our own, private beach," Agent Gatewood noted.

"I guess that's good for keepin' people out—or keepin' them in," Dale said. Agent Gatewood could tell where Dale was headed.

"You'll enjoy plenty of freedoms once you get used to the place and your new lifestyle," he said. Dale just nodded, flipped off his sandals and walked to the water's edge. The temperature seemed a near perfect match to the summer air.

"Nice and warm, doesn't even make you flinch," Dale said. "I've always loved that about the water in Hawaii."

As Dale let the waves roll over his feet, a figure appeared from the south, several hundred yards out and past the breakers. Dale watched as the sun-darkened man paddled his longboard swiftly through the water from a prone position. He could have been a postcard for the Hawaiian lifestyle. The boarder quickly covered the area that Dale could see and swung around to head back to the south. Agent Gatewood whistled loudly and waved at the paddler, who returned the gesture between powerful strokes. Soon he disappeared around the southern edge of the cliffs.

"He's very impressive," Dale said.

"His name is Ikaika, which means strength in Hawaiian, and as you can see it fits him very well," Agent Gatewood said. "I think you will learn much from him."

"Learn from him?" Dale asked.

"Ikaika has agreed to help in your training. Paddling is good for the mind and the body."

The idea of training with Ikaika and learning the ways of the native Islanders had great appeal for Dale. He wanted to immerse himself in his own new lifestyle—and let the old one go free.

"When do we start?" Dale asked excitedly.

"Soon, but we have some other things to take care of first," Agent Gatewood said, shaking Dale from his short daydream of paddling through the surf like a native Islander. "Shall we head back?" Dale was silent as they climbed the stairs and made their way back up the sandy path. Soon the white plantation style house loomed in the distance.

"Do you guys have a name for the place?" Dale asked.

"Hale ke`oke`o," Agent Gatewood replied, with some amusement at Dale's consternation.

"I remember one thing I never like about Hawaii," Dale said. "All the words sound the same, and I can't pronounce any of 'em right. What does it mean?"

"White house," Agent Gatewood said plainly.

Dale walked a few more steps before he acknowledged Agent Gatewood's dry wit.

"I guess you're going to have to teach me more of the native tongue," Dale said as he nudged his walking partner off the path and almost into a prickly bush.

Dale retired to his spacious room and spent the afternoon placing his belongings and making a list of things he would need. He found one of them in the bookshelf next to his bed: an authentic Hawaiian dictionary with English translations.

"I guess if I'm going to live here, I better learn the `olelo`," he said to himself after discovering the Hawaiian word for language.

Keloa rang the dinner bell at 6 P.M., and she gestured for Dale to join Agents McMahan and Gatewood on the veranda. Seated between the two retired agents at the outdoor table were two men that Dale didn't recognize. The first appeared to be around 50, with deep tan lines but definitely not the appearance of a native Islander. The other man was older and had a scholarly air about him. He, too, appeared to be not of Hawaiian descent.

"This is Dr. Martin Taylor," Agent McMahan said as the younger man arose, "and this is Dr. Avery Smythe."

"Nice to meet you both," Dale said as he shook both of their hands.

"Mr. Gant, I'm sure you are wondering why I've joined you this evening," Dr. Taylor said.

"Well, yes, the thought had occurred to me, especially with the doctor titles," Dale said.

"I am a plastic surgeon, one of the most sought after on the islands," Dr. Taylor said. "I'm sure Agent Johnson mentioned that some slight alterations to your appearance would be in order prior to you meeting anyone in public."

"Well, I've already met a few people with my current looks," Dale said. "I assume they—and you—are in on the secret."

"You don't have to worry about Keloa, Dale," Agent McMahan said. "I assure you she is completely unaware of your former identity. And the doctors are in the service of the FBI, in addition to their private practices."

Dale just nodded and waited for the rest of the news.

"Mr. Gant, the procedures are relatively minor," Dr. Taylor continued. "I don't recommend any changes in bone structure, but we can alter your look significantly by raising your brow and narrowing your cheek lines."

Dale had anticipated this moment for some time. The thought of looking like someone else—anyone else—had seemed appealing at times, but now he was facing the reality of permanently altering the looks that were part of his very being.

"I, uh, I don't know," Dale said. "I'm not so sure about this."

"Mr. Gant, feelings of anxiety are quite common when patients undergo plastic surgery," Dr. Taylor continued. "I can assure you, however, that you will be just as handsome as you are now, but in a different manner. Of course, changes in hairstyle, perhaps the addition of different facial hair, and contact lenses to change your eye color all contribute to the effect of changing your look as well."

Dale felt the feelings of confusion return, and his countenance gave that away.

"What will my fans say?" he asked to no one in particular.

Dr. Smythe motioned his hand for Agents McMahan and Gatewood not to take control of the situation as they had done the night before.

"Dale …" he said directly, and waited for his gaze to be met. "I'm a psychiatrist, and I'm here to help you with all facets of your transition. Do you understand?"

"Uh, yes, I think so," Dale said as his expression and thoughts cleared somewhat.

"It's perfectly normal to have feelings of anxiety from changing your appearance, and certainly from changing your life as a whole. Are you feeling anxious now?"

"Well, I just get confused sometimes."

"Again, that's perfectly normal in your situation," Dr. Smythe said. "We can talk about this more tomorrow and help you prepare mentally for the procedures. Does that sound reasonable?"

"Yes, I think so," Dale said. "I don't want to discuss it anymore now."

"Sometimes it helps to write down your thoughts when you are feeling that way," Dr. Smythe said.

"Keeping a journal of the day's events and adding in your feelings about them is a way to record things that you can read later. If you are feeling confused, you can look back through your thoughts in writing and see that things were fairly normal."

"Well, Mama used to have a scrapbook, which I guess is a journal of sorts. Sometimes I put clippings and other things in there, and Mama filled it with everything. We called it the Green Book, but it's gone now," Dale said with a distant look on his face.

"Ah, yes, I think I read somewhere that you kept a journal of sorts," Dr. Smythe said. "Would you like a new book, one in which you can write down your current events?"

"Yes, I think so," Dale said. "Right now, I think I just want to eat and maybe get some sleep, if that's OK?"

"Very well, then. We will leave you to your dinner with Agents McMahan and Gatewood," Dr. Smythe said.

The two doctors arose and clearly were conferring on Dale's condition as they exited the front door of Hale ke`oke`o. Dale quietly ate his dinner and said nothing. Agents McMahan and Gatewood looked at each other and wondered if a sedative would be required tonight.

Dale nodded off with just the aid of a mild sleeping pill. His dreams weren't frightening, other than a visage that his new face would resemble that of Roy Clark and he'd get a gig on *Hee-Haw*. When he awoke, Dale stood in front of the bathroom mirror and stretched his flesh into new shapes that Dr. Taylor might create.

"You'll get through this just fine, boss," he said to his reflection. "Who knows, it might even be an improvement."

When Keloa rang the breakfast bell, Dale felt ready to face a new day— and a new life.

"Richard, will you contact the good doctors and tell them I'm ready for my transformation?" Dale said as Agent Gatewood joined him on the veranda for breakfast.

Agent Gatewood had the latest issue of the *Star-Advertiser* under his arm as he settled into his chair.

"You can have the Comics. Mind if I take a look at the front page?" Dale asked.

"Not at all, Dale," Agent Gatewood said as he slid the paper across the table.

The front page wasn't exclusive to Elvis Presley, but the story of his funeral procession was above the fold with a picture that showed a line of white limousines heading out of Graceland for the cemetery. Dale read the sidebar that referenced the related stories throughout the edition: crowds were expected to reach near 100,000 along the route of the funeral procession; Memphis police were calling in reinforcements to handle crowd control; Vernon Presley and the rest of the immediate family were still in shock but doing as well as could be expected. Dale wiped away a tear and pushed the paper back toward Agent Gatewood.

"Nothin' is harder than hurtin' the ones you love," Dale said as he rose and walked a few feet away so his tears wouldn't be so public.

Agent Gatewood said nothing and waited for Dale to compose himself. After a few minutes, Dale returned to the table and the two men ate in silence.

"I know it's hard, but this too will pass," Agent Gatewood finally said.

"Thank you, Richard. We haven't known each other for long, but I know I can trust you. That helps a lot."

Agent Gatewood just nodded and returned to his meal. Emotional attachments weren't his strong suit. Gatewood had been engaged once, but his bride-to-be wasn't waiting for him when he returned from a two-year stint in Vietnam as a decorated officer in the Army's 75th Ranger Regiment. His stint in the Secret Service before joining the FBI included protective detail of several heads of state, so Gatewood knew the value of unfailing loyalty.

Dr. Taylor arrived at Hale ke`oke`o early the next day to perform the plastic surgery. He would be able to handle the procedures himself, and keeping the circle of people in the know small and tight was critical. Dale wore protective bandages for 10 days, and Dr. Taylor made several visits in the interim to put ice packs on the swelled areas of his new face and to provide emotional support.

"Just a few more days and we'll be able to take a look at your new self," he told Dale one week after the surgery.

Dr. Taylor made Dale promise that he wouldn't try to remove the bandages and see the new person inside until it was time. All the mirrors in the house had been hidden or draped to remove any temptation for Dale to take a premature peek. Dr. Smythe agreed that the unveiling could be an emotional event, and he insisted on being present when the day arrived. Finally, Dale stood in front of the large living room mirror as Dr. Taylor slowly stripped away the bandages. Everyone was silent as Dale looked up slowly and analyzed his new features.

"Gosh dang, if that ain't my Uncle Vester," Dale said.

The entourage held their collective breath for several seconds before bursting into laughter.

"He'd take that as a compliment, I think," Agent Gatewood finally said.

"So, you like?" Dr. Taylor asked eagerly.

"It'll do, doc," Dale said. "Thank you for not making me look like Roy Clark, by the way."

Dr. Taylor had a puzzled look, but Dale put him at ease.

"Seriously, doc, I can live with my new self. You done good."

"We have another surprise for you," Dr. Smythe said as he held forth an oversized, hard-cover book, all green with nothing else on the front or back. Dale opened the cover and saw blank pages save for an inscription inside the front cover. "Please chart your new journey in these pages. Congratulations, Dr. Avery Smythe." ~ Sept. 14, 1977

Dale was silent as the sight of this new book brought back memories of all the clippings from Mama's Green Book and a fresh wave of grief over her death. Those wounds never seem to heal completely. Dale closed the book and rubbed his hands over the smooth surface of the cover. This new Green Book would provide more comfort than anyone else present could imagine. In its pages, Dale would retrace the path that led him to this point in time. Though his intent was for his words never to be read by another human being, he would sneak down to his private study at night and retrieve the book from a safe behind a painting of The Last Supper. During the next few months, his journal entries would explain how he had made the hardest decision of his life.

"Thank you for this, Dr. Smythe," Dale said. "This is one of the nicest things anyone has ever done for me."

"It was my pleasure," Dr. Smythe replied in his formal tone, "and worth every bit of the effort if it helps you adjust to your new ... self."

With his new face sculpted, Dale was ready to get to work on his new body. He immersed himself in daily workouts to get back in shape. His afternoons were spent in the gym, working with weights and sparring with Agents McMahan and Gatewood. Three weeks into his workouts, Dale faked a front kick, spun to his right with the speed of a man 10 years younger, and brought a surprised Agent McMahan to the ground with a foot sweep.

"Nice move, Dale," Agent McMahan said as he gingerly regained his feet. "You're getting stronger every day."

While the afternoon workouts were providing the sweat that Dale's body needed to regain its form, his morning sessions on the paddleboard with Ikaika were providing balance—both physically and spiritually. Dale relished the challenge of navigating the waves to get to the paddle lanes, but the true reward was the wisdom that Ikaika imparted about the balance between mind and body.

"You have to feel the ocean, be one with it," Ikaika would advise as they cut through the water with powerful strokes. The area they covered grew by the day, and soon Ikaika had Dale logging at least 5 miles per outing on the paddleboard.

"What's the farthest you've gone in one trip on this thing?" Dale asked once.

"Distance is measured in the soul, not by the mile," Ikaika replied.

Dale spent a long time thinking about that reply, which was Ikaika's intent. Dale had traveled many miles on the paddleboard, but many more in his pursuit of a new existence.

"So, how do you know when you reach your destination," Dale asked after he and Ikaika reached the beach in exhaustion after their longest paddle yet. Dale was pleased that he posed the question in a manner that Ikaika, his physical and spiritual mentor, would respect.

"Why do you ask me this?" Ikaika replied. "Only the person who asks such a question possesses this knowledge."

Dale pondered that reply for many nights … and finally realized the answer wasn't coming to him anytime soon.

Dale spent the weeks paddling with Ikaika, battling Agents McMahan and Gatewood on the karate mat, and trying not to enjoy Keloa's cooking too much. The results were showing as Dale had dropped 20 pounds and turned his body a deep, golden brown as Thanksgiving approached. Keloa even noticed and described Dale's new shape as "wiwi," which made Dale blush for a moment before Agent Gatewood told him that it meant "skinny" in Hawaiian.

The hard work challenged Dale physically and exhausted him mentally. Wrapping his head around a new life was still his biggest challenge, especially with the holidays approaching. Dale made it through Thanksgiving—Keloa cooked half a pig in traditional Hawaiian luau style and added mashed potatoes and gravy at Dale's request—but Christmas was going to be a forbidding test. Dale accompanied Agent McMahan to the local market for some shopping a few weeks before "Kalikimaka," and Dale was keen on buying an authentic Hawaiian doll in the store. Agent McMahan agreed, but he had a feeling the doll wasn't meant for Dale's keeping.

"So, boss, you have plans to give that doll as a gift?" Agent McMahan asked on the ride home.

"Sure do," Dale replied.

"Mind if I ask to whom?"

"Well, you know, I've given Lisa Marie an authentic doll every year for Christmas, since the day she was born. I liked the one from Austria best, and it was her favorite, too. I found one from Spain and one from Mexico that had the cutest dress …"

"Dale, I don't want to be the bearer of bad news, but you need to realize that sending a gift to Lisa Marie just can't happen, especially a *Hawaiian* doll," Agent McMahan said.

"Why the hell can't I give my little girl a gift?" Dale asked indignantly as they pulled through the security gates and parked in front of Hale ke`oke`o.

"It's not my place to say exactly what you can and can't do," Agent McMahan said. "How about we go in and see what Keloa has for dinner, and we can discuss it later. Okay?"

"Yeah, I guess so," Dale said as he clutched the doll with no intention of letting it get away.

Dale retired to his bedroom with the doll in tow, while Agent McMahan made his way to the private study to make a phone call.

"Sir, I think it's time for you to have a discussion with our guy here," Agent McMahan said into the phone. "He wants to send a gift home for Christmas."

"Hmm, well thank you for the information," Agent Johnson replied. "I'll be in touch with all of you soon."

A week before Christmas, as they finished dinner on the veranda, Agent McMahan told Dale that they would have a visitor that evening.

"You'll have to be restrained and blindfolded, Dale," Agent McMahan said. "We hate to do that, but Agent Johnson insists that his identity remains concealed. I'm sure you understand."

"I'll go along with his little game," Dale said, "but one day, he's going to have to look me in the eye."

"Dale, it's in your best interests that doesn't happen," Agent McMahan said.

Later that evening a black SUV pulled through the security gates and stopped in front of Hale ke`oke`o. Agent Johnson stepped out of the SUV with two agents, who remained outside, on guard.

Dale was prepped and waiting in the meeting room downstairs.

"Good evening, Mr. Gant," Agent Johnson said in his usual cold and unemotional tone.

"I wish I could say the same, Agent Johnson," Dale replied through his black hood.

"I've received some good reports on your progress since arriving here, and I must say you are looking very healthy," Agent Johnson said.

"Why do I always get the feeling you're dancin' around what you really want to say, Agent Johnson? If everythin' was hunky dory I wouldn't be wearing this mask, you know?"

"True enough, Dale. Despite your progress, the reports that you wanted to make contact with your daughter … "

"Don't even say her name, goddamnit!" Dale interrupted.

"Relax, Dale, I don't mean to offend you," Agent Johnson continued. "But you do need to realize that the terms of our agreement require no contact of any kind with people from your former existence."

Dale remained quiet for some time as he processed Agent Johnson's terms.

"So, what *can* I do?" Dale said somewhat hysterically. "I've paddled halfway to freakin' Japan and back with Ikaika, played Bruce Lee with your agents here, but I need to start livin' life again, you know?"

"Your freedoms depend entirely upon your actions and our perceptions of those actions, Mr. Gant," Agent Johnson replied. "We are very much in accordance with your wishes, but only if they meet certain conditions."

"What conditions!?" Dale asked as he lurched forward in vain, wishing he could negotiate those terms physically with his unseen nemesis.

"We need to be certain that you have accepted your fate, Mr. Gant," Agent Johnson replied. "Which means you will make no attempt to contact anyone from your former life. Which means that all remnants of your former life no longer exist."

"And if I accept, if I show that I'm completely ready to leave everything behind, what then?" Dale asked in a slightly more subdued state.

"Well, then, Mr. Gant, of course we'll be much more comfortable in allowing—even encouraging—you to pursue your new life."

"If I do that, if I find a way to let everything go, once and for all, does that mean I won't have the, uh, pleasure of your company any more, Agent Johnson?"

"That depends entirely on you, Mr. Gant. If we don't talk directly, make no mistake, I'll be just a phone call away. Goodnight, Mr. Gant."

Dale awoke the next day and slowly made his way to the private beach. He looked from side to side throughout the half-mile stroll, checking in vain to see if he'd missed a route through the underbrush to escape. Ikaika was waiting on the private beach as usual. The native Hawaiian was waxing their boards and reading the surf as Dale approached and plopped down in the cool sand that hadn't yet been warmed by the morning sun. Ikaika sensed that something wasn't right with Dale this morning.

"I feel some sadness in you this morning, my friend," Ikaika said.

"Indeed, my friend," Dale said. He looked at his native Hawaiian compatriot and sensed that explaining his situation would not only be dangerous—who knows who was listening, even here—but fruitless. Dale needed to explain his despair in terms that Ikaika would understand.

"Ikaika, my friend, have you ever … not lost … but been separated from someone you love?"

"Of course," Ikaika replied, "but for how long?"

"Uh, I know the word that you will understand … it will come to me … Mau Loa," Dale finally said.

"Forever?" Ikaika replied.

"Yes, forever," Dale said.

"Dale, my friend, we believe many things are *Mau Loa*," Ikaika said. "The sea, the land, the fruits ... all these things. But people are not."

Dale sat and sifted the warming sand through his fingers. He wondered what to say to this person, a being so unspoiled by all the trappings that had led Dale to this point. Dale's faith had been shaken, to the extent of a soul-ravaging temblor, but he knew part of his being was still anchored to the beliefs he learned as a little boy in the small wooden Baptist Church that his Aunt Ada had built.

"Ikaika, my friend, let's continue this conversation in the sea," Dale said as he picked up his board and aimed it toward the surf. "We have much to learn from each other."

Dale was almost able to keep pace with Ikaika as they crashed their longboards through the surf and made their way to the channel beyond the breakers. Dale pulled up alongside his mentor as they paddled south around the point.

"So, my friend, what happens to your people after they die?" Dale asked reverently.

"This question has many answers," Ikaika said. "My great-great-grandfather and the people before him believed in the `aumakua. These were Gods who guarded each family and our entire people. They believed people passed into another world, but their spirits were still alive in this world, in animals and other things. During the time of my great-grandfather, many of our people began to be influenced by the missionaries who come to the islands. Many people now believe in one *akua*, He being Jesus Christ."

"And you believe this, too?" Dale insisted.

"Like some of my people, I like to believe that our ancestors were correct, that spirits do live in our world. So, you see, many things are *mau loa* ... the sea, the rocks ... but people are not, at least not that those who are living can see."

"We, Christians, I mean, believe that people have ever-lasting life in Heaven if they live their lives a certain way here on Earth," Dale said. "When you think about it, your version ain't that much different than mine."

Ikaika looked directly at Dale paddling beside him. After several strokes, he nodded to Dale in agreement, then churned through the surf with several powerful strokes that left Dale in his wake and effectively ended their discussion of religion.

After the two paddlers had made their rounds and played in the surf, they pulled their longboards to shore, sat on them and took in the never-ending beauty of the Pacific.

"My people celebrate the holidays much as you do," Ikaika said. "My family and I would be honored if you would join us in our celebration."

"I would like that very much," Dale said. "I may have to be escorted by Agents Gatewood and McMahan, however, if we are going to be away from Hale ke`oke`o."

"They would be honored guests as well," Ikaika said.

"Well then, my friend, as we like to say, count me in!" Dale exclaimed with a clap on Ikaika's shoulder. Dale was determined to bring some hipness into his mentor's means of communication, but that was a mighty calling. Ikaika just nodded, brushed the dried sand from his longboard, and dove back into the surf for his journey home.

Christmas Eve weighed heavily on Dale. He thought of the many good times and family traditions that had marked the years. Keloa had bought a medium-sized tree for the living room and trimmed it with some traditional Hawaiian ornaments. Agents Gatewood and McMahan added some trinkets they had collected through the years. The four of them shared a brandy and their own private laments during the evening. When Dale retired to his private quarters, he thought more of what he hoped would be happening at Graceland—or wherever his beloved daughter would be spending Christmas Eve. Dale clutched the doll he had bought for her and stared into the blackness of night.

"Goodnight, sweetheart," he said to the emptiness.

Christmas Day brought much more cheer to Hale ke`oke`o. Keloa prepared a delicious brunch, and everyone exchanged small gifts. Agent Gatewood was thrilled with his authentic Hawaiian spear, Dale a little less so with the ukulele he received in return. He did enjoy Agent Gatewood's twisted sense of humor, however.

"You never know, maybe you'll develop a new talent," Gatewood quipped as Dale thumbed the strings clumsily on purpose.

That afternoon, Agents Gatewood and McMahan were dressed in their beach casuals and waiting in the black SUV for Dale to make the short trek south on Highway 19 to the homeland of Ikaika. His family had inhabited the land for longer than the official registers could document. Ikaika liked to tell a story that one of his ancestors was the first to catch a fish from the reef that lay several hundred yards offshore.

"With a spearhead he carried from Mauna Loa!" Ikaika exclaimed as his guests gathered around the ample *ahi* (fire) that warmed the natives and would be the focal point of their evening luau with kalua roast pig, Christmas leis, and lots of singing and dancing. It felt like summer to Dale, but anything near 70 degrees was cold to the natives.

Dale didn't need any artificial warmth inside his body at that moment as he gazed at what almost appeared to be an angel on the other side of the fire. The late afternoon sun cast her perfect shape in a silhouette while flickers of light from the fire danced on her dark features. Dale couldn't tell for sure, but she appeared to be returning his gaze.

"She is my younger sister," Ikaika said as he nudged Dale from his reverie.

"What is her name?"

"She is Noelani, which means beautiful girl from heaven."

"Is she, uh, you know, with anyone?"

"Her husband died in a fishing accident three years ago. The period of mourning has passed, but Noelani still has kept mostly to herself since the accident."

"May I talk to her?"

"That is up to Noelani," Ikaika said with a slight grin.

"You know what I mean," Dale said. "I just want to be very respectful and not hurt anyone's feelings, especially on Christmas."

"The old traditions are changing, but very slowly," Ikaika said. "I know my parents would like her to meet and marry another island native. My advice to you, as her brother and your friend, is what we call akahele, be careful of what you seek."

Just then a young girl tugged on Ikaika's hand.

"Uncle Ikaika! Can we play?" the girl, who looked to be 7 or 8, said as she pointed to the nearby sand. Some of the other guests had just finished their game of pahi'uhi'u, which was lawn darts with palm fronds used as targets.

"Sure we can, but first I want you to meet a friend of mine. Pualani, this is Mr. Gant."

"Aloha, sir," Pualani said with the tone of respect that island boys and girls are taught to use when addressing their elders.

"Aloha, and the pleasure is all mine, young lady," Dale said.

Several guests were present who could have been Pualani's mother, but Dale was certain that Pualani belonged to the beautiful woman who was keeping a keen eye on his interaction with the young girl.

"I'd love to learn how to play your game," Dale said. "Can we play with three?"

Dale had played enough games of horseshoes and shuffleboard in his life to know that you always needed a partner at both ends of a target game. He felt only a slight pang of guilt for using Pualani to approach his real goal.

"Everyone knows you have to play with two or four," Pualani said in a teasing but playful tone.

"Perhaps you know someone else who would like to play, then?"

"Well, I can ask my mommy, but I don't think she likes games very much. Most of the time she doesn't like to play."

"But it's Christmas, Pualani, and that can change people. I'll bet your mother would be happy to join us. Why don't you run over there and ask her?"

Pualani ran excitedly to her mother's side and was tugging on her traditional grass skirt.

"Pleeease, mama? Just one game?"

The young girl's pleadings were persuasive as she grabbed Noelani's hand and led her around the fire. Ikaika had the good sense to know Dale would need a hand with the introductions.

"Noelani, this is my good friend, Mr. Dale Gant."

"Aloha `auinala, Mr. Gant."

Noelani caught Dale's puzzled gaze.

"It means hello, but in the time of day when the sun is moving toward the ocean," Noelani explained. "I see you have already met my Pualani."

"Yes, she is a lovely young lady," Dale said. "She wants to show me how to play paw ... uh, well, this game."

"Pahi`uhi`u," Noelani said in her perfect Hawaiian annunciation.

"Well, we'd call it lawn darts where I come from, but it looks just the same. Shall we?"

Noelani chose Dale as a partner, which put them on opposite ends. Pualani was tossing against Dale.

"Now, don't you go easy and let me win," Dale said with a wink to the young girl.

"I'll do my best," Pualani said as she launched her first throw, which plopped to the sand squarely in the highest-scoring circle.

Dale tried his best, too, but his aim was diverted by Noelani's beauty and the gaze that she seemed to be sending his way. The game ended quickly with Pualani and Uncle Ikaika on the winning side. Dale had achieved his goal of meeting Noelani, however, and he escorted mother and daughter back to the fire ring. Dale asked most of the questions in their ensuing conversation, but Noelani seemed genuinely interested in talking to him. Pualani eagerly shared stories of her days at the local school and her exploits in the surf with Uncle Ikaika. As the sun dipped toward the Pacific, the traditional Christmas meal of Kalua pig was pulled from the underground oven. The feast included fresh sushi made of poi and poke, lomi salmon salad, and Opihi, or freshwater snails.

"Aloha ahiahi," Noelani said as she and Pualani were seated next to Dale. "It means good evening." Dale nodded politely and returned the greeting while trying not to attack his dinner plate before everyone had been seated and properly welcomed to the feast. Noelani's father offered pule to the ʻaumakua—a prayer to the family gods—and ʻOkole maluna, a toast to the gathered family and their guests, before giving permission for the feasting to begin. With his Southern roots, Dale focused mainly on the pork, but he found the dessert of Haipua, a chocolate and coconut pie, much to his liking as well. He felt as stuffed as the pig itself and welcomed Pualani's invitation for a walk to the beach.

"Let's go, Uncle Dale," Pualani said as she clutched Dale's hand.

The practice of attaching family titles to friends was customary, but still Dale felt pleased to be welcomed into Pualani's good graces. Her presence couldn't replace being with his own precious daughter, but Pualani made the hole in his heart feel a little smaller. They made their way to the shoreline, where Pualani scoured the white sand for shells and other collectibles. Dale pulled off his sandals and let the warm water caress his feet.

"Did you get everything you wanted for Christmas?" Dale asked.

"Well, yes, everything for me, but..."

"But what, my dear?"

"What I really want is for mama to be happy again. I think having you here will help."

"Oh, *really?*" Dale said as he splashed some of the Pacific onto the girl playfully with his foot. Pualani responded by giving Dale a good splashing on his backside as he pretended to retreat. Dale let her prevail in the water fight before they walked hand in hand back toward the party. Dale could see Noelani watching them without trying to be noticed doing so. The sunlight was dancing off her dark features, and Dale realized he and Pualani had the same Christmas wish.

"If I can help make your Mama happier, I'll certainly do my best," Dale told Pualani.

"I know you will, Uncle Dale," Pualani said as she squeezed his hand a little tighter.

"You know, I have an idea that just might make both of you happier tonight," Dale said.

Dale set aside his urge to be impulsive and approached Noelani with his idea instead.

"I have a special gift that I would like to give to Pualani, but I'd like your permission first," he said.

"What is it?" she asked.

"It's a small token, something I bought in the village. It would mean so much to me to be able to give it to her, and I think she will like it."

Noelani paused for a moment as what seemed like a million thoughts raced through her mind. She was attracted to Dale despite her reservations about getting emotionally attached to anyone again. Maybe he was showing his attraction to her as well? Maybe he just wanted to be nice to Pualani? Maybe she should just relax and not let her emotions run wild …

"I think that will be wonderful, Dale," she said after what was just a brief pause in real time. Dale asked Agent Gatewood to drive back to the house immediately to retrieve the doll and to make sure Keloa wrapped the gift in a traditional Hawaiian Christmas package. Dale tried to be nonchalant in his gift giving, but the tears in his eyes gave away his true feelings.

"I bought this for a very special little girl," he said as he presented the gift to Pualani. "Now I would like you to have it."

Pualani was too young and too excited about the prospects of what was inside the package to take heed of Dale's words. They were not lost on Noelani, however.

"Oh, Uncle Dale!" Pualani exclaimed as she tore open the package and clutched the doll tightly. "I love it!"

"What else do you say, young lady?" Noelani interjected.

"Thank you, thank you, thank you!" Pualani said as she hugged Dale tightly.

"You are so welcome, my dear," Dale said.

Noelani walked away from the warmth of the fire and stood, staring longingly at the ocean in the distance. Dale waited a few minutes before approaching her. He said nothing, but stood next to her, taking in the beauty of the scenery.

"Thank you for making her so happy," Noelani said finally. "She deserves to be happy."

"And so do you," Dale said.

Noelani's thoughts were spinning rapidly again. She hadn't felt attracted to a man since her husband's death, and the feelings of excitement, guilt, and apprehension were swirling through her mind. She turned to look at Dale.

"I don't know anything about you, other than you and my brother are friends," she said. "What did you mean when you said you bought that doll for a very special little girl?"

Dale resisted the urge to tell her everything, to get the whole damn thing off his chest and throw caution to the breeze. A voice inside his head—perhaps his or perhaps Agent Johnson's—reminded him that would be a big mistake. Finally, he grasped Noelani's hand lightly and looked into her eyes.

"We both have demons in our past, Noelani," he said. "But maybe it's time we both look to the future."

In the months that followed, Dale courted Noelani slowly and in a traditional manner. They went for walks on the beach with Pualani in tow. Dale attended most Sunday services at Mokuaikaua Church with Noelani, Pualani and many members of the Akuma family. Most of the family members had converted to Christianity two generations ago, but many of the Akumas, particularly Ikaika, still believed strongly in the traditional Hawaiian gods. Their first kiss was atop Mauna Kea, after a Sunday drive and while Pualani was distracted in a search for native flowers. As the holiday season arrived once again in the islands, Dale knew what he must do. After making sure that Ikaika had Noelani and Pualani distracted by a paddling session, Dale called on Noelani's parents.

"Ah, Mr. Gant, to what do we owe this pleasure?" Noelani's mother asked with a look of mild surprise as she opened the door to see Dale standing alone and dressed somewhat formally for a Tuesday afternoon.

"I'd like to talk to you and Mr. Akuma, ma'am," Dale said.

A servant led Dale to the main sitting room of Hale Akuma, where he waited for what seemed an eternity. Finally, Mr. and Mrs. Akuma entered and seated themselves on the sofa opposite Dale's lone chair. Damn, I feel like a teenager, he thought to himself. Fortunately, the manners he'd been taught growing up in the South were fitting for the occasion.

"Aloha `auinala, Mr. and Mrs. Akuma," Dale said without too much stammering.

"Aloha `auinala to you as well," Mr. Akuma said. "To what do we owe the pleasure of your company?"

"Well, sir, and madam, I ... " Dale didn't stammer, but needed time to collect himself. You're a grown man, *damnit*, he told himself. Get it together! He'd rehearsed the line a thousand times ... "It's been a year now since I was welcomed into the good graces of you and your family. During that time, I have grown to love your daughter—and her daughter. I would like your blessing to ask Noelani to marry me."

Luana Akuma's mouth dropped open a little, but her main reaction was to look at her husband. Kilohana Akuma had spent his whole life in the islands other than a stint in the Pacific fighting the Japanese after being enlisted in the U.S. Navy following the bombing of Pearl Harbor. The "Day of Infamy" claimed the lives of Kilo's uncle, who was on the USS Arizona, and his paternal grandmother, who had enlisted as a nurse. Kilo, whose given name simply means "great," moved his wife and children into the main house on the Akuma plantation after the deaths of his parents. He had seen many changes to the traditional Hawaiian lifestyle during his 68 years, and he felt torn between belief in the ancient Hawaiian gods and Christianity. There was no dispute, however, of the patriarchal nature of the Akuma family and Kilo's position as its leader.

"I have watched you with my daughter and my granddaughter since you have been acquainted with our family," Kilo began while obviously measuring his words. "I've had a feeling that this day would come, and I appreciate the respect you have given to our family to wait a full cycle of the seasons. Our desire for Noelani—and Pualani—was for a 'kanaka maoli'—a native Hawaiian—or at least a local to take the place of her husband."

It was tradition to speak the names of the deceased only in certain situations, and this certainly wasn't one of them. From what Dale had gathered from Ikaika's tales, Konane Noma had embodied everything native Hawaiian parents wanted in a son-in-law: brave, loyal, and a tireless provider. Dale had the feeling his attributes weren't viewed nearly as appealing to the parents who were scrutinizing him at this moment. He had made his pitch, however, and Dale was enough of a skilled negotiator not to weaken his position with any more rhetoric. He loved Noelani—and Pualani—and he felt they loved him, too. That would have to be enough. After a pause that seemed like an eternity to Dale, Kilo finally spoke his intentions.

"I can see that you love my daughter and my granddaughter, and I think they feel the same way. You have the blessing of our family, but, of course, the choice will be Noelani's."

Dale reverted to his roots and embraced his future in-laws in a big hug before reverting to more reserved appreciation.

Dale's thoughts raced as he drove home. Kilo had stressed the final choice belonged to Noelani. Dale felt confident she would say yes, but he had the nagging doubts of every man who was about to ask a woman for a lifelong commitment. Dale awoke the next day and was excited for his regimen, especially his paddling session with Ikaika. After the two had made their way through the surf, Dale stopped paddling and sat upright on his longboard.

"My dear friend," Dale began with a look that prompted Ikaika to rise to the sitting position also.

"Our souls have been one since we first met, but now we will have union in a new way."

"Dale, I think you have been around me too long," Ikaika teased. "I spoke to my father this morning, so you can just spit it out."

Dale playfully clapped a spray of ocean water at Ikaika.

"Well, yeah, we're going to be brothers!"

Ikaika's lunge for an embrace caught Dale off guard, and they both tumbled off their boards. The two shared a laugh, and both were still smiling as they made their way back to the house. Dale's countenance changed quickly, however, as he saw what awaited. A large, black SUV, with government plates and tinted windows, was parked in the driveway. Dale didn't recognize the vehicle, but he was pretty sure what it meant. Agent Johnson's familiar bodyguards greeted Dale as he entered the foyer. At least Agent McMahan was present to keep the proceedings civil.

"Agent Johnson wants to see you, Dale," he said. "I hate to do this, but I think you know the drill." Dale held out his hands to be cuffed, and bowed his head to be hooded.

"I still don't like it either, James, but let's get this over with," Dale said.

The agents led Dale downstairs to the usual interrogation spot, where Agent Johnson was waiting patiently.

"Good afternoon, Mr. Gant. It's a pleasure to see you again," Agent Johnson said.

"Well, Ace, you know my feelings, so let's just get down to business. What is this about?"

"Well, Mr. Gant, I understand you have been to see Mr. and Mrs. Akuma about your intentions with their daughter," Agent Johnson said.

"Yeah, so what if I have? That's none of your business," Dale replied coldly.

"Well, Mr. Gant, as we have discussed many times, everything to do with your new life is the business of our organization," Agent Johnson said. "You asked Mr. and Mrs. Akuma for their blessing, but you forgot to ask for my permission."

"I don't need your permission to be happy, and I sure as hell am not going to ask for it!" Dale retorted.

"You need not worry, Mr. Gant. I have every intention of allowing you to bring your proposal to your would-be bride, but with certain conditions and understandings in place, of course," Agent Johnson said in his always even and emotionless tone.

Dale could envision himself slipping the cuffs, tearing off the hood and choking Agent Johnson to death with his bare hands. He shook off the dark reverie and decided his future life and happiness with Noelani and Pualani was too important to lose his cool.

"What conditions and understandings?"

"Well, Mr. Gant, we'll start with what you should already understand, which is it would be very unfortunate for everyone involved if your new family members were to realize your true identity."

"I certainly do understand that, Agent Johnson, and I have no intention of sharing anything about my former life."

"Yes, but don't you think your new wife will want to know where and how her husband spent the previous 43 years of his life? Don't you think she'll want to know why bodyguards will remain living in her new home? My God, she's a *woman*."

"I didn't think you knew anything about women," Dale said, regretting the insult as soon as the words left his lips. One of Agent Johnson's bodyguards grabbed Dale by the ear and squeezed. Agent McMahan smacked the bodyguard's arm hard enough to loosen his grip, and the two FBI agents squared off in their hand-to-hand combat poses.

"Enough!" Agent Johnson demanded in a tone that stopped both agents from striking.

"The conditions are you will share your alibi with Noelani," Agent Johnson said.

"What alibi?" Dale asked.

"An alibi that will explain why you live in an FBI safe house with two former agents as bodyguards. You will describe living conditions exactly as they are, Mr. Gant. The actions that resulted in those conditions will be much different from the truth, however."

"Christ! Do you take this much time to explain everything, Agent Johnson?" Dale asked. "Get on with it, so I can get on with my life!"

Agent Johnson explained that Dale would tell Noelani—and Noelani *only*—that he was not guilty of any crimes, but that he had become involved in business with some men who turned out to be extortionists and had ties to organized crime. One of them killed Dale's business partner, and had threatened to do the same to Dale and his daughter. The FBI placed Dale in its witness protection program in exchange for his testimony against the perpetrators. Since Dale was divorced, had no siblings, and his parents were deceased, the only family that mattered to him was his daughter. He had to live with no longer being able to contact her, but he was assured that she would be safe and living with her mother. In turn they would be told that Dale was alive and well, but he was forbidden from any contact with them. Since he wasn't a criminal, Dale was given his choice of locations, and the Big Island of Hawaii was it. That would be the story of how he came to reside at Hale keʻokeʻo.

"Doesn't surprise me at all that you are pretty good at stretching the truth, Agent Johnson," Dale said after the plan had been set forth. "I think it will work and, unfortunately, a lot of it is true. I'll sleep better at night knowing I'm not telling a complete lie to my new wife. At least I hope she will be."

"Well then, Mr. Gant, you have my blessing as well," Agent Johnson said.

Dale decided that he would "come clean" with Noelani before proposing. If she backed away based on his story, he would never ask her to marry him. The guilt he felt at deceiving her was offset by the true love he had for her and his complete dedication to making her and Pualani happy. As he had done at other key crossroads in his life, Dale opened his Bible and searched for guidance. Of course, he encountered many verses about the abominations of bearing false witness, but also one that provided hope that his means may in the end be justified: *Proverbs 12:22: Lying lips are an abomination to the Lord, but those who act faithfully are his delight.*

The next day Dale and Noelani took a walk from Hale keʻokeʻo near sunset to their favorite vantage point overlooking the Pacific, where Dale told his story. Noelani listened intently and quietly. Once the sun had faded into the deep blue ocean, she shared her thoughts.

"Dale, you have brought me much happiness since you came here. I remember you telling me that we both have some demons in our past, but that we deserve to be happy. You have also been like a father to Pualani. She loves you dearly … and so do I."

Dale hadn't planned his next move, but he was ready for what may come. He dropped to one knee and gazed up at Noelani's dark features, which were bathed in the growing moonlight.

"My darling, I have just one more question for you tonight," Dale said. "Will you do the honor of marrying me?"

"Oh, Dale, yes. Yes! Nothing in this world would make me happier."

An engagement party was held at the Akuma plantation on March 3, Girl's Day, a day of celebration in Hawaii as local families display collections of beautiful dolls. Dale presented Pualani with a beautiful Polynesian doll befitting the occasion. The wedding date was set for Saturday, May 5, during the annual celebration of Lei Day in Hawaii. Dale and Noelani were married in Mokuaikaua Church, and the Pastor offered dual blessings of the ancient Hawaiian gods and Christianity, according to the wishes of the bride and groom. Ikaika served as Dale's best man, and agents Gatewood and McMahan were groomsmen. Noelani wore a floral print dress instead of the traditional white reserved for first-time brides, and Pualani was a darling ring bearer in her matching print floral dress. Agent Johnson was not in attendance, but he received news of the nuptials soon afterward. He had already approved Dale's request for the couple to honeymoon in Tokyo—chaperoned, of course, by agents seen and unseen.

Dale soon became known as "Papa" to Pualani by mutual agreement. Her Daddy had perished at sea, and for Dale that term would always be sealed in his heart for a long-lost little girl. Dale knew it was time to lock away another part of his past life. One night while the residents of Hale ke`oke`o were asleep, Dale pulled the picture of The Last Supper from its place on the wall of his study and opened his private safe.

JOURNAL ENTRY: JUNE 5, 1979

It has been a year and a half since my last writing. Can it really be that long? Noelani and I are happy, and Pualani is so precious. I will love you and Lisa Marie forever, but it is time to move on.

Dale slid the Green Book inside the safe and quietly placed the painting back in place on the wall of his private study.

Many years of happiness followed for the Gant family at Hale ke`oke`o. Dale and Noelani agreed not to have more children, which reserved all of their love for Pualani. The Gant family attended services regularly at the Mokuaikaua Church. Dale joined the men's choir, but he resisted the choir director's pleadings for him to perform solo. The bond between Ikaika and Dale grew as well, to the point they were brothers in spirit more than in family. It was Ikaika who noticed a vague longing for something in Dale.

During a paddling session, Ikaika pulled his longboard to rest in calm waters and engaged Dale in conversation, an unusual occurrence.

"My brother, I think I know your heart and soul as well as anyone on this earth," Ikaika began.

"Indeed, you do," Dale replied.

"So, I am wondering what causes the longing that I see in you? I don't think it has anything to do with my sister or our family, but still I sense a sort of sadness, something that is missing in your life."

"Well, Ikaika, we all miss some things in our lives that are not attainable. I think that is one reason why people create things like art, and poetry, and music. They are a means of dealing with sadness in their lives. Of course, music also brings a great deal of happiness to folks."

"Well, Dale, perhaps it's time for you to find something that helps fill the holes in your life. I see the joy in your soul when you sing in church."

"Amen, brother."

Dale hadn't written in the Green Book for many years. Like his music, he mistakenly thought his journal entries were something he could bury in his past. That night, after Noelani and the rest of the residents of Hale ke`oke`o were asleep, Dale went downstairs, pulled the portrait of The Last Supper from the wall and opened his private safe. Opening the cover of the Green Book felt like saying hello to an old friend.

JOURNAL ENTRY: SEPT. 14, 1985

It's been eight years to the day since I saw my new self in the mirror. Now I'm staring at myself in the glass and thinking of doing something a little crazy—imitating my former self. Them Elvis impersonators have been around forever. Carl "Cheesie" Nelson started imitating me before I was even famous, and me and "Cheesie" were buddies for a while. There were lots of guys who played as me through the years, and mostly I got a kick out of it. I mean, if they imitate you when you're still alive and kickin', that has to be a good thing. I remember the joke in the *Weekly World News* that I once entered an Elvis lookalike contest and came in third place! Since I've been gone there are all sorts of Elvis acts out there. Ikaika was right. I've been missing my music real bad, probably more than I even know. So, what's to stop me from impersonating myself? Sounds kind of weird, but it might just be some fun.

Noelani had asked Dale to participate impromptu during open mic night at the Coconut Club in Kailua-Kona months earlier. Dale had refused then, of course, but now he saw an opening. He knew Thursdays were reserved for whatever local talent was ready to take the stage of the famous open-air eatery that was close enough to Kailua Bay to feel the ocean spray. Noelani's birthday was coming up, and Dale had an idea for a very personal present.

"Honey, why don't we drive into town this Thursday and get some dinner," Dale asked Noelani. "I'll bring my guitar and maybe even sing something at the Coconut Club. You can think of it as an early birthday present."

"Oh, Dale, would you!?" Noelani exclaimed. "That would be wonderful!"

"Ok, then, it's a date," Dale confirmed.

Tom Holmstrom was part-owner of the Coconut Club and an amateur musician himself. He enjoyed being part of the local music scene and ran the show on amateur night at the Coconut Club. The joint was busier than usual on this particular Thursday. Dale and Noelani sat near the back, farthest from the stage. Dale pretended to be nervous as he waited for Noelani to give him motivation.

"I don't know, it looks pretty busy," Dale said. "Maybe I'll pass this time."

"No way, Mister!" Noelani protested. "You promised. Besides, everyone is going to love you. I just know it. I've watched when you sing in church. It's like you have an aura around you, and the crowd sees it, too."

Dale smiled wistfully as the recesses of his mind played a quick highlight reel of his life spent onstage.

"OK, but only because I promised my sweet wife," Dale said.

He made his way toward the emcee stand where Tom was introducing the acts for the evening.

"Do you have a free spot?" Dale asked.

"Sure, how about 9:30?" Tom replied.

"That will give me just enough time to get over my stage fright," Dale said with a coy wink.

"OK, you're in. Print your name here and jot a short description of your performance."

Dale obliged and slid the paper and clipboard back to Tom.

"Mr. Dale Gant, singing some old country tunes," Tom read aloud. "That sounds like a nice change of pace from the typical island style. You need anything for your act?"

"Just some courage," Dale joked again. "No, I've got my guitar and the singin' voice ... Well, let's just hope it's still in tune."

Dale felt some genuine stage fright as the time ticked closer to his performance. He had always felt that nervousness, but like most great entertainers, he knew the adrenaline rush of stepping onstage would overwhelm any apprehension. An islander finished her native Hula dance, and it was Dale's turn to shine.

"Ladies and gentlemen, please welcome Mr. Dale Gant, who will be performing some old country tunes ..."

The crowd returned mild applause and took stock of Dale as he made his way to the stage. His style definitely stood out from the usual performers on the island. By the time Dale finished "Gentle on My Mind," the applause had grown considerably. He followed with "Don't Be Cruel," and the cheers grew to the point that everyone on the bay walk was wondering what the hell was going on at the Coconut Club tonight. He finished with a rousing version of "All Shook Up." Each act was slated for only 15 minutes onstage, but the natives weren't going to rest until they had heard more of Dale. "One more! One more!" they shouted in unison as Dale settled in next to Noelani.

"Well, are you going to give them what they want?" Noelani yelled above the din. "I told you they were going to love you!"

Dale knew how to draw out the suspense of an encore. Finally, he jumped to his feet, punched the air above his head to huge applause and headed back onstage. Tom Holmstrom was waiting at their table with Noelani after Dale put an exclamation on his performance with "Heartbreak Hotel."

"My God, that was incredible!" Tom exclaimed.

"Well, thank you," Dale said. "The applause never gets old."

"I need to get back to the show, but I'd like to meet with you when I have more time and talk about your music," Tom said. "Are you available during the day?"

"Sure thing," Dale replied.

"I have the perfect gig in mind for you," Tom said excitedly. "How about you drop by Monday, after the lunch rush?"

"I'll see you then," Dale said.

The crowd quieted down considerably as the following act was a local islander who played a guitar/ukulele combination. Not bad, but certainly not the quality that Dale Gant had provided on "amateur" night.

Noelani had been caught up in the excitement of Dale's performance like the rest of the crowd, but she was quiet as they started the 30-minute drive home, north on Highway 19.

"What's up, dear?" Dale asked as he could sense her change in mood.

"I guess I'm still a little overwhelmed by what I saw tonight," she said. "I knew you would be great, but I had no idea you could be *that* great."

"Greatness comes and goes, quickly," Dale replied as his thoughts were on a totally different track.

"So, you've experienced greatness before?" Noelani asked somewhat hesitantly.

Dale rolled down his window to breathe the salt air and clear his mind of the adrenaline rush that had consumed him—tonight and many times in the past.

"Maybe this was a mistake," he said. "I don't want anything from my past to be a problem for us."

Noelani paused to collect her thoughts as well. She had seen the change come over Dale while he was onstage, had seen the way he moved the crowd to a frenzy. She was excited by the experience, like many millions before her, but she also saw apprehension in Dale and felt vague fear that enjoying his music may come at a high price for both of them. She also felt that tonight had unleashed a force in Dale that couldn't be contained.

"I think you should keep playing," she said finally. "You should meet with Tom and see what he has to say. Just don't let this get too big, OK?"

"That will work, darlin', and let's keep this music business just between us. Nobody back home needs to know."

JOURNAL ENTRY: SEPT. 20, 1985

The last thing I need is a visit from Agent Johnson about getting back into performing. When the time was right, I'll go on offense and approach Agent

Johnson with a plan to play on without arousing any suspicions from the public. I'll see what Tom Holmstrom has in mind and make sure no one at home other than Noelani is aware of my intentions. I trust McMahan and Gatewood, but still, whenever they have key information it seems Agent Johnson is in the know shortly thereafter.

Dale was anxious but excited in advance of his meeting with Tom Holmstrom. What was this "perfect gig" he had described? That was Dale's first question when the two sat down in Tom's office toward the back of the bar Monday afternoon.

"Well, Dale, a few of the locals started a band a few years back, and I helped with management," Tom began. "They played lots of stuff, but mostly older rock 'n' roll and hillbilly rock. The lead singer was an Elvis impersonator of sorts. He didn't go all out like the guys in Vegas do now, but did his best to at least plant the idea in people's minds. It worked out pretty well for a while. They played here at the club and had quite a few local gigs, but he moved back to the mainland this summer. They need a lead singer, and you would be tremendous from what I saw the other night. To be honest, I'm not sure any of them are in your league, but I'm sure they'd be honored to perform with you."

"How much performin' are we talkin' about, Tom?" Dale asked. "I have time and all, but I don't want to get into anything big. If we can play here and there and do it for fun, then yeah: I'm interested."

"You bet, Dale," Tom agreed. "I've got a business to run here, and the others guys have jobs and lives, too. I just think it would be a helluva lot of fun."

"That sounds good," Dale said. "I need to discuss it with my wife, and maybe you need to do the same with the band. Then maybe we meet up and see what happens."

"I'll be in touch soon," Tom said and gave Dale a firm handshake.

Dale laid out the low-key plan to Noelani, and she agreed that it would be a great hobby. Some of the band members had heard about Dale's performance, and Tom sang Dale's praises enthusiastically, but they weren't prepared for what Dale laid down during their initial meeting and first practice session. Dale repeated his set from the Coconut Club performance and added in "Jailhouse Rock" for emphasis. Roger Morrison was on drums, Billy Forester played bass, Kiko Maheloa backed up on guitar and vocals, and Ronnie Mason manned the keyboards.

"Damn, boys, that's pretty good," Dale summed up after the last note. "We need to make up a few sets, practice a little, and we'll be ready to go."

The "boys" all nodded in agreement, too stunned by Dale's obvious star power to add much to the exchange. Tom had the business sense to chart their future.

"How about we shoot for opening night next Friday at the club?" he stated more than asked. "That gives you a week to practice. We've got a band booked for the main show that night, but you can open for them."

Dale hadn't been part of an opening act for more than 30 years, but this wasn't the time to nitpick. "That sounds great, Tom. We'll see you guys soon."

Dale managed to slip away from Hale ke`oke`o without alerting McMahan or Gatewood and led band practice for the next week. When opening night arrived, Tom was filled with anticipation.

"I don't think you'll be the opening act for long," he told Dale as the band members shared a dram of whiskey in Tom's office before hitting the stage.

A decent crowd had already gathered when Dale gave a 1-2-3 and started the evening with "Gentle on My Mind." Like they had during amateur night, the patrons became increasingly giddy as Dale led the group through a 90-minute set. The crowd demanded an encore, which Dale obliged again with "Jailhouse Rock." The main entertainment for the evening, a bluesy trio from the mainland, had no chance to match the fever pitch Dale and the boys had created.

"Man, that was awesome!" Billy yelled over the din as the boys gathered at the bar to mingle with their new fans.

"Yeah, that felt like the big time!" Ronnie replied as a cute blonde sauntered up to make his acquaintance. "Dude, I could deal with *this* every night."

Tom was busy keeping the rest of the night's entertainment on track, but Dale could tell his new buddy was ecstatic with the performance as well. Dale tried not to get too caught up in celebrating, and he knew Noelani was keeping a close eye on the women who were eager to meet the club's new star.

"You ready to head home, dear?" Dale asked, knowing that Noelani would want to elude the spotlight.

"Wow, that was amazing to see the electricity you created in the crowd," she said as Dale pulled onto Highway 19 northbound.

"It wasn't just me," Dale replied.

"You are the star, there's no doubt about that," Noelani demanded. "Everyone sees it, even if you are trying to share the stage."

"Does that bother you?" Dale asked.

"Like I said before, please let's keep this in perspective," Noelani said. "I love seeing you perform, and I can tell you love it, too, but all the attention scares me."

"I promise that I won't let this get out of hand, and believe me, I've been there," Dale said.

Tom called first thing Saturday morning to inform Dale that he could move some acts around and open up two weekend gigs for Dale and the boys.

"I don't know, Tom," Dale said. "Things are happening really fast, and I don't want this to spin out of control. I'll agree, but on two conditions: One, we stay local, and two, we play no more than one night a week."

"I'll take whatever I can get from you, Dale. Let me talk to the boys and we'll get something scheduled."

Dale reiterated the same conditions to his wife right after he hung up the phone. He figured she already knew that the early phone call was a reaction from last night. Tom called again before noon to tell Dale that he had opened up the next two Fridays already and would be working to keep at least one weekend night free for the, uh …

"We need a name!" Tom said excitedly after Dale had agreed to the first two bookings.

"I'll leave that up to you and the boys," Dale said.

Tom went to work right away on some names and had Dale back on the phone before dinner.

"How about the *Big Islanders*?" Tom asked excitedly.

Dale was silent for a minute as he ran through some checks in his head: 1. It is catchy, and not too complicated; 2. It has ties to the community; 3. Perhaps most important, it didn't identify Dale in any particular way.

"Sounds great," Dale said finally.

"OK, then, the *Big Islanders* hit the stage Friday night," Tom said. "This is going to be great, but I want you to know that I spoke to the boys, and we all agreed to respect your conditions."

"OK then, we have some practicin' to do," Dale said.

The group put in three late-night sessions that week to fine tune their sound. Dale made sure they added some works from a variety of artists and didn't get too close to the vibe of a particular "dead" rock 'n' roll icon. Still, the comparisons were inevitable. Their first Friday, Sept. 27, created a stir in the downtown tourist section. Their second Friday gig reached across the entire western side of the Big Island, thanks in large part to the ensuing Entertainment section of *West Hawaii Today*: "The Big Islanders have captured the local music scene much the same as rock 'n' roll took the world by storm some 30 years ago. If you want to experience the roots of modern rock 'n' roll, it's onstage with the Big Islanders every Friday night at the Coconut Club in downtown Kailua."

Noelani had left the story, which ran in the Wednesday, Oct. 9, edition of the newspaper, upright on the table for everyone to read, including McMahan and Gatewood. The agents didn't seem to make any connection at the time, but the next day Dale received word that Agent Johnson was ready for a pow-wow.

JOURNAL ENTRY: THURSDAY, OCT. 10, 1985

It can't be a coincidence that Agent Johnson seems to find out about anything out of the ordinary right away. McMahan or Gatewood—or both—are feeding him information. What does that mean? It could be they are just doing their jobs—or it could be one or both of them is working alongside that SOB Johnson. They're watching me—and I'll be watching them!

Agent Johnson wasn't available in person—much to Dale's delight—so they would hook up on a private phone call Friday morning when Noelani had her weekly brunch date with her mother.

"Good morning, Mr. Gant," Agent Johnson began in his usual business tone.

"Yes, sir," Dale replied while thinking maybe he could cut the conversation short by being succinct.

"I understand your new band is all the rage at the Coconut Club from what I hear and read in the newspapers, Mr. Gant," Agent Johnson continued.

"I guess so."

"Who gave you the idea that getting back into the music business would be acceptable under the terms of our agreement?"

"I came up with the idea on my own."

"I see, Mr. Gant. Well, I have to say my initial reaction would have been to remove that idea from your brain, perhaps even forcefully... "

"But ...?"

"You've managed to set this charade in motion without tipping off anyone, much to my surprise and disappointment."

Their conversation was on speaker phone, and Dale glanced at McMahan and Gatewood to see if he could figure out which one had failed in his duty to report to Agent Johnson. Still true to their training, neither man's expression changed perceptibly.

"Yeah, I'm kind of proud of myself."

"Shutting down the planned performances would only raise suspicion at this point, especially with your wife since she seems so pleased that you are back onstage."

"Actually, she's a little leery of my performin'. Call it women's intuition, but maybe for good reason."

"Yes, indeed, Mr. Gant, anything that reveals your true identity certainly is not in her best interests."

"Damn you and your threats!"

"I'm merely pointing out the obvious consequences that would occur."

"OK, so what's the deal? You always have an angle."

"Well, Mr. Gant, I have every inclination of allowing you to continue performing. Luckily, you already have demanded time and place constraints from Mr. Holmstrom and communicated those to your wife. I can agree to those conditions."

Dale realized that his every move still was under surveillance—even after all these years!

"So be it," Dale said. He wanted more than anything to end their conversation by hanging up, but resisted.

"Take care until we speak again." Click.

The Big Islanders became the hottest ticket on Kailua Bay during their Friday night performances, and the pressure was ramping up on Dale to increase the band's exposure. Roger and Kiko were mellow, and Tom had agreed to Dale's terms, but Ronnie and Billy had tasted the allure of the limelight and wanted more than a few hours on Friday nights. They were correct in thinking Dale could make them famous, but they had no idea of why he was so adamant against taking their act on the road. They put pressure on Tom, and he agreed to keep working on Dale.

Mike Martinez, one of Tom's friends and former bosses from his restaurant management days in L.A., was coming to the islands to vacation. Mike was in charge of booking acts for the Bonaventure Lounge, which had seen better times. Tom knew his buddy would love to get Dale onstage back in L.A. That might just be enough to get Dale thinking about performing outside the Coconut Club. Martinez caught the act on Halloween night, and it was a memorable one. Of course, Elvis props were readily available in any costume shop, especially this time of year. Dale played the part by wearing a black wig and mutton chop sideburns, just like the originals from his heyday in Vegas. Tom led Dale over to Martinez's VIP table during one of the breaks.

"Incredible, Mr. Gant!" Martinez yelled over the din of a packed house. "I've got a business proposal, but it can wait until tomorrow when we have a chance to relax." Tom had made sure to include Dale on their fishing excursion, which might be just the right environment to get Dale to bite.

"Dale, that was the best Elvis impersonation I've seen, and believe me there's a bunch of them that come down to L.A. when they're not working Vegas," Mike said as he leaned back in his chair on Tom's 30-foot clipper and sipped a cold one. "But to hell with that. You have enough talent not to rely on any gimmicks. I'd love to showcase that talent in L.A. The Bonaventure used to be one of the best haunts in the city, and I think people would show up again to see you."

Dale pretended to be checking his line for barracuda, mahi mahi, or a triggerfish, but he heard the proposal.

"I sure do appreciate your interest, Mike, and it would be fun, but there ain't no way I'm getting out of here," Dale said. "Even If I could get away, those days are way behind me."

Tom and Mike must have figured Dale's trouble with getting away was due to his wedding band. They couldn't have imagined the reaction Agent Johnson would have had to Dale wanting to make music on the mainland.

JOURNAL ENTRY: NOV. 1, 1985:

Perhaps I was a fool to think I could play music in public and stay completely anonymous. Creation is what drives a musician, or any artist for that matter, and those forces can't be controlled. On the other hand, music itself doesn't feed my soul. I need the crowd. I *need* to hear their applause, and I *need* to feel their worship. I guess for now we can just keep playing and try to keep the cap on the bottle. But I know it's getting all shook up inside.

Dale committed to Friday nights at the Coconut Club through the winter tourist season, but he wouldn't promise anything beyond that. Dale tried to keep the performances somewhat low key, but that artist's bug for creativity usually got the better of him. The performances were as popular as ever, and Billy and Ronnie were enjoying more and more of the fringe benefits. They kept pushing Tom to get Dale to commit to more, but to no avail. The answer came to Ronnie in an advertisement he saw in the November 1985 edition of *CREEM*, the pre-eminent rock 'n' roll magazine.

"Wanted: Performers to pay tribute to The King of Rock 'n' Roll on the 10th anniversary celebration of Elvis Presley at Graceland. The 10 best Elvis impersonators and others who represent his artistry will be invited to perform during the anniversary concert on Aug. 16, 1987. A group including Ms. Priscilla Presley will make the final selections. Please send studio tape along with identification of band members and return address to: 10th Anniversary applications, Elvis Presley Enterprises, 3764 Elvis Presley Boulevard, Memphis, TN 38116."

"Hey, man, check this out," he told Billy and showed him the clipped ad. "We should get some tape and send it in. We might get picked to go to Graceland! There's no way Dale could say no to that."

"I don't know, dude," Billy replied with a wary look. "Dale gets really riled up when we even mention playing anywhere else. What if he gets pissed off and cancels our whole gig?"

"Well, we won't give the contest people his name and we won't tell him until we hear back from them," Ronnie replied. "If they turn us down, then we've got ourselves one hell of an audition tape. And if they say yes ..."

"I guess we've got as good a chance as anyone," Billy agreed. "I mean, Dale is amazing when he gets into his Elvis stuff. It blows my mind."

"Yeah, and it's going to blow some minds in Memphis when they see that tape," Ronnie said. Ronnie had been banging one of the cocktail waitresses, and she agreed to give him access to the roof, the perfect spot to hide a camera and get a bird's-eye view of the Coconut Club stage. On Friday, Nov. 15, Ronnie made up a story about a girl he wanted to impress being in the crowd. He asked Dale to do his best Elvis stuff since she was a huge fan of The King. As usual, it didn't take much for Dale to ignore his best intentions and get carried away in the performance. He finished the third set with a spot-on rendition of "Love Me Tender" that was sure to impress.

CHAPTER FIVE

Nick Sartain had spent the final five years of his time on the Memphis PD force chasing the ghost of Elvis Presley. Of course, there were no shortage of leads thanks to the tabloids and their favorite fodder. The King had been spotted from Graceland to Greenland and practically everywhere in between. Nick's obsession had driven Eddie to request a new partner, and the retired Capt. Summerfield's successor had agreed to let Nick work alone rather than saddling someone else with a "nut job." Anyone who had seen the spare room of the Sartain household would have agreed with the assessment of Nick's mental state. Tabloid headlines screaming various Presley sightings were plastered all over the walls.

"Elvis working behind the counter of a burger joint in California!"

"The King visits Tut's tomb!"

Nothing seemed too outrageous for the media circus, and Nick couldn't pass a checkout stand without purchasing if one of the rags had a mention of Elvis' whereabouts. Jenny insisted that Nick pay separately for the tabloids if they were in line together. She hadn't set foot in the spare room in years, preferring to ignore Nick's obsession, and would lock the door whenever any guests were in the house.

Nick had watched in vain as the casket containing Elvis Presley's re-mains—allegedly—remained sealed and eventually were moved from Forest Hills Cemetery to their final resting place at Graceland. Nick used his access at the precinct to chase down all sorts of leads, local and across the globe, but nothing ever materialized. The other detectives never seemed to tire of ribbing Nick about his pursuits, however. When Nick finally retired, the detectives gave him a gag gift, an Elvis wig with sideburns and his signature sunglasses.

"Just in case you need to go undercover," Det. Larry Childress announced to great laughter. Nick played along, put on the disguise, and made fun of himself, but his outward appearances didn't change his inner drive to discover the truth. Now, instead of using his police access to stay in pursuit, he had a new home base with his part-time security position at Graceland. Any good cop knew perpetrators couldn't resist returning to the scene of the crime, so he poured over security tapes that captured every visitor on camera. Nick identified a few suspects, but nothing solid ever materialized.

In retirement, Nick did a good job of keeping his obsession limited to his part-time place of work. Jenny seemed pleased that he no longer seemed consumed by the chase—at least at home. She couldn't escape the near madness altogether, however. Nick mentioned his snooping around Graceland, and whenever they left town he was on a constant lookout for new "clues." The incident in Vegas nearly tipped Jenny to the point of divorce. Nick had gotten drunk while losing too much money on the craps tables and rousted an Elvis impersonator at the hotel bar. Nick was so certain the guy was authentic that he yanked on his sideburns to prove his point. Nick thought it was funny when the sideburns turned out to be fake and peeled off, but hotel security didn't agree. They let Nick go with a stern warning only when he showed his security credentials, which had to be embarrassing.

"Yes, sir, I do believe that Elvis Presley is still alive and hiding somewhere under an assumed name ..."

Jenny had reached her limit. She had put up with Nick's obsession for eight long years! She finally confronted Nick over breakfast one morning, and the only thing that saved their marriage was Nick promising to give up the pursuit for good. No more tabloids. No more tailing impersonators. No more spying on Graceland visitors. No more craziness.

"And we're going to turn the spare room into a guest room—and invite my mother to visit!" Jenny said while silently realizing she could never really leave Nick.

"Now you're going too far," Nick teased in return. "But I'm seriously done with this crap for good."

Jenny looked into Nick's eyes and believed him. Nick made good on his promise as he focused on beer and bass fishing in his free time. Eddie Baxter suffered his massive heart attack a few months later, and that shook up Nick enough for him to start exercising again and maintain his shape. Nearly a year had passed and Nick was finally starting to believe he could keep his promise. Up to that point, letting go had felt like trying to get rid of a bad habit, like quitting smoking, and knowing full well that you were bound to fail and burn through a whole pack.

Nick's willpower vanished when Priscilla Presley's big announcement for a 10th anniversary celebration showed up in the media in August of 1985. Performers from all over the world would be submitting their best Elvis material, and the chosen ones would perform at Graceland! Nick was certain this would be the moment that "he" would return.

As the audition tapes poured into Graceland—what Elvis impersonator wouldn't want to be included?—Nick had the perfect position to review them. He offered his services to do background checks on each of the performers as part of the process.

"You are brilliant!" he complimented himself as he popped in the first tape in the privacy of Graceland's security room.

Nick viewed hundreds of tapes, but the problem was telling them apart. Mimicking Elvis' sound and swagger wasn't all that difficult if you had some talent, and not being too convincing logically would be part of "his" disguise. Any number of these guys could be "him." And each one of them seemed more than happy to divulge their identity. That didn't make sense for someone who didn't want attention. Nick decided to stop watching the tapes, but he gave instructions for the other security personnel to alert him if any tape came in without identification of the performer. Several months passed, and Nick again was starting to get used to life without the pursuit.

Nick's last shift at Graceland before Thanksgiving would be his blessing—or perhaps his curse. "Hey, Nick, thought you might want to take a look at this one," read the note from a co-worker. "No Name."

"Bingo!" Nick said as he popped in the tape.

The performance was mesmerizing. Nick closed his eyes and thought the sound was unmistakable—Elvis Presley. The singer's looks definitely had some resemblance, but the voice was a dead ringer. Or was it? Perhaps Nick was just hearing what he had waited so long to hear? Perhaps he should just be done with this whole mess—for good this time.

But two words scrawled on the note had brought him back into the game for good: "No Name. Why would you send a package with some nightclub as the return address, with no band name, and stipulate that the name of the lead singer had to remain anonymous until further notice?" Nick asked himself.

The only information on the audition form was a contact name and phone number: Ronnie Mason (keyboards), 808-555-2573. Nick thought about calling Mr. Mason himself, but his police training prevailed.

"If someone doesn't want attention, then the last person they are going to talk to is a detective," Nick said to himself. "But a call from Graceland might cause some reaction."

Nick sealed the tape in his private locker before leaving work and left a note for Ms. Presley's PR staff to contact him first thing in the morning.

He managed to stay calm during the evening, thanks to more than one whiskey sour, but Jenny noticed a change in Nick in the morning. She had seen his cop's senses kick in when he was pursuing real criminals more than once, and she could read the intensity on his face.

"What's up with you, babe?" she asked while sliding a plate of eggs and hash browns in front of Nick at the breakfast bar.

"Nothing in particular, just some minor security issues with the fund-raising event next weekend," Nick replied. "Why do you ask?"

"Well, I've only seen that look on your face hundreds of times when you're onto someone or something," she said. "So, what gives?"

"Seriously, I think you're imagining things," Nick said as he put his hand on her forehead. "You feeling okay, Mrs. Sartain?"

"Don't screw with me, Nick," she said sternly. "You've finally seemed to relax these past few months, but now I'm getting a whole new vibe. One that I don't like."

Nick just shrugged and headed off to the living room with his wife's eyes following close behind.

"Damn, how does she read me so easily!" he whispered to himself as the phone rang.

"Graceland, for you," Jenny said as she handed the phone to Nick with a look of suspicion.

"Hi Janis.... Ok, good. Yes, I'll be there within the hour," Nick said while avoiding Jenny's gaze.

"Ok, babe, I have to run down there for a quick meeting," Nick said. "How about I trade you for a drive in the country this afternoon, maybe get a late lunch at one of those country barbecue stands?"

"Don't you try to change the subject, Nick," Jenny replied. "You're up to something, but I don't want to know. Just remember your promise."

Nick pulled into Graceland and headed for the business section of the mansion, where Janis Hansen worked as Priscilla Presley's public relations liaison. Nick asked Janis to meet him in the security room and fetched the tape from his locker.

"Check this out," Nick said as he inserted the tape.

Janis was spellbound as she watched.

"Who *is* this guy?" she exclaimed as the tape faded to black.

"That's why I contacted you. Carl flagged this entry and showed it to me. We have a return address and a contact person from the band—the bass player—but their information form stipulates that the lead singer remain anonymous," Dale explained. "I wasn't sure if we should pass this one through the process, but damn, this guy is good."

"Oh! Ms. Presley will want to see this," Janis said excitedly. "He's the best we've seen by far. I'll make the call myself and let you know what I find out."

Ronnie Mason couldn't believe his ears when he hung up the phone. Priscilla Presley herself wanted Dale to be included in the 10th anniversary show, maybe even as the final act. The performance was gratis, but all expenses paid for the entire band and their entourage. Ronnie leaned back in his chair and imagined himself with all the trappings of a famous musician: money, cars, girls ...

"Hot damn!" he exclaimed as he jumped up and headed out the door to deliver the news to Billy.

"Hey, man, we're in!" Ronnie said excitedly. "They want the whole band to come to Memphis and do the 10th anniversary show. This is our shot!"

"That's great, dude, but how do we tell Dale?" Billy asked. "I'm just afraid he'll be totally pissed that we went behind his back."

"Why don't we approach Tom with the idea and see what he thinks?" Ronnie replied. "He knows Dale best and will be able to convince him. Man, we gotta do this!"

Tom Holmstrom's reaction was decidedly less positive after Ronnie requested a meeting in the Coconut Club office.

"You've got to be fucking kidding me!" he screamed at Ronnie loud enough for the tourists on Kailua Bay Road to hear. "Dale will have a fit if he finds out, and that would be the end of our Friday nights. You keep your goddamn mouth shut, and give me the number of the people who called you."

Ronnie tried to protest, but he wasn't going against Tom—at least not yet. Tom promptly made a return call to the number Janis had provided and informed her that their generous offer would have to be declined.

"I'm afraid leaving the islands is just not an option for us," Tom said. "Please tell Ms. Presley that we are flattered by the offer, and we're sure there are plenty of other wonderful musicians who would love the opportunity to pay tribute."

"She will be disappointed, but I will let her know," Janis replied. "And please do keep my contact number in case you change your mind."

Janis summoned Nick to her office that afternoon to share the news.

"It did seem kind of strange, but I guess some people just want their privacy," Janis said.

"If you want privacy, why are you singing and playing guitar in a nightclub?" Nick asked.

"Good point. I don't know, but regardless we need to keep looking for more performers," Janis said as she turned her attention to a stack of tapes and audition forms on her desk.

Nick made sure to hang onto the mystery tape. He played it over and over, studying the mystery man on vocals and lead guitar.

"I need to meet you and decide for myself," Nick finally said to himself.

The next day Nick made good on his promise to take Jenny for a drive in the country and some home-cooked ribs for lunch. He knew it was the best place to ease her guard.

"You know, babe, it's great to get out of the city, but I think we're due for a real vacation," he said while wiping sauce from his chin.

"You have anywhere particular in mind?" Jenny asked without any hint of suspicion.

"Eddie used to always rave about how great the fishing and snorkeling is in Hawaii, the Big Island," Nick said.

"The beach does sound wonderful this time of year," Jenny said while closing her eyes to imagine the sea breeze.

"Things always slow down at the mansion right after New Year's," Nick said. "I think we still have time to get a cheap flight."

"Why not, let's live a little!" Jenny said happily.

Nick always put work before play, and he had some investigative work to do before any beach time in Hawaii. He still knew a private dick in Hawaii who used to do some work for the Manko brothers. Just the type of shady character Nick would need for a covert operation, if he remembered Jocko correctly. Two weeks before his trip to Hawaii, Nick made the call.

"Bill Jockowicz, what can I do for you?"

"Hi Jocko. This is Nick Sartain, from Memphis, do you remember me?"

"Yeah, sure, we did some stuff for the Manko boys. I remember you."

"Good, well, I've got some private work on the Big Island, if you are interested."

"Always interested, if the price is right and there's not too much skin involved."

"This one's pretty tame for $500. All I need you to do is follow a guy home from a club and keep an eye on him. Case his place to see who else is living with him," Nick explained.

Totally unaware of the tape's existence, Dale had continued to entertain the tourists on Kailua Bay through the holidays. It didn't take long for Jocko to get a description of the "amazing guy" who plays on Friday nights at the Coconut Club with a band called the Big Islanders. He sat quietly at the bar and watched Dale's performance two nights later. Jocko followed Dale home after the performance and noted the heavily gated entrance as Dale turned into Hale ke`oke`o. A vantage point in the hills above the residence and Jocko's trusty binoculars put him on Noelani's trail the next day when she left in the morning for her usual trip to yoga class and to visit her parents.

"I've got the scoop," Jocko said as he got Nick on a private line at one of the Manko Brothers' downtown hangouts. "Your boy's name is Dale Gant. Nothing comes up on him locally. Looks like he's been here for eight years or so, living off whatever he did before that. The band is called the Big Islanders. Gant is the lead singer, and he is *good*. He doesn't hang around long after the band is done and drives to a house about 20 miles north of town up Highway 19. Private entrance with big iron gates. Someone doesn't want anyone else getting in there. I hung out for three days and never saw him come or go. I did see a native broad leave the house every morning in a silver sedan at approximately 10:30. He's married to a Noelani Akuma, from a local family, so I'm figuring that's her. She stopped at a workout joint in Kukio Beach and then at the Akuma estate, which is just south of their house, off Highway 19. That all you need?"

"That's all for now," Nick said. "I know where to find you, and I'll wire the other half of the money right now."

Nick had a nine-day window in Hawaii—which he made sure spanned two Friday nights—to conduct his main investigation of the mystery man who plays with the Big Islanders. All he could do now was wait out the 72 hours before departing for Hawaii. He called in some favors at Memphis PD headquarters to help pass the time. Nick wanted to see the background report for himself, and he wasn't surprised when the name Dale Gant came back clean.

Nick and Jenny boarded a plane on Jan. 9, 1986, headed for the Kailua-Kona International Airport. One of Eddie's connections through the Manko Brothers had scored them a good deal on a beachfront condo rental just a mile south of Kailua Bay, a perfect location to do some recon on the Coconut Club. Nick made a cash arrangement and demanded that all transactions on the trip be paid with cash or traveler's checks. The last thing he needed was someone on his tail because of a credit card transaction.

Jenny came up with the suggestion of dinner on the bay Friday night, so Nick only needed to mention that he had read good reviews about the Coconut Club in the local paper that morning. Nick used a pay phone down the street from his condo to alert Jocko of his plan.

"You need me there to watch your back?" Jocko asked.

"Good idea, but don't make contact with me or him," Nick said. "We need to be careful just in case this guy has some people of his own on the watch."

When the Big Islanders hit the stage that Friday evening, Nick Sartain was seated less than 10 yards from a man he'd been seeking for nearly nine years. He watched Dale intently, studying the man's body size and shape, mannerisms, movements, all the things that a detective is trained to observe. Looking at the man's face was for amateurs, because a face can change.

Nick could feel the hairs on his neck dance as the band worked through its first set. If this was his man, Nick would need some proof. He couldn't just accuse this guy of being Elvis Presley, especially in front of his wife. Nick's initial investigation and subsequent combing through every death record he could find made him certain that proof wouldn't come in any tangible form.

Jenny seemed almost in a trance as she took in the music. Listening to Elvis after his death had brought mostly sadness in Jenny's heart for many years, but this was different. She hadn't expected to run across someone who sounded so much like him in a tourist bar on the Big Island of Hawaii.

"Oh, my God, he's spectacular!" Jenny told Nick as she swayed to the beat of "It's Now or Never."

"We have to meet him!"

Dale was trying to make his usual quick exit after the performance, but Jenny was not to be denied.

She wiggled through the crowd and made her way directly in front of Dale.

"You were amazing!" she said as she squeezed his hand.

"Well, thank you, ma'am," Dale replied politely.

"I'm here with my husband. May we buy you a drink?" Jenny pleaded.

"Well, ma'am, one of the promises I make to my wife is that I don't stick around to socialize after a performance," Dale said.

Dale tried to pull away, but Jenny was persistent.

"Oh, please, just for a minute?" she pleaded. "At least just come over and say hi!"

"I guess I can at least do that," Dale conceded, knowing that a quick conversation would get him closer to the door than trying to resist his fans. Jenny grabbed Dale's arm to make sure he wasn't getting away and pulled him toward Nick.

"Nick, this is, uh, I don't think the band ever introduced you," Jenny said. "What is your name?"

"Dale Gant, ma'am, and nice to meet both of you," Dale said politely. "Where y'all from?"

"Memphis," Nick said plainly and waited for any type of reaction. "From the sound of your accent, you don't hail far from there."

"Well, let's just say I've been around," Dale replied.

"Do you have time for us to buy you a drink, Mr. Gant?" Jenny interjected.

"Actually, I do need to get going, but thank you kindly for the offer," Dale said. "How long are you staying on the Big Island?"

"We just got here last night, so another eight days," Jenny said. "I know the time will fly!"

"We'll be playing here again next Friday," Dale said. "Hopefully, we'll see you then."

"Definitely," Nick said as he continued to scrutinize Dale's countenance.

"Oh, yes, we wouldn't miss it for anything!" Jenny said excitedly.

"Ok, enjoy your stay," Dale said and moved quickly toward the exit door.

Nick watched as Dale walked directly to a blue sedan and made his way out of the parking lot, heading north. Jocko was watching, too, from the seat of his medium brown Ford. Nick gave a nod for Jocko to tail and see if Dale Gant's habits had changed any. Nick wanted to put some heat on this guy and see if he had any cracks, but what could he do without any shred of hard evidence? Nick had nothing, save for a strong hunch that Dale Gant had a secret to tell.

Since the day he arrived at Hale ke`oke`o, James McMahan's assignment was to protect the identity of Dale Gant, at any cost. That included regular monitoring of all databases for anyone doing background checks on Dale Gant or anyone close to him. It had taken nearly a week to track down the names and locations behind the two recent background checks, but now McMahan was reading a fax with the key information:

Bill Jockowicz, age 64, gray/blue, 6-0, 245.
Location of inquiry: Kona, Hawaii.
Last known whereabouts: 1143 N. Kelowna, Kona, Hawaii

Nick Sartain, age 59, blonde/green, 5-11, 180
Location of inquiry: Memphis, TN
Last known whereabouts: Believed to be traveling in Hawaii; arrived through security on 1-9-86 at 15:35 local time, Kailua-Kona Inter-

national Airport; scheduled for departure from KKIA on 1-19-86 at 9:35 local time

———————

Shortly after receiving the fax, the phone rang on the multi-purpose machine.

"Hello, sir," Agent McMahan said as he knew only one person had access to this line.

"We've tracked the first inquiry to an address in Kona," Agent Johnson said. "We'd like you to put surveillance on Mr. Bill Jockowicz, priority status. All of his pertinent information has been faxed to you. I will be arriving tomorrow."

"Yes, the information has arrived, sir," McMahan said. "I'll initiate operations, priority status."

Jocko had followed Dale home Friday night, but there was no change in routine. He tailed Dale and Noelani as they made a visit to her parents on Saturday afternoon, but again nothing out of the ordinary—except for the black SUV that trailed Jocko's vehicle at a safe distance to avoid detection. Jocko took Sunday off and had plans for brunch downtown and a nap before an afternoon golf date. He pulled out of his driveway and later returned without noticing the black SUV parked across the street.

Jocko had another surprise waiting inside. He felt a stunning blow to the back of his head and a needle penetrate his neck, but he never saw the agent who delivered the silent attack as soon as the front door had closed. The next time Jocko opened his eyes, he could see nothing but blackness. His brain was refocusing, and he realized a black hood was covering his head. He could feel his hands bound tightly, but in front of him. The recliner in which he was trapped felt like his own, which was a slight relief, but he was strapped tightly to it.

"What the fuck …?" Jocko began before a hand covered his mouth.

"We'll talk first, Mr. Jockowicz," Agent Johnson said. "Then you will have your turn. Do you understand?"

Jocko could only grunt and shake his head yes.

"You searched the police databases for the name Dale Gant," Agent Johnson continued in his strictest business tone. "We need to know exactly who and/or what prompted your interest in Mr. Gant."

Trying to clear his mind and focus on the best course of action, Jocko hesitated to answer. Suddenly his balding head was jerked violently backward.

"Focus!" Agent Johnson hissed forcefully. "Your continued well-being may depend on your answers."

Jocko had been in many tough situations during his years as a soldier, cop, and private dick, but he sensed these guys were real dangerous.

"I'll tell you what I know, but it's not much," he said. "I got a job to find out the guy's name, put a tail on him and get some pictures, but that's it."

"Who hired you?" Agent Johnson demanded.

"The guy didn't give me his name," Jocko said quickly.

"The polygraph machine you are hooked up to says you are lying, Mr. Jockowicz," Agent Johnson said. "If you do not tell the truth, this ordeal will not end well for you. Now, what is his name?"

"Uh, Nick, I think. Yeah, that's it, Nick," Jocko stammered.

"Nick ... what?" Agent Johnson asked.

"I don't remember his last name, I swear. We did some stuff in Memphis, but that's it," Jocko said.

The needles on the polygraph were inconclusive this time. Jocko might be telling the truth that he didn't recall the last name. The FBI has ways of extracting memories, but Agent Johnson had enough information.

"His name is Sartain, Nick Sartain," Agent Johnson said.

"Uh, yeah, that's it," Jocko confirmed.

"Where are the photos?"

"In my desk drawer, by the kitchen table," Jocko mumbled while trying to rid the taste of stale garment from his mouth.

Agent Johnson motioned for Agent McMahan to retrieve the pictures. Agent Johnson flipped through a stack of Polaroids. Jocko was a shitty photographer, he thought to himself, but nonetheless, the faces of Dale and Noelani Gant were staring back at him. Agent Johnson handed the photos to Agent McMahan, who stuffed them inside the pocket of his jacket.

"Phone records show you've received several calls in the last few weeks, including one from Memphis on Jan. 2nd and one from a pay phone in downtown Kailua two days ago," Agent Johnson said. "What did you tell Mr. Sartain?"

"I gave him the guy's name and his address," Jocko said. "I told him I watched the guy for a few days, but he never left his house. That's it. He told me to sit tight."

"We know Nick Sartain is on the Big Island, but we don't know where," Agent Johnson said.

"He didn't say, I swear, and he didn't give me a number to call," Jocko said in anticipation of the next question. "I don't know how to reach him, but he's planning to come here tomorrow morning to look at the pictures."

"What time?"

"He arranged for his wife to be at the spa at 9 A.M., so right after that."

"I believe you, Mr. Jockowicz," Agent Johnson said. "Mr. Sartain will be here first thing in the morning, and we'll be waiting for him."

"I'm supposed to play golf this afternoon," Jocko stammered. "If I don't show up, my friends will come looking for me. Let me go. You can follow me, and I swear I'll come back!"

"Obviously you need the exercise," Agent Johnson while patting Jocko's ample stomach. "However, we can't take any unnecessary risks. So, I don't believe we'll be requiring any more of your services."

"What now?" Jocko asked with real fear in his voice.

"Don't worry," Agent Johnson said. "You won't feel a thing."

Nick and Jenny visited Hawaii Volcanoes National Park on Saturday. The churning and spewing of glowing lava from the active Mauna Loa volcano matched Nick's insides as he wondered if Jocko had any news about Dale Gant. Trekking through the park was an all-day affair. Nick managed to suppress his edginess when Jenny suggested that they find a hotel in Hilo rather than make the long drive back to Kailua in the dark. Breakfast on Hilo Bay and a trip to Rainbow Falls chewed up Nick's time for Sunday sleuthing. First thing Monday morning he slipped down to the pay phone while Jenny was planning her spa day. The spa service was expensive, but Nick insisted that Jenny pamper herself—while he would have time to do more digging.

"… You've reached Bill Jockowicz. Please leave a message after the beep."

Nick thought it was strange that Jocko didn't answer. He knew Nick would be tied up for the weekend but wanting to get back on the trail Monday morning. Nick tried again 10 minutes later. Still nothing.

"What the hell?" he muttered to himself after being careful not to leave a message. Cops knew how many times perps had supplied damning evidence in a voice recording. He hurried back to the room before Jenny missed him and told her he planned to tour the town while she was at the spa. Agreed. That gave Nick a solid three hours to see what was up with Jocko.

Nick's cop senses told him to leave the rental car at the condo and take a cab. He instructed the cab driver to pull up two blocks short of Jocko's residence as he surveyed the scene, one that provided a probable answer as to the private eye's status and tightened Nick's insides. An ambulance and a county vehicle marked "coroner" were parked in front of Jocko's house. Nick had worked enough crime scenes to figure out how to get information from the outside. He exited the cab and approached the small group of residents gathered two houses down from Jocko's.

"Does anyone know what happened? Is Mr. Jockowicz okay?" Nick asked innocently.

"I'm afraid not," an elderly Hawaiian woman replied. "One of his friends found him dead this morning. Apparently, he didn't show up for golf yesterday afternoon, and his friends were worried."

"Did they say what happened to him?"

"They said it was an apparent heart attack, but they haven't moved the body. The coroner has been in there for at least an hour."

Nick knew the rules surrounding any unattended death. The coroner might take several hours—or several days—to rule out anything other than natural causes. The last thing Nick wanted to do was question the cops and become a person of interest if there was anything suspicious about Jocko's death. His only play was to return to the hotel, try to relax, and not arouse Jenny's suspicions. Nick made brief eye contact with two men seated in a large, black SUV as he headed across the street and climbed back into the cab.

"Head back toward downtown," he told the driver while handing him two $20-dollar bills to prepay for the ride. "I may need to make a quick exit."

Nick watched in the side mirror as the cab pulled away from the curb. The driver of the black SUV gave them a one-block head start before following. Nick instructed the cab driver to take the busiest street in town, and he headed for Ali'i Drive, which follows the shoreline of Kailua Bay's busy tourist district. The black SUV gunned it through a yellow/red light to stay three cars behind. Nick's mind was whirring through the possibilities of who was tailing him and why. They must have been involved in Jocko's death, and that created a direct link to Dale Gant. Someone didn't want Nick—or anyone else most likely—investigating Mr. Gant.

Nick shook himself back to dealing with urgent issues first. He instructed the driver to create maximum distance between the cab and the car in front of it. Nick spotted the outdoor market across street where he and Jenny had weaved through crowds of tourists the day before.

"Then haul ass to close the gap, hit the brakes, and I'll be gone," Nick told the driver, who gave him a nervous glance in the rearview. "Do it, now!"

Nick jumped out on the driver's side and darted in front of oncoming traffic to reach the opposite boardwalk. He ducked into the main entrance to a market and sprinted through several packed aisles. He knocked a vendor to the ground and sent beaded bracelets flying before reaching a side exit. Nick doubled back toward Ali'i Drive and melted back into the crowd on the boardwalk. The black SUV had stopped abruptly and was partially blocking traffic. Nick could see the driver, but the passenger seat was empty. Nick moved down the sidewalk away from the SUV. He bought a souvenir "Kailua Bay" ballcap along the way and pulled off his t-shirt to go bare-chested. Another block away from the SUV, which was still blocking traffic, Nick crossed the street to the shoreline side and found a safe vantage point at the entrance to a small pier. He saw a man dressed in khaki shorts and a Hawaiian shirt climb into the passenger door of the SUV just as a traffic cop was telling the driver to move along. Nick stayed low and watched as the SUV passed, but he couldn't see much through the tinted windows. He marked the numbers on the U.S. Government plate, however: SPC 13 421

Nick knew enough about running plates that the SPC signified a special class of law enforcement vehicles that are exempt from registering as any specific agency. That meant even his Memphis PD contacts wouldn't be able to tag the vehicle's origin. The important thing was he knew someone was tracking him, but they wouldn't be able to trace him to the condo. He and Jenny were relatively safe moving about town, but that didn't get him any closer to Dale Gant. Waiting until the Friday performance at the Coconut Club wasn't an option. His pursuers surely would be on the lookout, and it was cutting too close to his return flight. Nick would have to up the ante.

Jenny scheduled another trip for Tuesday, and this time they were heading north on Highway 19 to visit the birthplace of King Kamehameha near the small town of Hawi on the northern tip of the Big Island. Nick would be driving directly past the Akuma estate and the entry to Dale Gant's secret residence. That excited his cop's senses, but what did it mean? Nothing, in reality, because Nick still didn't have any hard evidence. Nick went back through the notes he took during his phone conversation with Jocko. He had mentioned a native woman leaving every morning and a good vantage point on a nearby hillside.

"Hey, babe, let's take a little break?" Nick said shortly after he drove slowly past the entrance to the Akuma estate. "We can pull up the hill a bit and just check out the beauty of the ocean for a few minutes."

"Sure thing," Jenny said. "We can start in on the cheese and crackers, and hey, it's not too early for a beer because we are on vacation."

"You go ahead on the beer part, but a snack does sound good," Nick said as he spotted the turnout and short road up to Jocko's vantage point.

Nick had made sure to pack binoculars for "sightseeing," and he pulled them out under the pretense of wanting to get a better look at the fishing boat that was anchored a mile or so offshore. Jenny was lost in the beauty of the islands and didn't notice as a silver sedan pulled up to the highway and waited for traffic to clear before turning south. Nick had a good look at the car and the attractive Hawaiian woman behind the wheel.

Nick waited a few minutes to make sure she wasn't followed. His mind wandered as he pulled the rental car back onto Highway 19 and drove the 20 miles north to Hawi. He was reasonably certain that this woman, assumed to be Dale Gant's wife, would be leaving the compound every morning. She at least gave Nick a chance to put some heat on Dale Gant.

"You know, babe, I think I'll take you up on that offer to charter a fishing boat," Nick said. "You OK being on your own for a while tomorrow morning?"

"Oh, yes, there are some cute dress shops downtown that I'm dying to see," Jenny replied.

"OK then, I'm going to go out and catch us some dinner."

He staged the trip for Wednesday morning as a 1/2-day outing out of Keiki Beach, just north of Kailua-Kona. As Nick headed north toward his true destination, he stopped and purchased some mahi mahi from a roadside vendor that he could show for his alleged fishing efforts. He felt guilty deceiving Jenny, but he balanced the scales by convincing himself that he was looking out for her safety. Jocko had provided perfect directions to the fitness center in Kukio Beach where the mystery woman presumed to be Dale Gant's wife attended yoga classes. Nick parked as near the entrance as he could and waited. Just past 10:30 A.M., the woman he was trailing exited the building and luckily walked in Nick's direction.

"Mrs. Gant?" Nick said as he stepped in front of the woman and flashed his security badge from Graceland.

"Uh, yes, who's asking?"

"My name is Detective Nick Sartain, formerly of the Memphis Police Department and current head of security at Graceland, the final resting place of Elvis Presley," Nick said with the authority of someone who had questioned suspects all of his adult life. He made sure to add "Elvis Presley" at the end of his opening, hoping it would stir a reaction.

"What may I do for you, Detective," the woman said as she rubbed her cheek.

"May I buy you a cup of coffee?" Nick said as he indicated with his eyes the sidewalk café two doors down from the fitness center. "I'd like to ask you a few questions."

Noelani felt as if she was frozen to the asphalt of the parking lot. She felt her face flush, though that was impossible to perceive in her dark brown complexion. Finally, she felt her lips and tongue begin to move and form words into a sort of answer.

"Um, well, I really do need to get going," she said.

Noelani's reaction checked the first box on Nick's list of suspicious behavior. She had not stated the obvious "and what the hell does Elvis Presley have to do with me" that one might expect from an *innocent* detainee in this situation. Sensing Noelani's nervousness, Nick took control of the conversation.

"It will just take a moment," he said while lightly grasping Noelani's forearm and leading her in the direction of the coffee shop. Noelani allowed herself to be led, and Nick steered her toward the most private table.

"Two Kona coffees, please," he told the waitress. "Do you take anything in yours, Mrs. Gant?"

"Just a little bit of cream," Noelani stammered while clenching and un-clenching her fists.

"I hope I don't make you nervous," Nick offered while smiling inwardly that he had provoked exactly that state.

"No, I'm just a little confused as to what you want from me," she said.

"Well, ma'am, we're investigating some rumors, that's all," Nick said. He was using an old cop's trick of dragging out the real reason behind an interrogation, letting the subject's imagination conceive every reason imaginable.

"Rumors of what, exactly?" Noelani said as the waitress set down their refreshments.

"Do you read the tabloids, Mrs. Gant?"

"Well, I glance from time to time while I'm checking out at the grocery store, but that's all."

"No doubt you've seen tabloid stories that claim Elvis Presley is still alive and living out his days in some exotic location," Nick continued.

"Yes, I mean, they print trash like that all the time," Noelani said while obviously trying not to fidget in her seat.

"I assure you that we share your sentiments, Mrs. Gant, but lately we have reason to believe there may be some truth to those rumors."

The shock registered immediately on Noelani's smooth, dark face.

"You mean the rumors that Elvis Presley is still alive!?"

Noelani's statement and the alarm in her voice drew stares from a couple seated nearby. Nick paused and allowed Noelani's words to reverberate in her own ears. Time to move in for the kill.

"Well, yes, as strange as it may seem to you, we have reason to believe there is some credence to the rumor that Elvis Presley is alive and living here in Hawaii," Nick said with zero change in the volume nor intensity of his voice. "How long have you known your husband?"

Noelani felt her mind collapse. How *well* do you know your husband? Her inner voice had been asking this question of her conscience for years. She was keenly aware of the tabloids—oh yes, constantly scanning the front page for a picture of Dale Gant. Her suspicions began with Dale talking in his sleep. He'd call out, "Lisa Maria!" and less often "Priscilla!" Dale never seemed to remember anything about the dreams in the morning, and she never asked about them. But she *knew*. In that crawlspace deep inside your soul where you can't lie to yourself, she knew the truth. Dale Gant, her beloved husband, had been Elvis Presley.

When she heard him sing in church and later perform onstage, there was no doubt in her mind. But she had fallen in love with Dale years before he started to share his secrets in the dead of night. And she knew Dale loved her. Proof of that came from reading Dale's entries about her in his Green Book. She had stumbled upon the safe behind the painting of The Last Supper while trying out some rearrangements to the furniture in Dale's office. She had completely innocent intentions of wanting to surprise him with a new look that matched a fashion redesign of Hale keʻokeʻo. Figuring out the combination to the safe took numerous tries, but it made sense in the end: Dale's date of birth and month combined with Keloa's date of birth.

Noelani had a hard time reconciling her love for a man who would leave his birth daughter—and how that man could show true love for a stepchild in her Pualani. After reading all of the entries in Dale's diary, however, she understood how a person could be driven to desperation by the trappings of fame. She understood that once Dale had set events in motion, fiends like Agent Johnson wouldn't let him stop. She believed that in the end Dale had no choice but to go through with the plan to fake his death, and now he wanted nothing more than to be with her and live happily ever after. Her belief that a happy ending was possible, however, had been shattered by the confrontation with Detective Nick Sartain.

"You're crazy," Noelani said, but not with a piercing yell this time. She had lowered the volume of her voice but increased its intensity to a hiss. "Stay away from me, and stay away from my family!"

Noelani rose and walked hurriedly to her car parked nearby. Nick thought about following her, but what was the point? He knew where she was headed, and Nick had to be careful. The guys in the black SUV obviously meant business and would not hesitate to kill him or anyone else to keep Dale Gant's identity a secret. Nick had eluded capture once, but he didn't want to give his pursuers a second chance.

By confronting Noelani Gant, Nick had taken the only course of action he dared. He assumed she wouldn't be returning to yoga class anytime soon, at least not at the fitness center in Kukio Beach. If Noelani Gant confronted her husband, he likely wouldn't be showing up for the Friday night gig at the Coconut Club. Or would he? Smart people who want to stay hidden stick to their routines when they are confronted. If Noelani Gant said nothing, then her husband almost certainly would show up for his regular performance. Either way, Nick figured his best chance of exposing Dale Gant would come Friday night at the Coconut Club. Until then he would just have to sit tight.

Nick watched the blue sedan pull out of the parking lot and head north. The essential question arose: "I wonder what she's going to do?" he asked himself.

That question tortured Noelani as she drove more slowly than normal up Highway 19 toward Hale ke`oke`o. If she kept quiet about her confrontation, what would be Detective Nick Sartain's next step? What would happen if he tried to confront Dale, especially at their home? Dale trusted Agents Gatewood and McMahan, and so did she. But Dale feared Agent Johnson and what he might do if he felt threatened. She had never met Agent Johnson, but she was certain he had made visits to Hale ke`oke`o. Dale's entries about Agent Johnson in the Green Book had given her nightmares.

Perhaps she could approach Dale with calm and reason. Those traits had always been her strengths. Detective Sartain was looking for a reaction from them. They wouldn't oblige, just deny everything and continue to rely on the FBI to provide protection. She knew that removing Pualani from any potential harm was her first priority. She would approach Ikaika first and make sure he agreed to safeguard Pualani at all costs. Despite her attempts to remain calm, Noelani had the gnawing feeling her day of reckoning with the true identity of her husband would arrive soon. Nick scanned the parking lot for the black SUV, but it was nowhere to be seen. He turned south on Highway 19 and steered the rental car back toward Kailua. Nick's mind must have been focused on what to do next as he didn't notice two suits in a brown four-door that had pulled out behind him and were following a few hundred yards behind. Nick headed toward Kailua Bay, but instead of returning to the condo he pulled into the district reserved for industrial docks. The Manko brothers owned a building near the water that provided a perfect base for whatever black-market goods they were peddling at the moment. Nick had kept his nose clean during his days with Memphis PD, but Johnny Manko still owed him some favors. The building had only a few windows looking toward the waterfront, and those were obscured by years of salt and grime. Nick knocked on the rusty iron door. A hefty Hawaiian answered and sized up Nick.

"What the hell do you want, *haole*?" he asked with emphasis on the slur Hawaiians use for white trash.

"I'm looking for Johnny. I'm an old acquaintance from Memphis. Nick Sartain."

The hefty Hawaiian, who looked like an island version of Memphis' finest Irish-Italian thugs, stepped aside to let Nick enter a dimly-lit main room with just a few metal chairs for furniture.

"Hey boss, you want to talk to a Nick Sartain?" the Hawaiian yelled down the hall.

Johnny Manko was an authentic version of Memphis' Irish-Italian thugs. Johnny had put on some pounds and Nick figured he was tipping the scales at close to four bills, at least a quarter of the weight in his meaty neck and hands.

"What the hell you doin' here?" Johnny said with a grin as he stuck his head into the hallway. Nick relaxed because the greeting was about as gentle as could ever be expected from one of the Mankos.

"Well, mostly seeing the sights with Jenny," Nick said. "At least that is what she thinks. I'm also trailing a guy who might be causing some shit back in Memphis."

"Aren't you two renting the condo on the other side of the bay?" Johnny asked. "I thought Rico said he had you set up for the week in there."

"Yeah, yeah, it's great. We appreciate the hospitality," Nick said.

"And you figured you wanted to come and see how good ol' Johnny was doin'?"

"Well, yeah, that too. But I might need some muscle," Nick said.

"I'm getting' on OK, but all the pork they eat aroun' here has me fatter than a hog fit for slaughter. Guess I better watch myself after what happened to Eddie. Damn, I heard he just keeled right over in the middle of his garden, kind of like how Don Corleone bit the dust in *The Godfather*. How about you?"

"Well, I've been out of the real action since I retired from the force, but I've still got my gig doing security at Graceland."

After a long pause, Johnny leaned back in his chair and got down to business.

"How much muscle?" he asked directly.

"Well, a private dick I hired here to look into this asshole ended up dead. I went to check it out at his house and ended up with two guys in a black SUV chasing me through downtown. I lost 'em, but I think they were Feds."

"I don't need no shit with the Feds, Nick, no sir," Johnny said quickly. "They like to fuck with you where it hurts, like your taxes."

"I don't think it's anything like that," Nick said. "These guys are protecting the guy I'm after."

"Alright, so what you need from me?"

"I need someone to keep a lookout on the condo, make sure they don't know where we're stayin' because Jenny doesn't know anything is up," Nick said. "And if she finds out I'm back in the game, well, I might he hangin' out here with you guys full-time."

"We've already got Nui here and another one of our boys shacked up right next door to you," Johnny said as he nodded toward the hefty Hawaiian.

"Make sure he's on the lookout Friday night. This guy plays in a local band at the Coconut Club on Friday nights," Nick said.

"You mean the Big Islanders!?" Johnny exclaimed. "I love those dudes, especially the singer that sounds like Elvis."

"Yeah, that's him. I'm going to roust him a little bit Friday night, and I don't need nobody surprising me on the way home," Nick said.

"OK, I'll make sure Rico keeps an eye out. Hey, is this guy fucking with The King?" Johnny asked with a look of genuine concern.

"Yeah, something like that."

The brown four-door pulled out from across the street and followed at a safe distance as Nick pulled onto Ali'i Drive and drove three miles south to the condo. The two suits watched as Nick parked and walked around to the beachfront where Jenny could be seen sunbathing.

"Check this out!" Nick said as he pulled out the bag of fresh mahi mahi. "We'll be firing up that grill tonight!"

"Wow, look at you!" Jenny exclaimed as the brown four-door eased past the condo and continued out of sight.

"I don't remember this guy doing any fishing," Agent Tomkins told his partner as they parked a few blocks away by the nearest pay phone. "I need to call the boss."

"Sir, we've followed Mr. Sartain to an address, 1345 Kahakai Road, just south of downtown Kailua," Agent Tomkins said.

"Maintain full surveillance for now," Agent Johnson said. "Mr. Sartain is your primary target. Contact me if the situation escalates." Click.

Noelani spent Thursday morning agonizing over whether to confront Dale. Her mind whirred in constant motion from one plan to another. She finally settled on the one course of action she knew was right.

"Hello, my brother," Noelani said as she stepped into the Akuma Estate. "Where are mother and father?"

"They are visiting friends, my dear kaikuahine," Ikaika said, using his preferred Hawaiian expression for sister.

"Good, then we can be alone," Noelani said. "I have a very important favor to ask of you."

"What is it?" Ikaika asked without showing emotion.

"I'm not sure, maybe some trouble for Dale and me," Noelani said.

Ikaika did not reply, but patiently waited for his sister to continue the tale.

"You know that Dale has some demons in his past. I don't believe he has done anything wrong, and we love each other more than ever, but I fear some bad people are trying to locate him now. My only fear is for Pualani. If I bring her to you, I need you to promise that no harm will come to her. That is all I can tell you. Do you promise to watch over her, to be her, uh, 'aumakua?'" Noelani said. She struggled to find the right word for guardian angel, but she knew that the formal Hawaiian expressions carried great weight for her brother.

"I promise," Ikaika said directly. "I would ask if there is anything else you may require of me to help with the current situation, but surely you would indicate as much."

"Yes, my brother, my beloved Kaikunane, I would ask if there was more that you could do," Noelani said. "But I ask only for Pualani to be completely safe with you if the need arises."

Ikaika nodded and embraced his sister.

Nick and Jenny spent Thursday touring the southern Kona coast. Nick tried to relax as his mind kept leaping forward to Friday night and how he envisioned the encounter at the Coconut Club. What would he say, exactly? He was more certain than ever after seeing Noelani Gant's reaction, but he still had exactly zero proof. Somehow, he had to get Dale Gant to react—without arousing his wife's suspicions.

"Aw, to hell with it," Nick muttered to himself as Jenny tried to get him to appreciate the beauty of St. Benedict's Painted Church, one of the tourist attractions in the area.

"That's no way to talk in a place like this!" Jenny scolded him.

"Sorry, babe, I guess it's just the heat," Nick explained. "Why don't we head down to the beach?" They booked an excursion to the Captain Cook Monument that included snorkeling in the pristine waters of Kealakekua Bay. A cold Corona back on the porch of the condo helped wash away the saltiness of Nick's demeanor.

"That was awesome, babe," Nick said as he wrapped Jenny in an embrace. "Thanks for making me happy, always."

"Wait until you see what I have in store for you on Saturday!" Jenny said as she leaned in for a kiss.

"I can't wait," Nick said excitedly. "What is it?"

"I went ahead and booked that helicopter tour we were considering, the one to Waipio Valley!" Nick's expression turned dark, so Jenny kept going with the sales pitch. She worried that deep down his fear of getting in a helicopter again after Vietnam was the real reason for his apprehension.

"It's a really short trip, and you said yourself that the pilot seemed to know what he was doing. They say the valley is the most beautiful on all of the islands."

"It's not that," Nick said curtly. "I thought we agreed that it was more than we wanted to spend. Where'd you get the money to pay for it?

"I applied for a credit card a little while before we left, six months zero interest."

"Please tell me you didn't do that!" Nick yelled.

"I don't understand why you are so upset. We'll be able to pay it off easily before any interest even hits."

"It's just that using credit is … damn it!"

He wanted to explain that using a credit card was like wearing a homing beacon for the FBI, but that would be impossible to explain without admitting his ulterior motives for coming to Hawaii in the first place. Instead, Nick ducked from the fight and took off, leaving Jenny in tears. He would apologize later, tell Jenny what a jackass he had been, and beg her to forgive him, which she always did.

As Nick walked north along the shore, the blinking lights of the Coconut Club caught his attention. He saddled up to the bar and ordered a Corona, with a shot of tequila to further calm his nerves. Tom Holmstrom had been working the joint long enough to recognize a husband who had just endured a vacation spat with his wife.

"How's it goin', buddy?" Holmstrom said as he slid into the barstool next to Nick's and introduced himself as the bar manager.

"Ah, hell, pretty good, I guess," Nick said as the buzz from the liquor overtook the adrenaline in his veins. "I mean, it's hard to get too pissed off in a place like this."

"Yeah, there's nothing quite like a sunset on Kailua Bay," Tom said. "It's kept me here longer than I care to admit."

Tom ordered Nick another Corona on the house and went about his business of greeting more customers. Nick was well past the legal driving limit when Tom made his next round.

"You staying close by or are you going to need a lift?" Tom asked.

"I'm close enough to walk, but I'm not done yet," Nick replied. "You have any music going tonight?"

"It's open mic, but nobody seems too interested," Tom said. "You need to come back tomorrow night. The Big Islanders are the best act on the islands!"

"Hell, yes, they are!" Nick exclaimed with a little too much enthusiasm. "In fact, that's the reason I'm here right now. That singer is amazing. We'd sure like to get him back to Graceland, where he belongs."

The color drained slightly from Tom's face as he measured Nick's statement. This guy must be one of the people trying to get Dale to play in that anniversary show, he thought.

"Sir, he's comfortable right where he's at, and we should keep it that way," Tom said with finality. "Excuse me."

Nick wanted to pursue Tom into his office and press the matter, but thankfully his cop senses had overtaken his buzz. Nick had stirred the pot once again and added more heat.

Jenny was waiting up when Nick staggered back onto the porch and into the condo.

"You must have found a place to soak up your frustrations, I see," Jenny said.

"Yeah, I stopped in at the Coconut Club," Nick said before launching into his apology and blaming "vacation stress" for his outburst.

"Are you sure not wanting to fly doesn't have anything to do with your helicopter experiences from 'Nam?" Jenny asked with genuine concern as she helped Nick into bed and turned out the lights.

"No, it will be fine," Nick said. "It will be *fun*."

Noelani slept better Thursday evening with the comfort that Ikaika would protect Pualani with the ferocity of an island warrior if needed. She was more quiet than usual during Friday morning breakfast with Dale. She hadn't decided whether to confront him at all, but she at least assured herself she was not ready this day.

"My love, do you have to play in town tonight?" she asked innocently. "I was hoping we could do something together."

"You know I have a commitment to Mr. Holmstrom at least through the end of winter," Dale said. "I would love it if you came to watch us, though."

"No, no, I need to be here for Pualani," she said. "You go ahead, but please do be careful."

"Careful?" Dale asked. "You have no cause for fear, my sweet, but I certainly will take your advice."

"I would love to accompany you again one of these times, but Pualani needs me tonight," Noelani continued. "But Mr. Gatewood and Mr. McMahan would like to go with you. I heard them talking about it last night."

"Well, is that so? I'll go ask them right now," Dale said.

He found the agents eating together on the back patio.

"Boys, my beautiful wife tells me you might like to come to town tonight to watch another performance?" Dale asked.

"Well, yeah, boss, we haven't been down there to see you play for a while, and it would be nice to get out and hopefully see some pretty ladies at the same time," Agent Gatewood said.

"OK, then, we can all ride together," Dale said. "The train leaves at 7."

Agent McMahan was relieved that he didn't have to ask Dale directly if the agents could accompany him to town. They were on strict orders from Agent Johnson not to let Dale Gant out of their sights this evening.

The Coconut Club was packed as usual when Dale Gant and the Big Islanders hit the stage. Nick and Jenny had spent a restful day at the condo, and Nick's headache was just about gone when they snagged one of the last open tables near the back of the Coconut Club. Tom Holmstrom was working the crowd, but he didn't spot Nick and Jenny until the band's first break. Tom steered Dale away from the crowd at the bar and into his office, where Agents McMahan and Gatewood joined the meeting.

"Dale, I was hoping I wouldn't have to tell you this because I'm afraid it's going to be upsetting," Tom began. "Well, awhile back Ronnie and Billy came across an ad looking for acts to play at the 10th anniversary tribute to Elvis at Graceland. They thought it might get you interested in taking the band on the road, so Ronnie made a videotape and sent it in."

Dale sucked the air back into his lungs and tried to maintain his composure, but he was speechless. Even Agents McMahan and Gatewood were having a hard time not registering the shock of this news.

"You are well aware that Mr. Gant has made strict conditions on his performances," Gatewood said. "It would be quite impossible for him to even consider such an arrangement."

"That's what I told them when they called," Tom said.

"Told who?" Dale demanded. "There was a lady from Graceland who called Ronnie and offered the Big Islanders a spot in the anniversary show. I called her back and said no chance."

"You still have her name and phone number?" Dale demanded.

"Yes, it's right here in my desk drawer," Tom said as he handed over the slip of paper with Janis Hansen's contact info. "But, Dale, there's a bigger issue. I'm afraid there's a guy from Graceland here tonight."

"Where the hell is he?!" Dale demanded as he rose from his chair and started for the door. Agent Gatewood grabbed Dale by the shoulders and forcibly sat him back down.

"You need to let us handle this," Gatewood said. "That's what we've been paid for all of these years." McMahan nudged Gatewood and gestured toward Tom Holmstrom, who was suddenly an outsider in a very sensitive discussion.

"I don't know your business, and I don't want to know," Holmstrom interjected quickly. "I just don't want any trouble."

"The best way to avoid that is to go back out there and play like everything's normal," Gatewood said. "That will give us a chance to make contact with him."

Dale agreed, but he had to visit the restroom before going back onstage. He had puked before a performance many times before, but this time it wasn't from stage fright.

Gatewood and McMahan flanked Nick and Jenny's table when the music resumed, and Nick identified them immediately as security. McMahan made eye contact with Nick and gestured toward the bathroom.

"I'll be right back, babe," Nick said. Jenny was way too consumed by the performance to notice Nick gesturing for both agents to proceed in front of him.

"OK, boys, what's up?" Nick said when they were alone in the corridor. His cop's sense knew way better than to engage them alone in a secluded space like the restroom. McMahan turned to keep watch on the crowd and prevent anyone from joining them.

"Mr. Gant would like to speak with you personally in Mr. Holmstrom's office after the performance," Gatewood said. "Just you, and make sure the woman doesn't have any suspicions."

"She's a clever girl, but I know how to create a diversion," Nick said. He thought for a moment and hatched a plan.

"First, make sure Mr. Gant visits our table during the second break. Tell him that I won't say a word about my interests, and make sure he indicates to my wife that he will not be available after the show. As soon as the show ends, make sure Mr. Holmstrom comes to my table and asks to speak to me about a matter from last night. When I ask what's up, make sure he says it has nothing to do with me. Management is questioning guests from last night to see if they noticed anything suspicious about some of the employees. Make sure Mr. Gant is already in the office before I walk in with Mr. Holmstrom. And you two stay out here where my guys can keep an eye on you."

"One of us has to remain with Mr. Gant at all times, non-negotiable," Gatewood replied.

"OK, but the other one has to stay all the way in the back, farthest from the door," Nick countered.

"Agreed. We'll be watching," Gatewood said as he stepped past Nick and motioned for him and McMahan to reclaim their vantage points.

Nick had already made eye contact with the hefty Hawaiian who had "greeted" him down at the docks. Nick wasn't sure if the agents had spotted the big man, but he figured the odds were pretty even regardless. He sat down next to Jenny to enjoy the music.

The Big Islanders were playing "All Shook Up," and Nick grinned at the irony of the moment as he and Dale Gant made eye contact. Nick had interrogated enough guilty people to know this dude was rattled.

"The pot has been stirred, and now it's about to boil over," Nick said to himself.

"Oh, Nick, he's looking this way," Jenny squealed with excitement. "Maybe he remembers us and will want to come over and say hi again!"

"Maybe. When the next break comes, I'll go ask him," Nick said to Jenny's delight.

Nick made his way toward the stage as the Big Islanders finished their second act. He spoke something in Dale's ear, and the two headed toward Jenny.

"Oh, please sit down for a minute, Mr. Gant," Jenny exclaimed. "May we get you a drink?"

"I'm sticking to plain water tonight to keep a clear head, but thank you," Dale said with emphasis on a "clear head" in Nick's direction.

"I'm so glad we're able to hear you play again," Jenny said. "Do you ever play anywhere on the mainland? An act like yours would be perfect for Memphis!"

"No, ma'am, I'm not one for traveling much," Dale said. "We named our band The Big Islanders because that's where we like to stay."

"Well, we won't forget you, and maybe we'll be out this way again," Jenny said.

"I hope so too, ma'am, but now I better get back to business," Dale said. "Nice meeting both of you."

Nick made sure to remain calm and not make eye contact with Dale during the final set. He wanted him rattled, but not on the run. The ruse with

Tom Holmstrom worked perfectly. Jenny moved to the bar for a nightcap while Nick followed Tom to his office.

"I'll keep this short and to the point, Mr. Sartain," Dale said after the parties were seated with Agent Gatewood nearest the closed door. "I will not be doing any Elvis Presley tributes, at Graceland or anywhere else. You understand?"

Nick had imagined what he would say next over and over as he searched for exactly the right amount of impact.

"Mr. Gant, I'm not here to talk about you impersonating Elvis Presley," Nick said. "I'm here to talk about you *being* Elvis Presley."

Nick waited for the words to sink in before continuing. Dale Gant's face had turned the proper shade of ashen gray.

"I, I don't understand," Dale stammered.

"I was working as a detective for Memphis PD when you 'died' unexpectedly. I've been on your trail ever since, and I know the truth," Nick said and then paused to add the proper weight to his next statement.

"You *are* Elvis Presley."

Dale's entire body froze as Agent Gatewood's crisis intervention training took over.

"Ha!" Gatewood exclaimed to break the silence and shake Dale from his state of shock. "That's the biggest crock of shit I've ever heard!"

Nick's steely look as he turned to face Agent Gatewood advanced the conversation between the sudden adversaries more than words could.

"Even if there was a shred of truth—and I'm not saying there is—I'm sure you are not the kind of man who makes accusations without some proof," Agent Gatewood continued.

Now it was Nick's turn to twist under the weight of the moment. He knew damn well that he had nothing to prove this man was anyone other than Dale Gant. So, he fired the only bullet he had left.

"I know what I know, and I'll find a way to prove it," Nick said. "Perhaps another talk with Mrs. Gant will be worthwhile."

"*Another* talk?!" Dale exclaimed as a surge of adrenaline returned him to fight mode. "You've been in contact with my wife?!"

"Indeed, I have Mr. Gant, and she seemed very upset by the notion that her husband had been fooling her all these years."

"You leave her and my family out of your little charade or, God help me, I'll …" Dale said as he rose and lunged across the table toward Nick.

Agent Gatewood shot a forearm under Dale's chin to hold him off and shoved Nick toward the door with his free hand.

"You'll do what?" Nick challenged.

"You just leave us alone or you'll wish you had," Dale said and motioned for Gatewood to take action. "Take care of this asshole."

Gatewood reached behind Nick to open the door and moved him into the hallway. A service revolver was jabbing into Nick's right kidney.

"Do anything stupid and people are going to get hurt, mostly you," Gatewood hissed.

The hefty Hawaiian gripped his piece as he made eye contact with Nick, who shook his head as a signal not to engage. Agent McMahan advanced slowly from the back of the room with his hands clearly in front of him.

"Let him go," McMahan whispered to his partner.

"I don't think you understand the gravity of the situation," Gatewood said.

"Yes, I do. And I'm telling you, let him go," McMahan said more forcibly while trying not to arouse suspicion as Jenny was looking in their direction.

Gatewood holstered his service revolver and stepped back. Nick glanced to make sure the hefty Hawaiian had his back before moving to meet Jenny at the bar.

"Hey, babe, did you enjoy your drink?"

"Yes, but what was all that about, Nick?" Jenny asked.

"Like they said, just some stuff about employees dipping into the till last night. You ready for a moonlight walk on the beach?" Nick asked as he cupped Jenny's upper thigh and smiled.

Jenny was still too enchanted by the music to be suspicious, and the couple made their way to the beachfront exit.

"Make sure we're not followed," he whispered as they moved past the hefty Hawaiian.

Gatewood made a motion to follow Nick and Jenny, but McMahan clutched his partner's arm and stopped him.

"Let him go," McMahan said. "The boss has a plan for him."

Dale was silent on the ride home as he kept replaying in his mind Nick Sartain's vow to reveal his true identity. He thought only momentarily of the shame that could come to him and the incredible pain his actions could cause for those who had loved him. Dale's mind was focused on how he could protect his current wife and daughter.

"Try not to worry, Dale," Agent Gatewood said as they neared Hale ke`oke`o. "You heard that SOB detective. He doesn't have any proof that says you are anyone other than who you say you are. If he goes making accusations that Elvis Presley has arisen from the grave, people will just think he's another nut job. And if gets too close, I'm sure Agent Johnson has a plan to deal with him. Let's get some rest, and we'll figure things out in the morning."

"Thank you, Richard," Dale said. "You are a true friend."

Noelani was sound asleep when Dale peeked inside the bedroom, and he knew rest would be hard to come by on this night. He made his way to his office instead. He pulled the painting of The Last Supper from the wall, opened the safe and pulled the Green Book from its hiding place. The cover was less dusty than it should have been after lying undisturbed for nearly three months, but Dale didn't notice.

Dale couldn't form thoughts to put pen on paper, so he slid open the drawer of his reading desk. The Bible he kept there had gathered plenty of dust from not being disturbed. He still had an ominous feeling whenever he perused the passages after his experience in that Washington hotel room, but mostly they still brought comfort to his often-twisted soul. Dale paused to consider Matthew 10:28: *And do not fear those who kill the body but cannot kill the soul. Rather fear him who can destroy both soul and body in hell.*

Dale shook his head in affirmation as he began to write.

JOURNAL ENTRY: JAN. 17, 1986:

I was confronted by a demon this evening, but not in the form of Detective Nick Sartain, the man who is chasing me. No, my tormenter is doom itself, knowing that my actions are going to bring such pain. I no longer care about my own fate, but I must protect Noelani and Pualani. Agent Gatewood is right. We just need to lay low and let this pass. Tomorrow I will act like everything is perfectly normal.

Dale set the Green Book aside, and he tried to put the Bible back into exile as well, but he couldn't help reading through more passages. His finger stopped on Proverbs 14:12:

There is a way that seems right to a man, but its end is the way to death.

Dale sat back in the chair with his eyes closed tight and a look of wrenching pain on his face. For the second time in his life, he felt like God had spoken to him directly. Dale slowly opened his eyes and reached again for the Green Book. The wall clock chimed 12 times to signal the beginning of a new day, one that Dale Gant knew would determine his future.

JOURNAL ENTRY: JAN. 18, 1986:

We have to find a new hiding place. I cannot take the risk that Detective Nick Sartain will just go away, but I cannot trust Agent Johnson and how he will react. Somehow, I'll find the courage to convince Noelani to come away with me.

Nick arose early and sat on the patio overlooking the ocean and sipping his cup of steaming black coffee made from the renowned Kona coffee beans that are native to the Big Island. The waves were choppy and the water murky, much like Nick's train of thought. He would take the damn helicopter ride with Jenny ... and then what. His plane ticket back to Memphis was stamped for Sunday morning, so the clock was ticking.

Jenny slid open the patio door quietly and wrapped her arms around Nick's shoulders. He jumped at the surprise.

"Damn it, girl!" Nick said without any real anger.

"I got you!" Jenny exclaimed. "Now let's go for a real thrill ride!"

Nick had scanned the brochure and had to admit the scenery was breathtaking. Waipio Valley looked unlike any place in the world that he had seen.

Nick and Jenny pulled the rental car into the dusty parking lot of Big Island Adventures just north of downtown Kailua. Nick could see their ride on the landing pad. A pair of young native islanders appeared to be doing the prep work for their tour. The brochure said the helicopter could seat five, but it looked much too small to Nick as he surveyed the machine from behind the retaining wall.

"Don't worry, bro, it will do just fine."

Nick turned to size up the voice, surely that of the pilot who would be guiding them on this adventure.

"My name's Marty Scudmore, pilot at your service."

Nick sized him up and figured they were roughly the same age. Many of the chopper jocks who made it out of 'Nam ended up flying tourist and supply routes.

"The swashplate doesn't look like ones on any slick I've ridden," Nick said.

Marty Scudmore smiled broadly and chuckled at the obvious attempt to decipher his flying experience without asking the question directly.

"Yeah, it's a lot smaller than the Sikorsky seahorse I flew to lift our boys out of the A Shau Valley in '66," Scudmore said.

"I missed that one, thank God, from what I hear," Nick replied. "Marines. I was in country from 63-65."

"Well, no need to rehash any of that action," Scudmore said. "Today we're strictly on a pleasure cruise, and I think you're going to love it."

Nick and Jenny entered the office and filled out the necessary paperwork to go airborne. The couple that was supposed to take the tour with them had backed out suddenly due to the husband falling ill that morning. Nick and Jenny both had window seats in the second row behind Marty Scudmore.

Their route was straight up the coast and around the northern tip of the Big Island near the town of Hawi and the birthplace of King Kamehameha. Nick made sure to take the right rear window seat so he could scan the coastline. A few miles south of Dale Gant's compound he could see the flashing red lights of several rescue vehicles and a traffic jam from what appeared to be a fiery crash on the razor-sharp lava beds that usually leave few survivors. A single column of black smoke rose nearly to their 500-foot cruising altitude.

He recognized the big front gate of Dale Gant's compound and could make out the impenetrable hedges leading to the large white house. Several black cars were parked in the large cement driveway, and Nick could make out several people who appeared to be dressed in black. Nick had no idea of the commotion that was taking place on the ground at that very moment.

He was also ignorant of the phone call that Agent Johnson had made to the Pohakuloa Training Compound several minutes earlier to scramble a Bell 407 attack helicopter.

"This is Agent Johnson," he told the agent in charge of the Specials Ops Aviators that were on call for military engagements. "Your mission is hot." Click.

Marty Scudmore pointed out several landmarks, including the stone structure that marks the birthplace of King Kamehameha as they rounded the northernmost tip of the Big Island. The entrance to Waipio Valley is unforgettable. Rock walls rise 2,500 feet on either side of the narrow opening. They are completely covered in vegetation that cover every shade of green. Numerous waterfalls cut through the lush foliage and plummet to the valley floor where hikers delight in their pools. Marty Scudmore hovered to give Nick and Jenny a prime view of all 1,450 feet of Hiilawe Falls.

Nick caught a glimpse of smoke trails and felt a tremendous impact just behind him. His face and torso slammed into the seat in front of him. He could feel searing heat on the flesh of his backside from the explosion. Jenny was thrust sideways with such force that her head meeting the window sent cracks through the shatterproof glass. Nick could see she was unconscious and slumped forward. Blood was flowing down the left side of her face and turning her yellow capris a deep crimson.

Beep! Beep! Beep!

Nick could hear the warning siren as the thrust from the rotors sent the fuselage of the helicopter into a death spin. Marty Scudmore regained consciousness in time to keep his grip on the cyclic stick.

"We're going down!" Marty yelled above the roar of the faltering engines.

Nick could see the ground rushing toward them as the helicopter spun toward the valley floor like a toy going down a bathtub drain. The helicopter landed flush on a collection of umbrella trees with the rotors shredding hibiscus and bougainvillea before wrenching to a stop. The vegetation softened the blow for Nick and Jenny. Marty Scudmore was not so lucky. Nick could see that a branch of the tree had impaled the pilot mid-torso and pinned him to his seat. The former Vietnam rescue pilot had brought home his final pair of wounded passengers.

Earlier that fateful Saturday morning, Dale Gant approached his wife with news that she had been awaiting with both dread and anticipation to hear. Instead of the shock that Dale expected to see on her face, Noelani Gant was resolute.

"I've known the truth for several years," she said.

The shock Dale had expected to see on Noelani's face was now his mirror image.

"You called out the names of Priscilla and Lisa Marie in your dreams, but I had my doubts. The truth became clearer when I heard you sing in church. Then I accidentally found your journal while I was cleaning out your office. I was going to surprise you with new furniture. Everything is in there."

"How did you not lead on that you knew the truth?"

"My mind ran wild. I thought you might leave me if I confronted you. I figured Agent Gatewood and Agent McMahan were here for your protection. I had no idea what they might do to you, or to me, or even worse to Pualani if they found out I knew your identity. All I knew for certain was I loved Dale Gant, and that's who you are to me, who you will always be. Finally, I just decided to let fate determine our path."

"And here we are," Dale said. "I don't believe Gatewood and McMahan will harm us, but there is another—Agent Johnson—who I believe is pure evil. He will do whatever it takes to keep my identity a secret. For him, Elvis Presley and his secrets need to remain buried at Graceland."

"Then what can we do?" Noelani said with rising anxiety shaking her words. "That detective is onto you, and he's not going to give up. He made sure I knew that!"

"Did he hurt you? I'll kill the goddamn …"

"No, we just talked."

"Did he tell you what he planned to do?"

"No, but he made sure I knew that he was not going away."

"I got the same threat from him last night."

"Last night? You mean he was at the bar when you played?"

"Yes. He confronted me in Tom's office about my true identity, but he admitted that he didn't have any real proof."

"Oh my God, this is such a mess! I feel like we are trapped, caged in our own house just waiting for the walls to cave in!"

Dale grabbed Noelani in a tight embrace as she began to sob. Finally, when she began to calm herself, Dale laid out his plan.

"So, we leave—immediately," Dale began. "Tom can arrange for a helicopter flight to Honolulu and we can be in a foreign country before anyone knows we are gone."

"I'm not putting Pualani in that kind of danger," Noelani said with the resolute finality of a mother who would do anything to protect her child. "It has to be just us. I have already spoken to Ikaika about watching over her if the need ever arises."

"We can figure everything else out later," Dale said. "But right now, we need to go!"

Dale had the good sense to carry on the conversation in the privacy of the backyard, but that didn't matter. Agent Johnson had made sure that security cameras and sophisticated listening devices covered every inch of the compound. His thin lips curled into a sneer as he listened to Dale's escape plans.

"You're not going anywhere, my friend," Agent Johnson whispered to himself.

He picked up the phone in his concealed office and contacted another of his henchmen.

"This is Agent Johnson. You know what to do." Click.

Noelani was successful in convincing Pualani to make the trip with her to see her uncle and grandparents without giving away the gravity of the situation. She made up a story about having business in town to deceive her parents, and she motioned for Ikaika to join her on the back veranda for a private talk.

"Remember when you promised to take care of Pualani if I ever asked?"

"Yes," Ikaika replied without the need to inquire if this was the time. "She will be safe with me. May all of the gods be with you and Dale, my dear kaikuahine."

Noelani left her brother in silence and somehow was able to tell her beloved daughter goodbye without letting on that she feared it could be goodbye forever.

Noelani had driven her sedan less than a mile back toward Hale ke`oke`o when she noticed two large, black SUVs approaching fast from behind. The first vehicle sped around her and then slowed down while the second vehicle boxed her in from behind. The rear hatch of the lead vehicle rose just enough for a man to drop a puncture strip directly in the path of Noelani's silver sedan, which lurched violently as all four tires blew. The trailing SUV sped ahead while veering into the oncoming lane to miss the puncture strip. The driver jerked the steering wheel hard right to clip the silver sedan and send it careening off the road. The razor-sharp lava beds ripped open the sedan as if the car's body was nothing more than a can of tuna.

In the rush of emergency, no one noticed as a third black SUV stopped to retrieve the puncture strip before heading north toward Hale ke`oke`o. The third vehicle was the last to arrive at the compound. Agent Johnson slithered out of its backseat and couldn't suppress a grin as a helicopter with Big Island Adventures emblazoned on its tail section whirred northward along the coastline.

"Perhaps I should wave goodbye to Mr. Sartain and his lovely wife," he whispered to himself. In the driveway, several agents had surrounded Dale Gant. James McMahan held the man he was sworn to protect in a vice grip.

"Dale, it would be wise not to struggle," McMahan said. "Remember, our karate is better than yours."

"That was you in Colorado! You son of a bitch! I trusted you all of this time."

"I'm afraid loyalty goes to the highest bidder."

His partner's comment caught the attention of Agent Gatewood. The intense glare on his face showed he was just as surprised as Dale by Agent McMahan's betrayal.

Agent Johnson took command of the situation with his usual cold demeanor.

"I'm afraid there was an accident while your wife was returning to the compound," Mr. Gant. "Reports from first responders indicate she didn't suffer after hitting the lava beds."

"You killed her! You motherfucker!"

Dale Gant could feel the adrenaline surge through his body. He summoned the strength you read about when average people come face to face with deadly circumstances. With one mighty twist, Dale reversed the choke hold he was in and snapped the ulna and radius bones of Agent McMahan's lower left arm in the process.

"Now whose karate is better, you son of a bitch!?" Dale hissed.

Agent McMahan's initial screams could be heard all the way to the mainland. Fighting off shock, Agent McMahan's tactical training took hold as he pulled a knife with his good hand. Dale tightened his grip to stop the blade just inches from his exposed jugular.

Agent Gatewood hesitated for a moment, long enough for a flashback to his days on the battlefields of Vienam. A wounded soldier was calling his name for help ... Bob, Bob, Bob! Only it was Dale Gant's voice asking for Agent Gatewood's assistance. He snapped back to the present, aimed his Smith & Wesson .459 FBI service revolver, and fired a shot that ended his betraying partner's struggles. Moments later, the slug that shattered Agent McMahan's chest also ended his life.

Agent Johnson pulled his non-service revolver, but he made the deadly mistake of indecision. The tactical training part of his brain said to fire at Agent Gatewood while he had the chance. His emotions overruled, however, as he leveled the gun at Dale Gant. The slight hesitation gave Agent Gatewood a split second to swivel and fire another shot. The bullet pierced Agent Johnson's right lung and sent him staggering backward. He braced himself against the black SUV and tried to lift his arm and return fire. Instead, a look of terror flickered in his eyes as his mouth drooped open and a large red bubble formed of blood and spit. When the bubble burst, Agent Johnson slid down the side of the black SUV and died in the dirt. The driveway of Hale ke`oke`o, the white house, had turned a deep red.

The remaining three agents kept their sidearms holstered. Agent Johnson hadn't gained too much allegiance in his own circles. Agent Gatewood moved quickly to shield Dale and demanded surrender of their weapons.

"Relax, sir," the lead agent said as he placed his non-service revolver on the hood of the black SUV. "This stopped being an official FBI operation a long time ago. We'll make up a story to cover your tracks, but you don't have much time."

"Dale, you have exactly five minutes to grab whatever is of value to you before we get you the hell out of here—for good," Agent Gatewood said.

Dale Gant plucked a picture of him and Noelani off the wall as he rushed toward his office. He pulled the picture of The Last Supper from the wall and tossed it aside with disregard. The Green Book was the only item that truly mattered in his life now.

Keloa had been given the day off and spent it visiting relatives in Kailua-Kona. By the time she returned home and summoned police to the grisly scene at Hale ke`oke`o, a private plane was already shuttling Dale Gant to his new hideout.

CHAPTER SIX

Agent Gatewood had the foresight to avoid the FBI's legal attaché in Berlin, one of 11 field offices on the European continent that would be on the lookout for any activity out of the norm following the news of Agent Johnson's death. The pilot steered the private jet toward the town of Ramstein, where Agent Gatewood had called in some favors to gain entrance into an FBI safe house.

Sedated throughout the 15-hour flight from Hawaii to Germany, Dale was in a nearly catatonic state as Agent Gatewood led him to a bedroom inside the safe house. Dale awoke nearly 24 hours later, unsure if he was conscious or still living inside a nightmare. Sunlight was streaming through the window shade at a low angle, so he figured it must be close to sunrise or sunset.

He found an overnight bag near the foot of the bed stuffed with some toiletries and a few clothing items that were not his. The clothes he'd flown in lay in a heap by the side of the bed. He pulled them back on and caught a glimpse of himself in the full-body mirror. Dale couldn't tell what looked more wrinkled and fatigued: his clothes or his face. He stumbled down the hall and entered a kitchen where a small, stout woman was cooking what smelled like bacon and eggs.

"Good morning, Mr. Gant," she said in a thick German accent while still tending to her work. "I am told bacon and eggs are your favorite."

The dish was more like scrambled eggs mixed in a bacon and potato hash, but Dale didn't care. He ate heartily, something he had always been able to do despite his psychological state, which currently was teetering between the shock and denial stages of grief.

"Thank you, ma'am," Dale said after he had cleaned his plate.

"You may call me Fraulein Dichau, Mr. Gant," the stout woman said.

Dale quickly realized there would be no warming up period to get rid of the formalities. This woman was all business.

"What day is it, ma'am?"

"You may call me Fraulein Dichau, Mr. Gant," she said with a stern look that ensured Dale wouldn't make the same mistake. "It's Tuesday."

"Damn."

Fraulein Dichau gave Dale a look of disdain and genuine concern at the same time.

"Why is that such a concern, Mr. Gant?"

"Well, you see, I was hoping it was still Sunday. What happened to Sunday and Monday, anyway? I must have been asleep for the whole plane ride. I need it to be Sunday because I need to do some prayin' in a real bad way."

"Sunday is not the only day for worship, Mr. Gant," Fraulein Dichau said without looking up from her sink full of dishes.

"Where do y'all *worship*, if you don't mind my asking?"

"Dale, I can recommend a fine clergyman to speak with you if that is what you wish," Agent Gatewood interjected after stepping into the kitchen from the adjoining living room. "Why don't you come in here and sit down."

Dale arose from his stool and walked slowly into the living room where he eased into an oversized lounger. He laid back his head and closed his eyes.

"I could just stay right here and let the world go to hell," he said.

"That's not your style, boss," Agent Gatewood said. "I've been around you long enough to know that much."

Suddenly, Dale's face clenched and tears began to stream from his still closed eyes.

"She's gone! And it's all my fault!"

"Agent Johnson killed her, not you," Agent Gatewood argued.

"No, Bob, it's my fault just as sure as if I had been driving the car myself. I signed her death warrant the day I met her."

Agent Gatewood's training included field trauma, but he knew Dale was experiencing the ultimate psychological despair in blaming himself for the violent death of his wife. No field dressing could numb that pain.

"Dale, you need professional help to get through this," Agent Gatewood said.

"What if I don't want to get through it! Maybe I just want to end it right now!"

"You are feeling the worst pain a man can feel right now, but I know it will get better," Agent Gatewood continued calmly. "I am going to reach out to a friend of mine who is of the religious order. He can help you. How does that sound?"

Dale just nodded and squeezed larger tears through his still clenched eyes.

"OK, my friend," Agent Gatewood said. "In the meantime, I want you to take these to help with the pain you are feeling."

Agent Gatewood held out his hand with two large, white pills. Dale swallowed them without bothering to ask what they were or even for water.

"I've been down this road before," Dale said.

He spent much of the next week in a haze from the painkillers—prescription Demerol—but Dale ate enough of Fraulein Dichau's home cooking to stay somewhat healthy. Finally, Agent Gatewood cleared his senses with some good news.

"Dale, your morning medication was withheld for a reason," Agent Gatewood announced at the breakfast table.

"What might that be, Bob?" Dale asked as he rubbed his eyes and strained to focus his brain on the moment.

"If you are interested, I have made arrangements for you to meet with a friend of mine at a church nearby."

"Who is this friend of yours?"

"Capt. Norm McDougal was our Army Chaplain in Vietnam. He is now the head of Auftwazen Friary."

"What's a Fry, uh, whatever you called it?"

"This is a place of worship where Friars and Monks perform service to God," Agent Gatewood said. "Friar McDougal has indicated that you can take up residence and worship in a manner that suits you. I think this is the only way that you will be able to move on with your life."

"How long would I stay? Where will I go when I leave? What …"

"Listen to me," Agent Gatewood interjected as he grabbed Dale firmly by the shoulders. "You are going to have to take things one day at a time. And today, we need to make arrangements with Friar McDougal. OK?"

Dale nodded slowly. He felt comfort wash over him as he imagined himself in quiet contemplation. "Thank you, Bob. As always, you are a true friend."

"Fraulein Dichau and I will keep the place warm while you are gone," Agent Gatewood said with a genuine smile.

Capt. Norm McDougal had served in Gatewood's unit as Army Chaplain in Vietnam. He was also trained as one of the FBI's leading counteragents specializing in psychological warfare.

Dale spoke with Friar McDougal on the phone later that day and made arrangements to arrive at the Friary the very next day. He would have a room of his own, meager arrangements of course, but livable. Dale was expected to attend Mass at least once a day, and he was assigned work detail in the laundry. He could exercise with the monks. The rest of his time would be spent in whatever form of contemplation suited him, and he was allowed to speak, unlike the 30 or so monks who inhabited the Friary. Dale made no commitment to a timetable.

"You may stay here as long as you like, my son," Friar McDougal advised Dale upon his arrival. "I'm confident you will find God, and yourself."

Dale's favorite place for Bible study was in the garden. He could see the lush green foothills that were making their way to the Bavarian Alps, and a fresh breeze always seemed to rustle the leaves of the white aspen.

Friar McDougal joined Dale on March 31—Easter Sunday—to pray with Dale and to offer him the hope of Salvation.

"You seem to be more at peace, my son," Friar McDougal said. "I no longer sense such anguish in your soul."

"I am feeling better, Friar, but I still have much guilt to bear. I'm afraid I'll never find my way in the world again."

Friar McDougal handed his personal Bible to Dale and asked him to read aloud the passage that was bookmarked with a thin wooden cross.

Jeremiah 29:11-13:

"For I know the plans I have for you, plans to prosper you and not to harm you, plans to give you hope and a future."

Dale sat silently for a few minutes that seemed like days.

"A future?" he asked finally. "I'm not sure I deserve one."

"You wouldn't be here, my son, if God did not have plans for you. What I think you need is a pilgrimage, a time of discovery."

"What do you mean?" Dale asked with increased optimism in his voice.

"Some of the monks make a pilgrimage to the Holy Lands during the summer months," Friar McDougal explained. "I think you should join them."

"I think I would like that," Dale said as he gazed into the distance.

"Very well, then. I will make arrangements for you to join the next pilgrimage to Jerusalem."

Dale departed by train with a group of a dozen monks eight weeks later. They steamed through Austria, Eastern Europe, and into Greece, where Dale marveled at the Acropolis of Athens and the Parthenon before the group sailed across the Mediterranean. They embarked to the north of Jerusalem and visited the Sea of Galilee, where Jesus performed miracles according to the New Testament, such as his walking on water, calming the storm, and feeding the multitude. They visited Nazareth, the childhood home of Jesus and retraced many of his steps on their way to Bethlehem, where Dale prayed silently in the Church of Nativity. A priest there offered to hear his confession, but Dale declined. He was saving that for their visit to Jerusalem and the Church of the Holy Sepulchre, which contains the two holiest sites in Christianity: the site where Jesus was crucified and Jesus's empty tomb, where He was buried and rose from the dead. The Greek Orthodox, Armenian, and Roman Catholic denominations share custody of the church. Friar McDougal had reserved a meeting for Dale with one of the Roman Catholic high priests. Dale was nervous, and he toured all of the sacred sites before he mustered the nerve to enter the confessional. Dale had confessed his grave sins of the past, including to Friar McDougal, but never the mortal sins that he was carrying now.

"Bless me Father, for I have sinned. It has been three months since my last confession. I have confessed lesser sins, but what I am about to tell you I have not confessed prior."

"Go on, my son."

"Father, I have contributed to the deaths of two people, if not by my own hand, by my actions."

"I see. Were these accidents that you speak of?"

"No, Father. I knew the gravity of my actions, the gravity of the danger that I posed. But I felt helpless to stop these events once they were set in motion."

"Sometimes, when someone dies, we blame ourselves for circumstances perhaps more than we should."

"I understand, but I must accept all of the blame."

"God still wishes to forgive you, my son. Are you truly sorry for your mortal sins?"

"I am more sorry than I can ever express, Father."

"Repeat after me: O Almighty God, merciful Father, I, a poor, miserable sinner, confess to You all my sins and iniquities, with which I have ever offended You and justly deserved Your punishment now and forever."

Dale repeated the Prayer of Confession, and wept.

"Your eternal punishment is absolved. However, your temporal punishment can only be absolved through a penance."

"I understand, Father. What would you have me do?"

"God commands your penance, my son. You will live the rest of your life in the service of good, always putting the well-being of others before yourself."

Dale resolved to complete his penance after he returned to the Friary. He felt at peace until the approach of the holidays, which had represented some of the happiest times of his life but now were cloaked in sadness. The only solace Dale could achieve on Christmas Eve was to pull the Green Book from the bureau drawer in his tiny quarters.

JOURNAL ENTRY: DEC. 24, 1986:

Nothing is really stopping me now from going home. I could easily slip away and book a flight to Memphis tomorrow. I miss my Little Injun so much. But I must remain on the path of my penance. The best thing for her is for me to stay away.

Dale made another pilgrimage in early spring, this time to Rome and the Vatican City. He marveled at the work of Michelangelo in the Sistine Chapel and the supreme extravagance of the Roman Empire. Dale didn't seek the confessional during his visit to Italy, however. The path of his penance had been set in Jerusalem, and he vowed not to steer from it while kneeling in St. Peter's Basilica.

Dale returned to his simple life at the Friary, but he was growing increasingly restless. The struggle to avoid his destiny was becoming overwhelming. He sought solace in Bible study, but sometimes Dale felt like the lines of scripture were just that, lines on a page. Other times he felt power in the words of the disciples. On rare occasions, Dale felt as if God was speaking to him directly. April 19, 1987—Easter Sunday—was one of those days. Dale sat in his usual place in the garden, but his Bible study was anything but ordinary. Without trying, his hands turned pages and his eyes focused on passages about fate and destiny:

> Proverbs 16:3.
> Commit to the Lord whatever you do, and he will establish your plans.

> Proverbs 16:9.
> The heart of man plans his way, but the Lord establishes his steps.

Dale was ready to put his ultimate path in the hands of the Lord, but he wanted to control the first steps. He rose from his seat in the garden and walked toward Friar McDougal's quaint office. Dale requested access to a private office with a telephone to conduct some important business. He pulled out a piece of paper with Mike Martinez's private line written on it at the Hotel Bonaventure. Tom Holmstrom had introduced them while Mike was vacationing on the Islands. Mike had caught Dale's act early on at the Coconut Club and practically begged him to come work in L.A.

"With a voice that, Hollywood will make you famous," Mike had promised.

"Hollywood is a place where they'll pay you a thousand dollars for a kiss and fifty cents for your soul," Dale replied.

"Ah, I see you were a fan of Miss Monroe."

"Yeah, but I ain't no fan of how she ended up, you know?"

Dale had turned Mike down flat, but Mike was persuasive, so Dale left the invitation open-ended.

"We'll see what happens, but don't count it," he told Mike before giving him an Aloha back to L.A. Mike sounded surprised but excited when Dale called to accept the invitation to perform in L.A. The nightclub manager had no idea just how much circumstances had changed for Dale Gant during the past 16 months.

Dale would do a six-week gig at the Bonaventure Lounge on Hollywood Boulevard, four sets a night, Tuesday through Saturday. The contract included a suite in the hotel at Dale's insistence, just the way The Colonel would have done it.

Dale's next call left the person on the other end even more surprised and excited that Dale would be accepting an invitation.

"Oh my gosh! Priscilla will be so happy that you are going to play, Mr. Gant!" Janis Hansen gushed from the office telephone at Graceland. "Do you want to tell her in person? She's out at the moment, but I expect her to return soon."

"Oh no, that won't be necessary," Dale said quickly. He would be ready to return to Graceland in a few months, but talking to Priscilla directly now was more than he could handle. Dale requested to have detailed plans of the 10th Anniversary performance sent in his name to the Hotel Bonaventure to avoid any chance of them being lost in cross-country postal delivery.

JOURNAL ENTRY: APRIL 27, 1987:

I have set my path toward my destiny, and I know there is no straying from it. I don't know what will happen when I finally arrive in Memphis, but I know there are many forms of salvation. Music has always been mine.

He spent his last days at Auftwazen engrossed in Bible study and taking ample time to say goodbye to Friar McDougal.

"I'll never forget you, Friar, nor what you and this place have done for me," Dale said on his final day.

"I shall not forget you either, my son," Friar McDougal said. "I have seen much of the sadness and pain lifted from your soul during your stay here. I'm certain you still have a journey in front of you, however."

"I do indeed, but I'm ready now."

Agent Gatewood arrived and drove Dale back to the safe house, where he would rest another day before his flight to Los Angeles. The two men were silent as Agent Gatewood drove Dale to Berlin's Tempelhof Airport, but they met in a warm embrace before Dale was called to board his flight.

"You are a true friend, Bob, and I wouldn't be here without you," Dale said. "I am truly grateful."

"The pleasure has been all mine, Dale. And you know where to find me if you need anything."

CHAPTER SEVEN

"Enjoy your stay in L.A., sir," the Hawaiian Airlines stewardess chirped as Dale began his stroll down the jetway.

"Mr. Gant?" the inquisitor wore a black chauffeur's suit and cap and looked like a good-natured fellow, a year or two north of 40.

"Yeah, Ace, who wants to know?" Dale said with a warm smile.

"Jerry Skeen, sir. Mr. Martinez has hired me to be your driver during your stay in L.A."

Dale knew he would grow to be good friends with Jerry Skeen. Getting along with Jerry was easy. Like most good service people, he always waited for the conversation to start, but he always had something interesting to add, just enough to always keep the focus on his passenger. Jerry fetched Dale's bags from the carousel and led him to a stretch limousine that would be their ride— at least for now. Dale felt good sliding into the leather roundabout backseat, but then he remembered that riding in the back of a limousine in L.A. is about as unusual as hopping on a camel in the Sahara. Jerry's boss hadn't provided much information on Dale: part-time singer from the Islands who had spent some time in L.A., most of it in the '60s. Jerry knew enough that he figured the 405 Freeway would scare the hell out of this guy, even on a Sunday afternoon.

"Mr. Gant, how about I cruise through Venice a little, and then we can take Santa Monica Boulevard all the way up?"

Dale slid forward and gave Jerry a good-natured slap on the shoulder.

"I already told you. It's Dale to you. But yeah, that sounds great."

Dale rolled down the window and choked in the Southern California air.

"I guess it's not *quite* as clean as Hawaii, eh?" Jerry said with a chuckle.

"Yeah, but I tell you what. There's always excitement in the air here, too. Let's go sample some of it. I always loved walking on that pier."

"Santa Monica Pier?"

"Yeah, that's it. You must think I'm some kind of dumbshit! It's only the name of the city for goodness sake."

Jerry slipped a $20 to the parking lot attendant and rolled the limo into a spot right up front.

"You want me to wait here for you?"

"Hell no!" Dale said. "It's a sunny Sunday afternoon, so there should be plenty of bathing beauties for the both of us to admire."

"Yes, sir!" Jerry said as he jumped out to open the door for Dale, whose feet had already hit the pavement.

"You can drive me around, Jerry, but you don't have to treat me like nobody special, okay?"

"Whatever you say Mr.—uh, Dale."

They strolled leisurely down the boardwalk and past the shoreline on the pier. Dale was gazing over the Pacific, watching surfers work the swell that would be considered blown-out chop on the Islands. He saw a large shadow moving up from behind on the hot concrete.

"You want some white?" the shadow asked.

Dale turned his gaze straight ahead and kept walking, but he could still see the frame of a tall, slender man in his periphery. *Really* tall. This guy obviously doesn't play for the Lakers, but he's got the size, Dale thought to himself.

"Well, Ace, I'll tell you what," Dale said to the empty space in front of him but loud enough for the big guy to hear as they continued to move forward. "I don't know what white is, but then you probably don't know all that much about karate. I figure neither one of us wants to find out what the other one knows."

Dale saw the shadow vanish and didn't care to where the dude who cast it had disappeared.

"You really know karate, Dale? If not, that was a hell of a bluff."

Dale ducked behind Jerry with surprising speed and cocked Jerry's head back in a half nelson without applying hurtful pressure.

"What do you think?"

"I'd say you can handle yourself, and good thing, too. Things have changed in L.A.—and not for the better—since you were here last."

"You got that right, Jerry."

Dale couldn't help but notice the changes as they climbed back into the limo and rolled northeast on Santa Monica Boulevard. He thought he recognized a few of his old haunts, but it was hard to see past the maze of cars and crazies. At the stoplight on Overland, a group of teens sauntered in front of the limo, the leader sporting a red sequined jacket and periwinkle blue hair that was glued straight up, two feet in the air, in a wide arc.

"Damn, that dude looks like he's got a Cadillac fin on his head!"

"Punk rockers, the latest fad. At least we hope it's a fad," Jerry said.

"Yeah, I've seen some of that on TV," Dale said. "At least he's got good taste in jackets."

Jerry raised an eyebrow at the remark as he rolled the limo forward, but a glance in the rearview told him Dale wasn't kidding.

"If you say so, Dale. Maybe we can stop off in Hollywood and get you one of those for your show."

"Red ain't my best color, Jerry, but I bet they've got something in a nice, gaudy gold."

Dale thought about his gig at the Bonaventure Lounge, four sets a night, Tuesday through Saturday. Dale hadn't worked that much in a dozen years or so. It would be good to get back in front of a crowd that was paying to watch him perform. His recent sleepless nights were spent going through old lyrics and past performances. His first night in the suite's king-sized bed, Dale's mind made it all the way through "I Can't Help Falling in Love with You" before he finally nodded off.

Dale awoke early Monday morning and caught his reflection in the mirror on the way to the shower. He was still over 6 feet tall at age 52, his black hair showing distinguished streaks of gray. The karate bit he pulled on the pier was no bullshit, and training had kept him fit through the years. Only the eyes looked tired.

Promptly at 8 A.M. there was a knock on the door. Dale smiled at the thought of Jerry being someone he could count on. Trust had to be built, and being on time was a good start. Jerry was at the ready in a chauffeur's outfit, but Dale had other plans.

"Jerry, you look to be about the same size as me. How 'bout we go casual today?"

"I am working, you know, and I don't think the boss would go for that."

"Boss, my ass. It's Mike's day off, so we won't be running into him today. Here, throw these on, and let's go have some fun."

Jerry caught a pair of khaki shorts and an authentic Hawaiian shirt, not the crap they sell on Waikiki.

"You need some sandals, too?" Dale asked.

Jerry knew he was along for the ride, even if he was doing the driving.

"Damn, you could break some hearts!" Dale said as he spied a now laid-back Jerry, even if the look on the chauffeur's face wasn't completely relaxed.

"Now, you got a ride that people won't see comin' a mile away?"

Jerry nodded yes, and told Dale his Mustang convertible was down in the parking garage.

"All right, my man! Let's put the top down and cruise ourselves up to Malibu for some breakfast. How does that sound?"

Jerry nodded yes and didn't blink when Dale hopped in the front seat beside him.

The 45-minute drive was more than pleasant. Dale chatted about old times and shouted, "Hey, I remember that joint!" more than once. Jerry recommended a quaint spot right on the beach that served a mean plate of bacon and eggs, sensing somehow that's what was on Dale's palate this morning. They were promptly seated and handed their menus. A few minutes later a beautiful waitress stopped by their table, tall with streaked blonde hair, a beautiful complexion adorned only by a light shade of lipstick.

"Hi, I'm Trista. May I get you started with some coffee or juice?"

Dale couldn't keep his eyes from following the tanned, shapely legs as they strolled back to the kitchen. He reminded himself that Mama had taught him that staring wasn't polite as Trista returned with two steaming cups of coffee. She had noticed the gaze, however, and countered with a flirtatious smile.

"You sure look familiar. Have we met before?" she asked.

"Honey, I don't think so," Dale said with a slight blush coloring his cheeks. "I would remember someone as good looking as you."

Dale always had a way with women, and Trista was no exception. Jerry spoke up and told her Dale was performing at the Bonaventure Lounge.

"Ah, you're a singer. You look like the performing type," she said with a hint of suggestion.

Trista asked Dale how long he would be in town and what nights he would be performing.

"I'll be playing Tuesday through Saturday for the next month, but you might be able to convince me to stick around longer," Dale said.

"I guess I will have to catch your act one night," Trista said, adding a wink as she turned to stroll away.

"You do that, honey," Dale said.

This would be Dale's last day off for a while, so they continued up the coast to Point Magu and back.

"You know, Jerry, Hawaii is beautiful, but there is electricity here in SoCal that you don't find in many places," Dale said as the now clear, clean air blew through his hair.

"Well, from the looks of it you had some sparks going back there, Dale," Jerry said with a mischievous tone.

"We'll see. The last thing I need right now is a female to foul up things, but I couldn't help flirting with her a bit."

"I wish I could talk to women the way you do," Jerry said. "Who knows, maybe I'll pick up a few pointers."

"I wasn't really sure about coming out here to play in front of an audience again, Jerry—I left behind all the 'perks' of playing in a band a long time ago—but I think I'm really warming up to it now."

"Sounds like you have had some good times," Jerry said casually. "What's the biggest crowd you ever played for?"

"Well, this one time in Houston we filled the biggest damn building in the world, the Astrodome," Dale blurted out before he could catch himself.

"Yeah, right, boss!" Jerry laughed. "It sounds like you're full of stories, but I don't think you'll see too much action at The Bonaventure. Nice place, but the crowd is usually pretty tame."

"We'll see about that," Dale said and turned to give Jerry a wink.

Dale had made a reservation at Vicenti's and talked Jerry into joining him. The entry way felt like a portal to the Hollywood that Dale remembered. There on the walls were all the greats, Sinatra and the Rat Pack, and The King himself with a buxom brunette on each arm.

"I love looking at all these old photos," Jerry said. "Seems like it wasn't that long ago."

"I know the feeling," Dale said as he turned his attention to the menu that still served the best Italian food in L.A. The taste was just as Dale remembered it, with classy yet unassuming service still in vogue as well.

"That comes right over here," Dale said as the check arrived.

Jerry made a move to object, but he knew the gesture was going to be received as nothing more than good manners.

"Thanks for a great day, Jerry," Dale said. "If the rest of the month goes like today, I just might stick around a little longer."

Dale's inner voice spoke of impending doom that threatened to spoil the moment—Dale did realize that his month in L.A. was a brief respite before his day of reckoning would surely arrive—but it felt good to daydream a bit.

"The pleasure was all mine, boss," Jerry said. The moniker seemed to fit Dale well, and he didn't object.

Back at the hotel, Dale headed straight upstairs, entered Room No. 32, grabbed a quick shower and exhaled deeply as he flopped on the bed. Tomorrow was going to be a big day: practice early in the morning with the band, and then tomorrow night was his opener. He made it through just one imaginary set before falling into a deep and restful sleep.

Dale awoke to the sound of the alarm—that hadn't happened for months, he thought—dressed and headed downstairs to meet the musicians with whom he would share the stage for the next month. As Dale entered the darkened lounge, he saw four figures seated at a table in front of the stage. Dale approached with a friendly manner, but one that was naturally used to being in charge. "Hey guys, I'm Dale. You ready to do this?"

"Ready when you are, boss," Jack Sperling said. He would be on drums, with Billie Denning on bass, Al Stevens on lead guitar, and Perry Bransen on keyboards. All were studio musicians who had been in L.A. for years and had played with some of the best. Dale informed them that each set would have seven songs and leave time for them to honor requests. At Mike's request, the mix would be three lounge-style crooner tunes for every up-tempo song. They would play blues, early rock to contemporary, all of which could be revised to match the mood of the audience.

"Sounds like you've done this a time or two, boss," Jack said.

"Yeah, this isn't my first ride, but it's been a while, you know?" Dale said.

"No problem," Billie said. "We've got your back."

They opened the practice set with "Sweet Caroline," always a crowd favorite.

"Let's ramp that up a notch, boys," Dale said. With the pace quickened just a little the sound started to gel. They rolled through a few more songs, tapping all the desired genres, and Dale caught a glimpse of Mike standing in the doorway with a smile as he tapped his foot in time with the melodies.

"You guys are going to knock 'em dead," Mike said as the band wrapped up the practice session with Dale's moving rendition of "Gentle on My Mind." "Hey, Dale, why don't you open with that?"

"Yeah man, you nailed it!" Al said.

"Sounds good, boys," Dale said. "It's always a good idea to start on a high note, so to speak. See you soon."

Mike invited Dale to join him for lunch in the Bonaventure's main dining room.

"I'll take a pass on the chow, but I could use a nice glass of lemonade," Dale said. "I ate enough last night at Vicenti's to last me a month!"

"Ah, great place," Mike said. "They still have that stunning brunette behind the bar?"

"I didn't see any of that, but the atmosphere was just how I remembered it, and their spaghetti and meatballs are still the best dish in town."

"You and the boys sounded great from what I heard during rehearsals," Mike said. "You ready to go? Need anything before tonight?"

"No, sir. I can tell the boys are professionals," Dale replied. "We're ready to put on a show."

"I like your style," Mike said. "You seem like a natural."

Dale thanked Mike again for setting up the gig and headed up to No. 32 for some reflection. Good thing I got a good night's sleep, Dale thought to himself, because there's not going to be much relaxing going on between now and show time. Dale tried on his trim black suit more than once as he passed the hours in his hotel room. The worst part of stage fright is the anticipation. Dale knew he'd be fine once the lights came on, but that wasn't helping his roiling stomach right now. He finally decided to end the battle between seltzer water and nervous stomach acid by throwing up a bit around 6 P.M. It was mostly dry heave, of course, because he knew better than to perform after any kind of a heavy meal. He could still taste a bit of Oregano from that beautiful meal at Vicente's, though.

"Just like the old days," Dale said to himself in the mirror. "Now it's time to rock 'n' roll."

By the time he got to the lounge Jack, Billie, Al, and Perry were already tuning their instruments.

"Ready to roll, boss?" Jack asked from behind his seven-piece kit.

"It's now or never," Dale replied.

Jack rolled back a little in his seat and cocked his head to the side with a somewhat bemused look.

"I think I've heard that somewhere before," he finally said with a nod of approval.

When the clock struck seven, the band began to play softly as Mike handled the introductions for the evening.

"Ladies and gentlemen, please welcome Mr. Dale Gant!"

...That keeps you in the backroads,
By the rivers of my memory.
That keeps you ever gentle on my mind.

Dale nailed it, just like he had done in the warm-up that morning, just like he had so many times before. The feeling never got old.

The crowd was light as people were still dining, but as the first set came to an end the lounge was almost full. At first break Dale went up to the bar and grabbed a soda water.

"You're sounding damn good," Larry the bartender said as he slid Dale a glass of soda water.

"Thanks, man. You getting any requests?"

"Hell, yes. I haven't seen this placed hopped up like this in a while. They want you to crank it up a bit."

A part of Dale wanted to bring the house down, but that would be over-doing it. Better to bring these folks along slowly. He teased them a bit with a stirring rendition of "Heartbreak Hotel" to close out the night.

"Y'all come back and see us again!" Dale said as the crowd pleaded for more. "We'll be here every night, Tuesday through Saturday, for the next four weeks. Goodnight, folks!"

Dale hung around a bit as Larry pitched last call.

"Man, you were great," a middle-aged man crowed as he clapped Dale on the back. "We'll be coming back for sure!"

Billie and Perry were headed to a late-night haunt down in Hollywood and pleaded with Dale to come along.

"Sorry, boys, you go ahead and have yourselves a good time, but don't forget showtime is at 7 tomorrow night," Dale said good-naturedly, but with a tone of authority.

These guys were already *his* band, and they seemed to be just fine with that. Sleep wouldn't come easy or early for Dale tonight. Too much natural adrenaline, but that was a good drug.

Dale's pleasure with opening night was confirmed at a late breakfast the next morning as he plowed through a meal of sausage, eggs, and grits. He was pleasantly surprised that the cook knew how to make grits southern style, per his request.

"I've heard nothing but compliments from last night," Mike said as he pulled up a chair. "Keep it up, Dale, and we might not let you get away."

They both laughed, but for different reasons. Mike was pleased to have an act that promised to breathe some life into his joint. Dale knew this new scene was too good to be true. He met with the band to tighten up a few things and headed up to No. 32 to try to get some rest. The soda water won the battle with his nervous stomach this time, but the nerves were still there.

"That means you've got this," he said to himself in the mirror. "Show time."

The lounge was crowded as he opened again with "Gentle on My Mind"—no reason to mess with karma—and was standing room only by the end of the first set. Larry slid him a request for "Blue Suede Shoes," and Dale couldn't resist. Word spreads quickly in Hollywood, and as the week-end approached The Bonaventure was the place to be if you wanted to hear music the way it was meant to be played. At least that's what it said in one of the local entertainment rags.

Saturday arrived in a flash. Dale was about to finish his first week, and he had loved every minute of it. The place was already packed midway through the first set. Midway through the third set, Dale could only see a pair of stunning legs swing around on a barstool. When the crowd parted a little, he could make out the familiar face, angular yet feminine. Her streaked blonde hair was down, splashing over a colorful sun dress. Dale could see her smile from the stage. His heart raced and he heard his voice skip a beat as Trista gazed at him seductively. A thousand faces of girls who'd had the same look flashed through his mind's eye, but something told him this one was different. Dale finished the song, and another, never losing the connection. "Ladies and gentlemen, I'd like to dedicate this next song to a friend of mine who has graced us with her presence here tonight."

He mouthed "One Night With You?" to Al, who nodded that yes, the boys knew that old number. Dale always knew when to bring the emotion to a climax.

One night with you
Is what I'm now praying for.
The things that we two could plan
Would make my dreams come true.

When Dale finished the crowd paused momentarily, as if stunned by his energy, before erupting.

"We'll be right back, folks," Dale said over the din as he stepped off the stage and moved slowly toward the bar, his eyes never leaving Trista's.

"I love your hair down," Dale said. "You look gorgeous."

Trista broke the connection only to lean forward and kiss him on the cheek.

"Thanks for the song," she said. "I've never heard it done quite like that."

"Honey, it was truly my pleasure."

"Your voice is so clear and beautiful," she said. "I still have goose pimples."

Dale stroked her arm and felt the heat build in his face.

"Trista, I am so glad you came tonight."

The final set went by in a blur, and Dale was glad that it did. He wanted to make his way back to the bar and Trista. The crowd had been moved by the music, though, and fans wanted Dale's attention.

He was used to the feeling.

"Your rendition of "Blue Suede Shoes" was, well, *amazing*," an attractive middle-aged woman in a stunning red dress told Dale as she gently tugged at his suit lapels and pulled him closer. The look in her hazel eyes signaled keen interest in continuing the conversation upstairs, but Dale could feel Trista's gaze upon him.

"Thank you, ma'am. I'm glad you enjoyed the show," Dale said, trying not to look too interested in her attentions. "Please come back and see us again."

Dale pulled himself away and graciously acknowledged more fans as he slowly made his way toward Trista. As he casually chatted with fans, he was constantly aware of Trista's eyes on him as she sipped her drink. Finally, he broke free and slid into the seat next to her.

"You look amazing," Dale said as he lightly stroked her silky forearm.

Trista blushed, but with a flash of great pleasure as her golden features turned slightly crimson.

"Where's Jerry?" she asked, but her look belied her true intentions.

"He has the night off and is visiting some friends," Dale said with a return look that signaled Jerry—and anyone else but Trista—was furthest from his thoughts.

"Well, I hope I get to see him again sometime because he's really nice," Trista said and looked away.

Dale hadn't played this game for a while. The many women he had known through the years rarely bothered to be coy. They had wanted to be with him for whatever satisfaction it gave them, to roll with a star, get their 15 minutes of fame, tell their girlfriends about the encounter, but not for *him*. "I don't think you really came here to see Jerry, did you?" Dale asked.

Trista blushed again slightly, and returned the volley.

"Well, no, I really wanted to see you again," she said. "I never imagined you could sing that way."

"I almost forgot what I was singin' when you walked in," Dale said.

The chase continued, back and forth, as Dale and Trista exchanged small talk, both knowing the bigger questions were coming soon. Where are you from? What do you like to do? What's your favorite music? ... Uh, are you seeing anyone? Trista took the lead on that one.

"A guy like you has to have a girl somewhere, hopefully not one with a wedding band," she said. Dale moved his left hand slowly to the tabletop and left it there for inspection.

"That spot's been taken before," he said, "but not for a long time. How about you?"

Trista sensed that the details of Dale's past would be best kept for later. It was her turn to fill the sudden void.

"I grew up in the Midwest, the name of the town doesn't really matter," she said. "Main Street, same old friends and families, doing what they had done since their great-greats settled the place. I had a boyfriend all through high school, Charles Jeffries, stud football player, goin' nowhere other than to his daddy's tractor. We were *supposed* to be married. God damn! It was almost like someone else was living my life for me, you know?"

Dale said nothing, but returned a high, soft lob of a nod that indicated, "Keep going, honey. Tell me all about it."

"Well, I hung around for a few years after high school, but then I had to get the hell out of there!" Trista continued. "I had some money saved up, so I took a trip to the coast, booked a plane straight for L.A. I know it sounds stupid and cliché, country girl comes to Hollywood to find herself, you know? But the first time I stuck my toes in the sand and smelled the ocean, I knew I had found the place that I really wanted to call home. Well, that was almost eight years ago! I've been through a bunch of roommates and bullshit, but I've worked hard and saved my pennies. Finally, I had enough to get an apartment of my own. Well, it's more the size of a closet, but the location is what I really wanted. I can walk out my door and stick my toes in the sand in less than 5 minutes. That's enough for me."

"So, it's safe to say Charles didn't follow your path to the Pacific, eh?" Dale asked.

"Hell no!" Trista said as she flicked a good-natured forearm into Dale's ribs and took advantage of the opportunity to nearly lose her balance on the bar stool and be steadied in his arms.

"Well, darlin', I wish my story was that simple." Dale said.

"I hope it's not too complicated," Trista said.

"Nothin' that can't be overcome. Let's just enjoy the moment, OK?"

"It looks like we'll have to continue that outside," Trista said as Larry was shoving the last revelers out the front door.

"Oh, let me walk you to your car," Dale said.

He hooked Trista's arm gently and led her to her feet. She clasped his hand and leaned in close.

"Right this way," she said with a wink.

Her white Honda was parked nearby, and Trista made sure to take some time rummaging through her purse for the keys. How come this guy makes me feel like I'm back in high school, waiting for my first kiss, she asked herself. She could feel Dale move closer, warming with anticipation, but sensed his hesitance.

"Trista, I, uh ..."

She seized the moment and whirled around to stop Dale's stammering with a long, wet kiss. After their lips parted, Dale rocked back, looked to the starry night above and wondered why this girl made him feel so young and alive.

"I was going to ask if you are free tomorrow," he finally managed to say.

"My calendar is open," Trista said.

"Well, the Dodgers are in town. How 'bout we catch a game and have some laughs?" Dale asked.

"Sounds great," Trista replied.

"OK, it's a Sunday afternoon game. Jerry and I will pick you up around Noon. Sound good?"

"Yeah, but don't you need to know where to find me? Silly boy."

"Uh, yeah, I guess I do," Dale said, not the least bit ashamed of being lost in the moment.

Trista wrote down her address in Santa Monica and sealed it with another kiss.

"Goodnight, princess," Dale said.

Dale awoke more refreshed than he could remember. What a great opening week, what a great crowd, what a great rush to be back on stage ... what a great woman. Images of being with Trista blocked out any demons that tried to invade his thoughts. Dale took his time showering, shaving close and making sure he was mentally ready for a date with the new woman of his dreams. Jerry was ready and waiting with the Limo when Dale finally arrived downstairs.

"Ready to go, boss?" Jerry said with a genuine smile.

"Hell, yes, and don't be afraid to show what's under the hood," Dale said as he slid into the Limo's living area.

Jerry showed off his driving skills a little as they headed toward the Pacific and found their way to Trista's apartment complex.

"Here we are, boss," Jerry said as he pulled the Limo toward the curb in front of a two-story complex. "You got it from here?"

"Well, no, I thought I'd have you hold my hand and maybe even ring the damn doorbell for me," Dale joked. "Yeah, I got this."

Trista swung open the door to her second-floor apartment before Dale could push the call button.

"Hi there," she said with a fun-loving smile accentuating her ballpark outfit. Snug shorts showed off her tanned, shapely legs with a pair of aqua Chuck Taylor tennis shoes for accents. Her top half was equally attractive with a halter top that accentuated her golden midriff offset by a half-cocked Dodgers ballcap.

"You sure you're not one of those hot ballgirls who hang out down the baselines?" Dale said as he wrapped an arm around Trista and pecked her ear with a kiss.

"Well, they haven't asked me—yet," Trista giggled with delight.

They looked like anything but royalty as they climbed into the living area of the black limo.

"Hey, Jerry!" Trista said.

"Nice to see you again, Miss Trista," Jerry replied, ever the professional.

"Let's head for Dodgertown," Dale said. "I think we've got some champagne in here someplace, honey."

Trista and Dale acted like school kids on Prom night as Jerry navigated the freeways toward Dodger Stadium.

"Here we are, boss," Jerry said as he pulled the limo into the V.I.P. parking section. "You two have yourselves a great time. I'll wait here and listen to the game. Gettin' paid to sit here in this leather seat and have Vin Scully call the action isn't too bad."

"Thanks, Jerry," Dale said. "You're the best, man."

Jerry had made sure their seats were in the "important people" section, four rows up from the Dodgers' dugout. Trista was impressed.

"Hey, how'd you get us in the seats with all the movie stars?" she asked as Dale whistled for some hot dogs, peanuts and sodas.

"I guess Jerry has some connections," Dale said with a wink.

Trista spread mustard all over her famous Dodger Dog and piled on a few onions for good measure. Dale was impressed.

"I sure like your style, honey," he said.

The Dodgers were headed for a dismal fourth-place finish in their division, well behind the hated San Francisco Giants, and this Sunday was typical of the season so far. Dale and Trista hardly noticed the visiting team taking a 2-0 lead in the top of the first inning, however. They were lost in each other, Dale happily drinking in Trista's beauty. She was more determined, trying to crack the shell surrounding Jerry's personal life the same way she was crunching and munching through her bag of peanuts.

"So, did you grow up in a baseball town?" she asked innocently.

"I was always more of a football fan," Dale said, trying not to cut the words short but leaving no opening.

She snuggled closer and nuzzled Dale's ear as he pretended to be interested in the game.

"You know," she whispered, "I'm going to get you to open up eventually, Mr. Gant. You can't resist me for long."

"Well, you got that second part right, honey," Dale said as he pulled her closer. "But there are some things I'm just not comfortable talking about right now and my whole past is one of them."

"Uh, *okay*," Trista said. She was trying not to look hurt or confused, but she naturally pulled away a little and felt tense to Dale's embrace.

"Hey, honey, you ain't got nothin' to worry about," Dale said. "I'm not a serial killer or anything like that, you know."

She didn't know much about Dale, but her intuition told her she was perfectly safe in his arms.

"*Okay*," she said with a big smile. "I'm just going to enjoy being with you."

Neither of them noticed as the Pittsburgh Pirates scored four more runs in the sixth inning and the infamously fickle L.A. crowd began to thin considerably. They stayed to the end, enjoying the late afternoon sunshine and each other's company.

Jerry had a slightly disgusted look on his face as they climbed into the back of the limo.

"That has to be one of the worst bullpens in the league!" he said, listening to the radio crew recount another loss. "We've got to get some offense going, or this season will be over in a hurry."

Jerry glanced in the rearview and quickly realized Dale and Trista hadn't heard a word. They certainly didn't care that the Dodgers couldn't muster a clutch base hit.

"Okay you two, whereto?" he asked, loud enough to break their embrace.

"Oh, hey Jerry," Dale said. "The beach, definitely."

"Well, there's a few of those around here, boss," Jerry said good-naturedly.

"Hell, I thought they were all the same!" Dale said. "I'm a tourist around here, you know?"

"Well, I never get tired of Santa Monica, but I'm in the mood for a little wackiness. How 'bout Muscle Beach?" Trista said.

"Next stop, downtown Venice," Jerry said. "Maybe Dale will show off his pipes a little bit!"

"They are pretty impressive, babe," Trista said with a wink as she grabbed Dale's biceps and he pulled her close to put an end to the small-talk. Jerry could see conversation wasn't going to distract him as he swung south on the 405.

"I'll leave you two alone for a bit," he said while sliding the privacy barrier into place.

The muscle-builders were out in full force as Dale, Trista, and Jerry walked along the crowded Venice Beach promenade. Dale playfully put his hands over Trista's eyes as one of the young studs in a European-style thong smiled at her.

"She's all mine, big boy," Dale said with a laugh.

Trista spied a billboard with cutouts of a muscle man next to a bikini-clad bombshell.

"Oooh, we have to get a picture!" she said and stuck her head through the cutout of the girl.

"You're up, Jerry!" Dale said.

"Aw, man, really?" Jerry said, but he was flattered at being included in the fun.

Dale paid the photographer for two shots and laughed out loud as Trista and Jerry stuck their heads through the wrong holes.

"You're a knockout, Jerry!" Dale said.

They all admired the Polaroids after Dale agreed to take his turn.

"These have to go in my album!" Trista said.

"Oh, great," Jerry said. "Now you have evidence!"

Trista headed for the ice cream stand for more fun.

"Triple-deckers all around, my treat," she said, "Vanilla is out of the question!"

Dale ordered up Bananarama. Trista opted for Cherry Garcia, and Jerry requested a Karamel Sutra, much to Dale's delight.

"You lookin' for some action, tonight?" Dale said as he gave Jerry a little bump that left a splotch of chocolate on the limo driver's nose.

"I'll bring some home for Mrs. Skeen and see what happens," Jerry said. "So long as you two don't keep me out too late."

"Well, it's been a great day, but we probably need to get headed home before long," Dale said.

"Not before we catch a little of the sunset?" Trista pleaded.

Jerry had enjoyed the company, but he knew his time was up.

"I better make sure the car is safe with all these hooligans around," he said. "You two take your time. Mrs. Skeen isn't going anywhere."

"Thanks, Jerry," Dale said genuinely. "We won't be too long."

Dale and Trista pulled off their shoes and walked through the still warm sand to the water's edge. Trista wanted with all her heart to know more about this charming man walking with her hand-in-hand, but she remembered the uncomfortable exchanges at the bar and again at the ballpark when she had pried. She stepped in front of Dale and looked up at him with emotion in her eyes.

"I don't care about anything in your past, so long as you keep me in your future," she said.

"You can count on that, darlin'," Dale said as he pulled her close. "I've never felt more comfortable with anyone. I just want you to know that I'm a good man—at least I always try to be—and I would never do anything to hurt you. Someday, when the time is right, I'll tell you everything."

Dale and Trista shared a long, passionate kiss as the sun dipped toward its reunion with the darkening blue of the Pacific.

"I guess we have to fire up the carriage and take our princess home now," Dale told Jerry as he and Trista climbed into the limo.

"Yeah, too bad, but even the best days have to come to an end," Jerry said as he steered the limo north toward Santa Monica.

Jerry jumped out to open the door for Trista when they arrived at her place.

"Seriously, I had a great time today. Thanks for letting me tag along, Miss Trista," Jerry said.

"It wouldn't have been the same without you," Trista replied and kissed Jerry on the cheek.

"I think I need to keep an eye on you two," Dale said with a wink as he grabbed Trista's hand to lead her up the walkway.

"Honey, if you aren't busy tomorrow evening, I'd like to take you out for a real nice dinner," Dale said at the doorstep. "I have a reservation at Chasen's for 5:30. May we pick you up around 4:30?"

"I'll be counting the minutes until then," Trista said.

They shared one last kiss and Dale held Trista's hand lightly as she met his gaze while slowly pulling away and closing the door.

Chasen's was located in West Hollywood, close enough to Beverly Hills to have a host of A-list entertainers as regulars. The Ronald Reagan booth gained fame as the spot where he proposed to Nancy. Groucho Marx, Jimmy Stewart, and Frank Sinatra all lent their names to private booths through the years. The place had started out as nothing but a shack, but its notoriety grew quickly off a famous chili recipe.

"Lots of places can entertain movie stars and put their pictures on the walls, but not all of them know real southern cookin'," Dale said as he opened the door for Trista.

Dale was dressed elegantly in gray slacks with a white shirt and black vest, but no tie. He knew he needed room to use a bib at this joint. Trista wore a simple, stunning black dress that hugged her fit and shapely physique. A pearl choker accentuated her tanned neckline.

"Reservation for Gant, table for two," Dale told the maitre d'.

"Ah, yes, right this way," the distinguished elderly gentleman said. "How is this, madamé?"

"It's perfect," Trista said as she tucked her dress and slid into the crimson leather seat of the booth.

"Is this one of the famous spots?"

"Yes, madamé, you're sitting in the very spot Nancy was when President Reagan proposed to her," the maitre d' said.

"Oh my gosh!" Trista said and blushed to half the shade of the booth's interior.

"You're even more stunning in this light," Dale said, thoroughly enjoying Trista's reaction to the surprise.

"Thank you," Trista said, regaining her composure as their waiter arrived.

"Good evening. My name is Charles," the handsome man in his mid-30s said. "Would you care for some drinks and appetizers before dinner?"

"I'd love a cosmopolitan," Trista said.

"I'll have a glass of wine with dinner, but I think just a rosemary citrus spritzer for now, thanks," Dale said. "And we'll start with some oysters on the half-shell, with your southern vinegar sauce on the side."

"Very good, sir," Charles said and bowed slightly before heading for the kitchen.

"I didn't ask if you like oysters," Dale said.

"Love 'em!" Trista replied quickly. "I've never been here before, but I love the ambience. It's elegant, but with not too much attitude."

"It started out as a shack, but with the best chili in town," Dale said. "Me and the boys used to come down here all the time. We even had 'em haul chili over to our place."

"Ah, so you used to be a regular?" Trista said with a hint of pleasure that she had finally cracked Dale's shell, if only for a peek inside.

"Well, yeah, you know, their chili was the best," Dale said.

His shell had snapped shut again, but she took the closure in stride and turned her attention to the delicacies that Charles had set upon the table.

"I don't know about your heat meter, but this sauce will make it rise," Dale said as he dipped an oyster in the red sauce and popped it into his mouth.

"I can handle some heat," Trista said as she did the same.

Trista's eyes watered as the juices hit her tongue and the roof of her mouth, but the taste was exquisite.

"Holy moly!" she said as she finally gave out and grabbed for some water. Dale chuckled slightly.

"I told you. It's damn hot!" he said. "Sorry if it burned too much."

"I'm not a wussy girl!" Trista said between gulps. "Maybe I'll skip the sauce next time, though."

They shared a laugh and finished off the oyster plate. Dale had to relent and gulp some water, too, as he finished off the last of the sizzling sauce. Dinner was just as satisfying, linguini with Alfredo sauce for Trista and lamb chops with garlic potatoes for Dale.

"My gosh, I can't eat another bite," Trista said as she pushed her plate to the middle of the table. "I won't be able to fit into this little number if I keep this up."

"I can't imagine you looking anything but stunning in it," Dale said.

Charles interrupted the moment with an offer for dessert.

"Oh no, but I think we'd like some after-dinner drinks," Dale said. "Would you like another cosmo, honey?"

"I don't need to have anything with alcohol, if that bothers you," Trista said.

"Oh no, go right ahead, honey," Dale said. "I mean, I'm not trying to get you drunk or anything, but I want you to have a great time."

"That's easy to do with you, Dale," Trista said sincerely. "We've only known each other for …"

"Seven days, 10 hours, 11 minutes," Dale interrupted as he slid closer to Trista.

"One of the best weeks of my life," she said before they shared an intimate kiss.

They were quiet, but close, on the ride back to Santa Monica. Communication came without words in the subtle touches between them. Dale was glad he had asked Jerry to chauffeur instead of driving himself tonight. He'd have to be a gentleman … what would she do if he did make a move? He wanted to be with Trista, but he knew she would be worth waiting for, no matter how long that was. Trista couldn't help thinking about how special Dale made her feel whenever they were together … and how special he could make every one of her senses feel. She knew that wouldn't be tonight, except in their dreams, but soon.

Jerry opened the door for them, and Dale held Trista's hand as they walked toward the apartment door.

"I'd love to see you tomorrow, but I have the early shift and I'm covering for someone all week," she said, proud of herself for not letting on that she really wanted Dale to stay with her.

"I guess Jerry will have to keep me company," Dale said. "I can't wait to see you again, though."

"I'm off early Saturday," she said. "I'll come see your whole show, and you'll be in my dreams until then."

They shared a kiss that left them both breathless and wanting each other more than ever.

"Sleep tight, princess," Dale said as he pulled away reluctantly. "We'll be together soon."

The Bonaventure gained even more attention in the L.A. entertainment scene as Dale and the boys refined their groove.

"If you want to experience the roots of rock 'n' roll, catch the act at The Bonaventure," an article in the *L.A. Times* Entertainment section teased. "We don't even know the name of the band, but that doesn't matter. They've captured the soul of early rock 'n' roll, and they'll take yours along for the ride ..."

"Can you believe that?" Mike said as he slid the paper in front of Dale at breakfast Friday morning. "You guys are a sensation, and that's hard to be in this town. Maybe we need a 'name the band' night, eh?"

"It's enough for me just to make people enjoy the music," Dale said. "They can call us whatever they want, so long as they enjoy the show."

"They're enjoying it alright," Mike said. "I've got people calling from all over, wanting reservations. Hell, we haven't reserved a table in this place forever. I can't tell you how much I appreciate the buzz you've created, Dale. I'd really like to talk to you about what happens from here, and I know a music producer, Mr. Walker, who would really like to get you down to his studio."

"Mike, I'm really glad the place is jumpin' and all, and I can't tell you how much I've enjoyed it," Dale said.

"But ...?" Mike asked.

"But it's not going to last, at least not for me," Dale said. "I have to face some things that I've put off for a long time. I'd love to stay here, live this dream, just keep playing to the crowd, but that's not going to happen. If things work out down the road, I'd love to help you out some more, but I don't like to make promises I can't keep."

"Well, okay, my friend," Mike said. "Just let me know if I can do anything for you. And in the meantime, kick some ass for a few more weeks. Okay?"

"Yes, sir," Dale said.

His sleep rolled between dreams of Trista and nightmares of relations past. Ahead in the darkness lay an unknown specter, one he must surely face, and very soon.

When Dale awoke, he reached for The Bible on the nightstand. He wasn't expecting God to speak this time, but Dale was searching for truth in His words just the same. The words of John the Baptist provided solace, but conflict just the same:

If we say we have no sin, we deceive ourselves, and the truth is not in us.
1 John 1:8

Dale was prepared to pay for whatever sin may come with loving Trista out of wedlock, but a just God surely wouldn't punish them for what seemed so right, so pure, so good. The truth, however, was waiting to be told. Dale had killed a man, if not by his own hand then surely by his actions. He slowly closed the Book, rubbed his throbbing temples, and faced the future in the only way he knew. Time to knock their socks off.

Al and Jack were in the bar, doing some tinkering and tuning when Dale arrived an hour before showtime.

"Hey, boss, you ready to roll?" Al asked.

The intense, borderline crazy look on Dale's face provided the answer.

"Tonight, we're going to show 'em how it's done, boys," Dale said. "Be ready."

Dale felt a surge of energy he hadn't experienced for years. "Blue Suede Shoes" was even more amazing than last Saturday, and he brought the house down with "Jailhouse Rock" at the end of the second set. Dale was so enthused, he barely noticed that Trista had slipped into a seat Larry had reserved for her at the bar and was gaining ample notice from the male players in the packed house.

"Hey, baby," he said and kissed her on the cheek after fighting his way through the crowd of well-wishers. "I sure missed you."

"I missed you, too, immensely!" Trista said. "I've got some bad news, though. I can't stay long. You know my friend Debbie, from the diner?"

"Yeah, I think so," Dale said as Larry tossed him a towel to wipe the ample sweat from his brow.

"Well, her mama is sick in the hospital. They found out today that it's cancer. Debbie is going to see her at UCLA Medical Center tonight, and I promised I would be there with her when she goes into the room."

"I know what it's like to have your Mama sick and dyin'," Dale said. "Well, what about tomorrow? I have to see you!"

"I'm off all day," Trista said. "Why don't you come down to my place? We can relax on the beach, and I'd love to make a home-cooked, southern-style meal for you."

"How'd you know my taste?" Dale asked.

"I am a woman, you know," Trista said.

"Yes, you are. I'll see you tomorrow," Dale said. "But kiss me before you go, and stick for just the first number coming up. I think you'll like it."

Trista obliged on both counts, and Dale never took his eyes off her while crooning "Love Me Tender." Trista blew him a kiss as she disappeared out the door.

The band played two encores, "Surrender" and "All Shook Up," before Larry flipped on the lights and started hustling people out the door. Billie and Perry begged Dale to come out and party with them—they had some groupies in tow—but he turned them away as usual. As the crowd began to thin, the woman in red from the previous Saturday saw her opportunity.

"Hi, my name's Connie, and I just love your act," she said as she slipped into the now open bar seat next to Dale.

"Hi, sugar. I'm glad you liked it," Dale said.

"It's too late for a drink here, but maybe we could have a nightcap back at your room. I guess your girlfriend had to leave. Too bad for her," Connie said as she caressed Dale's inner thigh and winked seductively.

Dale was tempted, as he'd always been by the attractive women who came calling.

"I'd love to, honey, but I'd never forgive myself in the morning," Dale said. "I hope you come back and see us again, but I have to say goodnight now."

Dale rose and headed for No. 32, congratulating himself on eluding the charms of a seductress—for one of the few times in his life. The energy he burned on stage made sleep come easily, but Dale felt a strange sensation as soon as he awoke.

"I'm nervous as hell," he said to himself as he climbed out of bed.

Dale pulled on a pair of shorts, sandals and khakis. He looked at his razor and toothbrush … what the hell, he thought, might as well pack for whatever may come as he stuffed overnight items into his black toiletry case.

This was a twist, he thought. He had always sat and waited while the girls came to him, gave him everything he wanted, whenever and however he wanted it. For as long as he wanted it. Dale hadn't driven himself on a date, well, for longer than he could remember. The hotel didn't have a big ol' limo at his beckoning, but Dale felt freer than ever behind the wheel of the "mid-size sedan" they had for rent. The 30-minute drive breezed by, perhaps too quickly as he approached Marina Drive. Maybe I need to roll around the block, just to make sure I'm in the right area, he thought, knowing damn well that the directions were perfect. Dale parked within walking distance of Trista's apartment, and gave himself a heart-to-heart in the rearview mirror.

"Quit actin' like a damn rookie, Ace!" he scolded himself. "So, you like this girl? Just be yourself, and everything will be just fine."

As the apartment door opened Dale gazed upon one of the most beautiful women he had ever seen. Trista's blonde hair was down and across her shoulders. She was wearing a swimsuit with a short beach robe to cover it up.

"Good morning, Dale," she said with a bright smile and leaned in to give him a kiss.

Dale stepped into the modest apartment, small but decorated in hip beach decor. Candles were still burning on the coffee table, and a brooding charcoal drawing of Jim Morrison dominated the main wall.

"Gotta love *The Doors*," Trista said as she watched Dale scan the room. "I cried my eyes out the day he died."

"I guess fans really do have a hard time lettin' go," Dale said. "It's not any easier on the other end. I can assure you of that."

"Say what, honey?" Trista asked.

"Oh, nothin', darlin'. I'm just ramblin' because you look so damn good!"

Dale grabbed Trista in a full embrace and gave her a playful peck.

"Where can I change into my trunks?" he asked.

Dale left the door slightly ajar as he peeled to his birthday suit and pulled on a pair of swim trunks. Trista caught a glance of his toned body, much to her delight. Wow, he looks downright delicious for being an older man, she thought to herself.

Trista hoped the golden tan color was returning to her flushed cheeks as she waited for Dale with a packed lunch. He sent the color careening back toward deep red by pulling her close, nibbling at her ears and neck. Trista's body tingled, and she felt faint with warm pleasure.

"How the hell does he expect to walk to the beach after that?" her mind asked. She wanted to stoke the fire, let it burn! Being a decent girl, her eyes opened long enough to spot a diversion: the guitar.

"Hey, honey, why don't we take the guitar down to the beach? Maybe you can serenade me."

"Anything for you, princess," Dale said.

They walked, hands entwined, the two blocks to the pedestrian bridge that crossed the main boulevard to the beach. Santa Monica pier was on their left and miles of sand and sunbathers lay to their right. Dale spread out the checkered blanket down close to the water where they could watch the waves gently roll in and crash on the shore. Trista rubbed sunscreen all over her body while Dale enjoyed the view.

"Would you rub some on my back?" she asked, snapping Dale out of his short reverie.

Trista laid face down and untied the back of her string bikini. Dale squeezed a little too much lotion into his hands as he was distracted by Trista's naked back and the allure of her curves. He began gently massaging the lotion into the smooth skin of her shoulders and soft, toned back. Trista let out a sigh of pleasure as he worked his way down to the backs of her legs. She moaned unexpectedly as Dale's strokes came tantalizingly closer to her womanhood. Dale was becoming aroused and knew he needed to finish quickly before that became more obvious.

"Would you like some?" Trista asked.

"Some ... lotion?" Dale asked with a sheepish grin.

Trista gave him a playful shove as she dripped a long bead of lotion down the middle of Dale's back. He could feel Trista's soft hands moving rhythmically down his back and wished she would never stop.

They laid with their backs to the sun, facing one another, talking about the beautiful weather and enjoying each other's presence. Dale could have stayed in that moment forever. Trista finally sat up, opened the lunch basket, and pulled out a homemade chicken salad sandwich and some potato salad she had gotten up early that morning to prepare. She poured each of them a glass of fresh mango juice to quench their thirst in the warm sun.

"Honey, that was delicious," Dale said genuinely. He missed home cooking and was looking forward to dinner. Trista reached for the guitar and asked Dale to sing her a song. Dale took the six-string acoustic from her and plucked on each string until it was in tune.

"It's not an original Fender, but it's all I have," she said.

"It will do just great, honey, and you know your guitars. I'm impressed," Dale said as he softly started to strum the guitar and began to sing:

I bless the day I found you,
I want to stay around you.
And so I beg you, let it be me.
Don't take this heaven from one,
If you must cling to someone.
Now and forever, let it be me.

When he finished Trista was smiling and thinking to herself, "He is the one!" People who were sitting nearby could hear Dale's singing and began to applaud.

"Please don't stop," one lady said. "Sing one more song for us."

"Encore!" Trista pleaded.

Dale thanked everyone and obliged the woman and Trista by singing a gospel favorite of his, "How Great Thou Art." Even more folks gathered around as he sang this time, and the small crowd cheered enthusiastically when he finished.

"That was beautiful!" the woman said. "Did you know that Elvis won his first Grammy for that song? You sound so much like him!"

Dale nodded and put the guitar down, grabbed Trista by the hand, pulled her up and trotted to the water. The surf was cold at first, but refreshing. Dale playfully splashed Trista as she stood in knee-deep water and coaxed her to come in deeper. As she moved closer to Dale, a small wave crashed on them and she reached out for his arms. Dale grabbed her, pulled her in tight and kissed her over and over again. Trista melted in his arms. He could feel how relaxed she was and how natural she felt up close to him.

"Just like *From Here to Eternity*!" he said playfully as they rollicked in the surf.

"Are you ready for dinner ... and dessert?" Trista asked overtly as they dried off and let the sun warm their bodies. Dale smiled and nodded. They quickly packed up and walked briskly back to Trista's apartment.

Trista fumbled nervously with the keys as she unlocked the door and stepped inside with Dale close behind. She turned and kissed him, then skimmed his neck tantalizingly with the tip of her tongue before pulling away.

"I'm going to take a quick shower to wash off the salt and sand," she said.

Trista wiggled her shapely behind as she walked through the bedroom door and left it purposely wide open. Dale watched as she flicked her bikini top aside and slid out of her bottoms. She looked back at him with a smile as she dropped them to the floor. Her body was angel like, soft, golden and without a blemish. Dale watched as she turned and stepped in the shower.

"Honey, could you bring me a fresh bar of soap?" she asked. "It's in the cabinet above the bathroom sink."

Dale handed her the bar through the open shower door.

"Come in and wash my back for me," she said as her hands moved over her own naked body. Dale smiled, slipped off his trunks and stepped into the shower with her. She rubbed her body against his growing arousal and kissed him passionately. They began to wash each other all over, gently exploring. Trista turned off the water, grabbed the large bath towel hanging on the shower door, and wrapped it around them. Still wet and glistening, she took Dale's hand and led him to her bed.

Trista lay down on the bed and beckoned Dale with her eyes, her hands, and her exquisite beauty. He snuggled up close and began to gently stroke her face with one hand, while the other moved over naked form. Trista moved even closer to him, running her fingers through his hair with one hand and caressing his manhood with the other. Dale softly kissed her on the forehead, cheeks, and was soon at her luscious lips. She smelled like heaven, a mixture of soap and perfume that she had sprayed on her neck as they left the shower. Trista couldn't stand the anticipation any longer.

"Oh God, I want you," Trista whispered softly as she moved on top of him. With her graceful body on top of him, Dale looked at her face with eyes closed, a smile on her lips as she rocked back and forth. Trista and Dale let out audible moans of joy. Dale rolled on top of her and continued to make love to her with more passion than he had felt for years. Their bodies were in perfect harmony, and their souls followed.

"I knew it would be like this, Dale," Trista said as they separated slightly, keeping their hands attached.

Trista's head nuzzled Dale's muscular chest as they fell into a tranquil early-evening slumber.

Dale awoke first. He stared at Trista for a few minutes, thinking how beautiful and peaceful she looked lying there. He moved slightly to get out of bed. Trista stirred, but was still asleep, with a satisfied smile still on her lips. Dale got up, shuffled through his bag, and grabbed the robe he had packed away just in case something like this happened.

"I'm so glad it did!" he said to himself. This was a special woman, and he wanted her close to him from then on. Dale walked into the kitchen and opened the refrigerator door to see what was inside. Great sex always did arouse his appetite. He found a package from the local fish market sitting on a plate with two wrapped halibut filets. This must be dinner, he thought. He knew Trista would be up soon, so he scavenged the rest of the refrigerator and found makings for a salad, some fresh fruit, and asparagus. Dale laid everything on the counter and went through her cupboards to find everything he would need to make dinner. He enjoyed cooking, and started to prepare the salad. Dale sliced the fruit, boiled water to blanche the asparagus, and heated up a pan to cook the fish. A few pats of butter, some fresh garlic and a little pepper on top, and the halibut filets were prepared. Just then he heard Trista stirring in the bedroom. Dale was finishing setting the table when she walked into the kitchen.

"What are you doing?" she asked.

"I thought you might be a little hungry when you got up, so I found the fish and started dinner," he said.

She walked over and gave him a kiss and hug.

"I have never been with a man like you," she said in her sexiest voice.

Dale smiled at her.

"The feeling is mutual, sugar," he said with genuine affection.

Their bond was becoming stronger with every passing minute they were together. Dale tossed the asparagus into the boiling water and gently slid the filets into the pan. Being careful not to overcook, he kept a keen eye on the pan, which was difficult because he couldn't help looking at Trista. He picked up a plate and filled it with a filet, asparagus, fresh fruit and salad, and handed it to Trista. He did the same for himself, and they sat down on the same side of the table, staying sensually close.

"You felt so good," Trista said. "I enjoyed every moment with you."

Dale had the same feelings, and asked if he would be spending the night.

"You aren't going anywhere tonight, mister," Trista said. "I've waited long enough to meet you. Stay with me ... forever! Oh God, listen to me. I hope I'm not moving too fast, but I really do feel that way."

Searching his feelings, Dale knew he felt that way, too. Making it happen may be the difficult part—given the challenges he knew were coming soon—but the future could wait. In fact, to *hell* with the future. Trista was brave to take the next step and admit her feelings. She deserved to know where Dale stood.

"I already love you," he said. "I hope *that* isn't too soon, but I really do feel that way."

She moved forward quickly to kiss him, bumping foreheads in the process. She giggled for a moment, then her face glowed with intensity.

"I love you, too," she said.

When they had finished dinner, Trista made quick work of cleaning up the kitchen. Dale sat down on her sofa, flipped on the television and watched some of the Dodger game.

Trista came over to the couch, sat down next to Dale, put her arm through his and leaned her head on his shoulder.

"I have to drive to the San Fernando Valley in the morning for a very special appointment," Dale said.

"Who are you going to see?" Trista asked.

"I am going to a clothing store in North Hollywood. I have to have a special suit made, and they are the only ones that can do it. Do you want to come?"

"Yes, I'd love to, but a special suit for what occasion?" Trista asked.

"There is something I have to tell you," Dale said.

"Oh no, you're getting married! Maybe you already are married. I ..."

Dale grabbed Trista and kissed her warmly.

"I'm not doin' anything of the sort, silly," he said. "I've been invited by Priscilla Presley to perform at the 10th anniversary, at Graceland, in three weeks."

"By Priscilla Presley, at the 10th anniversary of Elvis' passing?" she asked excitedly.

"Yes. They have a whole day of remembrances planned, including performances by a bunch of impersonators. Priscilla asked me to do the final set."

Trista sprang from the couch. "Can I ..."

Before she could finish, Dale touched his fingers to her lips and said, "Yes. I want you to be there with me."

"Dale, that's so exciting! You will be perfect," Trista said.

"Well, not as perfect as you," Dale said as he switched off the TV, grabbed Trista's hand and led her back to the bedroom. Their passions ignited again, Dale and Trista made love until they were both exhausted. The sleep that followed carried through to morning. Trista awoke minutes before the alarm went off and roused Dale in a much more sensual way.

"Each time we make love is even better than the last," Trista said as she lay on the bed, craving more sleep—and more of Dale.

"Come on, honey, I'd love to stay here all day and kiss every inch of your body, but we have things to do," Dale said.

He gave Trista a light slap on the rump and headed for the shower.

"Last one in has to do all the washing," Dale said with a laugh as he stepped in the shower and turned on the spray.

"No fair!" Trista said playfully. "But I guess if I have to lose ..."

It was already past 8 A.M. when they hit the 405 Freeway, but they were headed out of town, so the traffic wasn't too bad. Still, Dale glanced at his watch and hoped they would be on time.

"These aren't the type of people who are used to waiting for customers," Dale said. "Nudie was the best clothes man in the business, and Mrs. Cohn knows her stuff, too."

Trista was just glad to be along for the ride, no matter where Dale was headed. When he put his hand on her lap, she returned the favor in a spot that made Dale nearly swerve.

"We don't have time for a rest stop, honey," Dale said with a laugh. "Soon enough, though. When you see me in that gold suit, you won't be able to resist."

Nudie Cohn had passed away a few years earlier, but the legacy he had built from adorning Elvis in his gold suit and being the clothier to Hollywood's greatest stars had endured.

"Right on time!" Dale said as they pulled to a stop in front of Nudie's Rodeo Tailors.

Since Nudie's death his wife and granddaughter had taken over the operation, and they had agreed to make a replica of the famed gold suit for Dale to wear at the 10th anniversary.

"May I help you?" a young man asked as they stepped to the front counter.

"Yes, my name is Dale Gant, and I have an appointment with Mrs. Cohn."

"Eddie, send them right back here," a voice said from the back.

They headed to the back of the store where Mrs. Cohn had shimmering gold material laid out for inspection.

"This is the exact same material Nudie used for Elvis," she said with pride. "I hear you are going to be the last performer at his tribute. What an honor! Priscilla must think very highly of you."

"Well, yes, I guess so," Dale said with an unusual tone that made both Trista and Mrs. Cohn cast a quizzical look at each other.

"Well, when you called, I thought the gold suit would be a perfect touch," Mrs. Cohn said.

She called for James, her master tailor, to get Dale's measurements.

"42 chest. 34 waist. 33 inseam," James said as he worked his cloth tape measure.

"Remarkable. If I'm not mistaken, those numbers are exactly matched to Mr. Presley's, God rest his soul," Mrs. Cohn said. "It will be a rush, but we will have your suit ready for you, Mr. Gant."

Dale cupped her hand and kissed it lightly.

"You are a goddess, Mrs. Cohn," he said.

"You just be sure to do us proud in Memphis," she said.

"I will indeed, ma'am," Dale replied.

Dale and Trista bade farewell and headed out to the car.

"Trista, I think it is time to do some shopping for you," Dale said.

"I really don't need anything, as long as I'm with you," she said.

"Oh yes, you do, honey. The Anniversary Show is going to be a special event, and I want you to have the dress of your dreams to match," Dale said.

"You are the kindest man I know. Thank you," she said.

They headed out to the west end of the valley where all of the major department stores were located. They shopped in store after store until finally Trista found a navy blue, printed dress that matched her natural beauty perfectly.

"What do you think?" Trista asked as she held the dress to her body, with a look of assurance that she knew it would make Dale swoon.

"I think you will look spectacular!" he said. "Go try it on. I can't wait to see you in it."

Trista disappeared into the ladies dressing room and took her time to make sure she looked perfect before her entrance. The dress fell just above her knees, with thin shoulder straps, and hugged her form perfectly across her bust and waistline. The deep blue accentuated her golden tan.

"Wow!" was all Dale could say.

That was all Trista needed to hear.

"Why, thank you, sir," Trista said in her most formal tone as she struck a regal pose.

"We'll take it," Dale said to the clerk, who already was preparing to wrap the gown in chiffon and place it in a leather bag.

They headed to the shoe department, where Trista picked out a simple toeless pair of navy blue high heels that were the perfect complement. Dale insisted on a matching purse and some other accessories she liked before they left the store.

"Let's grab some lunch," Trista said before they reached the freeway again. "I like pure pleasure food when I'm so happy."

On the corner was a small stucco building with a sign on top that simply read, "Hot Dogs." Dale pulled to the curb, and they headed to the small window to order.

"How 'bout four of them chili dogs, with everything on 'em, and a couple of Cokes," he said to the girl inside.

They sat side-by-side at one of the small tables next to the stand and gorged themselves. Trista wiped a hunk of chili from the side of Dale's mouth and popped it in her mouth.

"Delicious!" she said with a girlish laugh.

"Will you kiss me even with nasty onion breath?" Dale asked.

Trista leaned over and gave him a chili kiss on the cheek.

The drive back to Santa Monica didn't seem to take too long as even the infamous L.A. traffic couldn't spoil their moods.

"Let's go down to the beach again," Dale said. "I'll even walk you down to the end of the pier to work off some of those calories."

"That sounds fun," Trista said. "I always like to see if the fishermen are catching anything."

They got into their suits—the thought of just staying naked crossed both of their minds—and headed for the Pacific. They walked slowly down the pier, people-watching as they held hands tightly. At the end of the pier four fishermen were enjoying the day even though their buckets were still filled mostly with chopped bait.

"How's the catch?" Dale asked.

"Well, it's a little slow today," one elderly man said. "But even if the fish aren't biting, it's still great to be out here with all the pretty girls like your wife."

Trista and Dale both laughed, a little nervously.

"She's not my wife, at least not yet," Dale told the old codger. "You can enjoy how pretty she is just the same."

Trista looked up at Dale with a shy smile on her face.

"What do you mean, *yet?*" she asked honestly.

"I was just playin' along," Dale said. "But I figure give us enough time and maybe we'll get there."

"Maybe," she said coyly and squeezed his hand tighter.

They stayed at the end of the pier to watch the burnt orange sun merge with the Pacific, ending what both were thinking had been one of the best days of their lives.

"Dale, will you spend the night with me again?" Trista asked.

"There's nothing I want more," he said. "I don't want to be any farther away from you than I am right now."

"I feel the same way," Trista said.

As they ambled, hands entwined, back along the pier toward the beach, they both spoke of their hopes and dreams.

"I want a quiet life, quality time, travel, and to be with the woman I love," Dale said. "Trista, you make me feel a special somethin' that I haven't felt in a long time. You are smart, gorgeous, and just a joy to be with."

"Thank you," she said shyly. "I have been waiting for someone like you, Dale. I wasn't sure you would ever come for me, though."

Dale leaned over to give her a kiss, and said, "Let's walk down the beach a bit. It's such a beautiful evening."

They pulled off their sandals, let their toes mingle with the sand, and searched their souls. Dale asked Trista how she wanted to spend her life, where she wanted to go, and what were her dreams.

"My dreams are to be with someone like you," she said honestly. "I want a home by the beach, a special place to grow old with the man I love."

Trista put her arm around Dale's waist and pulled him closer.

"I guess we are of the same mind—and body," she said as they embraced tightly, fell on the sand as one and kissed passionately. They barely noticed as a surge of surf from the incoming tide rolled up and over their bodies.

"Oh God, we're soaked!" Trista giggled as she rolled on top of Dale.

"Hold that thought, honey," Dale said as staggered to his feet.

They walked through the sand, laughing at each other's wet predicament but loving the innocence of the moment.

"Is it OK if I jump in the shower?" Dale asked as they reached her apartment.

"Only if I can jump in with you, cowboy!" Trista said.

"You're on, honey, but remember tomorrow it's time to go back to the real world," Dale said.

"Do we really have to do that?" she pleaded.

"Maybe one of these days we can just shut out the world, get lost in each other," Dale said.

"But not tomorrow," Trista said.

"No, but we still have tonight," Dale said as he pulled her naked body into the shower.

Their lovemaking grew more intense, more intimate, as they discovered the secrets of each other's desires. Dale barely heard the first note of the first set as he fell into a deep sleep, with Trista tucked in his embrace. Their bodies had barely moved when the alarm shocked them both back to reality at 6 A.M.

"I just want to lay here with you," Trista said, "but the breakfast boys will be showing up at 7:30, as usual."

"Yeah, and Mike said he has someone he wants me to meet today before the next performance," Dale sighed. "Still, these were two of the best days of my life."

They stole one last, desperate embrace, each wishing the intensity of their passions could keep the world at bay.

"Are you coming to the show tonight?" Dale asked.

"Well, I have the morning shift again Wednesday, but can I stay at the hotel with you?" Trista asked.

"You bet," Dale said. "No problem at all."

"So long as you don't wear me out, baby," she said and gave him a quick kiss while cinching up her apron.

"I'll do my best," Dale said.

"Mmm, promises, promises."

They parted outside the doorway with a passionate kiss that prompted Trista's neighbor, old Mrs. Langley, to let out a wolf whistle.

"You go, honey," Mrs. Langley shouted as Dale and Trista climbed in their cars and shared a silent laugh before departing.

Trista spent every night at the hotel, and every night both of them gleefully broke their dual promises not to wear out the other before the next day's duties. By Saturday night, Mike had hired two more bouncers to keep the crowds in order. Larry and the boys working the door were making a nice side business taking $100 for the best seats in the house and half that for *any* seat. Saturday's first set started off with a bang encouraged by an enthusiastic crowd. Dale and the boys played "You Were Always on My Mind," and the crowd exploded with applause. They worked in some requests. Between breaks Dale would mingle with the crowd and spend the rest of the time with Trista. By the time the band struck up a chord for the last song of the third set, it was standing room only in the lounge. Dale Gant had turned The Bonaventure lounge, previously a spot where a guy could get a drink in peace while listening to a dead-end act, into the hottest spot in Hollywood. Good thing the Fire Marshal wasn't around because he would be trying to shut down the place … or be seen stuffing a Benjamin into one of the bouncer's palms for a table with a view of the dance floor.

"I'd like to dedicate the last song of the night to the beautiful woman at the bar," Dale said.

Several females perked up at the thought of being honored, but Dale's intentions were clear.

"It's called "What's She's Really Like," and this one's for you, Trista," Dale said.

He worked the crowd with a deft touch for making people feel special after the final number. A tall, handsome man in his mid-30s didn't bother to vie for Dale's attention. He knew the best way to get noticed.

"Hi, my name is Dan Walker," he said to Trista. "I'd like to buy you a drink, and I ensure you my intentions are in the best interests of Mr. Gant. But I must say you look very beautiful this evening."

"Why, thank you, Mr. Walker. I'd love another lemon water," Trista said.

Larry the bartender knew his important clients well, and he was quick to serve Mr. Walker.

"Two lemon waters, Larry, as I'm sure Mr. Gant will be thirsty as well, and a whiskey sour for me," he said.

Dale noticed the competition and quickly cut a swath through the crowd, headed for the open bar stool next to Trista.

"I took the liberty of ordering you a lemon water," Mr. Walker said as he motioned Dale to sit down next to Trista.

"I'd like to talk business for a moment, if that is OK with you, Mr. Gant," he said. "I haven't seen this place so lively in years. I hear it used to get hoppin' once in a while, but not since the Rat Pack stopped in back in the '50s. Your performance was very impressive."

"Why, thank you, Mr. Walker," Dale said and made no bones about pulling Trista close. She greatly enjoyed his show of jealousy.

"What do you have on your mind?" Dale asked.

Mr. Walker pulled a decorative case from his pocket, and handed a card to Dale.

"I am the President of Artist Development for CBS Records," Mr. Walker said. "I'd like you to come into the studio and do some recording."

"Oh, my God, Dale!" Trista said. "You have to do it. Everyone needs to hear your gift. He really is amazing, Mr. Walker."

"Well, I wouldn't be here if we didn't recognize some real talent," Mr. Walker said. "What do you say, Dale?"

"Well, I don't know for sure," Dale said, his reply just a stall to get his thoughts in order. His inner voice was running this dialogue.

"Hot damn, Ace!" he heard from within. "You've been out of the spotlight for 10 long years. This is you, what you were born to be. Show these people what music is all about!"

Dale shook his head noticeably before speaking aloud.

"Thank you for the opportunity, Mr. Walker, but I am only here for another week," Dale said, trying to convince himself that he wasn't enticed by the offer. "Then I'm committed to an engagement in Memphis. After that, who knows? I plan on returning home for a while, I guess."

Trista wanted to stay out of the conversation, but her enthusiasm couldn't be contained.

"Baby, every time I've heard you play, people are amazed. I'm amazed," she said. "Why wouldn't you want to share that?"

"Well, maybe you just don't understand yet that music is my sanctity—and my curse," Dale said. "God, I wish it was just that easy to share with people for the pure joy that music brings. But there's always the other side, the demons that come with it. I just don't think I'm ready to go there again."

Trista, more so than Dan, was stunned by the emotion of Dale's response, though neither could question his sincerity.

"Are you OK?" Trista said as she cupped Dale's hands.

"Yeah, baby, I'm fine," Dale said. "I just don't know what I'm thinkin' or feelin' right now."

Mr. Walker, being used to dealing with artistic genius, was unflappable.

"Well, Dale, we'd love to have just a few hours of your time. Come over and take a tour of the studios, if nothing else. I'm sure you would at least find it interesting."

"Let me think it over," Dale said. "And thank you for coming down tonight, Mr. Walker."

"OK, Dale, you have my card," Mr. Walker said. "I think you have a very promising career, if you choose to pursue it. If you don't believe me, just listen to the crowd tonight."

"Yeah, the crowd can be intoxicating, Mr. Walker," Dale said, "but, you know, those people aren't always your friends."

Dale was quiet as he and Trista made their way back to No. 32.

"You sure you are OK?" she asked as Dale disrobed and climbed into bed.

"I'll be just fine, sweetheart," he said. "I just have some things weighing on my mind right now. Heavy on my mind."

Tuesday morning he rousted Jerry earlier than usual and asked his friend to accompany him to North Hollywood to pick up his suit from Nudie Cohn's.

"Jerry, I have some things I'd like to talk to you about," Dale said as they pulled onto the freeway heading north.

"Go ahead, boss," Jerry said.

"A guy needs people around him who can be trusted," Dale said. "You know, someone to go to with the tough questions. Someone who will come back with the right answer, and not just because they're being paid for it, you know?"

"Yeah, I guess. What's your point?" Jerry asked, which made Dale smile because that was exactly what a trusted confidante should say in that situation.

"Well, Jerry, I have this gig coming up in Memphis. We've talked about it," Dale said, not getting to the point.

"Yes, we have," Jerry replied, pushing the conversation back to its resolution.

"Well, I'm wondering if you would take a job being my driver for the week while I'm in Memphis?" Dale asked.

"Why do I get the feeling that driving won't be my only occupation, Dale?"

"Because you are the right guy for the job, Jerry. I'm not sure what I'm walking into out there. I don't think there will be trouble, not like in dangerous stuff or anything, but still it could get a little sticky. I've asked Trista to come. I just need a guy with a good head on his shoulders to keep an eye out for me, keep a cool head, give me the right advice. I really think you are that guy, Jerry."

"Well, boss, I'll have to clear it with Mrs. Skeen first, that's for sure. Other than that, I'm no tough guy, so don't get me into anything I can't handle."

"Driving and advice, that's all, plus a free ticket to see what should be one helluva show."

"Sounds like fun, boss."

"Perfect. I'll make sure Mike gives you the time off. He's wantin' to do anything to get me back at The Bonaventure for another gig," Dale said as they pulled up to Nudie's. "Now, how 'bout you come in with me and make sure that gold suit looks good."

Mrs. Cohn was expecting them, and she sounded excited on the phone to show off her latest masterpiece.

"Mr. Gant, it's so nice to see you again," Mrs. Cohn said as the bell on the shop door snapped her to attention. "James, please bring up Mr. Gant's suit. You are going to look divine in it. I just know it!"

214

James arrived packing the suit in both arms since it weighed an astonishing 35 pounds with gold sequins adorning the entire front from head to toe. The sequins were set against gold and white leather patterns. Red sequins added the look of flames licking up each sleeve.

"Absolutely amazing!" Dale said. "I'll be right back to show it off."

While Dale took the suit to the changing room, Mrs. Cohn pulled out some old pictures of Elvis Presley in the shop with Nudie and showed them to Jerry.

"That's one of Elvis and Nudie in 1969, right before The Comeback," Mrs. Cohn said.

Dale emerged from the dressing room and struck a pose for everyone to admire.

"My gosh, if that doesn't bring back the memories!" Mrs. Cohn said.

"Yeah, Boss, some sideburns and a little black hair dye and you'll have everyone thinking they're seeing a ghost in Memphis," Jerry said. "Speaking of which, check out these pictures in Mrs. Cohn's scrapbook. They're amazing!"

Dale looked down at the faded Polaroid as if trying to access the memory in his brain.

"Yeah, that was a good one," he finally said, prompting quizzical looks from Jerry and Mrs. Cohn. "Well, anyway, let me take care of the bill right now, and I can't thank you enough, Mrs. Cohn," Dale said.

"Like I said, honey, you just make us proud on that stage in Memphis," she said.

"Will do, ma'am. Will do."

Dale had some news for the boys when they met Tuesday afternoon to warm up for the coming week.

"Boys, I'll cut right to the chase," Dale said. "An executive for Sunset Records has asked me to come down to their studios and do some recording. At first I told him I wasn't interested, but I've been thinking. You've all been true professionals and have had my back every step of the way since we've been playin' here at The Bonaventure. It's been like old times, like when I first got started and played music for the sheer joy of performing and making people smile. I've been wonderin' how I could ever repay that debt, but I think a studio session to lay down some tracks just might do it. I'm game if you boys are up for it, but I'm not goin' without you. And that's final!"

"Hell, yes!" Jack said excitedly. "I think I can speak for all of us when I say we're with you all the way."

Billie, Al, and Perry quickly nodded in agreement.

"When are we going?" Perry asked.

"Well, I'll call Mr. Walker right now and make arrangements," Dale said.

The Boys couldn't hide their smiles, and the thought of recording in a major studio had them all in tune as The Bonaventure welcomed another raucous crowd that evening.

Dale called Dan Walker first thing Wednesday morning to set up a session.

"Mr. Walker, we're ready to come over and lay down some tracks at your studio," Dale said. "But the deal includes all my guys who have been playing with me at The Bonaventure."

"That is certainly good news, Mr. Gant," Walker said. "By all means, you may choose the recording artists to accompany you and the material. Of course, we'll have to discuss rights to the material. We have a studio open Thursday morning."

"We want rights to half of whatever comes from what we record, however it's used." Dale said. "I trust your people can have a contract ready for us before we take the stage."

"Absolutely, Mr. Gant," Walker said. "Of course, there are no promises as to what may come of the session. We just want to bring you in, see what happens, and go from there."

"We'll be there with bells on, Mr. Walker," Dale said.

He broke the news to the Boys before their Wednesday gig, which produced synergy in the group that brought them to new heights. Trista showed up midway through the third act, and Dale couldn't wait to share the news.

"Hey, I've got some good news," Dale said as he slid into his spot at the end of the bar that Larry kept reserved for the two of them. "We're doing a recording session tomorrow at Sunset Records. I'm taking the Boys with me."

"Dale! That's wonderful," Trista said. "You all have to share your gift with the world!"

"Don't get too excited, honey," Dale cautioned. "We're just gonna do some recording and see what happens. I'm more excited for the Boys than anything. I'm gonna take them along for the ride, but I'm not sure I want to get on that roller-coaster again. It's kinda hard to get off, you know?"

"Damnit, Dale!" Trista said with a scolding but loving tone. "What you need is a good manager, someone who has your best interests in mind, someone you trust won't screw you."

"Well, honey, I guess that rules you out," Dale said while pulling back quickly from the elbow he knew would be forthcoming.

"Don't be a jerk! I'm serious," Trista said.

"Well, as managers go, I've had me one of the best—and worst—dependin' on how you look at it," Dale said. "Let's just let it ride, okay?

"Okay, mister, but just know this conversation isn't over," Trista said as she leaned back in to give Dale a kiss but gave his earlobe a soft bite instead.

"Dang, girl, don't you know I'm destined to be a star someday? You've gotta treat me nice!" Dale said as he pulled Trista in for the real thing.

He and the Boys looked the part of budding stars as they brought The Bonaventure crowd to a boil. Just a few more nights, Dale thought as they finished a rousing encore, and this roll will be over. When Thursday morning arrived, Jerry brought out the limo to deliver Dale and the Boys to Sunset Records headquarters. Dan Walker was there to greet them and led the way to a conference room where some suits and secretaries were already seated.

"Welcome, gentlemen," Walker said. "I'd like to introduce you to Mr. Lewis, our lead attorney who has your recording contract for today at the ready. I could have him go through the entire contract, line by line, but basically it boils down to this: Whatever comes out of this session, and you have the lead on that note, will be shared mutually, 50-50, by all parties involved. That's all of you and Sunset Records. Just know that we have everything to gain by treating you 100% fairly. You are the talent, and we are the vehicle that drives that talent. One doesn't benefit without the other. And, most importantly, you have my word."

"That sounds good to me," Dale said. "Boys, you good with signin' on here?"

Jack took the lead as the unofficial spokesperson for the group of musicians, who'd never been this close to fame before and wouldn't be anywhere near this close without Dale Gant.

"We're all on board, Mr. Walker," Jerry said. "Let's just go play some music."

They put pen to paper, slid the documents toward the suits, who in turn inspected the signatures briefly and shuffled the papers toward the secretaries.

"Okay, then, right this way gentlemen," Walker said with a genuine smile.

They were led through a maze of corridors and into a studio fit ... for a King.

"Damn, I wish my apartment was half this big," Al said.

"Yeah, and I wish mine was a quarter this clean," Perry echoed.

A tall, skinny dude wearing jeans and a tie-dye shirt with horn-rimmed glasses and a neat ponytail was in charge.

"My name's Tony, everyone. Just go ahead and settle in wherever you feel comfortable. We'll do some tests and get started whenever you are ready."

Jack settled in behind the 10-piece Gretsch Classic drum set. Perry hammered a few chords on a Music Man Sterling 4 Classic bass, and Al made time with a Gibson Firebird. Dale just sat back and took in the scene with an amused, contented look.

"Just like old times," he said to himself before showing everyone who was really in control.

"Okay, Boys, you ready?" Dale said as he picked up an acoustic Gibson and stepped in front of the mic. "Let's show 'em what we've got."

They started with "Gentle on My Mind" to ease into things and rolled through everything that had made them a sensation at The Bonaventure. After two hours of listening to their magic, Tony only had one question.

"You guys have a name?" he asked. "I need to put something on the label."

"Nothing official," Dale said, "but for now you can call us the 'Venture Kings. Sound good, Boys?"

"Call us whatever you want so long as I hear some of that on the radio," Jack said.

"That kind of thing can happen mighty quick," Dale said with a wistful look.

Dan Walker stepped into the studio and shook hands all around. He knew what greatness looked—and sounded—like, but he didn't get to the top of a media conglomerate by overreacting.

"Gentlemen, I'd say that was a major success," Walker said. "Of course, nothing will move forward without your blessing, but I'm very optimistic."

"Thank you, Mr. Walker," Dale said. "If nothing else, I'd say this was an experience to remember." The look on the faces of the Boys more than agreed.

The 'Venture Kings had three more nights together to rock their home turf, and they would make them count. Larry had makeshift valet parking in place by Friday night, and you needed to be—or at least know—someone to get a seat at The Bonaventure for Saturday's closing act. Mike Martinez stepped to the mic to introduce an act that he hoped would make a return appearance, but knew was one that had outgrown his stage.

"Ladies and gentlemen, I introduced Mr. Dale Gant here just a few short weeks ago," Mike began. "I knew he was great then, but I had no idea what he would bring to this stage. It has been, truly, an incredible run. So, without further ado, Mr. Dale Gant!"

Dale had thought about this moment for some time. It represented a return to the past, and all the while a glimpse into an uncertain future. All he knew in his heart was that he had found his roots.

"Folks, I want to thank Mr. Martinez for bringing us together," he said with a sweeping hand to the Boys. "I get the fanfare, but you are going to be treated to a group of musicians tonight who are true professionals. Ladies and gentlemen, we are going to tear the house down! I give you the 'Venture Kings! Hit it, Boys."

Dale was spent when the show was over, but tonight he'd make sure the music played on.

"Boys, y'all are coming up to the suite for a while tonight," Dale said after the final encore. The newly-minted 'Venture Kings obliged, with a bunch of their new friends. Trista was there, too, wondering where she fit in with the throng of party-goers.

"Dale, honey, how are you?" Trista said as she pulled him aside for some attention.

"I'm good, just windin' down, you know?" Dale said.

"Yes, what I caught tonight was amazing," she said. "I'd like to have some alone time, though. I want your lovin', and we have to talk about being ready for Memphis, too."

"Yeah, baby, we'll get there," Dale said as he double-timed with the crowd that was bursting the walls of the suite.

"So, is this what you were like when you were 'famous'?" Trista asked above the din. "If so, maybe I don't really want to know all about it."

Her words separated Dale from the throng, retraced his mind's eye to many years past, similar scenes when he paid attention to the wrong people.

"Honey, you're right," Dale said as he grabbed Trista and gave her a re-assuring hug. "I'll send them home, and we can be together. OK?"

"Yes. I'll be waiting," she said.

Billie and Perry headed off into the night with a new batch of groupies. Al gave Dale a big hug and headed for who knows where. Jack commanded a quick pow wow before exiting.

"Boss, you're the best thing that ever happened to this group of nobodies," he said. "If that record deal amounts to anything, we'll be forever grateful. But, most importantly, you've made some friends who will do anything for you. I don't know what you're heading for in Memphis, but I can tell you are a little wary about it. I ain't asking, and I don't expect you to be telling. Just watch your ass. And if you need anything, you know where to come."

"Thanks, man," Dale said as he clapped a big embrace around his drummer. "You are the best."

Dale sensed Trista still had hurt feelings over last night, so he had a proposition to brighten her spirits at breakfast.

"I'll tell you what, let's borrow Jerry's convertible and get out of town. Just drive up the coast, find a nice, quiet place to stay and leave the city behind for a bit. How's that sound?"

"Well, we have to pack for the trip, but I can take Wednesday off, too," Trista said as she quickly showed a smile of forgiveness. "I'm with you. Wherever that takes me."

Jerry was more than happy to lend Dale and Trista the Mustang. They headed north, caught the 101 past Oxnard and breezed past Santa Barbara in no time. Trista chatted some more about her past. Dale seemed lost in his thoughts, but was obviously enjoying the freedom of motoring with the top down and no particular destination in mind.

"How far are you planning to go?" Trista asked as they put Santa Maria in the rearview mirror. "Not sure. What's next on the map?" Dale asked.

"Pismo Beach. Past that, I'm not really sure because I haven't been any farther."

"Well then, honey, we need to go!" Dale said with a laugh. "Pismo sounds good for tonight, though. Isn't that the famous place for clams?"

"Yeah, it's a fun little tourist town," Trista said. "I was up there a few years ago for the Clam Festival. That was a crazy adventure!"

"You can tell me all about it while we walk on the beach tonight," Dale said. "Then tomorrow maybe we can drive up and see the Hearst Castle. I've read about it and always wanted to go there. If ever there was a dude that was driven crazy by too much fortune and fame, ol' William Randolph Hearst has to be the man. Did you know he has a full-sized pool, decked out all in real gold tiles?"

"Then what, all the way to San Francisco? Seattle by sundown, maybe? You plan on taking me back home anytime soon, Mr. Gant?"

"I'll have you back in L.A. before sundown tomorrow evening, young lady," Dale said. "But it sure does feel good to get away."

Dale had the urge to just keep driving, to run away forever with Trista. But he knew that was fool's gold. No amount of running would separate him from the future that was waiting for him in Memphis.

They booked a room at the Pismo Beach Hotel, an historic getaway where Clark Gable filmed *Strange Cargo* in 1937. After dinner at the famous Shell Beach restaurant, the ocean beckoned.

"There are some things I'd like to talk to you about," Dale said as he clasped Trista's hand and led her along the shoreline.

"I'm listening," she said, hoping that this would be the moment Dale would open up about his past.

"Everything has been such a whirlwind since we met," he began. "We really haven't had time to talk seriously."

"Yes. Go on," she beckoned.

"First, I want you to know that I've never been more honest in my life than when I told you I love you," Dale said.

"I love you too, and I mean that with all my heart," Trista replied.

"Second, I want to know how much you trust me?" Dale asked.

"Well, my head tells me to ask why, but my heart is with you all the way."

"I'll tell you why … because I really don't know what is going to happen in Memphis."

"What do you mean? You're going to play at the Anniversary, right?"

"That's the plan, but my past might … not might, *will* catch up to me there. I just know it. I'm not really sure what will happen then. I'd give anything to be able to tell you about it, but I just can't. I don't think you will be in any danger, though. So, like I said, I need to know how much you trust me."

Trista continued to walk, pretended to have her gaze captured by the setting sun, but she couldn't hide the tear that was running down her cheek.

"Dale, I'm scared," she said finally. "I know I love you. I know you are a good man. I know, more than anything, I want to be with you. But … what is it? What can't you tell me? If you love someone, you are supposed to be able to tell them anything!"

Trista shook her hand free, turned from Dale and sobbed openly.

"I *will* tell you. I promise on everything I hold sacred. But only when it's safe. Only when we are safe. If you want to walk away, I won't blame you. So, I ask you again, how much do you trust me?"

"With my life," Trista said as she turned to face Dale once again. "Is that enough?"

Dale pulled her close and tried to wrap his arms around her entire world, as if his embrace could protect her from whatever harm may come her way because of their relationship.

"Trista, your life is my life," Dale said.

They made love passionately and desperately that evening, both feeling if this was their last night together it would also be their best. They made the trek to Hearst Castle in the morning, marveled at William Randolph's gold-flaked pool, and wondered how someone who had it all could end up leading such a tragic life. By sundown Monday evening, Trista was back in her apartment, preparing for what would turn out to be her last day of work at the diner.

Dale used an early meeting with Mike as an excuse to return to the hotel Monday night. What he really needed was some alone time to contemplate his strategy for what promised to be one of the most eventful weeks of his life, former and current.

Sleep overtook Dale easily that evening. His dreams could not escape the rising anxiety he felt about what awaited him in Memphis. Dale was sitting on the bluff that overlooks the Pacific Ocean at Hale ke`oke`o. He was scanning the sea and surf for the familiar form of Ikaika as he had done so many times in the past. Instead, a huge, ghostly image arose from the sand and hovered directly in front of Dale. Noelani's features were unmistakable despite the wavering form of the visage.

"God has given you a second chance … don't waste it," Noelani said in a hollow voice that echoed off the lava walls.

Dale tried to speak, but his mouth was clenched tight. A second image arose from the sand and joined Noelani. Dale recognized the chiseled features of a native islander, but it was not Ikaika.

"I've returned to the sea to be with my beloved husband, and now you must live your life," Noelani said in her hollow whisper.

The images turned to sparkles and swirled as one into the shape of a spear. The spear darted toward the sea and danced over the surf before disappearing into the horizon.

Dale stayed asleep through the dream, but it was still vivid when his eyes opened slowly in the dawn hours. He lay in bed for some time, staring and thinking. He became certain of what must be done before he rose to face the daylight.

Dale had planned to spend his final days in California with Trista at her place as she packed for their trip, but instead he asked Mike for at least one more night's lodging when they met to close out Dale's contract. Mike was more than happy to oblige as he continued to do anything possible to secure more performances from the 'Venture Kings.

Dale did anything he could to stay busy ... other than watching the big clock in his room count down the minutes to when Trista would be off work and expecting him. Jerry would be waiting at 2 P.M. sharp to escort him in the Mustang. At 1:55, Dale pulled the Green Book from its hiding place in the hotel safe and placed it in a large shopping bag. He plodded his way downstairs.

"You're a little quieter than usual," Jerry said as they pulled onto the 405 in the growing afternoon traffic. "Worried about the Memphis gig?"

"That too, but more what I have to do before we take off," Dale said before turning his gaze out the window and away from Jerry.

"Wait here," Dale said to Jerry as they pulled up to Trista's apartment. "I won't be long."

Trista threw open the door with a big smile that wasn't returned from her beau.

"What's wrong, babe?" she asked immediately.

Dale walked to the couch and sat down without speaking a word. The look on his face set the tone to way beyond serious.

"Wow, you look stressed," Trista said. "Can I get you ... ?"

"No, just please sit down," Dale said emphatically. "There's something you must know."

Dale struggled mightily. Just blurt it out, "I'm Elvis freaking Presley!" his mind suggested. Finally, he found the words to relay that message, but not the courage to speak them directly.

"When we were up north you said you trusted me with your life," Dale began.

"Yes, I do," Trista insisted.

"What I'm going to tell you, what I'm going to let you discover, will come as a shock. Perhaps not.

"Perhaps you've wondered about my true identity. Well, I can't say the words. I can't utter my former name." Dale's voice trailed off as he felt a return to the dream state.

"And ..." Trista demanded.

"And it's all here," Dale said as he pulled the Green Book from the shopping bag. "My life story, from the beginning."

Trista sat with a look of shock and disbelief on her face. Dale thought of passing the Green Book to Trista right then, but he stuck to his plan.

"You can't open this until I have gone," he said. "I'll go back to the hotel and give you space. I'm going to Memphis, with or without you. Once you've read what's in these pages, you can decide. I stayed silent once, thinking my past wouldn't catch up to me, but I was wrong. Someone I loved very much paid the price for my selfishness, but I can't let that happen to you. I have to tell you the truth, and you can decide where we go from here."

Huge tears were streaming down Trista's face.

"How will I know what to do?" she asked.

"In times like these, I've always asked for help from above," Dale said.

That actually brought a chuckle from Trista through her tears.

"Thank you, silly, but I meant how will you know what I decide?"

"I want you to take tonight and the whole day tomorrow to think about it. We're staying at the Radisson near the airport tomorrow night to beat the traffic Thursday morning. Jerry and I will be here tomorrow evening to pick you up. Then you can tell me if you are ready to face the future with me ... or not."

Dale set the Green Book on an end table near the door and turned to leave. He had one last message before leaving Trista to discover the truth.

"No other living person has read this. I'm sharing this secret with you and you only. As you read this, please remember how much I love you and want to spend the rest of my life with you."

"I love you, too," Trista said as Dale nodded and walked out the door.

Dale was exhausted, emotionally at least, when he arrived back at No. 32. Sleep came easily, a surprise that Dale took as a good omen when he awoke. Dale summoned Jerry and thought of anything they could do to keep busy and not dwell on what Trista may be thinking. They had one last lunch with Mike Martinez and stopped by Sunset Records to see how things were going with production. Finally, it was time to hit the freeway and head for Trista's apartment.

"Jerry, I have to level with you about my situation with Trista," Dale began. "I told her about what may be waiting for me in Memphis and gave her time to consider if she really wants to be involved. She may or may not be going with us. We'll know soon enough."

"So you know, I promised Mrs. Skeen I'd stay out of trouble," Jerry said. "I hope you're not talking about anything illegal or too dangerous."

"Jerry, I would never put you in harm's way or ask you to break the law," Dale said emphatically. "I trust your instincts and may need your advice, that's all. I don't believe I will be in any danger, either. But there could be a major revelation that will affect the rest of my life. Best-case scenario is we avoid any confrontations, play a great show, and move forward."

"OK, I trust you too, boss."

Dale was never more nervous in his life as the Mustang turned onto Trista's street. He wanted to give her space, encouraged her not to contact him, but now he wished she had ignored that advice and had made the first move. As the Mustang pulled to the curb, Dale and Jerry could see an array of colorful items adorning the rail leading up to Trista's second-story door.

"Those are yellow ribbons, lots of 'em," Jerry said.

"Yeah, I can't believe it," Dale said.

He'd crossed paths with the members of Tony Orlando and Dawn more than once and loved their "Tie a Yellow Ribbon Round the Ole Oak Tree," which topped the charts for four weeks in the spring of 1973.

Dale sprinted up the stairs because he also knew a yellow ribbon signified the welcome return of a person from exile. Trista threw open the door before he could knock.

225

"That's a lot of ribbons, babe," Dale said.

"100 to be exact, my love," Trista said as they leaped into each other's arms.

"I'm ready for all of it," Trista whispered into Dale's ear.

He was still too stunned to respond. The pressure of carrying a secret all those years finally was being released, and Dale wept.

"Does Jerry know?" Trista finally asked.

"No, only you, and I plan to keep it that way," Dale said as he tried to regain his composure.

Trista motioned Dale into the apartment to help with her bags. She unwittingly had that star-struck pose and jaw hanging open look that Dale had seen so many times before.

"Dale, I have so many questions," Trista said excitedly. "I can't believe that you are, or were, or … it's so strange! I can't believe that you were *him*."

Dale grabbed Trista firmly by the shoulders and moved his face directly in front of hers.

"First, thank you for not using that name," he said. "Second, take a good, long look at me. I'm Dale Gant, and to you that's who I always will be."

Trista shook off the reverie of being with "him" and returned to the moment. She kissed Dale, exploring to see if the sensation would be the same.

"OK, I'm coming to grips with this, but I still have a million questions," she said.

Dale cut her off before she began a conversation that may take days, even years, to exhaust.

"We can talk at the hotel, all night if you want," Dale said. "Right now we need to get on our way and not keep Jerry waiting any longer."

During the ride to the airport hotel Trista sat close to Dale in the back seat and kept scanning his face for any hint of plastic surgery. Dale eventually grew tired of the scrutiny and pulled the skin on his temples to make squinty eyes at Trista.

"Relax, babe, it's still me," he whispered into her ear.

Jerry settled into the room across the hall, which put Dale more at ease as Trista launched into her questions.

"How'd you manage to leave your daughter behind? That seems so cruel and selfish."

"Well, I didn't realize that at first. It kind of started out as a fantasy, you know, and I was only thinking about escaping the spotlight. Once I set things in motion, though, it was impossible to stop. In the end, I went through with it because of the undying love I have for my daughter. I had to protect her."

"Was your life really that miserable? I mean, you had everything a person could ever want."

"I had all the things that regular people think they would want if they were rich and famous. But I had none of the good things in life that people take for granted."

"Such as?"

"Such as being able to walk down the street and not have people screaming and tearing at your clothes. Trust me, it's really weird."

"Your wife in Hawaii, Noelani, what was she like?

"Very quiet, but very beautiful inside."

"Did you love her more than you love me?"

"I think God has given people unlimited ability to love, in many different ways, but we let other emotions get in the way. Ikaika, Noelani's brother, and my brother in spirit, taught me that. Our love is different, but even stronger."

"Will you love me forever?"

"Yes, and I'm going to prove it," Dale said as he gently pulled Trista onto the king-sized bed. Dale started his massage on Trista's feet and worked his way up her calves and thighs, lightly brushing over her womanhood. He worked her entire back and finished with a deep shoulder rub.

"See what I mean," Dale whispered into her ear before rolling over and pretending to sleep.

"Not getting off that easy, mister," Trista said as she rubbed Dale and gained an immediate arousal. They made love with their usual intensity—enough to make Dale doubly glad that Jerry was across the hall and not next door—but also with a sense of freedom that didn't exist before. At least for now, the nagging doubts in the recesses of their minds over where their relationship was going had disappeared. The doubts of what awaited them in Memphis were stronger than ever.

"I want to know more about Memphis," Trista said after she caught her breath.

"Well, we're going there to do the show," Dale said.

"Aren't you afraid of this detective, and what he might do? What if he shares your secret with the world?"

"Well, he still has no proof, just his word. And who's going to really believe such a story? The tabloids have been making it up for years. He'd likely just be seen as a fool. It's up to us to make sure we play it cool."

"You're bound to meet your first wife and your daughter. What happens then? How do you know how you will react?"

"I don't know for certain how I will react, but I've finally lifted the burden of keeping that secret by sharing it with you. Now I have to make sure it stays just between us."

"Oh, God, Dale! Why can't we just get a plane ticket to the other side of the world and start a new life? The FBI is out of your life now. We don't have to go through with this!"

"Something inside tells me that I have to go through with it, that I'll never be rid of my demons until I take that stage and perform, until I make peace with my former life and the people who were in it."

"You're going to tell them who you are, your wife and daughter! I know it!"

"No! Seeing them will be enough. One last performance will be enough. I swear it!"

CHAPTER EIGHT

Trista slept like a buzzsaw throughout the flight, but Dale was lost in thought, staring out at the passing clouds and the patchwork of jagged mountains, desolate mesas, and occasional farms on the ground below as the plane made its way east across Arizona, New Mexico, and Texas. His somber spirits lifted as the scenery below turned mostly a deep, lush green as the plane approached the Deep South. Even 35,000 miles in the air, Dale imagined he could smell home. He drifted into a light sleep and could see his mom and dad as a young couple on the porch of their home in Tupelo.

"Ding, ding, ding … This is your Captain speaking …"

Dale stirred from his reverie and Trista gave one last snort before waking from her deep slumber.

"Are we there yet?" Trista teased as she opened a second eye and leaned over to kiss Dale on the cheek.

"Not quite, but everyone can take out their earplugs now that you're awake," Dale said.

Trista ground an elbow into his side, not too hard but enough to draw a reaction.

"Just kiddin'," Dale said quickly. "Truth is you look even more beautiful when you're sleeping." Trista seemed satisfied with the retraction as Dale pulled down their carry-on bags and they shuffled toward the exit.

"Welcome to Jackson, The City with Soul," the airline representative said as Dale, Trista, and Jerry emerged from their four-hour flight. Dale chose

229

Jackson because he wanted to show Trista around the South some, but also to be as incognito as possible coming into Memphis. He didn't want Nick Sartain or any other interference waiting to greet them. Dale had demanded to make his own hotel reservations as well, instead of staying at the reunion hotel with the other musicians. Jerry was in on the idea of laying low to avoid any trouble, but he was below Dale and Trista's knowledge level.

"We'll get to see a little of the countryside before heading into town," Dale said as they packed their bags into the minivan. "Jerry, I know this ride isn't your usual style."

"It'll do just fine, boss," Jerry said as he climbed behind the wheel. "Next stop, Tupelo, the home of the one and only Elvis Presley. Those people will think The King has come home for sure when they see you."

Trista and Dale shared a sly smile at their private joke. The three checked into a downtown hotel close to the tourist sites. In the morning, they set out to tour the Elvis Presley Center, which includes the Elvis Birthplace, the Elvis Presley Museum and Memorial Chapel, and Elvis Presley Park.

"This is pretty much like I remember it," Dale announced as he stood on the wooden porch of the small white house from the 1930s.

"You didn't tell me you've been here before," Jerry said.

Trista was wide-eyed when she looked at Dale, but he remained calm.

"Yeah, I visited here once, but it's been quite a while," Dale said.

Inside the house, they looked at the living room scene that had been pre-served exactly the way it was in the early '50s.

"My gosh, you sure do look like him," an elderly lady said as Dale stood reminiscing over the scene.

"Why, thank you, Ma'am," Dale replied.

"And you even sound like him!" the lady said. "It's uncanny."

"It's all part of the act," Trista said as she rescued Dale from a growing crowd of onlookers and led him back outside.

"I'm starting to see things a little better from your point of view," she said after making sure Jerry was still inside and out of earshot.

"Darlin', times that by 10,000 and you're still not approaching the way it used to be," Dale said. "Even that much attention seems strange now after all these years. I don't miss that part one bit."

"It's such a small place. Dale, were you happy here during your childhood?"

"We were dirt poor, but yes, we were happy," Dale said. "My mom and dad both worked hard, but we spent evenings talking and singing. Sundays were reserved for church, and I enjoyed that, too. That's where I first learned the beauty of music. I've thought about my childhood often as I went through life being rich, but unhappy. I think it's one of the driving forces that brought me to where I am now."

"Well, I'm glad you made it here," Trista said as she gave Dale a heartfelt kiss on the forehead. Jerry stepped onto the porch just then.

"Hey, Jerry, I've had enough sightseeing for one morning. How about we hit the road and make our way toward Memphis? We can stop and get some real Southern cookin' for lunch along the way."

They pulled off at a barbecue pit along Highway 22 and sampled the spare ribs.

"Man, that's good," Jerry said as he wiped sauce from his lips. "How'd you know about this place?"

"The band used to stop here all the time when we were tourin'," Dale said. "Best ribs within 500 miles."

"When you were touring?" Jerry asked. "When was that? I'm realizing there's just so much I don't know about you."

Trista was wide-eyed again.

"It was back in the day, but that's not important now," Dale said, clearly shutting down any further inquiry.

Dale was quiet on the remaining hour-long drive into Memphis as he was literally rolling down memory lane. He'd made this trip hundreds of times and was amazed at the amount of development since his last visit. Trista, meanwhile, was getting excited.

"I can't wait to see Graceland, Beale Street, all of it," she said.

"Yeah, I've heard Memphis is really cool," Jerry replied.

"We can get out and about, but we're keeping a low profile all the same," Dale said. "Keep your eyes open for strangers."

The Memphis Hilton was the main hotel for the musicians and others who would be putting together the anniversary show for a crowd of 10,000 at Ellis Theatre. Dale instead requested a room at Heartbreak Hotel, right across the street from Graceland. He wanted to be as near home as possible. And he figured the last place a detective looking for him would suspect is the hotel right across the street from Graceland. Little did he know that Nick Sartain, head of security, knew exactly where every guest would be spending their nights in Memphis.

Dale was growing more nervous by the minute, but his stomach was never too upset for a good meal.

"Hey, you two, I am really in the mood for a good, old fashion cheeseburger," Dale said. "There is a place not too far from here called the Gridiron, and they make the best burgers in the South."

"That sounds great, but you're going to have to take me for a walk afterward," Jerry said. "This is stacking up to be at least a 10-pound trip."

"It's right downtown, so we can walk Beale Street, take in some of the shops, and even listen to some amazin' blues," Dale said.

"Ooh, that sounds wonderful," Trista said.

Graceland was on Dale's side as they pulled out from the hotel, and he took a long, foreboding look at his former home before turning to face Trista. She had been looking over his shoulder at the Presley Mansion in the distance and squeezed Dale tight.

"It's going to be OK," she whispered in his ear.

Entering the Gridiron was like walking right into the 1950s. They were greeted by the hostess who led them past pictures of Chuck Berry, Buddy Holly, Jerry Lee Lewis, and of course, The King of Rock 'n' Roll himself. A waitress who looked straight out of the Golden Era approached their table.

"Hi folks, I'm Mary, and welcome to the Gridiron," she said without making eye contact. "Are you ready to order, or do you need a few minutes?"

"We're ready now, ma'am," Dale said.

Mary let out an audible gasp, and she took a step backward when she saw Dale's face.

"Oh my, a shiver just went up my spine," she said. "Your looks and your voice! I have been here a long time and used to serve Elvis Presley in this very booth. You look almost like he did when I first met him. He changed a bit over the years, but I still remember him when he was young."

Now Dale was the one who looked like he was seeing a ghost. Trista spoke first and told Mary that Dale was in town for the 10-year Anniversary Tribute Concert and was going to be the final act of the night. Mary smiled and told them that Elvis used to come in at all hours of the night dressed in disguise and eat.

"Scotty Moore!" Mary exclaimed. "He would come in with Elvis and was always so nice to me. He came by the other day and couldn't believe I was still here. He gave me two tickets to the show!"

"Well, now, I hope I don't disappoint with my performance," Dale said.

"Something tells me you'll be wonderful," Mary said. "Now what would you like to eat? My treat." Dale tried to argue, but Mary would have none of it. They chowed on cheeseburgers, hush puppies, and fried pickles until they couldn't eat another bite.

When they returned to the hotel later that evening, they noticed an envelope with an ornate gold seal had been slid under the door while they were out. Dale bent over and picked it up as Trista and Jerry watched.

"What is it?" Trista asked excitedly.

Dale opened the envelope and announced it was a letter from the Presley Estate.

> Mr. Dale Gant,
>
> Thank you for being part of our celebration this week. We hope you find your hotel accommodations suitable. The concert is going to be held at Ellis Auditorium here in Memphis. Elvis sang there years ago, and we thought it would be the right venue to hold his memorial concert. The Ellis seats 10,000 people and was sold out within a day of our announcement of Elvis' 10-year tribute. Enclosed you will find seat assignments for the guests you have invited.
>
> All performers will have an opportunity to practice with the band this week. Your practice time is on Saturday afternoon at 1:00. Scotty Moore and other members of Elvis' band will be there. You are the only performer who will have The Jordanaires as your backup singers, and they will be there to work with you.
>
> On Friday evening, everyone along with their guests are invited to a private party at Graceland. Dress will be casual as that is the way Elvis would have liked it. Graceland

closes to the public at 6:00 P.M. and festivities will start at 8:00 P.M. We look forward to seeing you there and to your performance on Saturday night.

Respectfully,

Priscilla Presley

"Wow, this is so exciting!" Trista said.

Dale had managed to slip the card that was attached to the letter into his pocket without being noticed. He found privacy in the bathroom, pulled out the card, and scanned the information with a sense of dread:

Nick Sartain, Head of Security

GRACELAND

Elvis Presley Blvd, Memphis, TN 38116

(901) 555-2376, ext. 21

"I'm watching you," was scrawled on the back.

After Jerry retired to his room, Dale showed the card and its ominous message to Trista.

"Oh, shit!" she exclaimed. "Do you think he's dangerous?"

"No," Dale said flatly. "I just think he's on a quest to reveal the truth. Fortunately for us, he still has no tangible proof, just a wild, unbelievable story."

They awoke early and surprisingly refreshed the next morning despite both having dreams of being chased around Graceland by various villains. They were heading to the Arcade for breakfast down on Main Street and then some shopping on Beale Street before Dale had an appointment to practice with the band.

"Boys and girls, you are going to have a good ol' southern breakfast this morning," Dale said with a smile.

"I am going to get fat if I keep eating this way," Trista teased.

"Sugar, I will love you skinny or fat," Dale said with a laugh.

Dale ordered for everyone: sausage patties, eggs over easy, white toast, and grits.

"What do you put on grits?" Jerry asked as he and Trista were both new to the Southern delicacy.

"I always put a pat of butter, salt and pepper," Dale said. "Give it a try."

"They're amazing," Trista said. "I can't believe I have never tried them before. I love how you are always showing me new things."

"Well, they're an acquired taste, and I wouldn't expect you to find any good ones in California," Dale said as he popped a tender piece of sausage in his mouth. "This is a great way to start the day. If the rest of it goes like this, I'll be a happy man."

Jerry drove by Humes High School, where Elvis first became famous, on the way to Beale Street.

"I don't want to be a third wheel, so I'll stroll around on my own and see you two back here, around 12:30?" Jerry said.

"Maybe I'll go with you and avoid the dress shops," Dale said with a wink, but he was already being pulled by Trista in the direction of Beale Street's fashion district.

People were already filling the street, and the stores all had good crowds in them. It was only going to get busier as the week progressed with all of the folks coming to pay homage to their idol. Dale and Trista walked hand in hand past antiques stores and music joints that were already pumping the sound of the blues. They came upon a classy women's clothing store.

"It looks like a really nice store, but it might be expensive," Trista said.

"I am sure we can afford it," Dale said as he opened the door for her.

The store was filled with everything from gowns to cute sun dresses, shoes and accessories. Trista picked out a red dress with a delicate print on it. She was also captivated by a gorgeous light blue dress and a sheer white gown that brought a sheepish grin from Dale.

"I will be right out," Trista said seductively as she headed into the dressing room.

She looked gorgeous in the red, radiant in the blue, and stunning in white.

"Which one do you like best?" Trista asked.

"All three," Dale said without hesitation. "I want you to have all of them."

"But they are very expensive," Trista said.

"I don't care because you look so beautiful in all of them," Dale replied.

Dale implored Trista to get matching shoes and purses as well. The final stop was at the jewelry counter where she picked out several pairs of earrings and a gold heart bracelet.

"Your total comes to $4,735, sir," the clerk said.

Trista gasped, but Dale didn't even flinch as he took care of the bill with his American Express card.

"You are worth every penny and more," Dale said.

Trista blushed slightly and gave Dale a passionate kiss, not caring if they had company. They stepped out onto Beale Street that was even more crowded. This time they stopped at Lansky Brothers, an iconic men's store that provided much of Elvis' wardrobe back in the day. Dale picked out some black slacks and a red polo shirt with a 1950s rockabilly look.

"That outfit will be perfect for the reception tonight," Trista said. "I'll wear my red dress to match."

A voice in the back of Dale's mind recognized that red is the color of fire, and blood, and is associated with danger as well as passion, desire, and love. He remembered that Red enhances human metabolism, increases respiration rate, and raises blood pressure. Dale chose to focus on positive thoughts rather than the dread that was building as he moved closer to seeing all sorts of people from his past.

"It's the color of love," he said while giving Trista a tight squeeze.

He wasn't sure if the motivator was that growing sense of dread or his unquestionable love for Trista, but Dale made a decision right then that he had been considering for weeks. He invited Trista to shop in an antique store while he made a phone call.

"It's going to be part of my surprise," Dale told her when Trista asked who he needed to call. "And I think you're going to love it."

Dale stepped into the phone booth, pulled a piece of paper out of his wallet, deposited coins, and dialed the number.

"Hello, this is Lowell," a man said. "How can I help you?"

Lowell had made a number of things for Elvis out of his small shop on 10th Street and was a trusted and well-respected jeweler.

"My name is Dale Gant, and I was referred to you by people who knew Elvis Presley," Dale began.

"And what may I do for you?"

"I need an engagement ring," Dale said. "I want it to come from you, but I need it by tomorrow morning. Can you do that?"

Lowell had some items in store that fit what Dale wanted: a classic gold band with at least a 2 carat rock. Dale made arrangements to stop by Saturday morning.

Jerry was waiting for them back at the car to make the short drive to Sun Records, the birthplace of rock 'n' roll and perhaps the site of its resurrection as Dale would be reunited with members of his former bands. Scotty Moore was back from the original band, The Blue Moon Boys, to play lead guitar. The rest of the group hailed from the TCB Band, which performed in Elvis' later days, with Jerry Scheff on bass, Ron Tutt on drums, and Glen Harlin on piano.

It was another hot humid day in Memphis, and the air conditioner in the car barely got cold by the time they pulled up to Sun Studios and parked the car.

"This is where rock 'n' roll as we know it all began," Dale said as he held the door open for Trista and Jerry.

As they walked into the studio Dale thought back to the first time he went through this door to cut a record for his mother's birthday. It was about nine months later when he got a call from Scotty Moore that basically launched his career. Sun looked almost the same as it did in the '50s, just a little more touristy as it had become a popular attraction. Dale stared at his reflection in a photo from the '50s on the wall where all of the musicians who had gold records were immortalized.

"Are you ready to make some music?"

Dale's reverie was interrupted by Tommy Stanwood, the studio manager for his practice session. "Yes, sir," Dale replied.

"Right this way, Mr. Gant," Tommy said. "Your band is waiting."

Dale had never felt such stage fright. He had played in front of every size of crowd, but performing with four ghosts from his past was going to be surreal.

"Ok, here we go," Dale said to Jerry and Trista. "I need you two to be my eyes and ears."

Scotty Moore was the first to hold out his hand as Dale approached the recording area. Dale grabbed his hand but kept going for a full embrace.

"Wow, man, it's so great to see you," Dale said, much to Scotty's astonishment.

"Well, uh, nice to meet you," Scotty said. "Damn! I've seen lots of Elvis impersonators, but none like you. The look is close, but the voice ... and the mannerisms. It's uncanny!"

Dale shook his mind loose from the shock of seeing Scotty and was much more normal as he shook hands with the three other visages from his musical past. That old feeling of always knowing how to take charge was returning.

"Ok, boys, let's get to it: shall we?" Dale said.

As the final performer, Dale would be performing four of Elvis' greatest songs—"Hound Dog," "Suspicious Minds," "Jailhouse Rock," and, ultimately, "Can't Help Falling in Love With You." The last two were planned for an encore.

"First thing is tempo, always," Dale said. "We've got to hit a groove and keep turning it up. Usually, I like to let that build, but we've only got four songs. We're going to build quickly to that big finish."

The four musicians sat and stared at Dale, transfixed by this man who looked like Elvis Presley but absolutely sounded and acted like him.

"Hey, let's go!" Dale said.

They rolled through each of the songs, with Dale making adjustments mostly to get the tempo just right. After two hours, all of them were sounding like their old selves.

"Man, we're going to kick some ass!" Scotty said.

"Always," Dale replied, drawing more strange looks from the boys. "I'll see you Saturday morning for a tune-up at the Theater. Get some rest and be ready to rock 'n' roll."

Jerry and Trista watched the show from behind the glass and were mesmerized as always by Dale's talents. They had a visitor who stood some 20 feet away and rotated his gaze from the band to Trista and Jerry. After a nervous half hour of feeling she was being highly scrutinized by this stranger, Trista decided to make a move.

"He's really amazing, don't you think?" Trista said after moving to stand within a few feet of the stranger.

"Mr. Gant, you mean?"

"Yes, Dale Gant, we're here with him for the anniversary show. My name is Trista," she said and held out her hand.

"Nick Sartain, *Detective* Nick Sartain."

Trista jerked her hand back and stared at the man Dale had described as his pursuer.

"I hope for your sake that you know what you're getting into," Nick said. "Things didn't end up too well for his last lover."

"That was his wife," Trista said in a low hiss as Jerry had noticed their encounter.

"Whatever their relationship, it's definitely over now," Nick said.

"What do you want?" Trista demanded.

"What I've always wanted, the truth," Nick replied.

"Knowing the truth is one thing," Trista said. "Proving it is quite another."

"True enough, but pressure has a way of changing things," Nick said. "Eventually, it gets to everyone. I'm sure we'll see you this evening at the reception. That should be really interesting when Mr. Gant reunites with another of his, shall we say, old flames."

Nick had used his best interrogation techniques to rattle Trista, but she remained calm and steadfast.

"There's one thing you haven't taken into account," Trista said.

"What's that?" Nick replied.

"That Dale Gant is a wonderful man … and a crime needs a victim."

Dale burst out of the recording area just then and didn't notice Jerry and Trista had company at first. Nick made sure to ramp up the pressure another notch.

"Wonderful performance, Mr. Gant," he said. "I hope you can be as convincing tonight at the reception. We'll see you there."

The two men stood looking directly at each other, trying to gauge what was in each other's soul.

Jerry stepped into the contested space, turned, and slowly pushed Dale and Trista out the door of Sun Studios.

"We'll see you soon, Mr. Gant," Nick said just before the door closed.

"Who the hell is that?!" Jerry demanded.

"One of those people from my past that I thought would make our acquaintance," Dale replied. "Just keep an eye out for him."

"Dale, I have an idea," Trista said after they were back in the relatively safe confines of their own hotel room.

"I'd like to hear it," Dale said.

"First, I need to know something," Trista said. "Do you trust me? I mean, do you really trust me, the way you asked me to trust you?"

"I do, with every bit of my being," Dale said.

"OK, then I have a plan," Trista said with an intensity to her look Dale had never seen before. "We need to give detective Nick Sartain exactly what he wants."

"And what is that?" Dale asked.

"The truth," Trista said. "We show him the Green Book. Let him see what I saw. Let him see that you were tortured in your former life. Let him see that, yes, you wanted out, but ultimately you were forced into the actions that you took to escape. Let him see that your final decision was made to protect your ex-wife and daughter. And let him see that you are a good man. No, a wonderful, loving, incredible man. I think he will make the right choice. Otherwise, he's never going to leave us alone."

Dale leaned back in his chair, took a long, deep breath and exhaled slowly. The look on his face was that of a man who had been to war.

"I just want this ... to end," he said finally.

"Snap out of it, you asshole!" Trista screamed. "I know you want to put your past behind you, you and a million other people. But it's time to focus on the future! We need to *truly* put all of this behind us, your demons and this detective. He's not going to stop until he has the truth."

"OK, my dear," Dale said as he cupped Trista's hands. "I trust you ... with my life."

Jerry donned a red polo to match Dale and Trista's wardrobe for the reception.

"Well, it looks like we're ready for love ... or war," Dale said as they exited Heartbreak Hotel. Trista drew the crowd's attention as she strode through the grand entrance to Graceland and stepped into the foyer.

"It looks like you're the star tonight," Dale said.

"What do you mean," Trista asked shyly.

"All their eyes are on you," Dale said. "They've seen plenty of Elvis impersonators, but you are the real deal in that dress."

Trista blushed, but she obviously was loving the attention. Guests were taking in the majestic style of Elvis' mansion before gathering on the back patio for hors d'oeuvres and drinks. That's where Priscilla surely would be waiting to greet all of the musicians. Dale delighted in showing Trista the upstairs Jungle Room, the social hub of Graceland during his heyday. The Jungle Room looked frozen in time to Dale, with its green shag carpets and carved wood furniture. Dale was more than relieved to see that his former bedroom, the site of his crime, the core of his guilt, was off limits to all visitors.

Jerry was keeping vigil near the entrance to the patio as he scanned for detective Nick Sartain, who was nowhere to be seen. Back downstairs, Trista and Dale found an unoccupied corner of the living room where they could talk.

"How are you feeling about seeing all of this again?" Trista asked.

"It's surreal for sure, but I don't feel any real connection to the place like I thought I would," Dale said. "It feels exactly like what it is, snapshots from a former life."

"Are you ready to see ... her?" Trista asked.

"Yes, I think I can get through it, but I'm relieved that my daughter isn't here tonight," Dale said. "I'm not sure how I'm going to deal with that when the time comes, which it surely will."

Trista took Dale's hand and led the way to the patio. The crown numbered around 50 as only the musicians and their guests were invited. Dale counted at least six Elvis impersonators, including one who was decked out in one of his vintage Vegas outfits.

"Howdy, ma'am," one of the clones said.

"My God, do I look like *that*?" Dale asked after he had passed.

"Not at all," Trista said. "You look, um, like yourself."

"Now that's a mind-blower," Dale said.

Just then, a stunning beauty in her early 40s, with jet black hair and dark blue eyes, stepped into their circle.

"You must be Mr. Dale Gant," she said. "I've been so looking forward to meeting you."

Dale looked up at the face that had stopped his whole world on the day they met almost 30 years ago. His head was spinning, and he felt as frozen as the Greek statue that stood close to him. Trista gave him a nudge that reminded him to breathe again.

"Oh, yes, ma'am," Dale said as he took her hand and kissed it lightly.

There was another gulf of silence as Dale wondered what to do next and the woman felt slightly embarrassed at not being introduced to Trista.

"And who is this lovely person with you?" the woman finally offered.

"Oh, my gosh, this is Trista Sloan," Dale said.

"Welcome to Graceland, both of you," the woman said. "My daughter is so excited to meet you, Mr. Gant."

"Dale, please call me Dale," he said.

"I remember her squealing, 'He sounds the most like Daddy!' when we received your tape," the woman said. "I'm so glad you changed your mind and decided to join us."

"Well, I'm just flattered that you asked me to be a part of all of this," Dale said.

"Wonderful, now please let me know if you need anything, anything at all," the woman said. "You had your practice session, right?"

"Yes, this morning," Dale said. "Scotty and the boys were amazing, as always."

The remark drew Trista's wide-eyed look as Dale was being anything but coy about concealing his past, but the woman hardly noticed.

"That's wonderful," she said. "I'm so looking forward to your perform-ance. Now, please excuse me."

The woman moved into the crowd to engage another clone. Dale stood looking at Trista with a vague expression she hadn't seen before.

"It's strange," Dale said. "We've met so many people who were struck by my resemblance to him, but she didn't seem moved at all."

"How does that make you feel?" Trista asked.

"Again, like it's all part of a dream, just snapshots of a former life," Dale said. "That makes it better. I know more than ever that my future is right in front of me, with you my love."

Dale and Trista embraced and kissed like they were the only people on Earth. Their escape was interrupted by a tap on Dale's shoulder.

"Over there," Jerry said, pointing to the darkness, where detective Nick Sartain had stepped from the shadows and was watching them intently.

"Let me handle this," Trista said. "You two have a drink and relax. I'll see you back at the room."

"Detective Sartain, may I have a word in private?" Trista asked after approaching the detective.

"Sure," Nick said.

"We have to go to my room. Can you drive us?"

"Why can't we talk here?" Nick asked.

"I have something to show you, something that will blow your mind," Trista said.

When they were alone in the hotel room, Trista opened a dresser drawer and pulled out the Green Book.

"This book has everything you seek," Trista said.

"And what's that?" Nick countered.

"The truth."

"The truth about ..."

"You know," Trista said. "The truth about a ghost you've been chasing for 10 years. It's yours to read, the proof you seek. But I have one favor to ask."

"What's that?"

"That you consider how many lives could be ruined if the truth you seek is shared with anyone. Dale Gant is a wonderful man, and we're in love. I think he plans to ask me to marry him. The people he left behind have moved on and have loved ones in their lives. You'll read about a man who was desperate for a new life and was eventually forced to seek it. In the end, his decision was made solely to protect the people he left behind. I'm sharing a secret with you, and I'm pleading with you to keep it locked away, forever.

"Please," Trista said finally as she held out the book. She pulled it back slightly. "Also, please don't take this as a bribe, but we'll need someone here at Graceland who can protect the secret, and who better than the only man who knows it? You can secretly be on the payroll and help with any security needs that may arise. Dale said he respects your tenacity and believes you are a man of honor. You've solved the mystery. Now, please, I beg of you to keep it locked away."

"I won't promise anything," Nick said after taking possession of the Green Book. "If I feel a crime has been committed, it's my duty to pursue justice."

"In this case, there's absolutely no good in justice being served," Trista said. "It will bring only pain. Whatever you decide, please wait until after the show."

"I *can* promise you that," Nick said before he turned to leave the hotel room, the Green Book in hand.

Dale and Jerry returned to the room 15 minutes later to find Trista sitting on the couch, weeping.

"Oh, God, Dale! I hope I haven't ruined our lives."

Dale wrapped her in his arms and just rocked. Jerry looked more than concerned.

"Jerry, it's going to be fine," Dale said. "I'll fill you in more in the morning, but for now can we have some privacy?"

"Sure thing, boss," Jerry said and headed for his room across the hall.

"So, how did he react?" Dale asked when he and Trista were alone again.

"I don't know: like you'd expect from a cop, I guess," Trista said. "He could do anything."

"Or he could do nothing," Dale said. "Let's just try to get some sleep. Things will look better in the morning."

They made love passionately, desperately, like this was their last night together, before falling asleep in each other's arms.

Dale awoke early and was glad he had things to do to keep his mind busy.

"I have to meet the boys at the Theatre for a tune up and a mic check," Dale said as he slid out of bed and got dressed.

Trista was still a lump under the covers and showed no signs of going anywhere.

"I'll wait here for you, babe," she said. "If I'm not here, I'll be laying out down by the pool. I've got to find a way to relax."

Dale sat down on the edge of the bed and retrieved Trista's hand from under the covers to hold in his.

"I feel like we've put our fate in the hands of the Lord," he said earnestly. "We have to trust that his grace and his mercy will carry us through."

Dale tuned up the boys even more as they worked through the set one more time and made their final adjustments. Afterward, he stopped at Lowell's and picked up a stunning piece of jewelry.

"A gal's gonna have a hard time saying anything but yes to that," Lowell said as he showed the ring to Dale. "When are you planning to ask?"

"I haven't figured that out quite yet," Dale said. "I've got some hurdles between now and then, but I want to have this ready for when the time is right."

Dale arrived back at the room just before noon. Trista was awake, but only in the literal sense.

"OK, babe, how about some lunch and maybe some pool time?" Dale said.

"No, I want to see it," Trista said.

"See what?"

"The grave. We were close to it last night, but I want to go see it. Something tells me it's the right thing to do."

"I don't know if I can do that," Dale said with a frightened look on his face.

"I think that's the last demon we need to confront," Trista said. "I think then you'll be free. We'll be free."

"OK, let's do it," Dale said.

Dale and Trista decided to walk the quarter mile across the street to Graceland. They didn't want to attract any attention, so Dale paid for two tickets rather than asking for any special privileges. Once inside, they stopped at the flower shop before moving slowly toward the grave marker that bore the name of Elvis Aron Presley. Trista placed the single rose she had purchased on the marker as Dale stood staring at *his* gravestone. He dropped to a knee, and sobbed.

"Oh, Lord, please forgive me, for I have sinned," Dale said quietly.

He and Trista remained there, silent, for some time. Detective Nick Sartain remained silent, too, as he watched the scene unfold on his surveillance camera.

The 10th Anniversary Tribute to Elvis Presley at Ellis Theatre would prove to be one of the most epic musical performances of all time, with 10 different performers playing all 40 of The King's top 40 hits. Dale and Trista grabbed a quick afternoon meal and retired to their room to prepare for the evening. For Trista, minutes seemed like hours as she envisioned the myriad outcomes that were possible with so many variables. How would Dale react in front of a huge crowd? What will he do when he sees his daughter for the first time in 10 years? What will detective Nick Sartain do? ... and, most of all, does he really love me? How many other women have asked that same question of this man?

For Dale, the routine was much more familiar. He was able to push his angst over what the future may hold and focus on the performance, as he had done so many times before. Surely, that would mean a trip to the bathroom to "pray to the porcelain god" as someone had profoundly described the unseemly act of throwing up before a big performance. Dale sat and wondered how many times he had been through this routine. Maybe a thousand? Two thousand? Dale ordered room service for dinner, and he and Trista were unusually quiet as they picked at a plate of shrimp and vegetables. The clock chimed 6, just three hours before Dale's ultimate performance.

"I'm scared," Trista said, finally breaking the silence.

"I'm scared, too," Dale said. "It's been so long since I've been in front of a crowd like that. And the pressure to perform ..."

Trista cut him off in mid-sentence.

"You just don't see it, do you!!?" she demanded.

"See what?" Dale asked.

"The gravity of this situation. This could change your life forever, maybe even put you in jail for the rest of your life, and all you are worried about is your damn performance."

"In order to be brilliant, you have to block out all the other light," Dale said.

"I'll see you after the show, and I hope you're still the man I fell in love with," Trista said as she walked out and slammed the door behind her.

The words registered too late for Dale to intercept her. He sat alone on the hotel room couch, as he'd done thousands of times before, and contemplated his position.

"She's right, *damn you*," he said aloud.

Dale leaned back, closed his eyes, and let his mind run through the scenarios.

"The truth is you don't have any idea what will happen when your set ends," he said finally. "But one thing is for sure. You better be ready to play."

Dale arose, visited the bathroom to empty whatever was left over from dinner, and headed downstairs to meet Jerry for the ride to Ellis Theater.

"Trista blew through here a few minutes ago, and she still looked upset," Jerry said. "She took a cab to the theater and said to tell you she'd be waiting for you when it's over. You still sure all of this is a good idea, boss?"

"No," Dale said. "But it's too late to turn back now. The show must go on."

Dale sat quietly as the makeup artists applied his signature fake sideburns and tinted his hair jet black. When he donned the sequined jumpsuit, the transformation was complete. Dale Gant looked—and felt—like his old self.

"My God!" one of the stage hands said as Dale entered the staging area at 8:45. "You're a dead ringer for The King. If I didn't know better, I'd swear I'm seeing a ghost."

"Stick around for the show and you might start believing in ghosts," Dale said and gave the man a wink.

Artie Cornette, a renowned Elvis impersonator out of Vegas, was finishing his set with "Blue Suede Shoes" as Dale scanned the crowd from the left wing. He could see Trista, front row, low left, and she appeared to be loving the show. *Maybe she has forgiven me already,* he thought.

The notion brought a smile, not because things would be back to normal with Trista, but for the hundreds of times he had been given a reprieve for his transgressions with the ladies.

"Maybe I can go back to being ... me," he said to himself before ducking backstage.

Artie Cornette brought the crowd to a fever pitch before he exited the stage.

"You're up, man," Artie said as he soaked in the applause.

"Don't worry, Ace. They're just getting started."

The lady of the evening took the stage for one last introduction.

"Ladies and gentlemen, are you enjoying the show?!!" she asked and received a thundering return.

"We've saved what I think is the best for last. When we were looking at audition tapes, my daughter squealed, 'He sounds the most like Daddy!' Without further ado, Mr. Dale Gant!"

When he sauntered onstage, the gasps of surprise equaled the cheers. A lady in the second row fainted as he struck an iconic pose.

"Evenin', folks," he said to wild applause as several more females swooned to the ground. "I can't thank you enough for having me here tonight. And now, let's get it goin'!"

He strode away from the crowd, counting beats to the band, before making a dramatic turn.

You ain't nothin' but a hound dog
Cryin' all the time.

The scene could have been straight out of 1956, the year Elvis' version of the iconic blues song was released. Numerous people fought to stay on their feet. Others jumped, shrieked, or shook uncontrollably. And those were just the men.

"Suspicious Minds" is about a dysfunctional relationship, and various feelings of mistrust within it. It was originally written by Mark James, but Elvis turned it into a hit during his comeback, the same time he was going through his separation and eventual divorce.

We're caught in a trap
I can't walk out
Because I love you too much baby.

The irony of the lyrics brought both a chuckle and a tear as he locked eyes with the lady of the evening, who had returned to her front-row seat to witness the end of an historic night of rock 'n' roll. The band members finished and hustled offstage, everyone in the house knowing they would return.

"One more! One more! One more!" the crowd chanted as the band members hovered just backstage and waited for the precise moment to create a frenzy. As Scotty and Jerry teased the crowd with the familiar guitar and bass riff of "Jailhouse Rock," Dale could see a woman's features framed through an opening onstage. A million thoughts raced through his mind. His first performance in church, followed by his first hit in high school. All of the road trips, the girls, the parties. Good times. Bad times. Friends. Enemies. His beloved father. Mama. And the woman he truly loved.

Suddenly, Dale threw back the curtain, sprinted onstage, and slid on his knees before popping up, shaking and shimmying.

The warden threw a party in the county jail
The prison band was there and they began to wail.

By the time Dale hit the final refrain, the entire crowd was "Dancin' to the Jailhouse Rock." Dale stood and relished the moment as the crowd's reactions to his music grew even stronger. He scanned the huge crowd and acknowledged each section with waves, blown kisses, or a simple thumbs up. Dale also noticed detective Nick Sartain, low and left, flanked by what appeared to be Memphis Police officers, directly in the path of Trista's nearest exit.

"Can't Help Falling in Love" was not Elvis' greatest hit, but he often finished performances with the heartfelt song. It was also the last song he performed live, at Market Square Arena in Indianapolis on June 26, 1977.

Wise men say, only fools rush in
But I can't help falling in love with you.

Dale had been thinking about the parallels ever since he learned it would be the last song of the evening. Was he rushing in, being foolish, or was he certain that the path he would take at this moment was the right one, with the right woman?

Take my hand, take my whole life too
For I can't help falling in love with you.

When Dale finished and bowed, the applause was lesser in volume but much greater in reverence. The lady of the evening had tears pouring down her face, which was a common sight throughout the crowd. It had taken 10 years, but at that moment, millions of fans were finally able to let go of The King.

Dale Gant was one of them. As he arose from his bow, he locked eyes with Trista and held out his arm, beckoning her to join him onstage. She shared a brief glance with detective Nick Sartain as she passed his vigil and climbed a short flight of stairs to the stage. As Trista approached, the crowd let out a collective gasp.

Dale dropped to one knee and pulled out a small black velvet box. He used the microphone so the entire crowd could hear his words.

"Miss Trista Sloan, darling, love of my life, will you marry me?"

"Oh Dale, yes. Yes!"

The crowd could barely hear her words, but they cheered as she shook her head emphatically and held out her left hand. Dale slipped the glittering rock on her finger, and they embraced and kissed for what seemed to them like forever. When the forever moment expired, Dale and Trista waved to the crowd one last time and exited backstage.

Staff had put together a reception area where the lady of the evening was greeting musicians and other VIPs along with her daughter, who gasped when Dale and Trista approached. Dale's insides felt like he was in a clamp, tightening to the point where he questioned whether he would be able to even speak to this young woman, let alone coherently. He was shocked and proud to see that she was so beautiful in approaching womanhood … and so much like her mother. His emotions were a strange mix of yearning and trepidation.

"You were amazing, Mr. Gant!" the young woman gushed.

At first, Dale could only smile and stare. A single tear rolled down his left cheek.

"Thank you, my dear," he said finally. "Always remember that your daddy loves you, and he's watching over you proudly."

"I know, Mr. Gant," she said. "It's still hard, after all these years, but somehow your performance makes it better. I can't ever thank you enough."

She lunged forward and embraced Dale, who tightened at first but soon gave way and wrapped the young woman in a loving embrace.

When he finally let go of the girl and looked up, he was staring at the face he fell in love with so many years ago. Dale felt a tug of the same attraction he experienced upon seeing her ravishing beauty for the first time.

"Dale, you have to come back and play for us again," the lady said as she reached for Dale's hand. A strange look came over her face as her fingers clutched his. She shook her head as if attempting to rid herself of some strange thought.

"I'm sorry, you were saying?" she said to Dale.

"Oh, no Ma'am, you were saying I need to come back and ... play again," Dale said. His hesitation was forced by noticing detective Nick Sartain standing in front of the main exit, flanked by two Memphis Police officers. At least he has the courtesy to allow me some dignity and to say my goodbyes, Dale thought.

"I'm not sure that will be possible, but I'll never forget you or this night," Dale said.

That same wistful look passed over the woman's face before she released Dale's hand and backed away, finally turning to greet other guests.

Trista joined Dale in the middle of the reception area, and they stood, hand in hand, eyes locked with the gaze of detective Nick Sartain, who held the Green Book under his left arm. Finally, Trista and Dale took two steps forward, which were matched by the detective's advance. The police officers remained at their guard posts. Two more steps each. Followed by four more. They stood, sizing up each other for what seemed like an eternity to Dale and Trista. Finally, detective Nick Sartain stepped forward and ended the standoff.

"I believe this belongs to you," he said as he extended the Green Book with both hands.

Dale and Trista both looked stunned. Detective Nick Sartain just smiled.

"You haven't visited a copy machine?" Dale asked.

"No, sir, I haven't. I've decided you are free to live your lives in peace. And now I can do the same."

"Then I have just one question for you, Nick."

Dale paused, and squeezed Trista's hand hard enough for her to wince.

"Can you keep a secret?"

"Yes, boss."